THE KISS OF LOVE

JEL JONES

PublishAmerica
Baltimore

Softcover 9781630842079
PUBLISHED BY PUBLISHAMERICA, LLLP
www.publishamerica.com
Baltimore

Printed in the United States of America

Chapter One

It was early on Friday evening about half past seven; I was already dressed, buttoning up my long burgundy wool coat. Smiles danced inside of my contented heart as I stood outside my bedroom door, propped against the door frame. I was consumed with excitement of what lied ahead for the evening with me and my father. I looked up and saw Mom heading down the hallway toward me. She didn't appear to see me standing there as she was busy looking down raking lint from her blue sweater. When she reached me, she smiled.

"I see you are dressed and all bundled up for your evening out with your father. But come with me for a second. I have something you need," she grabbed my hand and led me two doors down to their bedroom.

"Something I need," I asked laughingly. "Another birthday present; I don't mind even if my birthday was last week."

Mom nodded. "You figured right. It is another gift, but I forgot to wrap it. But don't get too excited. It's just a little something that will come in handy this evening."

"Okay, sure, what is it? Tell me already."

"Just hold your horses, you'll see in a moment," Mom mumbled in a low voice.

"Okay, sure." I rubbed my hands together excitedly. "But how long is this going to take? I need to get downstairs. Dad is probably ready by now."

"This will only take a minute; besides, your father will not be leaving without you," she assured me.

I lagged behind her into their huge pale blue and white room; and was always aware of its enormous size compared to all the other bedrooms. She immediately stepped across the large room to the wide double-dresser and pulled out a drawer, rambled through it and seconds later handed me a pair of snow white mittens that matched the white scarf around my neck.

"These are for you," Mom said, and then she took a seat on the bed. "I forgot to wrap them with the scarf. Make sure to put them on and don't pull them off for a second while you and Daniel are walking around in this awful weather," she said, glancing toward the window at the blustery conditions." She shook her head. "I hate to think of you freezing, walking down those streets in this chilly March weather. It's pretty cold out tonight," Mom stressed, as she kept looking toward the window. "I don't know why Daniel has to insist on taking you out on a windy night like tonight." Then she paused and looked at me. "You should speak up, sweetheart, if you don't care to be out in this weather."

I smiled. "Its okay, Mom; he didn't insist. I want to go."

"No matter what the conditions are, I guess," Mom said disappointedly.

"It's not that bad out," I mumbled. "It's just raining a little and the wind is sort of blowing."

"Mandy, you almost paint the picture of a summer evening." She held up both arms. "All because you don't want to miss an evening out with your father; and that I do understand. But if you'll admit it, you know how chilly and windy it is this evening." She pointed toward the window as branches shook on the tall evergreen next to the window.

"Mom, I know. It won't bother me," I assured her.

"Mandy, you are not going to convince me that you enjoy walking around in cold windy weather like this? That's nonsense."

"Mom, I know it's cold and windy this evening, but it's not always like this," I mumbled, wanting her to change the subject.

"That's my point, the two of you need to forget about walking this evening and just stay inside the theater."

"Mom, don't worry. We'll be okay and I promise we won't freeze or get blown away by the wind," I teased to calm her down.

She stared at me and gave me a half smile. "There's no getting through to you, young lady."

"Thanks for the mittens. I promise to keep them on during our walk. I'll put them on right now." I stepped over to the bed where she was seated and gave her a kiss on the side of the face.

Mom stood up and adjusted my coat collar and the scarf around my neck. She was about five foot five, one hundred and twenty pounds with long black hair sweeping across her shoulders. She had deep brown eyes that were slightly narrow and a smooth perfect shaped mouth. She was just the opposite of my father and seemed somewhat entitled. She had been raised with a silver spoon in her mouth and saw things from a different perspective. Although, from her perspective, she and my father both were raised with silver spoons, her spoon came from old money and Dad's spoon came from new money. Her inheritance had rolled in from five generations and his inheritance had rolled in from just two generations.

Besides courageous and not afraid to speak her mind, she was also quite attractive. The older of two children, spoiled by her very wealthy family, and was told by her family that she married down when she married my father.

Before I turned to leave the room, she kissed the side of my face and then said as I headed toward the door, "You might want to mention to Daniel how much I fell in love with Bonne's car."

"Mom, what did you say?"

"Tell Daniel your Aunt Bonne visited this afternoon."

"What about her visit, Mom?"

"Just let him know she was showing off her new car again."

I glanced over my shoulder, "Mom, Dad doesn't care about Aunt Bonne's new car," I sort of teased, laughing. "He barely looked at it when she first drove over."

"Maybe he doesn't care about it; but he admits it's a nice car," Mom seriously uttered. "I would love to own that red Mercedes she's driving. It won't hurt for your father to know how much I fell for that car."

Mom caught me off guard and made me feel uncomfortable. It felt as if she was being sneaky about it. It didn't feel right.

I turned and glanced at Mom, but I didn't reply; I just stood there in the middle of the room staring at her, and then she repeated. "Did you hear what I just said? While you're out this evening with Daniel, I want you to mention Bonne's car."

"Mom, I know you want me to mention Aunt Bonne's car, but why?" I asked for clarification.

"I just want you to mention to your father in around about way, how much I love her new car; and how much I would love one identical to hers," Mom said seriously.

I smiled at my mother and paused for a moment. "Mom, don't you remember?"

"Remember what?" She asked.

"That you already mentioned that to Dad? You told him how much you loved Aunt Bonne's car when she was here last week."

"Of course, I remember, sweetheart, but I just want you to mention it away from my presence."

"But Mom, you already have a new Mercedes," I protested, feeling uneasy about mentioning to Dad what she had asked.

Mom's brow wrinkled. "You don't understand, sweetheart. Yes, of course, I have a nice car, and it's a Mercedes, but it's hardly new. It's actually sort of old and it's time for a new one," Mom explained, headed across the room toward me.

"It looks brand new to me," I said.

"But, dear, it's not brand new and I want a new one."

"Just go out and buy one," I suggested.

"I could." She smiled. "But that's my point. I could easily go out and buy one. But that would not sit well with your father."

"Why not, you can't buy what you want?"

Mom shook her head and smiled. "Not if I want to keep the peace around here." Mom adjusted the scarf around my neck again. "Your father has made it quite clear that he doesn't want us to spend any money on a new car for me right now."

Bitterness poured through her words like they came from a deeply cold place. "He doesn't care about what makes me happy anymore," Mom mumbled in a sad distant voice.

"Mom, I'm sure Dad wants to make you happy."

"Yes, sweetheart, once upon a time. But now is a different story. I'm afraid your father resentment toward me has grown over the years."

"Mom, Dad doesn't resent you. What resentment?" I asked, feeling awkward to hear her confession.

"Something you wouldn't understand. It happened when we were in college. About a promise I broke."

When Mom mentioned a broken promise, I walked away from her and stepped over to the window and stared out. My mind flashed back to an argument that I had overheard between my parents when I was six-years-old:

"When we started dating at the university, you had promised to wait until we were married, then a few weeks after we become engage, out of nowhere we broke up and you started dating Robert Dieringer again; and apparently not waiting when you got together with him," Dad said in a disappointed tone.

"Why are you bringing that up now? That was years ago, and besides, I was no longer obligated to that promise since we had broken up," Mom explained.

"Yes, Francis, a break up that came out of nowhere. Everybody on campus was gossiping about the whole thing," Dad shouted.

"Daniel, my goodness, everybody at that university gossiped about everything. I thought you had gotten that out of your system."

"Well, apparently not if I'm still talking about it. Besides, you might as well know. It broke some of my trust in you."

"How could that incident break some of your trust in me when I wasn't dating you at the time?" Mom asked.

"Francis, that's simple enough to explain. We broke up and were apart for three weeks; you dated Robert Dieringer for two weeks and then you broke off with him and got back together with me."

"So, what are you getting at Daniel? We got back together and I married you."

"Yes, we got back together after you had broken your promise."

"I didn't plan to break the promise. It just happened. I think you should forget about the past," Mom stressed.

"Mandy, Mandy," Mom voice interrupted my memory of their argument. "Why are you looking out of the window? I told you how nasty it is outside. Have you changed your mind about getting out in that weather with your father after all?"

I rushed across the room toward Mom, shaking my head. "No, I haven't changed my mind.

"Well, in that case don't forget to mention Bonne's car. I'm sure he'll listen to you," she said with a tint of sadness, giving me a firm look. "All you have to do is just mention Aunt Bonne's new car and how much I have fallen for it."

"Mom, it doesn't feel right to say that to Dad."

"Why doesn't it feel right? You would be stating the truth. Besides, Daniel listens to you more than he does me."

"Maybe Aunt Bonne could tell Dad," I suggested.

"Sweetheart, Daniel will not listen to Bonne anymore than he will listen to me."

Aunt Bonne Jamison had also married rich when she married Uncle Scott Jamison, but their parents felt Aunt Bonne had married a step up with Uncle Scott and not a step down as they felt Mom had with Dad.

At that moment, Dad called out loudly. "Are you ready, yet, Mandy?"

With a quick wave to Mom, I rushed out of the room.

"Remember what I said," Mom mumbled in a low voice as she headed right out behind me. We walked quickly down the hallway and down the staircase.

Dad was waiting at the bottom of the staircase, near the front door. He was a handsome man with dark brown eyes and black hair against a smooth shaven face. He looked quite stylist standing there smiling, dressed in a long burgundy wool coat and burgundy leather gloves, with a brown scarf accenting his bronze complexion. He was a tall, slender man at six foot two inches and always dressed very business-like; and on many occasions Mom had mentioned how young he looked at his age of 41, just three years older than her.

"Sweetheart, you look swell, all bundled up," Dad said. "Are you ready for our evening out?" He smiled. "It's quite chilly and windy too. We don't really have to take a walk in town. We can just drive around if you like."

"I don't mind, Dad. A little cold and wind is not going to hurt me. I'm all bundled up," I said smiling, holding out both hands. "Even my hands won't get cold." I smiled and glanced at Mom, who didn't seem pleased that I had decided to walk in such cold windy conditions after Dad had suggested we didn't have to. But I wanted to stick to our routine.

But while Dad and I walked the streets of downtown Barrington with the cold wind blowing against our backs, Mom's suggestion was nagging me at the back of my mind. I didn't like the thought of pretending it was my idea for Dad to buy her a new car? The whole thought made me anxious and uncomfortable. Our time together was our time and I didn't want to spoil it with pretense. He always tried to clear his schedule to spend time with me on Fridays so we could do something together. Our routine included taking walks in downtown Barrington and discussions about my school work and other activities, along with discussions about his job as a vice president of Lakeland Investments in downtown Chicago. We also discussed how he spent his time during the week, whenever he stayed over at his hotel room in the city. We never mentioned my mother or the growing tension at home. Therefore, to break the good cheer of our time together, by bringing up what she suggested, didn't feel right. She wanted me to pretend something that wasn't true, so she could end up with a new car. She felt it was a harmless ploy, but I couldn't do it.

Our evening was a fun night out for us. I saw my first scary movie. I was never allowed to watch horror when I was younger, but was promised I could start once I turned fifteen. Therefore, when I turned fifteen on February 24, I was given permission to see: Scream 3, starring Neve Campbell and Courtney Cox, which had been released in early January. The movie theater was noisy and filled with teenagers screaming and hollering every time someone got stabbed. I was enjoying the movie, seated next to Dad, but I was somewhat distracted going in and out of thought about the growing tension between him and Mom.

Chapter Two

I was too young to spend so much time thinking about Mom and Dad's troubled relationship. But I was burdened down with frightening thoughts of the possibility that they would get a divorce; since day-by-day nothing seemed happy about their relationship anymore. They appeared to be just two people living under the same roof making each other miserable with anger and rudeness. Being around each other was a constant exchange of rude remarks that grew into bitter arguments. They were both equal at dishing out insensitive remarks and comments toward each other. Their contempt for each other left a feeling of dread in the entire household, like a permanent dark cloud hanging over the place that kept me uneasy and worried.

In the still of the night I could hear their arguments and would lie awake shaken by their bitter exchanges. On this particular night, an airplane flying over the house broke my sleep. However, after the engine faded away into the distance, I could hear my mother and father quarreling in the room down the hall. Their voices were strong and firm with anger.

"What absurd egotistical human being you men are!" Mom shouted angrily. "You're all alike. It's all about what you think and say!"

"There's no room for criticism from you, Francis. You women are just the same! It's all about what you think and say as well, and let's not forget what you want! And you want plenty from where I'm standing!" Dad shouted sharply.

"I was used to plenty before I ever met you!" Mom yelled coldly. "If you couldn't wear the hat why did you even try?"

"I think it was more like you chasing after me, Francis. Seriously, at the time, getting serious with some female was the farthest thing from my mind."

"Of course it was Daniel, that's why you asked me out when you knew I was already dating some other boy."

"You said yes on the spot before I could finish asking you," Dad reminded her.

"That's because I was silly at the time and all hung up on your school status. You were the bright college student that all the other students were singing praises. You were the young man who was voted most likely to succeed in whatever business you tackled. All the girls wanted to date you."

"And that's why you dated me; I was like a prize and you couldn't allow anyone else to take the prize over you?"

"It's not a joke and that's not the whole reason why I started dating you. But it was part of it. Although, if I had only listened to my parents. They were never that keen on our engagement, that's for sure. But I wanted to marry you and have a life with you. Probably because I could see in you what the rest of the campus could see."

"And what was that?"

"That you had a bright future. You were in a class above most, considered one of the brightness. You were going places and I was excited about your future."

"And how long did that last?"

"Not long since you didn't go that far."

"What is that suppose to mean, Francis?"

"You know what it means. Think about it, Daniel. You left Springfield to end up here in my family's home. You didn't have to buy me a dream home; you could just stay in my parents' home."

"At the time, it seemed Bo and Mabel was more than a little pleased about my move into Mandy Manor."

"Sure my folks didn't want me stuck in Springfield, but it didn't mean we had to be struck in this town either," Mom fussed.

"Are you saying you would have sold Mandy Manor after your parent's death?"

"Maybe I would have if you had encouraged it."

"No, Francis, it wasn't my place to encourage you to sell your family home after you had just lost your parents in such a tragic way. Besides, you can say whatever you want at this time, but fifteen years ago when your folks were both killed on that cruise, you were in no condition to sell this place. You were caring for a seven month old baby; and if I recall correctly, you were pleased that you had inherited Mandy Manor instead of your sister."

"Yes, I was pleased but not for the reasons you think. Bonne and I inherited everything equally. She wanted me to have the estate since you and I already lived here and had lived here since our wedding, two and a half years before my folk's death."

"Regardless you still ended up being the sole owner of Mandy Manor and it never crossed my mind that you wanted to sell the place. A place your daughter was named after, I figured you wanted to keep it in the family."

"You are probably right and I probably wouldn't have sold Mandy Manor," Mom agreed.

"Okay, what's all this fuss about then?"

"All the fuss is about how we are stuck in a middle class suburb like Barrington, when we could have lived anywhere in the world."

"Excuse me if I thought you wanted to stay in this town. For goodness sake, Francis. I thought you wanted to reside here in Barrington. After-all, you were born and raised here, not me," Dad explained.

"If I had married Robert Dieringer, I'm sure I wouldn't be stuck in this little boring town. Just because I was born here didn't mean I wanted to spend the rest of my life in this place."

"How would I have known that, Francis? I uprooted and left my home for you!"

"You didn't do it for me, Daniel. Go tell that lie to somebody who might buy it!" Mom shouted. "We both know that you told me at that time that you wanted to leave Springfield. Your exact words were: I can't wait to get out of Dodge."

"Yes, I did say that, but only because you made a remark that you didn't think you could live in Springfield."

"And I didn't think I could live in Springfield, but you sounded like you couldn't wait to leave the place. Furthermore, saying I didn't want to live in Springfield didn't mean I wanted to continue living in Barrington."

"Well, how was I to know. I relocated here because this is where I thought you wanted to be," Dad explained.

"Daniel, as usual, when it comes to me, you always guess wrong."

"So what Francis, it's pretty ridiculous for you to bring this up now. What purpose does it serve other than something else to bitch at me about?"

"It serves a purpose to me. I thought you should know how you have absolutely disappointed me in this marriage."

"Whatever Francis, if that's the way you feel. So, I guess you gambled on a jet-set life with me and lost, according to you."

"We have never lived the jet-set life, that's for sure. I can't even get you to cross the Illinois border. So, I surely do not feel like a winner," Mom snapped.

"That makes two of us because I took a chance on your love and look what I ended up with, someone who was born with every single advantage! And on top of that I have given you the world, but it's still not enough?"

"Think about it Daniel, by most standards, we are considered quite well off and we could live mostly anywhere in the world, but here we are in this town."

"Francis, what are you bitching about? Maybe you could live anywhere in the world, but you're living here. And I might add you're living in the lap of luxury on the outskirts of Barrington in a huge estate that showcases a three-story brick home."

"So What, Daniel, I have lived here all my life. What's your point?"

"My point is, you should count your blessings. Mandy Manor is one of the largest and oldest homes in Barrington, housing five generations of Redford's before you were born," he reminded her.

"That is probably more sentimental to you than it is to me."

"Is anything sentimental to you, Francis? What about the fact that your daughter was named after this house? Does that mean anything to you?"

"Of course, it does. It's a very special memory that I will always hold dear. I'm not likely to forget how my own mother delivered Mandy in the foyer by candlelight during a severe rainstorm that knocked out all the electrical power."

Chapter Three

By the time summer rolled in, even more gloom took a foothold at Mandy Manor when Lakeland Investments where my father worked experienced a devastating quarter that resulted in a major loss for the company. The unexpected financial crisis set a lot of anguish in motion, like temporary pay-cuts, including my father's. Then my father made immediate household budget cuts. That despair brought even more shouting and bitter fights between my parents. They could barely tolerate to be in the same room with each other without pouring bitter remarks at the other. Therefore, Dad started staying in the city at his hotel room most of the time. Then Mom fell into self pity and depression complaining to visitors and friends that she suffered with pain and aches. She started moping around the house a lot, and attended less functions and events, spending a lot of time in her room, lying in bed.

When Dad dropped by on Friday, he was surprised to hear that she was lying in bed again complaining of a headache. He removed his gray suit jacket and threw it across the arm of the sofa and reached in his back pocket and pulled out a bundle of cash. My eyes widen with surprise. I had never seen that much money at one time.

Dad looked at me and smiled. "I know this seems like a lot of cash to be carrying around, but I pulled it out for our shopping trip tomorrow," he said, smiling. "We need to take you downtown to do your school shopping."

"So we are going shopping downtown tomorrow?" I asked excitedly.

"Yes, we are going shopping," he said as we both hurried up the staircase and down the long hallway toward their bedroom.

The door was propped half open, so we stepped into the room. Mom was lying in bed under the covers, with her head propped on two pillows with a thin blue blanket pulled up to her chin. Her eyes looked red as if she had been crying or maybe drinking wine. She had been crying and drinking white wine a lot lately; and I couldn't tell the difference.

Dad was propped against the door frame with his arms folded. Disappointment poured from his eyes. "In your under the weather condition, Francis," he said across the room. "I'm sure you couldn't perhaps have enough strength to handle a car ride into downtown tomorrow, could you?" he said teasingly in a double talk manner.

Mom sat up in bed and yelled at Dad as if she was looking for a fight. "Do I look like I'm up for a trip, Daniel?" Mom pointed to her face. "I feel just awful. I have been lying in this bed all day."

Dad frowned. "What's the matter with you, Francis?"

"I just told you I feel awful."

"I heard that part, but what I would like to know, what is your condition? There has to be a reason for whatever is causing you to feel this way. Really, Francis, for the past few weeks you have been struggling with one thing or another; and I have yet to hear what's causing your ill feelings. So what is your condition?" Dad asked firmly.

"My condition is that I feel awful, isn't that enough?"

"No, it's not enough," Dad said sharply. "Mandy is worried about you, and frankly I'm starting to get concerned as well."

"Well, there's no need for any concern on your part, Daniel. I'm just under the weather, okay? I'm not dying," Mom shouted.

"Francis, nobody said anything about dying; but have you been to see your doctor?" Dad asked with a curious look on his face.

"No I have not," Mom quickly answered. "Not today." She waved her hand. "It's not that bad that I need to see the doctor?" Mom stared hard at Dad. "Besides, I haven't felt like getting out of bed and making a trip into town."

"I can give Dr. Horton a call and I'm sure he'll drop by the house and give you a check up," Dad quickly suggested.

"Don't bother, Claude Horton, Okay? I just told you I'm not feeling that bad right now."

"But it's bad enough to keep you in bed all day?"

"Yes, it is. I'm exhausted, okay?"

"What are you exhausted from?" Dad held up both arms. "Tell me, what do you do all day? The staff waits on you at your beck and call." Dad shook his head. "Yeah, I guess it can be pretty exhausting having people wait on you hand and feet," Dad joked.

"Stop your wisecracks, Daniel, and just get out and let me be?" Mom pointed toward the door.

"I'll let you be, but one question. If your condition, whatever it is, isn't that bad are you up to going downtown tomorrow?"

"Take a hard look at me, Daniel. Do I look like I'll be up to a trip downtown tomorrow?"

"I'm just checking, Francis. It's for Mandy school shopping, remember?"

"I remember that we never set a date for that yet," Mom reminded him.

"No, we didn't set a date, but I'm suggesting it now." He held out the bundle of cash toward her. "This is for Mandy's school clothes."

Mom shook her head. "Why did you pull out all that money anyway? What happened to your credit card?"

"I wanted the cash so I wouldn't go over budget. When the cash is gone I'll know the shopping is done."

"You and your budgets are ridiculous! You can do the same thing with the cards." Mom threw up both arms. "But it's your money to spend in whatever method you choose."

"Francis, this is about a shopping trip for Mandy. Do you have to be so rude?"

"I'm not being rude. You are being rude to have planned a shopping trip when you clearly knew I wasn't up to it."

"I'm sorry you feel that way, but we can hardly plan our household agenda around your moods," Dad said firmly. "And for the record, I didn't clearly know you were not up to the drive. Frankly, I don't know from one day to the next whether you're going to be out of bed or in bed. I have no idea what's the matter with you lately. But the one thing I do know is that your strange moods are disrupting things around here."

"My strange moods, what is that supposed to mean?"

"Francis, you know it means just what I said. I never know from one day to the next if you are going to be in a good mood, a bad mood or a sick mood. Lately, it's been all about these sick moods. Tell me if that's not strange?"

"Daniel, there's nothing strange about being sick."

"If there's nothing strange about being sick, you might as well know that I ran into Claude Horton the other day, and asked him about you, he said he has diagnosed nothing medically wrong with you. So what gives here?"

"Who cares what Dr. Horton said to you? I think I know how I feel more than my doctor does."

"Of course, you do Francis; and nevermind his medical degree."

"Yes, that's right; nevermind his medical degree. I know what discomfort feels like. I'm not manufacturing these aches and pains, okay?"

"Maybe you're not manufacturing them, but you seem just fine not doing anything about them, other than complaining to whoever will listen." Dad shook his head in disbelief. "So, if you want to lie around here and complaint, and do nothing about it, but still expect for people to feel sympathy as if there's something the matter with your health." Dad paused and shook his head. "Then so be it; but life goes on, Francis, like taking Mandy downtown tomorrow to do her school shopping. So, if you don't mind, I'll just keep this cash and take Mandy downtown myself."

"Don't put Mandy in the middle of this," Mom yelled.

"What's with you, Francis? She's already in the middle of it. It's about you and I doing our parental duty to take her shopping for school clothes," Dad stressed.

"No, it's about a trip you planned. Just give Mandy the money. She's old enough to shop for herself. She doesn't need the both of us lagging along."

"Yes, she's old enough to shop for herself, of course, but I'm not handing over this kind of cash to a fifteen-year-old," Dad said firmly. "I will drive her downtown and I plan to take Miss Smith along to help. She can help carry packages and give Mandy some suggestions."

Miss Doris Smith was Dad's secretary, who had worked for him for the past seven years, but her salary was one thing that Mom had relentlessly fussed about. In the past two years, Mom's attitude had changed toward Miss Smith from cordially to contempt.

After a moment of silence of Mom and Dad staring at each other, Dad asked. "So Francis, let's hear it, what do you think about Miss Smith coming along to help Mandy shop? I'm sure you have a few words to say about that."

"Yes, I do and none of them are good, so why are you asking me, Daniel? I'm sure you will do whatever you please," Mom snapped.

"That's why I'm asking you, Francis. I would like to know if this is acceptable to you, or would you prefer that we wait until you are feeling up to the trip, so you can also go along?"

"You just said we couldn't plan our household agenda around my moods. Now you say you'll wait until I'm feeling up to it. Which is it?"

"I know I said that and I meant just what I said, Francis. We cannot put everything on hold and plan around your moods, but for argument sake, if you want, we can postpone until you'll feeling up to it," he grumbled. "But it needs to be sometime within the next two or three days."

Mom shook her head. "No, I'm not going to change your plans. You made them and you should keep them. Besides, I happen to believe that you planned it this way. You can't say one thing and then turn around and say another. And you are right; it is for argument sake just to throw me a bone," Mom snapped and waved her hand. "But just leave me out of it. Go on and do the shopping without me!" Mom said angrily. "I don't buy it for a second that you want to wait until I'm feeling better. I think you planned this trip, to go shopping without me so you could have an excuse to take that Miss Smith instead," Mom shouted. "So don't stand here and try to make me think it's not what you want!"

"Francis, there's no talking to you!" Dad shouted, walking closer to her bedside.

"And there's no talking to you, Daniel." Mom pointed her finger toward Dad. "Because if you wanted to prove that it's not all about Miss Smith, you would trust Mandy, your own daughter, with that shopping money and let Miss Smith pick Mandy up and take her downtown to shop."

"Think about what you just said, Francis. You think it's just fine for Miss Smith to drive from her apartment in Chicago all the way here to Barrington, pick up Mandy and then drive back to Chicago and help Mandy shop all day; and then after a long exhausting shopping trip, drive Mandy back out here to Barrington and drive herself back to the city," Dad said agitatedly and held out both arms.

"So, what's the big deal? The woman works for you. She needs to start doing something to show that she deserves that big salary you are paying her. Really, Daniel, you are paying her a small fortune. A lot more than you pay the rest of the household staff combined."

"That's a complete lie, Francis, and you know it," Dad yelled.

"It's not a complete lie. You are paying that woman too much money, and why? What does she do other than general office work and a few errands here and there?"

Dad's eyes were filled with anger as he threw the bundle of cash toward Mom. "Francis Redford Clark, I'm not having this conversation with you," he yelled angrily as he grabbed the back of his neck with both hands, and then turned on his heels and hurried across the room. Twenty and fifty dollar bills landed all over the bed and floor.

"That's right, get out! Why did you bother me in the first place?" Mom yelled at his back as he headed toward the door. "Was it something I said, like bringing up Doris Smith? I don't care what you say; with the insanely high salary you are paying that woman I think she needs to do more to show that she has earned it."

Chapter Four

Dad and I arrived in downtown Chicago around noon. We stopped at Miss Smith high-rise apartment and picked her up as planned, but realizing Mom's huge dislike for the lady, I had mentioned to Dad enroot to the city that I didn't need Miss Smith help. I suggested that he and I could manage just fine. However, he wouldn't accept any explanations that would eliminate his secretary from our shopping plans. His reason was, "Since your mother isn't here to help, Miss Smith will be a big help to you, you'll see."

The three of us spent the entire afternoon shopping and after a fun-filled exhausting time of shopping, and visiting what seemed like every store on Michigan Avenue, we ended up with over twenty bags of school clothes, shoes and purses for me. We were done shopping around six-thirty that evening and after we carried all the bags and locked them inside the trunk of the car, Dad took Miss Smith and me to dinner at the Hilton Hotel, the same elite hotel where he roomed at during the week. It was the hotel peak dinner hour and lots of people were sitting around waiting for a table, but the management knew him and seated us at once at one of their reserved tables.

The hotel was fabulous and elegant with white table cloths on all the tables and what seemed like several waiters per table. People were dressed in fine clothing with fine jewelry highlighting their necks and hands. A live band was playing and the delicate sounds of their even tone music floated in the background displaying a feeling of calm and relaxation.

Sitting at the table in the middle of the room, the lighting seemed to hit Dad's face. I stared at him for a moment and smiled. I hadn't seen him look so relaxed and in such a happy mood in a very long time. He appeared to be having a great time and seemed quite interested in the dancing as he kept observing the couples on the dance floor. After dessert, he asked me to dance. It was my first dance in a public place. We danced to just one song, and then he danced with Miss Smith. They danced to two songs before they were seated. Watching the two of them dance made me smile and feel happy inside. It was good to see my father enjoying himself. His secretary was smiling as she had both arms around his back. She seemed content as if she found comfort dancing closely with my father. Watching the two of them dance made me smile and brought warmth to my heart to see Dad enjoy himself. But the vision of him dancing with Miss Smith also brought hopeful thoughts to my mind, that someday in the near future, I would see him and my mother on the floor dancing with each other and enjoying an evening out. I was hopeful that Mom and Dad would get out of the house for dinner and dancing to enjoy themselves together the way he was enjoying the evening with Miss Smith.

When Dad and Miss Smith were seated back at the table, he looked at her and smiled. He reached across the table and gave her a quick touch on the side of her arm.

"Thanks for the dance, Doris."

"You are welcomed, thank you," she said, smiling, not looking across the table in his eyes, but looking down at the glass of white wine in front of her. "I can't remember the last time I was on a dance floor." She lifted her wine glass and took a sip and then gave Dad a quick glance before she looked toward the dance floor.

"It's been awhile for me as well, but I must admit, it was a lot of fun," Dad said, smiling as he lifted his glass and took a sip of his red wine. He looked toward me with a big smile on his face. "Mandy, I think it's safe to say you had fun out on that dance floor as well."

"Dad, that was so much fun, I must say. I had no idea this evening was going to turn out so swell. I can't wait to tell Mom what she missed by not coming."

Those words brought a bit of silence among us, as I noticed Miss Smith and Dad quickly exchanged looks. Bringing up Mom's name seemed like a sore spot for Dad even when she wasn't around.

When she wasn't noticing, I discreetly stared at Miss Smith for a moment. I had never paid much attention to her physical appearance. Now it was like seeing her for the first time. It was clear that she was quite an attractive lady. She was tall at 5'8 and slender with a model figure. She frequently wore her neck length black hair pulled back in a French roll that complimented the stylish glasses that she wore. She seemed somewhat reserved with the look of a librarian. She was ten years younger than Dad, divorced with one child, a son by the name of Dale. Her son, Dale, was three years younger than me. He and I had played together when Miss Smith first started working for my father. In the beginning she came to our home and worked in his study; and during that time she would bring her son and the two of us would play. Sometimes Mom and Dad would pay her to look after me as they went out for an evening.

Noticing how comfortable Dad appeared in the company of with Miss Smith, it made me want to get to know her better. She was seated to my right and I realized at that moment that I had never really paid her that much attention. I knew little of her personally, except she was Dad's secretary and Dale's mother. She always seemed rather quiet and respectful around my father and was always soft spoken and kind to me when I was much younger. However, since I had grown up, I knew her mostly as the woman that my mother had constantly fussed about. Mom frequently argued with Dad regarding how much salary he was paying her. The arguments had never fazed me, since I had always thought of Miss Smith as a nice lady who was just another one of my father's employees. But seated at the table with her, it was clear that she and Dad were more than just boss and worker. They were interacting as if they were close friends. Somewhere along the way while working with each other, they had apparently become good friends and maybe my mother knew of their friendship and felt jealous or threatened by it. But Dad needed a friend to make him smile, and if his secretary was his good friend, someone to make him smile, I could see no harm in that.

Chapter Five

All during the summer of 2000, Mom and Dad continued to grow farther and farther apart and the fact that my father was having financial problems with his firm made the tension between them greater. I prayed on my knees every single night that things would get better between them, but I felt as if my prayers were going unanswered as the household money situation continued to worsen. Dad chose to make cuts to the family budget. He didn't cut the salaries of the household staff or the groundskeeper, but he cut Mom's and my allowance and reduced his secretary salary.

Seated at the breakfast table with my parents that Saturday morning, the spread of food looked delicious: Buttered wheat toast, scrambled eggs, ham, fresh fruit, coffee and orange juice. But in spite of the beautifully set table and wonderful meal before us and all we had to be thankful for, we were all seated with miserable looks on our faces. I could feel the bitter tension between Mom and Dad as they dared to look at each other. It was obvious they were both upset with each other when they made a big deal about an item on the breakfast menu.

Mom rolled her eyes toward Dad, who was seated at the opposite end of the long dinning room table that seated eight. Why did they have to sit so far apart? I always had to pass the food back and forth since I always sat in the middle.

"Daniel, I thought you asked the cook to squeeze fresh orange juice for breakfast this morning?" Mom sipped her orange juice while looking straight at Dad. "I'll have you know that I can tell this is not fresh juice."

"Francis, what's the difference?" Dad lifted his juice glass and sipped his orange juice without glancing toward Mom. "This tastes just as good. I can't tell the difference."

"Well, I can taste the difference, and the point is, I prefer fresh squeeze," Mom snapped. "If you forgot to mention it to the cook, why didn't you tell me?"

"Because maybe I forgot to mention it to the cook and you," Dad barked right back, still not looking her way.

"Maybe you didn't forget. Maybe you chose that frozen can garbage over fresh just so you could save the ridiculous extra dime," Mom said angrily and held an angry stare toward him.

"So, what if I did, Francis? What's the big fuss about? I'm sure we'll survive drinking the frozen can garbage, as you put it," Dad said firmly with an angry stare as he pointed his finger toward Mom. "Besides, Francis, it's ridiculous to sit here at this breakfast table and bitch about such petty things when so many people in the world are starving."

"I dare you to throw something like that in my face to diminish my wants! What does the world starving have to do with the fact that I like fresh squeezed juice?"

"I'm just making a point, Francis. Maybe you should be a little more thankful for what you have," Dad said firmly as he sipped his coffee.

"Daniel you are an inconsiderate bastard to sit here at this breakfast table in front of this child and make me feel guilty for wanting fresh juice when you know we can afford all the damn oranges in this town."

"That may be true, but I'm sure we should be able to drink frozen juice, considering I had to cut my own secretary salary to a ridiculous rate."

"So, that's what this is about! You feel if you have to cut that woman's pay, then surely you can deprived me of a few of the things I want. Did I hit the nail on the head?"

"No, you did not, Francis. The two are not related. But maybe they should be when you thought it made excellent sense to help the budget by cutting Miss Smith salary. But you don't see the same logic for cutting back on unnecessary kitchen items."

"Daniel, you can spin it anyway you like but you know I'm right. You're pissed for cutting that woman's pay. And even though you should have, I'm just surprised you did."

"Francis, you're off base as usual; I'm not pissed. I'm just embarrassed to expect full time work from the woman when I'm giving her part-time pay at the moment."

"You're embarrassed to hand that woman her pay? That's a laugh and it's news to me, considering you're not feeling any shame in asking me to cut back on what I spend around here," Mom snapped angrily, pointing to her juice glass. "Like my fresh orange juice for instances."

"Francis, get over it! It comes with the territory," Dad stated.

"What territory?" Mom asked.

"It's your sentence, I guess," Dad laughed.

"And what is that suppose to mean?"

"The sentence that comes along with a marriage certificate," Dad explained. "One of the penalties for being my wife," Dad laughed again.

"But really Daniel, there's nothing funny about it. This is ridiculous," Mom stressed. "We really don't need to cut back to the degree you are pushing us."

"I happen to disagree. I'm in charge of this budget and I think this is the right choice."

"The right choice, for who?" Mom took a bite of toast and then took her fork and poked in her scrambled eggs.

"You mean for whom?" Dad teased at her word selection.

"No, I mean for who and I'm not trying to be proper and say whom?" Mom snapped. "So just tell me, Daniel, who is this choice actually suppose to benefit?"

"It's the right choice for the household, and that includes all of us." Dad dipped his knife in the butter dish and placed a tad of whipped butter on his toast. "We will all benefit," he said, cutting into a piece of buttered toast. "Think about it. My pay has been cut in half for now and we need to live accordingly."

"But for what, Daniel? Why should we?" Mom argued.

"Francis, it's the sensible thing to do." Dad took a sip of coffee and glanced toward the doorway. "We need to lower our voices otherwise all the staff is going to hear our business."

Mom smiled, shook her head and seemed indifferent. "I'm sure they already know."

"Just the same, they shouldn't be privy to our disagreements."

"You are right, Daniel. We do disagree on this issue. You call it sensible and I call it unnecessary."

"That's because you were born with a silver spoon in your mouth, Francis," Dad said firmly, staring hard at Mom.

"And you weren't born with a silver spoon in your mouth, Daniel Clark?"

"He stared at her hard. "Is that a statement or a question?" Dad asked, biting into another piece of buttered toast with his eyes looking toward Mom, "Because we both know the answer."

He shook his head. "So I was born into money, so what?" Dad asked.

"Sometime I wonder about you. The way you carry on at times, you act as if you were born in a paper box," Mom mumbled.

"Francis, you don't wonder. We just have different viewpoints about wealth. You see it as entitlement, but no way do I see it that way. I was born into wealth but I refuse to allow it to swell my head or make me think that I'm somehow entitled," Dad explained calmly. "Because, really, think about it Francis. We are not entitled; we are just two people who were lucky enough to be born into the wealth of someone else's hard work and sacrifice really. I for one, I'm thankful for all that we have and don't see it as I'm better than anyone else because I'm more fortunate. Therefore, all this ranting and raving from you about these little things is just you being snobbish and difficult as usual."

"I'm not being snobbish and difficult! I'm just stating my case!"

"So, you're stating your case and I stated mine; and the bottom line here, Francis, is that I'm trying to make a point. Why can't you see that, Francis?"

"I can't see it because it doesn't make sense to me. Why should we sweat and change our living habits when our bank account has more zeros than we can count on one hand?" Mom stressed. "More money than we will ever spend; and you're treating this little situation that happened at your job as if we are about to stand in the soup line."

"That's not the point, Francis." Dad pushed his plate aside and leaned forward, placing both elbows on the table.

"Why isn't it the point?" Mom raised both hands. "You tell me, are we just supposed to let money set in the bank and rot? My folks didn't do that and there's no reason why we should."

"Francis, come on and work with me here. I'm sure you see the bigger picture I'm getting at."

"No, Daniel, I do not see your bigger picture. All I see is how you're trying to make us live beneath our means." Mom pointed her finger toward Dad. "I'm telling you right now, I will not continue to do it. Is that clear Daniel Clark? I see no reason to put Mandy through this preposterous notion of yours to live according to your paycheck when we shouldn't have to."

"Francis, I think your thinking on the matter is more preposterous than my proposal. You would have us throw the budget out of the window just because we have money in the bank. That makes no sense. I'm good with finances and I think I know a thing or two about numbers."

"Okay, Daniel, if that's the case, try counting the numbers in your own bank account," Mom stressed seriously.

"Why should I bother, I'm sure you already have! Really, Francis, get a clue. Finances and numbers are what I do. That's why I have my job helping others figure out theirs. So let me ask you this question, just how long do you think our numbers in our account would last if they were not managed?"

"Daniel, I don't care what you say. Cutting our allowance is unacceptable. Clearly I'm upset about it and I'm sure Mandy isn't happy about it."

"She hasn't complained to me," Dad snapped. "But so be it, I'll reverse the cut," Dad said calmly and held up one finger. "But, you need to know right now that it will be a cross the board reversal, which means my secretary pay cut will also be reversed to her normal salary."

Chapter Six

For all the financial matters and the angry arguments between Mom and Dad, particularly when Dad got so upset and cancelled our annual two week summer vacation trip to France, it was still a fun summer for me. For one thing, I was getting older and going through a particular romantic dreamy period, indulging myself with every love story I could get my hands on. I kept my nightstand stacked with romance novels that put me to sleep each night with a smile on my face and love in my heart for some imaginary couple. I was particularly interested in stories of well-mannered gentlemen of fairly tales long ago, mostly stories that included a handsome dashing prince that always ended up with his princess. And my monthly trips downtown with my father seemed to intensify my enchanting and romantic daydreams. It wasn't what we did on our trips that mattered, whether we took a walk along the lake, a picnic at the park, or lunch at some nice restaurant; it was the fun, the laughter and the freedom from all the bitter arguments between him and Mom that overshadowed our house when we were all at home together.

They had gotten to the point where they disagreed about nearly everything they discussed. There was no middle ground for the two of them. If Dad liked something, Mom would usually find fault with it and if she liked something, he would usually find fault with it. It seemed more and more that they were disagreeing with each other just for the sake of disagreeing. Therefore, the tension increased in the fall, when Dad wanted Mom support and consent in his efforts to sell a piece of property that they jointly owned. She refused flatly. She also made a big fuss and talked him out of selling a piece of property that he owned. He was so upset with her that he talked to me about some of the things that were burdening him.

It was a Friday evening after Mom had left for bingo. Dad and I were seated in the living room watching a movie. I was curled up comfortable on the long white sofa and he was relaxing in his favorite comfortable white chair when he glanced over at me and said.

"Mandy, I'm sorry that your mother and I keep having the same disagreements over the household budget and our financial issues altogether." He had both legs propped on the ottoman with both arms behind his head as he stretched back in the chair.

"Its okay, Dad; I try not to listen," I mumbled.

"I'm sure you try not to pay any attention to what you hear when your mother and I are going at it, but we have gotten more and more vocal lately; and I'm sure it's hard to avoid our ridiculous arguments."

"That's because sometime you and Mom can get pretty loud," I mumbled.

"You're right, we can get pretty loud. I'm sorry that we haven't been exactly discreet with our arguments lately." He shook his head. "But never-the-less, I'm sure you don't understand all this money talk. It's just that Francis and I totally disagree about how to handle the budget in this situation. Not to mention the fact that even though I'm not bringing as much home, I still need extra funds for a few projects and would prefer to sell unused property than to pull out cash."

"What about borrowing from yourself, Dad, and when everything is okay again, just pay yourself back?" I suggested.

Dad looked at me as if what I had just said surprised him. However, he didn't comment on what I had said.

"Once Lakeland survives this rough patch within the next couple months, and stay on track without falling into the red again, and I'm sure it will stay on course," he said with overwhelming confidence. "All will be good with the world again. Everything will balance out with the books and Lakeland Investments will be on solid footing just as before; and I'll receive a substantial bonus to boot."

"You'll receive a substantial bonus?" I asked. "That sounds like a lot?"

"Well, that's what it will be, which will actually replace all the pay that has been cut from my salary and more," he stressed seriously. "So, by no means do I want you to think that my job is headed downhill or that this family is in any real financial trouble. This is just a phase. The company is solid. We just stumbled upon a block in the road, which is a normal pitfall for any business from time to time," he explained.

"I think I understand, Dad," I said.

"Well even if you don't, it's not your place to understand all this stuff. Your mother understands, but doesn't seem to care."

"Why wouldn't she?" I asked.

"Your mother is your mother. She won't listen. Her priorities are in a different place. I tried to explain a few things to her, but as I said, she won't listen to anything that has anything to do with me selling any of our properties; and just because it was my idea she instantly slammed the door on it."

"In that case, maybe you should have told her that you didn't want to sell any properties," I suggested, laughing to myself.

Dad glanced at me and right back at the movie we were watching. It was almost as if he ignored my comment, not commenting on my remark. "Your mother just won't listen to anything I have to say," he continued.

"Just like you won't listen to Mom about taking a withdrawal from the bank," I glanced at him and mumbled softly."

Dad stared hard at me again. He had a certain look in his eyes as if he wondered if I was being sarcastic with my comments. However, he was right about Mom. She was just trying to punish him for punishment sake. I could still hear her words in the back of my mind.

"Your father thinks he's a financial genius so let him figure out a way on his own. If he thinks he's clever enough to take care of all of our financial business with just half of a regular salary without withdrawing a dime from the bank, then let him figure out how. Back when your father and I attended the University of Illinois together, everybody on campus called him the boy genius Daniel Clark; and now I would agree that he's a man genius at not spending money," Mom said disappointedly.

Mom had her doubts, but I had complete faith in my father. And whatever else I had doubts about, I kept my faith in him. I knew both of my parents had their faults, but because of Dad's smart business mind and his no non-sense personality, I had a tendency to give him more leeway with his shortcomings.

Chapter Seven

In early October, something shook me awake in the middle of the night. I quickly sat up in bed with the thought that Mom and Dad were probably arguing again. Their arguments were interrupting my sleep regularly. I sat quietly almost holding my breath, clutching the bedspread up to my chin. For a moment as I sat there looking toward my open door into the dark hallway, all I could hear was dead silence and the sharp tick-tock of the little silver clock that sat on my bedside table. Then just as inhaled sharply and fell back on the pillow to try and fall back to sleep, the racket started again and this time I could hear Dad's voice, loud and shouting with a bitter edge.

"Certainly there's no point in our going on and on like this, Francis," he yelled. "You seem to have zero respect for me and disregard with everything I say, do you not?"

"Well, I guess we are even there," Mom shouted bitterly.

"You think we are even, I wouldn't say so. I'm not as difficult about everything as you are, Francis. Whatever I say or the slightest suggestion I make, you flatly disagree with it. It's clear to me that you are not interested in putting any efforts toward this marriage anymore!"

"You are accusing me of not wanting to put any efforts toward this marriage anymore?"

"That's right, as far as I'm convinced, actions speak louder than words; and that's the bottomline as far as I can see it," Dad yelled.

"Bark all you want, Daniel. But this is a two-way street. You can turn the tables and try to place all of this into my lap if you like, as if you are putting forth all the efforts in the world?" Mom shouted.

"Francis, I know we both need to do better and try harder," Dad said in a calmer voice. "But you just don't try to meet me halfway. You constantly carry a chip around on your shoulder and you won't let me in on why."

"I'll give you one clue," Mom snapped. "There's no affection in this room!"

"There's no affection in this room," Dad repeated. "Is that your answer?"

"Yes that's my answer, and I think that says it all. There's no affection in this bedroom, none, zip! Is that clear enough an answer for you, Daniel?"

"Francis, please, that's also a two-way street."

"Oh, is that right? It's a two-way street now? It's funny how you didn't worry about my lack of aggression in the past. So, what has changed?" Mom shouted angrily.

"I think you know what has changed," Dad quickly remarked.

"Yes, Daniel, I do know. I'll tell you what has changed! You are probably spreading your affection too thin, elsewhere!"

"Think whatever you like, Francis," Dad stumbled with his words, not defending Mom's assumptions.

"That's actually what I'm doing. I'm putting two and two together. You're not giving me any affection anymore and it makes me wonder," Mom yelled.

"That's my point, Francis. It's hard to be affectionate to an unwilling bitter person."

"I'm the one who's bitter and you're not?"

"Yes, Francis, you're the one who's bitter to put it mildly; and you won't meet me halfway on absolutely anything. I just want you to meet me halfway."

"The way you meet me halfway? Give me a break, Daniel. When have you ever listened to anything I had to say or accepted any of my suggestions?"

"Like I said, I agree that we are both at fault," Dad said.

"Okay, if you agree that we are both at fault, why do you always twist all the blame for our troubles to clearly fall on my shoulders?"

"Francis, I'm not doing that. It's all in your head to think so."

"It's not all in my head," Mom shouted angrily. "You blame all our problems and disagreements on me!"

"Well, we're even, because you blame all our problems on me," he said firmly and paused. "And I guess it makes sense since we have long since fell out of love. All the love in this marriage left with the wind long ago!"

"So, you're telling me there's no love left in this marriage?"

"Francis, that's exactly what I'm saying," Dad stated sadly.

"I see, so you think we're all out of love now; is that what you're saying? Is that what you think, Daniel?" Mom cried.

"Yes, Francis, that's what I'm saying! I do believe we are out of love for each other!"

"And what brought you to that conclusion?" Mom asked.

"It should be as clear to you as it is to me. We can't be in the same room with each other without ripping into each other. Our behavior with each other doesn't sound like love to me, if you ever loved me in the first place. Therefore, to continue this farce of a marriage is ludicrous if you ask me."

"Is it ludicrous that we have a young daughter in the room down the hall who needs both of her parents?"

"Francis, do not bring Mandy into this conversation."

"Why not bring her into this conversation? The decisions and choices we make will affect her as well, or have that slipped your brilliance mind?" Mom cried.

"I can assure you, Francis, nothing has slipped my mind, but this is our mess and Mandy doesn't need to know all of our dirty laundry!"

"She's not blind and she's not deaf, Daniel. She can see and hear what's happening in this house between us."

"You are right, Francis. I'm sure she can see what is happening in this house! If nothing else, we have neon signs taped to our backs that read: miserable couple. And that's one of the points I'm trying to make," Dad explained.

"I'm sorry but you have lost me as usual with your rambling on," Mom snapped.

"Francis, don't you get it. Mandy is a smart young lady, and I'm sure she can feel this awful tension and bitterness between us," he said calmly and paused. "What we have here is just not working!"

"So, if it's not working, we need to fix it," Mom cried.

"Why should we even try?" Dad asked.

"Why should we try? I'll give you a hundred reasons why we should try," Mom said tearfully. "I honestly cannot believe you just asked me that question."

"Well, believe it, Francis. Because I'm about to repeat it; I really don't think we should try saving a dead in the water marriage."

"I'm sure you don't, Daniel. As I said before, you are no longer interested in this marriage; and I guess the vows you made for better or for worse have been crossed off your list."

"It's not off my list, I just feel it's useless to try," Dad said regretfully.

"You need to think again, because we have one real good reason. I think for our daughter's sake is a good enough reason," Mom continued to speak through tears. "And I think it's a reason that should matter."

"Yes, I agree. Mandy deserves to grow up in a home with both of her parents. But not like this. Maybe, if our hearts were really into it. But why should we prolong something that's not going to get any better. Think about it, Francis, and just be honest. You and I have long since passed the point of really caring for each other in that way," Dad said sadly.

"Speak for yourself, Daniel. Don't pretend to know how or what I'm feeling, especially where you are concerned," Mom yelled angrily.

"Francis, if you have feelings for me, you are good at keeping them to yourself. When was the last time we were really together?"

"Are we going to get into that conversation again?"

"I think it's the conversation that we should be having if you have any kind of notion that this marriage can be fixed," Dad stated firmly.

"Daniel, there's more to a marriage than that."

"I agree, but there's not much of one without it," Dad snapped.

"Okay, I get it. Now, you're going to say that's the reason for the breakdown of this marriage?"

"I'm not saying that, Francis. But you just said a few minutes ago that I don't show you any affection anymore; but have you ever thought how you don't invite it. Well, have you?"

"Daniel, that's not the be-all to end-all! Translation, it's not everything," Mom tearfully snapped.

"Maybe not, but I'm just saying, it's another nail in our coffin along with all the other stuff that we can't seem to get a handle on or see eye to eye on."

"So just like that you feel this marriage is doomed and can't be fixed?" Mom asked firmly.

"That's right, Francis, it's doomed for sure. And it doesn't take a rocket scientist to figure that out. We can't even have a simple discussion without yelling and jumping down each other's throats. If that's not a sign of doomsville, what is?"

"It sounds as if you want it to be doomed!" Mom spoke in a defeated voice.

"Francis, I don't want it to be doomed. It just is. It just can't be fixed. It's broken to the point of no repair," Dad stressed.

"Why can't we just try? We can go to a marriage counselor or something," Mom calmly suggested.

"Francis, we have been over this before. Why should we throw good money after bad? It would do no good. All the counseling in the world can not drain all the bitterness and contempt out of this marriage!"

"How do you know, Daniel, if we don't at least try to fix this?"

"Francis, you speak of trying to fix it. Where would we start? Frankly, I see absolutely no way out of this rudeness and anger that we seem to have for each other, other than just to end this mockery that we call a marriage."

"Okay, I get it. Our union is a mockery to you and I don't plan to continue pleading to you. If you are so willing to throw in the towel, then so be it!"

"Give me a break, Francis; I wouldn't have all this gray hair in my head at 41 years of age if I had been willing to throw in the towel. I would have thrown in the towel long before now; because frankly, we should have ended this misery between us years ago!"

"Why didn't you?" Mom cried out.

"Because I wanted to try to fix it," Dad mumbled sadly.

"But no more trying I guess. You're done trying, is that right Daniel Clark?"

"Yes, Francis, I'm done up to my neck!"

"Whatever, see if I lose any more sleep over it. If you can't stomach being married to me any longer, then I don't want your pity. Go right ahead and get your divorce if that's what you want Daniel Clark," Mom cried.

"Francis, this is not about me and what I want. It's about you and me, the two of us and what we need to do for the sake of our sanity."

"Blah, blah, blah, you can preach until the cows come home, but I'm not on board with you ending this marriage," Mom said tearfully.

"What marriage? Do you call what we have a marriage? I can think of a few names for it, but marriage isn't one of them," Dad stressed firmly.

"And is that because we are always fighting at each other's throats?" Mom asked.

"You said it, I didn't," Dad mumbled.

"Well, think about it, Daniel, we are usually always fighting because you get on my nerve or upset me about something, just like now," Mom shouted.

"Okay, Francis, as usual it's entirely my fault and I guess you bear none of the blame for the breakdown of this marriage," Dad pointed out. "You can sit there and cry as if you want to keep this marriage together, but I'm not buying it. Actions speak louder than words. I don't think you want to stay in this union anymore than I want to accept the fact that it's over."

"If you want to leave this house; and separate yourself from me and your daughter, then do it! But do it with the knowledge that it's not what I want. Don't sit here and put words in my mouth and make this my choice. When we talk to Mandy, make it clear that it's what you want. Just you, Daniel," Mom said sadly.

"Whatever, Francis, you never admit to how you really feel. Why should now be any different."

"I dare you to give me such disrespect, totally disregarding what I say and how I feel. I think I know if I want out of this marriage or not. I agree that you totally get under my skin more than I would like. But I'm not ready and willing to throw what we have away just because we have reached a critical point in our marriage. However, if you don't think what we have is worth fighting for, then that's you. But this sudden burst of urgency of needing a divorce makes me wonder about your motives. That maybe your motives go deeper than the problems between us."

"Francis, what are you trying to get at?" Dad asked.

"I'm just trying to figure you out and your sudden rush to end this marriage."

"It's not a sudden rush. Our marriage has been on the rocks for a very long time now. I know and you know it, and by now I'm sure the entire staff knows it as well."

"But why now? If you could stomach the rocks for a very long time as you say, why you can't stomach it now? What has changed?"

"I have changed. I'm fed up with all the anger and disrespect. Focusing on my work and Mandy is hard enough. I don't need the added pressure of coming home to such animosity and hostility. There is never a kind exchange between us anymore."

"Whatever, Daniel, if you want to walk away without even trying to fix what's broken between us. Just go ahead and do that, but listen to me good, if you go through with this divorce, Daniel Clark, I will make you pay through your wallet big time. I will hit you right in the two places that seem to matter the most to you: your bank account and Mandy. And of course, after she realizes how you have broken up our home, she'll probably grow to resent you; and will probably cut the amount of time she spending with you."

I leaped out of bed and dashed down the hall into their room. I stood in the doorway with tears falling down my face. Mom and Dad looked around stunned to see me standing there. Mom's face was covered in tears and her eyes looked swollen as if she had been crying for a long time. She was wearing a long sky blue nightgown. But Dad was fully dressed as he stood there staring at me with a cross of surprise and anger in his eyes. Then he grabbed his suit coat that hung across the nearby settee and threw it on. I ran to him and threw my arms around him.

"Dad, where are you going? Please don't leave us, Dad," I cried.

"Mandy, don't you worry about a thing. Everything is going to be fine, just go back to bed," Dad suggested.

"Dad, I'm not some ten-year-old. I can see what's going on. How can you say everything is going to be fine? It's in the middle of the night and you are fully dressed. I know you are leaving. I heard you say it," I cried.

"I know it's in the middle of the night and I'm dressed, but I promise you, I'm not leaving," Dad assured me. "I'm just going outside for some fresh air. I need to clear my head. I'll be back I promise."

I wouldn't let him go. I kept my arms wrapped tightly around him. "Dad, I think you are leaving us." I shook my head as tears rolled down my face. "I don't think you are going outside for fresh air. I think you're leaving us and not coming back."

"Mandy, I'm not leaving. Why would you think that?"

"Because I just told you, I heard you and Mom arguing about a divorce. You are going to get a divorce and leave us," I cried uncontrollable.

"Mandy, listen, sweetheart, I'm sorry you heard us, but nothing is going to happen tonight. I'm sorry our voices were so loud that we awakened you and you overheard us arguing." He gripped my shoulders and held me at arm length staring at me with concerned eyes. "But please calm down, sweetheart, and don't let our silly argument upset you like this. Your mother and I are always arguing about one thing or the other. And some of the stuff you may have overheard, we may not have meant," Dad explained.

"But did you mean it?" I stared up in his eyes hoping he would say no.

"Did I mean what, sweetheart?" Dad asked.

"Did you mean it about getting a divorce?"

He just stared at me with sad eyes as if my question had stunned him. And then, Mom spoke up. "Just tell her the truth, Daniel. If you won't, I will."

I glanced at Mom and then back at my father. "So, Dad, is it true?"

"Mandy, we didn't want to tell you like this, in the middle of the night, in between one of our arguments, but since you have asked and I wouldn't dream of lying to you. The answer is yes. There is a possibility that your mother and I could get a divorce."

"I beg you two, please don't." I looked toward Mom and she pointed toward Dad.

"Don't look at me, sweetheart. Make no mistake about this. This is entirely your father's decision. This is what he wants."

"Mandy, it's not what I want. It's where your mother and I seem to be headed. And if we can't work things out, I think it's for the best."

"I hate this, Dad, and I hope and pray with all my heart that you won't get a divorce and leave us. But if you do, I hope you'll still come see us and spend time with me."

He held me to him for a long moment and then kissed the top of my head.

"Of course I'll still spend time with you. You are my precious daughter and that will never change."

Mom cried sadly, as though my words had punched her in the stomach. "Mandy, don't let your father off the hook by hoping he'll spend time with you. He shouldn't leave you in the first place. He's trying to break up this family?"

I looked at Mom not sure why she suddenly seemed upset with me.

"Mom, I just asked if he would still come see us and spend time with me."

"I know what you asked. How can you make him feel better by asking if he'll still spend time with you, when he is the one who's destroying this family? And I know you don't mean too, sweetheart, but saying that to your father is like letting him off the hook for breaking up this family," Mom said sadly, and then fell back onto her pillow in tears.

"You're mad at Dad and he's mad at you. I'm not trying to take any sides or let him off the hook for wanting to leave us. I don't want Dad to leave us," I cried, ran to her bedside and threw my arms around her. "I love you both so much. The thought of you two breaking up is like a nightmare to me."

Mom sat up, held me in her arms and yelled at Dad. "Daniel, I dare you to upset this child as you have with all your talk of breaking up this family with a divorce. So, if you want a divorce, go out and get one," she said tearfully as she nervously shook all over. "But I would like to know what grounds are you going to divorce me on? Maybe you'll lie and say I have been a louse of a mother; or maybe you'll lie and say I have been an unfaithful wife or maybe you'll lie and say something else appalling about me just to help your case."

"I'm not going to lie about you, Francis," Dad said, standing next to the door. "The truth is enough for any judge to grant our divorce. We are constantly upsetting and hurting each other. We can't continue this way. Those are the grounds."

"But a divorce, Dad," I said softly, staring at him. "Why get a divorce to end your marriage? This is a huge house, why can't we all stay together under the same roof?"

Dad shook his head. "Mandy, I'm going to take that walk now. This isn't the time to continue this conversation."

"But if you divorce Mom, you'll stay at that hotel all the time and never come home." I flew off the bed, leaving my mother's side. I had to stop my father from leaving the house, even if he was only taking a walk. But suddenly as I headed across the large room toward him, reaching middle-ways the room, a sharp pain ripped through my stomach.

I grabbed my stomach and screamed. "Oh, my goodness, I'm in pain."

"Are you okay, Mandy?" Dad asked as he rushed toward me.

"I feel sick like I could vomit. I feel extremely sick in my stomach."

Mom hopped out of bed and she and Dad held me up, one on each side of me and took me to the kitchen where I sat at the kitchen table as they both fussed over me to make me a cup of hot tea. My upset stomach and nerves settled after the cup of hot mint tea. The sick feeling vanished and I didn't feel the urge to throw up, but the thought of their pending divorce made me feel as if I needed to.

Chapter Eight

Three weeks after their big fight, he started staying permanently at his hotel room downtown. They had minimum communication with each other but he still came home on Fridays to spend time with me. I was crushed and extremely sadden by the distant between them, but pleased that he was sticking with his routine of spending time with me.

Looking forward to seeing Dad, when I arrived home from school that Friday, I had an anxious feeling in the pit of my stomach. I ran throughout the entire house asking everybody I could find, the housekeeper, the cook, the laundress, just one question. I wanted to know if my father had telephoned and what time he was coming out. None of the staff that I asked seemed to know, and to make matters worse there was no message from him. Mom and I had an early dinner and then she left the house with some of her friends to go play bingo. I figured she left so early because she didn't want to be home to see Dad when he arrived to pick me up. And on the other hand, if he was thinking the same way and didn't want to run into her, he probably wouldn't arrive to pick me up until around seven-thirty, since that was the usual time Mom left for bingo on a Friday night.

Very excited about his visit, I quickly dressed and then settled down in the living room to wait for him, but when an hour passed and I heard the grandfather clock in the far corner of the dinning room ring ding dong at eight-thirty, my nerves tightened at the thought of something being wrong. I hopped off the sofa and strutted across the living room floor to stand at the living room window. I looked out into the darkness across the grounds with my mind in wonderment. I stood there for over fifteen minutes staring out, hoping Dad would pull into the driveway but his car never showed. I walked across the room and flopped back on the sofa and grabbed the phone off the end table and anxiously holding the phone on my lap, I dialed his work number. I listened to at least six rings before I hung up the receiver. Sitting there on the sofa with the phone still in my lap, cold fear settled over me. I thought to myself, "Dad wouldn't disappoint me. He never forgot to pick me up on Fridays. Something awful must have happened to him!" But I didn't know what to do. Then I thought of Miss Smith. But I didn't have her number. I thought for a second, placed the phone back on the end table, hopped off the sofa and ran down the hallway to Dad's study. I took a seat on the big brown leather chair and searched around on his desk and through all the drawers with no luck until I flipped through the rolodex near his phone. I located Miss Smith's number and dialed it quickly from the phone in the study.

The phone rang and rang and finally on the seventh ring she answered. "Hello," she said as if she was out of breath.

"Hi Miss Smith, this is Mandy."

"Hi Mandy, hold on just a second, I need to place these bags in the kitchen. You caught me just getting in from the market."

A few minutes later she was back on the phone. "I'm sorry to keep you waiting. Is everything alright?" she asked in a concerned manner.

"I'm sorry to bother you, but I'm trying to find my father."

"You are trying to find Daniel?" She asked with surprise in her voice.

"Yes, do you know where he is?" I asked.

"Mandy, I can't help you there. I have no idea where your father could be."

"You must know or have some idea since you make all his appointments."

"But not after work hours. I'm sorry, Mandy."

"I was sure you would know. I don't know what happened or where he could be. He has never stood me up when we have plans. He didn't come home to pick me up, and he didn't call."

"Something probably came up; I'm sure you'll hear from him soon?" she said.

"But it's already far past the time; and I think you know he always comes home on Fridays to see me."

"Yes, I'm aware of his schedule and knew he would be driving out to see you this evening," she said.

After a moment of silence, she said. "Although, he keeps me abreast of his appointments, and his plans with you are listed on his agenda, I'm not sure where Daniel is. Does your mother know? Did he call her?"

"I don't think he called Mom. They are not getting along that well. Besides, I'm sure she would have mentioned it if he had called and cancelled. But I didn't ask her and she's not home right now," I said sadly.

I didn't know what else to say to Miss Smith. She didn't seem to know where my father could be and I was positive when I dialed her number that she would be able to tell me exactly where he was.

Then after another moment of silence, Miss Smith asked. "Did you try calling him on his cell phone?"

"He doesn't have a cell phone."

"You're right he doesn't," she said. "What about his office? Did you try calling his office?"

"Yes, I called his office and punched in his extension, but I didn't get an answer. That's why I called you."

"Mandy, if your father is not answering his phone at his hotel room or his office, I'm not sure what I can do," she said softly without concern in her voice. "I didn't list any other appointments for him other than the one with you."

"I was hoping you could do me a huge favor and go back to the office and check on him," I mumbled humbly.

"Mandy, you're asking me to go back into the office to see if Daniel is there?" She asked, puzzled.

"Please, Miss Smith, since you only live a few blocks from your job."

"Mandy, I want to calm your fears, but I guess I don't feel the alarm that anything is wrong with your father."

"But I feel alarmed and wish you would go back to the office and see if he is there and call and let me know," I insisted.

"So, you want me to go back into work to check if he's working late?" She asked, sounding a bit distracted. "Mandy, I understand your concern but a drive back to the office is really uncalled for," she said firmly. "I'm sure your father is fine and will call you as soon as he gets a chance."

"Maybe you're right but I feel uneasy about this whole thing. It's not like Dad to not call or show up. So could you please just do me this favor and drive back to the office to see if he's still there working late?"

"Mandy, it hasn't been that long since I left the office and Daniel wasn't there, sweetheart. I'm sure he's okay and will call you soon," she tried to assure me.

"But he hasn't called," I said anxiously, thinking the worst. "So please tell me how long ago?" I asked.

"Calm down, Mandy. How long ago...? What are you referring to?"

"You said it hasn't been that long since you left the office. How long ago did you leave the office?"

"Maybe an hour," she said.

"An hour is a long time. Maybe he went back to the office, could you please go and check. I'm worried about him because he has never missed coming out on a Friday for our evenings together. He has always called long before time if he had to work late," I stressed. "So, please Miss Smith, will you go back to the office and check and then call me back, please."

"Okay, Mandy, I can tell you are quite worried about Daniel and quite persistence. "I'm sure he's okay, but I'll take a drive over to the building to see if he went back into work for some reason," she said, not sounding too pleased to bother.

"Thank you, Miss Smith."

"Mandy, remember, I asked you to call me Doris and would appreciate it very much if you would," she said politely but firmly through the phone.

"Okay, Doris. Thank you so much."

"You are welcomed and I'll give you a call or have Daniel give you a call if I locate him," she said and hung up the receiver.

It was a full hour before the phone rang again. I was sitting on the living room sofa with the phone sitting in my lap. I picked up the receiver on the first ring and without checking the caller ID assumed it was Doris.

"Hello, Doris. Did you find Dad?"

Her voice sounded a bit anxious. "Yes, Mandy, all is okay with the world again," she said, laughing. "I found Daniel here at his hotel room; and you were right to be concerned about him not showing up at the time he promised. I guess you know your father quite well."

"Oh, no, did something happen? What do you mean I was right?" I asked anxiously, not giving her a chance to speak.

Then I paused as fear ran through me. I took a deep breath and braced myself during those few moments of silence as I felt panicky. But figured her news couldn't be too bad since she was laughing with relief in her voice.

"Are you still there, Mandy?" She asked.

"Yes, I'm here," I said, wondering what her next words would be.

"Your father is just fine," she said slowly and softly. "He just ran into a little car trouble and ended up getting stuck at the auto shop longer than he anticipated, but he said to let you know that he's still heading home. He said don't fall asleep because he wants to have a late snack with you when he gets there."

Chapter Nine

Swiftly Dad's job was back on track again. It kept him extremely busy to the point that he was making so much in bonuses that Mom seemed almost happy again. Plus, my own emotional state and peace of mind rose when it seemed like peace had settled over the house. However, it was just an illusion of happiness, since Mom and Dad were still basically separated. Dad was still staying at his hotel room downtown most of the time and only coming home on Fridays to see me.

Then suddenly, all hope and happiness as I had known in my life, died for me that breezy afternoon in the spring of 2002, when I arrived home from school. It caught me off guard since I had developed a false sense of hope about Mom and Dad's marriage. We were so wrapped up in happiness and good cheer that Dad's firm was back on track, until their fragile marriage had slipped to the back of my mind.

When I stepped off the school bus that mild Wednesday in April, and headed up the driveway, I swallowed hard as anxiety settled in my stomach when I didn't see Mom standing in the door. Without fell for as long as I could remember, rain or shine, she always waited sandwich between the doors as the school bus dropped me off. On edge because of all the chaos that was going on with my parent's trouble marriage, I ran toward the house in tears thinking the worse. I stumbled up the steps and across the porch with my textbooks in my arms; and in no mood to dig through my purse or book bag for my house key, I rung the doorbell. A couple minutes later, our cook, Mrs. Ronda Lawson opened the door.

I tore past her and rushed inside without saying hello or thanks, but didn't get far when I tripped on the rug in the foyer, falling on my knees. At that moment, the laundress, Mrs. Erica Staten, was walking through with an armful of fresh folded linens. I had startled her and caused her to stumble and drop the bed sheets to the floor.

"Oh, my goodness, Mandy, are you okay?"

"Yes, Mrs. Staten, I'm okay; I'm sorry I caused you to drop the linens."

Mrs. Erica Staten had only worked as our laundress for three years. She was a short stout built middle-aged very nice and polite little lady, but didn't talk much. She seemed anxious as she assisted Mrs. Lawson, as the two of them gathered me and my textbooks up off the floor.

Mrs. Staten patted my back and handed me my books.

"Be careful Mandy," said as she gathered up the linens off the floor and went on about her work.

Mrs. Lawson was still standing there with a concern look on her face.

"Mandy, you seem bothered about something, tripping like that." She placed her hands on her hips. "Is something the matter?" She asked with concern on her face.

Mrs. Lawson was somewhat overweight, a grandmother type and seemed too elderly to be a cook in someone else's kitchen. But she loved her job and made the best meals ever. She and her husband, Isaac, the groundskeeper, and her daughter, Vanessa, the housekeeper seemed like a part of the family. They had all worked for us since the time I was seven years old.

I stood looking at her almost shaking. "Is Mom okay?"

"She was just fine ten minutes ago when she gave me the menu for dinner. Why do you ask? Is everything okay?"

I stared at Mrs. Lawson for a moment, realizing I was probably alarming her needlessly. "I'm sorry to alarm you," I mumbled. "But I was just wondering since she's always standing in the door when the school bus drops me off."

Mrs. Lawson smiled and looked at me as if I was being silly. "Is Francis still doing that? My word, you are a big teenager now."

I smiled. "I guess I am, but yes, she does."

"Young lady, not seeing your mother standing at the door is what have you in such a knot, tripping over the rug and dropping your textbooks, or is there something wrong that you're not telling me?"

Mrs. Lawson could be quite curious but my mother had stressed how she didn't want me burdening the staff with my problems; and since Mrs. Lawson wasn't aware of my parents' marital problems I didn't feel comfortable mentioning it and confiding their personal business to her.

I nodded. "I know it's silly, but I'm okay now."

"Okay," she touched my arm and headed to the left toward the kitchen.

"What's for dinner," I asked.

She glanced over her shoulder and smiled. "It's Wednesday, so it's your favorite, baked chicken and..."

I didn't hear the rest of what she said because I had headed up the staircase toward my room to change out of my school clothes. I was almost singing, so relieved to hear that Mom was okay. But it was out of routine for her not to meet me at the door, at three o'clock on the head, whenever the school bus dropped me off at the end of the driveway. If I had outgrown that routine, she had not enlightened me.

I quickly changed and headed down the staircase. I wanted to find Mom and give her a hug before turning on my computer to start my school assignments. I usually would hug her the moment I got home from school but since she wasn't at the door to greet me I hadn't gotten the opportunity.

When I reached the bottom of the staircase, I took a seat on the bottom step to tie my shoe lace; and as I sat there tying the strings on one of my gym shoes, I could hear sobbing. I hopped off the step and ran toward the living room. I grabbed my face with both hands, stunned to find Mom in a panic. She was sitting on the living room sofa with her face in her hands. I rushed to her and dropped to my knees in front of her.

"What happened?" I asked hysterically. "I figured something was wrong when you were not standing in the door when the school bus dropped me off." Kneeled in front of her, I gripped her knees with both hands. "Did something happen to Dad? Please tell me what's the matter?"

She raised her head and wiped her tears with her fingers. Her eyes were red and swollen as if she had been crying for awhile. She shook her head. "I'll tell you what's the matter, but I really don't like putting this on your shoulders."

"Putting what on my shoulders? You have frightened me now. Please tell me what's wrong."

"Everything is wrong!" she said sadly.

"Everything, like what, I don't understand," I cried.

"It's your father, Mandy. It's all about your father." She grabbed her face and cried a bit harder.

"Oh no, not my father," I cried. "Did something happen to Dad?" I anxiously asked with my heart in my throat. "What happened to Dad? Is he sick?" I asked with my heart racing.

"Yes, I'll say he's sick," she snapped. "Your father is sick with love for another woman!" She dried her eyes with her fingers.

"What?" I asked, stunned at her words.

She looked at me with dry eyes and smiled in a sad sort of way. "Yes, another woman; and I know you can't be surprised."

"Mom, I am surprised. I still don't know what you are talking about. Dad is with another woman? What woman?"

"Does the name Doris Smith ring a bell? That's the woman!"

"You can't mean Miss Smith."

"Yes I can and I do! I'm talking about Doris Smith."

"Doris, Dad's secretary?" I stared with unbelievable shock at her words.

"Yes, his secretary. He's living with that woman right now!"

I grabbed Mom with both hands. "It can't be true. I won't believe it."

"Believe it, it's true; and do you know what that means?"

I stared at Mom and sat back on the floor with my arms wrapped around my knees as the room seemed to spin and revolved around me. I could only stare out into space, as Mom continued.

"For months they have sneaked around behind my back seeing each other." Mom threw a pillow from the sofa across the room. "This beats all! I thought I was the lousy spouse. I know I'm not perfect and have my issues, but at least I'm not seeing another man behind your father's back." She threw another pillow across the room that landed against a corner stand, knocking a vase to the floor. "All this time, I thought your father was staying in his hotel room downtown. But he has been spending all that time with that woman."

"Mom, who told you this, how do you know it's really true?"

"Believe me, Mandy, it's true. I have had my suspicions for a long time but they were just confirmed today."

"Confirmed how? Who told you? Mom, it's all gossip. I'm sure. You can't believe that grapevine stuff." I grabbed my head with both hands with tight knots in my stomach. I couldn't believe it, because a betrayal to my mother from my father also felt like a betrayal to me and I refused to believe that my father would betray me.

"Mom, I tell you it can't be true. Dad would never do something like that. Besides, his secretary is a wonderful person. She wouldn't do something like that either." I wiped my falling tears with my fingers.

"Oh, wouldn't she?" Mom said sharply. "Mandy, please spare me your ill informed admiration for this woman. She isn't deserving of your high regards. You don't really know that woman at all. She is clearly a home-wrecker."

"But it doesn't sound like Miss Smith. She would never do something like that. I spent some time with her during my shopping trip and she's really nice."

"Mandy, you need to get over your fairy-tale about your father being perfect and this woman being so wonderful. They are not that. Your father wants to marry this woman. He has asked me for a divorce."

I grabbed my face and my mouth fell open. "He asked you for a divorce?" I managed to say after a long pause, and then suddenly tears rolled down my cheek. "I thought you had worked things out."

"I thought we had worked things out too, but he had other plans that included spending his time with your wonderful Miss Doris Smith."

"Mom, I'm so sorry for you and for me. What are you going to do?" I hopped on the sofa beside her and wrapped my arms around her in a tight hug and held on to her for a long time. When I released her I noticed fresh tears falling down her face.

"I'm not quite sure how everything is going to end up, but as soon as I can get an appointment I plan to visit my lawyer," she said in a heartbroken tone and then flew off the sofa and stepped over to the bar across the room. She stood there for a moment and stared at the different selections of wines and liquors, and then picked up a whiskey bottle and poured herself a shot of whiskey. She turned the glass up to her mouth and poured the liquid down her throat in one swallow and then shook her head and made a big frown from the sting.

I stayed seated on the sofa feeling too sad for words as I watched Mom down her second shot of booze. Then I hopped off the sofa, rushed to my room and threw myself across the bed in tears. The news Mom had just sprung on me was too unreal and felt like a nightmare that was making it hard for me to breathe. None of it seemed true. I kept picturing each visit with

Miss Smith. I had extreme faith in her, almost as much faith in her as I had in my father. To me she seemed nice and honest. I couldn't let her be bombarded by hearsay and gossip of such a nasty rumor that she was having an affair with a married man. I had to let her know what was going on. Someone had started a nasty rumor about her and my father. It would surely hit the press. She needed to know and Dad needed to know about the lies they were up against before the rumors snowballed into bitter grapevine gossip.

Chapter Ten

Wednesday evening dinners were always my favorite: baked chicken, boiled potatoes, green beans with onions and blueberry pie for dessert. However, this particular evening the food almost seemed invisible as I sat trying to enjoy my meal between the tears that wouldn't stop rolling down my face. However, by the time Mrs. Lawson served us a slice of blueberry pie, my spirits lifted a bit. I was encouraged that Mom seemed calmer as she sat there finishing her dessert. However, just as we finished our dessert, I glanced at her and she appeared to be crying again. Mrs. Lawson noticed Mom's tears as she walked in quietly with the coffee pot in her hand and offered us coffee. We both shook our heads and she turned and walked slowly out of the dinning room. From the look on Mrs. Lawson's face she seemed concerned and troubled that Mom was crying. But she was very professional and discreet and did not pry. But after she left the dinning room Mom and I glanced at each other and quietly got out of our seats and left the dinning room. We settled into the living room to watch a movie. Then by seven o'clock after Mom had curled up all relaxed and comfortable on the sofa with her head propped on two pillows, I hopped out of the recliner where I was seated.

"Mom, I won't be gone long, but I need to head to the library before it closes."

She glanced my way and nodded. "It's getting late. Isn't it already closed," she mumbled. It was obvious from the sad broken look in her eyes that she was hurting greatly over the rumors.

"It's not closed yet, but I need to hurry to catch it open." I ran upstairs, threw on a jacket and grabbed my purse and rushed back downstairs and out of the house to catch the eight o'clock metro train into Chicago.

I parked my car at the metro station and rushed into the station and purchased a ticket. After purchasing my ticket while waiting at the metro station to board the train, I pulled out my cell from my purse and called my father's hotel room and also his office without success. Then I called Miss Smith with the same results. With no luck of reaching either one of them, while on the train, I wasn't sure whether I should stop at my father's hotel or knock on his secretary's door. It was getting sort of late and maybe the best choice would be to go talk to Dad first to find out the real story and what really started the awful rumors about him and his secretary. In a panic of indecisiveness, when the train arrived downtown, I took a cab to Dad's hotel. Knowing he hadn't answered his phone and probably still wasn't there, I sat in the lobby, waiting and watching the door hoping he would walk in. I figured he had to come to his room soon or later and I would just wait until he did. But the hotel lobby had lots of traffic pouring in and out, and the hotel clerk kept looking back and forth at me between waiting on customers. She kept looking over at me as I sat anxiously and nervously staring at the door. She probably could sense there was something not right with me. Therefore, to keep from appearing so obvious, I grabbed a magazine from the nearby magazine rack, and continued to sat there for another five minutes, pretending to read the National Geographic until the huge clock on the wall made a quick ringing sound at nine-forty. It caught my attention and I realized it was getting too late to continue sitting there waiting for my father. I would have to leave and try my luck at Miss Smith's apartment. Hopefully she would be home and I could inform her of the nasty rumor that had spread.

Miss Smith's Lakefront high-rise apartment building was just three blocks from the hotel, so I decided to walk. Anxious to get to her apartment to inform her of the rumors, I hurried down the bright street almost running.

In the foyer before I could locate and ring her apartment bell, another tenant opened the door with his key. I followed him in and hopped on the elevator to hurry up to Miss Smith's apartment. When I stepped off the elevator and hurried down the hallway to her apartment, I was hoping she would be home. Standing at her door, I took a big breath and knocked softly a couple times.

I grabbed my face with release when she stretched open the door. She was dressed for bed wearing a long white nightgown.

"Hey, I'm so glad you're here," I said quickly. "And I know its sort of late in the evening and I apology for showing up so late, but I really need to talk to you," I said anxiously.

She just stood there not inviting me in. "Mandy," she finally said. "What are you doing here this time of night?" she said with surprise in her eyes.

"I know it's getting late, but as I said, I really need to talk to you. Is it okay if I come in?" I asked anxiously. "I see you are ready for bed and I promise I won't stay too long. I stopped at Dad's hotel but he wasn't there."

"That's because he's here." She stretched out her hand for me to step inside.

"You mean Dad is here?" I hurried into her living room. "I'm glad he's here because now I can tell you both about that crazy rumor."

"What crazy rumor?" She closed the door and glanced toward the bedroom.

"Where is Dad?" I asked.

"He'll be right out, but what crazy rumor did you want to tell us?" She took a seat on the sofa and stretched her arm toward a nearby chair for me to be seated.

"I'm too anxious to sit. I'll stand here and wait for Dad because you two will not believe the awful lie that's floating around about you."

A couple minutes passed and I glanced toward Miss Smith. "How long is Dad going to take in your bathroom?" I smiled.

She shifted in her seat and glanced toward the bedroom again. My eyes followed hers and I spotted a tall figure standing in royal blue pajamas and a robe. He was stepping from the center of the bedroom. At first glimpse I could only see the back of a man's head. "Is Dale here?" I asked. "Is that Dale I see in your bedroom?"

"No, Mandy, that's not Dale," she quickly answered.

I laughed. "I'm sorry for asking, I should have known it wasn't Dale. He's clearly taller with all that long black. Does he still keep it pulled back in a pony tail?"

She nodded and just then Dad stepped out of the dim room into the living room. When he saw me he seemed stunned and lost for word.

"I know it's a surprise but as I was telling Miss Smith I really needed to talk to you and her. I went to your hotel but you weren't there, because of course, you are here," I said anxiously.

He exchanged looks with Miss Smith and then glanced toward the grandfather clock in the corner. "It's getting quite late, sweetheart, what are you doing here?"

"Dad I just said, I have something important to tell the two of you." I glanced down and noticed he was standing in his barefoot. Then it dawned on me that he was also standing before me dressed in pajamas and a robe. Within a split second it all added up in my brain and at that moment, I was conscious only of the sound of my racing heart of disbelief.

In a concerned voice, Dad said, "What's the matter?"

I stood there in shock frozen for a second, as an awkward silence swallowed up the room. I grabbed both cheeks and held my face. "Dad, you do live with her," I repeated, over and over. "You do live with her."

The look in my father's eyes showed pure shock when I said that to him. It was as if someone had just stabbed him in the chest. It was a painfully sad look on his face. He looked exactly how I felt. He seemed at a lost for words as he stumbled for a moment. He glanced at Miss Smith and then stared at me with humble eyes.

"Mandy, I didn't want you to find out this way. You shouldn't have come here tonight. Whatever prompted you to come here at this time of night?"

"I'll tell you what prompted me to come here." I held out both arms. "This right here what I'm witnessing. That's the rumor I wanted to share, only I thought it was some made up tale. I guess the joke is on me."

Dad shook his head. "Mandy, we had no idea you would show up like this."

"Of course you didn't, Dad. You wanted to keep me in the dark!"

Dad held out both arms. "But it wasn't like that, Mandy."

I stumbled with my words, barely able to speak from shock. "That's exactly what you did! You're here in this apartment dressed for bed." I pointed to his pajamas.

"I was planning to have a talk with you on Friday," he explained in a solemn voice. "I guess your mother couldn't wait to fill you in before we could both talk to you together."

"It's not Mom's fault this time. Maybe I should start listening to her more often," I snapped.

"What did you say?" Dad asked.

"I said I should start listening to Mom more instead of always assuming she's wrong about everything and you're right.

"Mandy, you don't mean that," Dad said with great frustration. "You don't know what you are saying."

"I do know what I'm saying. My mother is not perfect, but she would never do something like this to you," I shouted angrily. "So you can bet, in the future I'll listen to Mom and not you. She was right about the two of you!"

Dad held out both hands. "Mandy, please calm down," he urged me. "I understand how upsetting it is for you to see Doris and I together like this, but Francis had no right and should have used better judgment than to drop this in your lap like this, especially before she and I had the opportunity to sit down and talk to you together."

I stood there shaking my head as tears fell down my face. I was so let down and upset until I thought I would be sick in the stomach. "Don't put this on my mother! It's not her fault that I found out. She only confided in me about what was going on between you two after I found her crying."

"Still, your mother should have shown more restrain for your sake."

"I can't believe you're mad at Mom because she couldn't control her emotions about your affair with another woman. She is so crushed over this. What about my mother and how she feels?"

"Your mother will be okay," Dad said.

"How will she be okay? I'm not okay. Nothing will ever be okay. The only way things can be okay is if you come home with me now and tell Mom you're sorry and that everything is going to be okay." I squeezed my hands together. "Can you leave here and come home with me and tell Mom everything is going to be okay?"

Dad shook his head. "Mandy, you are seventeen years old, plenty old enough to understand and get what's going on here," he stressed and paused for a second and then glanced up at the ceiling for a moment. Then he looked at me with sad eyes. "Although, it might be hard for you to understand, walking in on us so unexpectedly; but you need to hear this," he began slowly, "Doris and I have fallen in love with each other. We are happy together. We make each other happy and somewhere inside of you, I think you already know that."

I shook my head, refusing to hear him. "I don't already know that!" I shouted angrily. "I don't know anything except I hate you for breaking up our home." I glanced about the room, spotting his slippers near the big brown leather recliner with his briefcase on the coffee table. He seemed to be all settled in at his new home and the thought of him living with another woman that wasn't my mother, ripped at my heart in the most tormenting way.

"Doris and I are…"

I cut off his sentence. "You are not married to that woman! You are married to my mother," I shouted angrily. "You have no right to do this to my mother and me! No right at all." I held out both hands. "This isn't what you do! This isn't who you are! Did she make you move in here?"

"Mandy, nobody can make me do anything. Now, you need to calm down and have a seat and let me explain," he insisted.

I shook my head with my blood boiling inside. "If she didn't make you move in here, and you want to be here because you're in love with her! How can you explain that to me? How can you explain your right to be with another woman when you're still married to my mother?" I grabbed my face in my hands and cried. "You can't explain and I don't want you too, because you have no right!"

Miss Smith gave me a serious stare and then glanced at Dad before she softly said. "Mandy, I don't expect for you to understand what's going on between me and your father right now. This is probably too much for someone your age to take in right now, but we do have the right to be in love," she said humbly. "All is fair in love and war, sweetheart," she said softly with a slight nervousness to her voice.

I grabbed my head covering both ears. "Don't call me sweetheart." I shouted. "Don't call me anything. I hate you now for what you are doing to my father."

"Mandy, I'm not doing anything to your father. I would like to think I'm doing something for him."

"Yes, you're doing something for him. You're breaking up his home."

She shook her head and just stared at me with sad eyes.

"Besides, how can you say all is fair? How is it fair that you have broken up our home? Please answer that question, how is that fair to me and my mother?"

"Mandy, it's not Doris's fault what happened between us. It just happened. We didn't plan any of this. It just gradually happened. We understand and accept each other's faults. We enjoy each other's company." He held out both arms. "Sweetheart, I know you are very disappointed, but one day you will understand." He glanced toward Miss Smith. "Get her a bottle of water."

"No, please do not bother with getting me a bottle of water. I'm not interested in drinking any water."

"It might make you feel better," Dad encouraged.

"A bottle of water won't make me feel better. Nothing is going to make me feel better except to wake up from this nightmare."

"Mandy, I need you to try and understand," Dad explained. "I love you and need you to understand."

"Please listen to your father, Mandy. You mean everything to him."

"I don't mean anything to him or he wouldn't do this to our family," I snapped disrespectfully, trying to strike back at both of them at once. "Mom told me that everybody was talking about you two. But gullible me, I thought it was a rumor and that's why I jumped on a train this time of night to come here. It wasn't because I believed it, it's because I didn't believe it. I just wanted to come and let you two know. Not in all my life did I think for a minute that it was true. I didn't believe it, but it's true. It's true," I cried.

"Mandy, you don't understand," Dad insisted humbly, "Could you please have a seat and let me attempt to explain so you won't continue to be as upset as you are." Dad reached for my arm, gripped it and tried to lead me toward the long brown sofa, but I jerked my arm away from his grip.

"I don't want to sit and listen to your explanations," I snapped rudely.

"Mandy, dear, I realize how upset you must be, but please try to collect yourself and listen," Miss Smith pleaded. "We only want to try and explain things to you."

"If you were in my shoes and you walked in to find your father with another woman, would you collect yourself?" I pointed to my chest. "Besides, why should I collect myself and listen, there's nothing you can say that can explain things!"

"I know it seems like that to you, that there's nothing from us that you would like to hear, especially from me," she said calmly and then paused, looking in my eyes. "But, Mandy, when you think about it, you and I have something very much in common," Miss Smith said.

"We have nothing in common," I cried.

"Yes, dear, we do. I love your father just as you love him. We both love Daniel. That gives us a common bond. Plus he also loves the both of us."

"You love my father?" I cried uncontrollably. "How can you talk to me about how you love my father? What do you really know about love? What about the fact that my mother loves my father? What about that fact. What about that bond between my mother and me, since we both love my father? Don't stand here and tell me how you love my father. Because to me, it seems minor compared to the love between a man and his wife and his kid?" I shouted between tears.

"Yes, it's a different kind of love, Mandy; but it's just as real," she explained.

"It might be real, but it's wrong in my book. Any kind of love that brings tormenting pain to someone else is wrong.

And what you are doing with my father is bringing tormenting pain to my mother."

"I don't mean to hurt your mother," she stressed.

"But you are! You're a home-wrecker. My mother is going to get a divorce and I'll never see my father again. Is that what you want?" I screamed in her face and ran toward the door without looking toward my father.

I felt that I needed to get out of that room to breathe. I grabbed the doorknob with both hands and stretched it open and tore out of the apartment as Dad called out for me. "Mandy, don't tear out of here in the state you're in. Sweetheart, you need to wait and listen."

I paused for a second with my back to them, and then I closed the door shut. After I stepped into the hallway, suddenly it seemed too quiet and everything seemed too unreal. I suddenly felt weak all over as the disappointment and pain overwhelmed me. I stumbled about in tears as I headed away from their door. I paused, collected myself and ran down the long hallway to the elevator. I cried uncontrollably in the elevator as two strangers looked at me all the way down from the forty-third floor. And when the elevator stopped on the first floor and the three of us stepped out of the elevator, the two strangers stood there in the lobby and stared at me with a concerned gesture about them until I rushed through the lobby and out to the streets. I hopped in one of the cabs that were parked in front of the building and cried all the way to the metro station and then sat on my train seat and cried all the way home.

Shortly before midnight, I burst into the house and rushed to Mom's room. From the dim lamp light at her bedside table, I could see that she was lying in bed, but she was still awake with a magazine in her hand.

"Mandy," she said sitting up in bed. "I was getting concerned about you. What took you so long?" She stared. "I'm sure the library closed hours ago."

"Yes, I know," I said sadly, standing there with tears covering my face.

She reached over and switched on the other lamp light that sat on the opposite bedside table. The room lit up and the bright light showed my tear-stained face and she caught her breath. "What's the matter? Did something happen while you were at the library?" She asked. "Why are you crying?"

I slowly took a seat on the edge of the bed and wrapped my arms around her back. "Mom, I'm so sorry I didn't listen to you earlier."

"Listen to me earlier about what, sweetheart?"

"I just didn't believe you because I thought it was impossible."

"You thought what was impossible? What is it, Mandy? Why are you crying?"

"I'm crying because I found out that you were right about Dad."

"So, I'm assuming you didn't spend all this time at the library, which closed hours ago. You drove into the city to talk to your father?"

I shook my head. "No, I didn't drive into the city, I parked my car at the metro station and took the train," I mumbled sadly.

She removed my arms from her back and stared at me firmly. "I know you wanted more answers, sweetheart, but I'm not pleased that you hid this from me. You left this house under false pretense and that's not okay with me."

"Mom, I know it's not okay with you and it's not okay with me either. But I was driven to do it. I had to see Dad," I cried. "If I had mentioned it to you, you never would have allowed me to leave the house."

"Mandy, you are right. I would not have allowed you to hop a train into that city this time of night to see your father?"

I wiped my tears with my fingers. "I know that and that's why I sneaked out and told a lie that I was going to the library.

I just had to go see him because I didn't believe what you had said. I thought it was a rumor. I felt it had to be a rumor."

"Mandy, this pedestal that you have put your father upon is not realism," she said sadly. "In your mind he's perfect and has no faults?"

"I know I was wrong to doubt you. Everything you said is true."

"Did he actually confirm that he's living with that woman now?"

"He didn't have to," I sniffed.

"What do you mean he didn't have to?"

"Well, when I arrived downtown. I hopped a cab and went straight to his hotel room to ask him or more to let him know there was a rumor floating around about him and Miss Smith, but when I arrived at his hotel he wasn't there. I waited around for a while, but then left the hotel and walked down the street to Miss Smith's apartment; and that's where I found him." I grabbed my face and cried. "He was dressed for bed."

Mom waved her hand. "I bet he was plenty surprised to see you. I wish you hadn't shown up at that woman's door, but it serves him right that his daughter, who thinks he's perfect would catch him red-handed living with his mistress," Mom said with a voice filled with agony.

I shook my head in a daze of the whole evening. "Mom, I just can't believe Dad is living with her just as you said. I despise what they are doing."

Mom nodded. "You and me both, but Daniel does what he wants. Your self-righteous father has preached and fussed at me for years about making honorable choices and doing the honorable thing, now he's doing a very dishonorable thing by living with another woman while he's still married to me."

"Mom, I know. I'm so disappointed in Dad. What he's doing goes against the kinds of principles that he has taught me to live by; and the kinds of ethics that I thought he lived by. It just disgusts me and I don't care if I ever see him again." I threw my arms around her again. "Mom, we will me just fine without Dad," I cried with an agonizing burning pain in the pit of my stomach.

"Yes, we will. Now, head on to bed and try to get some sleep. If you don't feel like getting up for school tomorrow, just stay home," Mom suggested.

"Thanks, Mom, but I don't want to miss class because of this," I said and headed out of her room.

I walked slowly down the hallway to my room as if I was in a daze and didn't recognize what I was doing. I changed out of my clothes and hopped into bed and stared up at the ceiling in tears. My whole world as I had known it had instantly changed. I didn't want to sleep I just wanted to wake up from the nightmare that had captured me while I was still awake. Everything around me seemed unreal as I listened to the sound of the wind sweeping against my bedroom windows. I could feel a storm brewing inside of me that was bringing me unspeakable misery.

Chapter Eleven

Several months after the awful confrontation with my father at Miss Smith's apartment, I had tried hard to keep my focus off the separation of my parents. I was trying to focus more on my own social life or lack of. My heart was distracted with loving thoughts for the Chase brothers, Brad and Todd. They were not in any of my classes or attended any regular classes, they were in a special college program at school, but running into them in the hallway or the cafeteria always made my heart flutter. My heart especially flickered for Brad. Brad and I had spent time together talking in the cafeteria and we had spent time together talking on the school ground, but he had never asked me out or showed more than a casual interest in me. Yet, I was hopeful that our casual friendship would bloom into something more. And I was especially thinking of him that Monday morning during my math class. It was lightly snowing outside as I sat at my desk in thought, daydreaming about Brad, and then I heard some of the students in the rear of the classroom talking about a New Year's event that was going to take place at one of the Chase mansions. My curiosity made me motionless as I sat there in wonder of which one; it was several Chase mansions in the area. Then as I carefully listened to their conversation, I heard someone say," The party is taking place at Molly Chase house."

My heart raced for a second as I sat still at my desk smiling inside. I was in deep thought about the party and wondered if it was by invitation only. However, as I sat there waiting for the bell to sound, ending the class in the next few minutes, I got all the information I needed as the entire classroom started discussing the party. The teacher had stepped out of the classroom and it seemed every mouth in attendance was talking excitedly away about the party taking place at the Chase mansion.

"Get this, they are throwing an open house party," someone said.

"I doubt they are just letting anybody show up," someone said. "They never throw open parties at their house."

"Maybe not, but this time they are. Ask them if you don't believe me. The party is for whoever wants to come," someone said.

Just then, the bell rang. I hopped out of my seat with my purse across my shoulder, gripping my notebook against my chest, smiling as I rushed out of the classroom to head to the cafeteria for lunch. My insides were excited with the thought of going to a Chase party. My hunger for lunch had somehow faded since the party news had me so filled with cheerfulness. I was beside myself about the party and the wonderful opportunity to go and spend some time in Brad's company.

I walked into the cafeteria and spotted Kathy Gross, my best friend, already seated at a table with her lunch tray, I waved my arm above my head and she spotted me headed toward her table smiling.

When I reached her table I was smiling excitedly. "I have incredible news that I can't wait to tell you about." I placed my purse and notebook on the table and held up one finger. "I'll be right back and tell you," I said quickly and then rushed across the cafeteria floor to stand in line to order some lunch.

I asked the server for a glass of iced-tea and a ham sandwich, on wheat bread with lettuce, tomatoes and mayo. And with my lunch tray in hand, I headed toward Kathy's table. I spotted Rachel Gross, Kathy's older sister, walking away from the table. She had just handed Kathy something; and was now glancing over her shoulder waving goodbye as a group of boys at the next table was whistling and beckoning her to their table. But Rachel just flashed them a smile and headed straight out of the lunchroom. She had graduated the year before, but whenever she came around all eyes were glued to her because of her absolute striking good looks.

"I see I just missed Rachel. What did she give you?" I asked.

"She brought my wallet."

"She had your wallet?" I asked.

"Yes, I rushed out this morning and left it on the coffee table."

"So, how did you buy lunch?" I asked.

"Luckily for me, I found some extra money in my coat pocket."

"That's good, but I would have bought your lunch."

"I know, but I have lunch and I also have my wallet."

"That was nice of Rachel to drop it off." I placed my tray on the table.

"Yes, sometime big sisters will do something nice." Kathy grinned. "Then again it could be because she wanted to bump into Todd Chase."

"Rachel likes Todd?" I asked, surprised to hear as I took a seat.

"Does she ever? She has a huge crush on the guy, but he has never asked her out. So if you ask me, I'm sure she was glad for an excuse to drop by here."

"I had no idea Rachel had a crush on Todd," I said, smiling. "Although, I have to admit she has great taste to fall for a Chase."

"Yes, very good taste, I might add. But you don't have to worry because at least she's not after Brad," Kathy teased.

"I thought she was dating Dr. Horton's son, Jeffrey."

"That's correct, she is dating Jeffrey, but she still has a crush on Todd. If Todd ever looks her way, Jeffrey is history," Kathy said seriously and nodded.

"So in other words, according to you, Rachel actually likes Todd more than she does Jeffrey Horton, the boy she's dating." I stared at her.

"Why are you staring at me like that? I'm just calling it the way I see it. Rachel is into Todd more than she is into Jeffrey," Kathy assured me.

"That could be so, but don't spread it around because then it becomes gossip," I said. "Besides, if she does like Todd, I'm not sure I buy the fact that she made a special trip to the school in these cold temperatures, during her holiday break from college, just to bump into Todd Chase?"

"Mandy, I think I know my own sister better than you. And most likely she wanted to run into Todd or maybe she wanted to come and show off her new car."

"Rachel has a new car?" I asked.

"Yes, the folks surprised her with a new silver Mustang last week. It's a belated graduation gift?" Kathy pulled through the straw of her orange soda.

"She graduated last year and they are just buying the car?" I asked.

"That's because she wanted a diamond bracelet for graduation, and that's what they bought her." Kathy took another pull through the straw of her soda. "They decided to surprise her with the new car after she kept complaining about the old one. Plus, she had put a lot of miles on her old car traveling to and from Michigan State. They put two and two together and figured out that Rachel really wanted the diamond bracelet and a new car but they had told her that she could only have one."

"She picked the diamond bracelet, but ended up with both." I smiled.

"Yes, she got lucky, and now she's here showing off her new car. But either way I'm just glad she brought my wallet."

"I'm sure you are; but a new car for Rachel, that's great."

"I know it's great. I have my fingers crossed that they'll do the same for me and I won't have to keep driving around in my ancient car," Kathy complained.

"A new car would be great but your car isn't ancient. They bought it for you at the same time my folks bought mine, on our 16th birthday, remember? It should be fresh in your mind since it was just last year. So yes, our cars may seem ancient but they are still practically new," I reminded her.

"You're right they are, but if we are both lucky, which we probably will be, we'll end up with new cars for graduation, which is just around the bend," she said excitedly.

"If you do get a new car for graduation, what color do you want this time?" Kathy asked. "I'm thinking about white, what about you? Do you want another blue Mustang?"

"I'm not sure," I answered.

"You seemed in a good mood and now you seem down," Kathy noticed.

"These moods come and go, but it's been this way ever since I found out about my father and his secretary. The fact that he's living with that woman has given me trust issues," I mumbled with no zest to my voice.

"I'm sure it has, but your Dad moved out more than six months ago. You need to try to cope with it without allowing it to bomb out your days," she suggested.

"I know you are right, Kathy. But what happened with my folks has also motivated me to be a stronger female. I'm determined not to be a casualty of the male species that has befallen my mother."

"Mandy, what are you talking about? If you plan to stay away from the male population you need to keep that thought in the back of my mind as your feelings for Brad Chase keep growing out of control. Just seeing that guy drives you batty," she teased.

"You are right about that. Just being around him gets to me and makes me happier than anything else ever has. But if my parents splitting up and being in love with Brad, a boy who hasn't shown much interest or asked me out, isn't enough to shake up my world, look at the hassles I'm dealing with ever since I started writing those articles in the school paper."

Kathy waved her hand. "Oh, those articles, the ones telling teenagers they should wait," Kathy stared at me. "What were you thinking?"

"It seemed like a good idea at the time," I mumbled.

"Well, we both know, it was the worst idea ever as far as this crowd is concerned," Kathy stated seriously. "These pretentious students at this school do not want to read about your objections to premarital sex."

"I guess not. It was just my opinion on the subject and I thought it would have gone over a little better," I explained.

Kathy laughed. "Leave it to you to cause a commotion throughout the school like an out of control disease. Whatever prompted you to write those articles? In a perfect world teenagers would take heed, but not this pompous crowd." Kathy looked at me. "So do tell, what's the real reason behind those articles? I'm not buying your excuse that it seemed like a good idea at the time."

"You are right; there is a deeper reason behind the articles."

"Okay, what is it?"

"It's all about my parents," I confessed.

"What do you mean it's all about your parents?"

"Everything, those articles and staying celibate until marriage, all stems from the fact that in my mind it destroyed Mom and Dad's marriage."

"Mandy, I guess I don't follow you. You need to be a little bit more specific."

"I feel the root of my parent's marital problems is because my mother didn't remain celibate until marriage."

"And what makes you think this?" Kathy asked.

"I just do and I'm determined to change my fate from my mother's. I want my future marriage to last."

"We all want that, Mandy," Kathy grinned. "But writing your articles about staying celibate until marriage it not what these students want to read. To them it's outdated and prudish."

"I realize it's not what they want to hear, but its still how I feel. But from now on I'll just keep my opinion to myself."

"That's a good idea, because not writing those articles will shut them all up," Kathy said. "But you still haven't explained what you meant about your mother not remaining celibate until marriage. You believe that's what broke them up, right?"

I nodded. "Yes, I do believe that."

"But why do you believe that?"

"I believe it because it appears that Mom and Dad's marriage ended because Dad lost trust in Mom."

"He lost trust in her because she didn't remain celibate until he married her? Is that what you're trying to tell me?"

"Yes, exactly," I said and nodded. "It stems from a promise that my mother made to my father that he would be her first, but she broke the promise without good cause and slept with another boy."

"Wow, Mandy, that's very personal." Kathy grinned. "Did your mother tell you this information?" Kathy asked.

"Of course not," I shook my head. "Mom would never tell me something that personal. I overheard them arguing about it one night. So I guess in other words, I'm convinced that if I remain faithful to my viewpoint, once married, it will somehow keep me out of divorce court."

"Mandy, that's just hopeful thinking on your part."

"Why do you say it's just hopeful thinking?"

"I say its hopeful thinking because it's an honorable thought, but from what I have heard, men will find an excuse to leave, whether you broke a promise or did nothing wrong, if they want out of a marriage."

"So in other words, what you are saying is that my father was just ready to leave us and it had nothing to do with anything else."

"Mandy, I didn't mean it like that and I don't know why your father left. I know I'm sorry he's gone, but you need to cheer up and let your folks work out their own issues with each other," she suggested. "Does that make sense?"

"Sure it makes sense," I said and then looked across the cafeteria in the direction of all the commotion and laughter. Molly Chase and her gang had just walked into the lunchroom.

"What are you looking at?" Kathy asked.

"Here comes Miss Universe. Brad and Todd's show off sister," I mumbled.

"I see her." Kathy waved her hand. "You mean the senior class dictator. She's our most popular senior on campus according to her. She's nothing like those handsome brothers of hers. Maybe she's the milkman baby." Kathy grinned.

"She can be rude, but she's no milkman baby. She looks just like her brothers."

"I know, Mandy, I'm not being that nice. I was just kidding about the milkman but she is nowhere near as friendly and polite as Brad and Todd. Plus, every time she walks in here there's always several cheerleaders lagging along with her."

"That's because cheerleaders usually stick together," I said.

"Maybe, but just look at them," Kathy uttered annoyed. "They are always giggling about something when they walk in and strut across the floor toward the food counter. And it never fails how all eyes turn to Molly when she walks in."

"That's because she's always dressed in some chic outfit that most of us would save to wear to a party," I mumbled.

"I'm sorry, Mandy, I know I'm being extra vile toward Molly, but her snobbish arrogant manner gets under my skin and just rubs me the wrong way," Kathy admitted.

"I didn't know she got to you that much." I pulled through the straw of my iced tea. "I guess she gets to you even when she's not being rude or bothering you?" I looked Kathy in the eyes. "I know she's hard to take, but I don't let her get under my skin when she's not in my face being rude or bothering me?" I said seriously.

Kathy shook her head. "I'm not proud to admit how Molly arrogant behavior rubs me the wrong way. But it does very much, even when she's not being rude."

"If just seeing her sets you off, there's a word for that and it's not good," I said.

"I know there's a word for that and I'm working on it."

"Good, work on it hard," I suggested. "It's okay to be rude to her when she's being rude to you, but don't be rude to her just because."

"It's easy to say, but Mandy, I guess I don't have your depth of compassion. Because even when Molly is not being rude, I think of all the times she was rude and it burns me," Kathy explained and held up one finger. "That reminds me, I hear Todd has an arrogant, conceited side."

"Who said Todd is arrogant and conceited?" I asked curiously. "I haven't noticed that side of him. He seems nothing like Molly."

"Believe it or not, Ricky said it. If his own cousin calls him arrogant than I guess maybe he is," Kathy mumbled. "But he has never said that about Brad. So I guess your Brad is always nice." Kathy stared in Molly's direction.

I poked at Kathy's arm. "Stop staring at Molly's outfit. She wears a new outfit everyday."

"I know she does and she dresses like that to be the center of attention. But I'm not staring at her outfit," Kathy poked her fork in her salad and then placed the fork on the table and pushed the salad aside. "I was just looking her way because I wanted to see if she was giving out any invitations to their party."

"That reminds me," I said excitedly.

"That reminds you of what?" she asked.

"Remember I said I had something exciting to tell you?"

"You mentioned that before you got your food."

"I know when I first got to lunch before I went to the lunch counter to get my food; I told you I had something exciting to tell you. But after I got my food we got into talking about everything but the Chase party."

"So, your exciting news is about the Chase party?" she asked.

I smiled. "Yes, it is."

"Okay, what is it? Do you know if they are giving out invitations?"

"I can answer that," I said and then bit into my ham sandwich.

"Well answer it. I want to know if it's a private party," Kathy stared at me.

"It's not a private party," I quickly said. "I heard some students talking about the party before I left my math class. They said it's an open party and whoever wants to come can come," I said excitedly. "Isn't that the most exciting news ever?"

"You're kidding," Kathy said, excitedly with a big smile. "That's a first for a Chase party to invite whoever wants to come. Why are they doing that I wonder? Their parties are usually private by invitation only."

"I know, but that's what I heard. Besides, I'm especially glad it's an open party since lately invitations to after school parties haven't been coming my way."

"I guess not with all the uproar over your articles," she laughed. "You have built yourself quite a controversial reputation around here young lady, don't you think?" she teased.

"I guess I have when seniors like Molly thinks I'm somewhat of a stick in the mud trying to rain on their sexual freedoms," I said lightheartedly as if the uproar wasn't ripping at me. "Yeah, I have been painted as a regular crusader against teenager sex. Who would have figured, just three articles on the subject would have caused so much backlash and criticism against me?"

"Don't sweat it. Just don't write anymore."

"I don't plan to, but it won't stop the hostile emails and rudeness."

"I'm sure this crowd will find something else to criticize about soon. Just give them time and some other unsuspecting student will be on their hit list. But can we change the subject back to the Chase party?" Kathy suggested. "I still can't get over the fact that they are opening their doors to anyone off the street," Kathy said.

"It's not to just anyone off the street, its students from school. Besides, who cares why they are doing it? I'm just glad they are. Do you want to go together?" I asked, sure she would say yes.

She looked at me and laughed. "Of course we can go together." Then she paused and frowned at me. "Mandy, all shoot," she shouted and grabbed her face with both hands. "I just remembered I can't go. I already have plans for New Years."

"You already have plans and you can't go to a Chase party?" I asked, not pleased with her answer.

"I'm sorry, Mandy, but I really can't; I already promised my mother to attend a New Year's event with the family. And that's just my luck. The Chase first open house party and I can't attend because I already have stupid plans. Ricky is already upset with me that I have plans with my folks. I'm sure he'll be at his cousin's party."

"I'm sure he will," I said with no zest to my voice as I pulled through the straw of my iced-tea.

"So are you going?" Kathy asked.

"I was thinking about it, but I thought we would go together."

"But since I already have plans and won't be able to break them, I hope you'll go anyway." Kathy encouraged.

"But I didn't want to go alone."

"I know, but you need to be there so you can tell me all about it."

"I'm sure I'll probably go, but why can't you just break your other plans and tell your folks you're going to another party? They'll understand that you don't want to hang out with grown ups." I laughed.

"Mandy, if I could I would. But believe me, my mother would not understand," she said sadly. "If that was possible I would do it. I didn't want to disappoint Ricky by saying no, and I don't want to disappoint you, but I have no other choice but to attend the New Year's affair with my parents."

"Your Mom seems lenient with you."

"Yes, mostly, but you don't know her when it comes to events that she wants the entire family to attend. She planned this New Year's outing for the whole family and we all have to attend. If I were to even mention cancelling she would most likely have a fit, and no doubt cut off my allowance for a month or something else that would make my life miserable."

"Would she really?" I asked surprised.

"Yes, really," she assured me. "So go to the party, have fun and spend some quality time with Brad."

I nodded. "Okay, I will." I nibbled on my ham sandwich and touched Kathy's shoulder. "I know you hate to miss the party, but I'll tell you all about it."

"You promise."

"Yes, I promise and you know I have never broken a promise to you ever. You are my best friend," I said to her.

She smiled. "We are best friends aren't we?"

I nodded. "Yes, Kathy, I think our association constitutes best friends. Think about it, we spend all our free periods together, especially lunch and break. You are most likely the only person at school who hasn't given me a hard time about those articles that I wrote in the school paper."

"I did give you a hard time. I asked you why you wrote them."

"I know, but you asked out of concern and not malice."

"That's true; and since you're making a list, I always make you laugh about something or someone," Kathy added.

"That's true; and it helps that we live on the same block with parents who are each other's best friends. I actually heard the names Wesley and Deanna Gross and knew who they were before I knew who you were."

"Because you saw them in your parent's wedding pictures. They both stood up in your parent's wedding," Kathy remembered.

"When I was around ten they showed me the wedding pictures and told me that the four of them were best friends in college," I shared, but my conversation was distracted when I noticed Molly from the corner of my eye headed toward our table.

A moment later, Molly and three other cheerleaders walked past our table, looked over at us and smiled. Kathy and I both spotted the striking reflection coming from Molly's neck. We both admired her sparkling diamond choker that glimmered around her neck like a priceless treasure. She looked in my eyes with an arrogant assured look as if she owned the place, and after staring at me for a moment, she then placed both hands over her mouth.

"Hi Mandy, I'm sorry to trouble you and Kathy while you're still having lunch but I just heard something about you and I'm dying to know if it's true."

My heart raced with anxiety. I figured she could only be referring to some rumor that had circulated since I started writing the unpopular articles in the school paper. I kept my composure, but to mention some lie in front of all the other students would surely embarrass me. I shifted in my seat with my heart in my throat. "What did you hear?" I asked.

Molly exchanged looks with the other three cheerleaders who were all smiling and nodding. Whatever it was, the other three felt it was okay for her to tell me.

Molly stared at me and smiled and just as she was about to say something, one of the cheerleaders tapped her shoulder and whispered in her ear. And after a moment of silence, Molly grabbed her head and stared up at the ceiling for a second before exchanging looks with the other cheerleaders and nodded. She seemed surprised by whatever the cheerleader had just said to her. She looked at me and raised both hands, shaking her head. "Forget what I just said."

"But you didn't say anything. You said you heard something about me but you never said what you had heard," I said confused by her behavior.

Then one of the cheerleaders whispered in her ear again. The four of them stepped away from the table and discussed something among them, and then they stepped back over to our table with mysterious smiles on their faces.

"Mandy, I know I never said what I heard, and at this point I'm glad I kept my mouth shut," Molly said, laughing.

"When have you ever kept your mouth shut, Miss Molly Chase," Kathy snapped.

"Excuse me, Kathy Gross, no one is talking to you; but for your information I kept my mouth shut because I just found out that your little friend here is dating my brother." She pointed to me. "So, no matter what I think of Mandy's articles, blood is thicker than water. If I throw her under the bus, there goes Brad as well."

I exchanged looks with Kathy and stared at Molly speechless. Her little announcement that Brad and I were dating had stunned me.

"So, Mandy, what do you have to say for yourself?" Molly asked. "Do you care to enlighten us on how you did it?" She pointed to the four of them.

"I have no idea what you are referring to, Molly," I said politely.

"I'm referring to my brother. We are all curious to know how someone with your less than popular reputation at the moment managed to pull that off."

"Pull what off?" I asked.

"You know what I mean. How did you snag my big time player of a brother? When did you start dating Brad anyway? I'm surprise he puts up with someone who writes such outdated, prudish gibberish in the school paper." She held up both hands. "Nevermind, I don't need to know when. It's enough that it is."

My mouth fell open and I couldn't speak. I exchanged looks with Kathy, who was sitting there smiling and holding her mouth with both hands to keep from laughing.

"Excuse me," I finally said to Molly.

Molly smiled. "Why are you saying excuse me as if you have no idea what I'm talking about. I'm the one surprised. I just found out that Brad likes you."

"Did Brad tell you this?" I asked wanting to know where she got her information since it was news to me.

"But apparently it wasn't him who told me since I just now found out."

"Can you tell me who told you?" I asked.

She shook her head. "It doesn't matter who told me, what matters is that it's true. You guys are not really dating but I guess he wants to date you or you want to date him." She waved both hands. "Something of that sort, which is all I need to know. I'm not about to get on the bad side of that guy! Have you ever seen Brad when he's ticked?" She waved her hand. "Sorry, wrong brother. I'm thinking of Todd. He's the one with the arrogant attitude."

"I guess it runs in the family," Kathy said in a low voice.

"What was that you said Kathy?" Molly asked.

"I said it's your family," Kathy lied.

Molly rolled her eyes toward the ceiling at Kathy's comment and then she stared back at me. "Mandy, as I was saying, Brad is more easygoing than Todd, but I still don't want to be on the receiving end of ticking him off for meddling in his business."

"And saying whatever it was that you were going to say to me before, would be meddling in his business?" I asked.

She nodded. "Yes, it would. If you're his girl, and I think you are. He would let me have it for being impolite to you." She waved goodbye and headed across the cafeteria floor toward the exit doors with the other three cheerleaders right by her side.

My eyes stayed glued to Molly and the other three cheerleaders until they were no longer in view. I was stunned as I turned and looked at Kathy.

"What just happened here?" I asked.

"Molly Chase told you that her brother likes you." Kathy grabbed my arm excitedly. "Isn't that super? It came straight from her lips so it must be true."

"Kathy, just calm down," I suggested, touching her shoulder. "I'm sure you heard her when she said very clearly that she heard something of that sort. And I put emphasis on, something of that sort. So, yes, maybe she heard that I'm crazy for Brad."

She cut me off, "Or that he's crazy for you?"

I held up one finger. "Or just maybe Brad doesn't have a clue that I'm crazy for him and maybe he isn't really into me at all."

"Why are you saying that? You know Brad Chase is totally into you. He wouldn't spend time talking to you sometime here in the lunchroom if he didn't like you. Plus, I know he talks to you sometime outside when school let out."

I waved my hand. "So what, he still has not asked me out."

"But he will. I tell you, that boy is crazy about you," Kathy insisted.

"If he's so crazy about me, what makes you think so?" I asked.

"For one, he wouldn't look at you the way he does if he wasn't crazy for you," Kathy stressed, trying to convince me to be hopeful. "Whenever he's having lunch in here he always stares over at our table. I have told you this many times."

"So you have but I'm not buying it. If that boy was that into me, I would know it because he would have asked me out."

"Maybe he doesn't know if you want him to ask you out. Guys are afraid of rejection more than girls are," she explained. "But Brad is into you. If his sister Molly, who is not your biggest fan, thinks so, it must be so. So get excited already."

"I am excited, but I'm cautiously excited. I will go to the party and I guess I'll find out how much he likes me once I'm there." I noticed my hands trembling as I took a bite of my ham sandwich.

Molly hadn't just stunned me. She had shaken me and given me all kinds of emotions. Because before she confessed that Brad liked me, she announced that she had heard something about me that she was dying to find out about and that had somewhat gotten to me. Deep down I felt she was probably going to ask personal questions about the articles I was writing if she hadn't found out first that there was something going on between Brad and me. Therefore, as I sat there trying to finish up my lunch, I couldn't be excited that Brad possibly liked me because I couldn't stop thinking about how rotten I felt that so many students were on my case and unhappy about the articles.

When Kathy looked at my suddenly sad face, she could read my thoughts. She drew an attitude and suddenly seemed upset and just as shaken as I was from Molly's little scene that could have turned into a very uneasy moment for me.

"I know it's not easy for you to be excited about what Molly said about Brad when you are so on edge about the backlash from your articles," Kathy said.

I nodded. "Kathy, you are exactly right. I have to tell you, sticking to my guns and standing up against teenage sex is not making my life here at school a cake walk. It wasn't this awful last year. Remember, I wrote a few articles for the school paper and nobody made a big deal about it."

"That's because nobody was really reading the school paper that much until Molly became the editor. Now everybody at school reads it."

"And nearly everybody at school is in an uproar." I grabbed my face with both hands and shook my head. "What is wrong with these crazy kids at this crazy school? Why can't they look beyond my views on the subject? My opinion is not a roadblock against any of these students sexual freedom," I stressed. So, please, can you tell me what's wrong with some of these kids who are taking my articles so personal?"

Kathy stared at me hard and grinned. "I'll tell you what's wrong with them."

"Okay, I'm listening."

"This high school is packed with too many spoiled little rich kids like us." She pointed to her chest and then to me.

"Is that supposed to make me feel better?" I asked.

She shook her head. "Mandy, we are not like them."

"Thank you." I grabbed my head with both hands from her statement and the image that flashed in my mind. "My goodness, I hope we don't fall into that category. Besides, the ones who are so upset about my articles apparently don't have anything better to do than to nosy around in someone else's life! I'm fed up with all of the meddling and butting into my business."

"It's really not all of students," Kathy pointed out.

"I know it not all the students. I said the ones who are upset about my articles."

"That would be Molly and her crowd," Kathy stressed. "If Molly would but out, the rest of her crowd, which is all those high hat cheerleaders, would follow."

"You think so?" I asked.

"Of course, I think so. Molly is their leader and pulls their string."

"What is Molly's problem? Does she think being editor of the school paper gives her the right to butt into everyone's business?" I asked.

"Maybe she does, especially when she has to publish whatever is submitted to the paper," Kathy said, nodding. "I'm sure she didn't want to publish your articles, but she had no other choice but to publish them, since no student's article can be turned down no matter what the subject."

"I guess you're right and she doesn't want to publish mockery material."

"Since she's the editor, she no doubt thinks of the paper as hers. Besides, without your articles, she has extra space for her pictures of herself," Kathy laughed.

"You are kidding. Molly likes attention, but she's not that conceited," I said.

"I know, Mandy; but she's still a snob."

"No more than the rest of those cheerleaders she hangs out with." I pointed out.

"That's true. But if you ask me, I think Molly started the backlash against your articles."

"Why do you think that?"

"She's the editor and probably was the main person who didn't like the idea of you writing against teenage sex; and I wonder why?" Kathy smiled.

"Why would she make such a big deal about my articles and start such a commotion at school?"

"I'm not sure, but we both know how Molly likes attention. Giving you negative attention will make her shine more," Kathy suggested. "And who knows, maybe she's just plain envious of you."

"How could someone as wealthy as Molly be jealous of me? She's the one with all the boys chasing after her. Plus, she's the one wearing designer clothes, shoes and purses every single day. What do I have that she could be envious of?"

"As many shoes as she does?" Kathy grinned.

"Kathy, don't be funny. I'm serious and would like to know the root of her problem with me. I think it's just the articles because she wasn't this rude to me before they were published."

"Maybe and maybe not," Kathy said. "I still think she could envy you," Kathy humped up her shoulders.

"Get real, Kathy, you can't be serious about envy." I waved my hand.

"I'm very serious, Mandy. It's possible Molly could be jealous of you."

"But why would you think that?"

"Okay, let's think. Maybe your good looks." Kathy paused. "In case you haven't thought about it, you are the knockout she wants to be."

I stared hard and frowned. "Get real," I laughed. "What are you talking about? Molly is very beautiful just like the whole Chase clan. Wouldn't you agree?"

"Is that a trick question? I agree the whole Chase clan is attractive, but Molly I'm not sure if I'll put her on the gorgeous list with the rest of them," Kathy said.

"Well, she's on the list whether you want to put her there or not," I stressed with both hands out. "Get a clue, Kathy. That's why the entire school picked her as homecoming queen last year, remember; and she was picked this year, but she turned it down so it could fall to the first runner up." I paused. "That was quite generous of her, I might add."

"Yes, it was generous, but the first runner up was no other than her best friend and cousin, Lynn Chase. She probably would not have stepped aside for anyone else," Kathy stated.

"I don't know about that, I just know regardless to how you feel about Molly, she is very beautiful."

"Mandy will you keep something in mind?"

"What's that?"

"Beauty is in the eye of the beholder." Kathy pointed to her eyes. "For these eyes, it's not there." Kathy shrugged her shoulders. "I'm just saying."

I shook my head. "And we both know you are not bias toward Molly," I stated with a disappointed edge. "I thought you were going to work on that," I said, pulling the last of my iced-tea through the straw.

"It's hard to work on when I have nothing but contempt for the girl."

"Contempt is not good, but I wish she didn't have a beef with me. I just wish she would stay out of my face about those articles."

"Mandy, you have to stop paying Molly and the other kids around here any attention," Kathy said, biting into her tuna sandwich.

"How can I not pay them any attention? You just saw what happen. I'm not going to let Molly confront me like that! What am I suppose to do, just turn my head as if I don't hear them? No way do I plan to just sit still and take their constant criticism about my articles. I'm done being the quiet pushover! I plan to speak up for my opinion and viewpoint," I said firmly. "Why should I allow a few students around here to make me shy away from something I believe in?"

Kathy glanced at me and shook her head. Apparently she felt I was just blowing off steam. "What does your statement translate into?" She asked.

"It translates into the fact that I plan to fight back."

"Now you're talking!" Kathy said with conviction. "You need to stand up and let them all know that you're no more of a rich square than the rest of these rich bitches," she said firmly.

"You're right, that's what I need to do. Their outrageous statement that I'm pushing garbage in the school paper is just ridiculous."

"Keep thinking like that and you may build enough backbone to tell one of them off," Kathy grinned.

"I have enough backbone now and I plan to use it," I stressed seriously. "Believe me, the next time Molly confronts me, the way she just did not long ago, I plan to have a few words with her! You hear me, Kathy?"

"Yes, I hear you; and I'm sure you're not looking forward to confronting Molly or anyone else, but maybe that's going to be the only thing to get these rich snobs off your back," Kathy suggested.

"Maybe you are right, Kathy. Maybe a war of words with Molly will get her off my back."

Kathy shook her head. "Mandy, I'm having second thoughts."

"What are you having second thoughts about, confronting Molly?"

She nodded. "Yes, I don't think that's the answer."

"Well, what is the answer?" I asked.

"It just dawn on me that it's not a war of words."

"You thought so a second a go and cheered me on," I reminded her.

"I know I did, but really, what good is some argument going to do? Fighting doesn't solve problems." She pointed to her head. "Using your brains solve problems. You got to out smart that snob! She's the leader of the pact. If you can get her out of your hair, the rest of her group will fall out as well."

"Kathy, you make it sound so simple." I took a sip from my bottle of water. "Out smart her? How do you suppose I do that?"

"I can think of one way you can out smart her," Kathy narrowed her eyes at me and smiled.

"Okay, I'm listening."

"You can sleep with as many boys as she has, and make sure she finds out about it," Kathy joked. "I'm just kidding that's not it."

"I know you are kidding," I said, laughing. "Because I'm not about to do that, but how is this for an idea?"

"How is what?"

"Turn around is fair play, right?"

"Mandy, what are you getting at?"

"I was just thinking that maybe we can poke fun at one of her articles in the school paper. She always writes about fashion. Maybe we can make fun of the clothes she showcase or something."

Kathy held up both hands. "No, Mandy, that won't do. Her style sense is too cool to poke fun at. But I have something else in mind that just might do the trick."

"Okay, I'm listening. What just might do the trick?" I grinned. "If it's going to improve my quality of life here at school, I'm all for it." I glanced about to make sure nobody was standing near our table.

"Do you have an extra coach purse lying around?" Kathy asked.

"Do I have an extra coach purse lying around?" I grinned. "Get real, Kathy. What does having an extra purse have to do with what we're talking about?"

She glanced over her shoulder and scanned the room, and then looked at me and spoke in a whisper. "It has everything to do with what we're talking about. Now do you have an extra coach purse you would like to let go of?"

"Sure, I have a few," I whispered, with no idea what Kathy was getting at.

"Okay, this is my idea. Let's give one of your elegant purses to one of those cheerleaders."

"What? Give one of my purses to a cheerleader?" I grabbed my face, staring at her. "Kathy, have you cracked up? What are you talking about? You're not making any sense. Give one of my purses to which cheerleader?"

"You know who, that poor little rich girl, of course." She grinned.

"What poor little rich girl? Are you referring to Molly?"

"Not Molly, her cousin Lynn."

"You mean Ricky's sister?"

"Yes, that's who I'm talking about."

"Okay, you think we should give Lynn Chase a purse. To be precise, you think we should give her one of my coach purses, but not one of yours."

"It should be your purse since it's your problem that I'm just trying to help you with," Kathy pointed out.

"Okay, but you're still not making any sense. I don't follow what you're getting at." I shook my head. "Why should I give your boyfriend sister a purse when she owns enough coach purses to open a small boutique?"

"Mandy, you don't follow because I haven't finished explaining. Just let me finish explaining."

"Okay, sure, explain yourself."

"It's like this, Mandy. I figured we could give Lynn one of your nice purses to spread a bogus rumor about you. She'll do it," Kathy grinned.

"Spread what bogus rumor?" I asked.

"What bogus rumor do you think, the lie that you are no longer writing and speaking out against premarital sex," Kathy explained. "And when she spreads the lie she can say even though you have written about it, you are not practicing it."

"You are kidding, right?"

"No, Mandy, I'm not kidding. I'm dead serious that we need to spread a rumor about you, that you have changed your viewpoint on that issue," she said firmly. "We really need to do this since your articles seem to have so many at school in a tailspin thinking you are trying to cramp their style. I get the feeling that they think you don't know about the birds and the bees." She laughed. "That's why a little white lie brewing about you could help your fuddy-duddy not so popular reputation at the moment!"

Still holding my cheeks with both hands, a smile curved across my mouth. I nodded. "This could actually work." I slightly pounded my fist on the table.

Kathy kept nodding and grinning as she broke her tuna sandwich in half, passing one half to me. "For sure it can work; and I came up with this brilliant idea."

"Why are you giving me half of your sandwich?"

"I'm stuffed; that Greek salad did the trick," she said. "Do you want it? If not, it goes in the trash." She smiled, pointing to the trashcan at the end of the table.

I shook my head. "I'm stuffed. Did you notice my plate? I didn't even finish my own sandwich."

"Okay, we're both stuffed, so in the trash it goes," she said, throwing her half eaten tuna sandwich in the trash.

"Listen, Kathy. Are you sure about Lynn? She's not only Molly's right hand, they are first cousins and very close? This little plan could backfire on me, you know?"

"Backfire how?"

"She could refuse the purse for one. After all, she has plenty of purses already."

"I know she already has plenty. No other student at school own as many coach purses as Lynn Chase. Therefore, I'm sure she won't refuse the bag."

"Kathy, get real. I don't care if she owns every purse in town; she still could refuse the one we plan to offer her."

"Mandy, don't sweat it. Lynn will not refuse the purse. She's a coach purse junkie just like I'm a shoe junkie and can never have enough shoes. So believe me, Lynn will never refuse a new coach purse."

"I hope you are right, Kathy, because if you are not, she could run and tell everybody what we tried to do. That would put me higher on their detestation list. You know what I'm saying? I have no desire to find myself deeper in the doghouse with any of these snobs around here!"

"No, listen, Mandy, I told you, I'm sure about this. You really don't have to sweat this not one tiny bit. I have gotten to know Lynn quite well since I'm dating her brother and she's dating mine. So believe me, if you can give her a new coach purse, your troubles are over. You hear what I'm saying?"

"Alright, I'll do it. I'll bring the purse to school tomorrow."

"Well, consider your troubles over, because like I said, Lynn is a sure bet. She's going steady hot and heavy with one of my brothers, and if she can't do us this favor I'll spill my guts about what I know; and she knows I know quite a bit."

"Oh, that's right. She does like Justin, doesn't she?"

Kathy shook her head. "No, it's not Justin; he's into Molly, remember?"

"That's right; so she's crazy about which one of your brothers? You have three; I mean four, all one year a part in ages." I paused. "I guess I'm not sure who is dating Lynn. If it's not Justin, I'm not sure if it's Cody, Wesley or Kent?"

"No, it's not Cody or Wesley. Besides, Wesley only has eyes for you, remember. But you have yet to look twice at my poor lovesick brother."

"I do look twice at Wesley Jr. He's nice and cute too, and we talk sometime. But I just don't like him in that way."

"You mean the way he likes you?" Kathy waved her hand. "Besides, girls are calling him up all the time, I'm sure he'll get over you soon or later. But, yes, it's Kent who's crazy about Lynn. And just so you know, since you have forgotten, I have four brothers. Where is your head, thinking I only have three? You need to stop confusing my brothers with the Chase boys. Just remember there are three Chase boys, but four Gross boys," Kathy said teasingly.

"Give me a break. I can't keep up with that Chase clan." I smiled.

"Since you are madly in love with one of them, you should try," Kathy teased.

"You're madly in love with one of them also," I teased her back.

"So we are both in love with Chase boys, but listen closely; Molly has two brothers as you know: your dreamboat, Brad; and that other dreamboat, Todd. But add my honey, their cousin to the mix, and that makes three Chase boys," she paused. "If you are following me, Ricky is Lynn's brother and not Molly's. But still, two plus one adds up to three Chase boys. Is that where your mind is right now, on a certain Chase boy?" Kathy teased.

"Let's stay focused and not get sidetracked by my wreck of a love life or lack of," I mumbled, not wanting to discuss my feelings for Brad. "Now, it just registered. I do remember that Lynn likes and is dating your brother, Kent," I said, smiling.

"I wouldn't use the word like. I would use the word worship. She worships the ground Kent walks on and then some," Kathy stressed.

"She's that into Kent?"

"Yes, she is, "Kathy nodded.

"That's great. I had no idea she was that serious about Kent. But is she so into him that she would lie for us and fool her best buddy?"

"Of course she is." Kathy hit my arm in a playful way. "Like I said, you don't have to sweat this mess anymore. Lynn is stone in love with Kent." She paused for a second. "He loves her too, but their relationship is fragile right now, because they are living in a glass house."

"What are you getting at, Kathy?"

"I could throw a brick through the window of that relationship, a brick heavy enough to break up her playhouse!"

"That would be cruel. I don't I like the sound of that."

"I'm not saying I'll do it, I'm saying I could. She hasn't always been truthful to Kent. She knows I know it. So, like I said, if she tries to come out of left field and shoot down our plan, I can throw a stone in her glass house so quick it will make her head spin," Kathy grinned.

"But, you won't, right Kathy?" I shook my head.

"Mandy, of course I won't, I'm not that cold," she assured me. "But Mandy, the point is: she knows that I know about her deception to Kent. But she doesn't know I won't tell him.

You know I have a reputation for being bold and nobody's pushover, so most likely Lynn will think I'll tell her deception to Kent if I tell her I will."

"What are you talking about? What deception might that be?"

"It's not something you would know about."

"But you do know about Lynn's business?"

"I clearly found out by accident when I overheard her telling Molly in the restroom. It's about the time last year when she lied to Kent about not feeling well just so she could attend some family dinner with some other rich boy that her family had introduced her to and invited over. In case you didn't know, her folks can't stomach Kent because he's not rich enough for their poor little rich girl. But that wasn't the only time she lied to Kent. Not that long ago she told Kent she was sick so she could break their date. Then she went to a house party with Molly and a few other cheerleaders. She has kept those lies from him. That's why I'm so sure she'll come through for us."

"How do you know all of this stuff?" I asked.

"I'm not gossiping. I know it because I was at the same house party that Lynn and Molly showed up at after she had called our house to tell Kent she was sick."

"Whatever, if Lynn will do this, it's great. But listen, Kathy. I'm not trying to make trouble for anyone else. I just want Molly off my back and out of my business about those articles. After she drops it, I'm sure everybody else will chill out about it. After-all, writing my viewpoint in the school paper and speaking out about my objection to teenage sex is something I'm proud of. I'm just cooling it and want this rumor to work because I want Molly and the other students off of my back and out of my business. "

"I know what you mean. Just like we already figured out, Molly is the main one who has made a big deal out of it, and caused the other students to get upset with you over it. As if your viewpoint is going to somehow block some of their fun.

It's your opinion and you are entitled to it," Kathy explained seriously.

"I am entitled to my opinion. But just the same, please do not cause any trouble for Lynn and your brother. But promised me you won't do anything to hurt their relationship. Doing this isn't worth breaking up their relationship," I stressed firmly.

"Look, Mandy, don't look so serious. Don't lose any sleep over what I just said, okay? I don't have a beef with Lynn. I actually think she's okay. She just hangs with the wrong crowd," Kathy said firmly.

I nodded. "Okay, because I'm really not trying to cause any trouble."

"I'm not planning to cause trouble for Lynn," Kathy assured me.

"Yeah, but you just said if she turned us down you could," I reminded her.

"Yeah, Yes, I know I said I could, but I didn't say I would. And I won't, okay?" Kathy assured me. "So just chill about that, Mandy; and you'll see that everything will work out just as I have predicted."

Chapter Twelve

Kathy and I approached Lynn in the cafeteria that Tuesday during our lunch period. We cornered her when we caught her alone at the water fountain. She was busy filling her cup with water when she glanced around and noticed the both of us standing on either side of her.

"Lynn, do you have a minute?" Kathy asked.

"Sure, what's up?" She put the cup of water to her mouth and took a sip, then glanced at me and gave me a hard stare. After a moment of silence, she pulled Kathy by the sweater away from me. Kathy was her boyfriend's sister, so she didn't mind talking to Kathy, but she could damage her reputation with her crowd, especially Molly, if she was spotted mingling with the little rich square, that they called me, that was causing all the commotion on the school premises with my outspoken articles in the school paper about my objections to premarital sex.

Kathy jerked her arm away from Lynn. "Lynn, let go of my sweater. I just need you to listen to me for a minute. What I need to talk to you about includes both of us." Kathy pointed toward me.

"It includes both of you? What is this all about?" she said, and then looked across the cafeteria at Molly and the rest of her crowd beckoning for her. She kept looking their way, until they walked out of the lunchroom. Molly stuck her head back in the door and hollered across the room.

"Lynn, we'll be right back, okay?"

Lynn nodded; no doubt pleased they stepped out of the lunchroom.

"Lynn, I know we are catching you off guard, but we need a huge favor from you," Kathy said seriously.

Lynn put her hands on her hips and gave us a downcast look as if we had just stunned her.

Kathy exchanged looks with me and smiled at Lynn. "I'm sure you can not imagine what this is all about, but it's important to us; and I'll make this quick," Kathy said and gestured her head and eyes toward the cafeteria exit.

"We saw your crowd beckoning for you, "I quickly added. "We know you are anxious to get away from the school unpopular big mouth and her shadow. I think that's what I'm being called at the moment," I said calmly. "So you can keep your reputation in tack with them."

Kathy stared in her eyes. "We know they'll be back soon. So the sooner I get to the point, the better."

"Okay, get to the point already," Lynn nodded anxiously.

"Okay, it's like this." Kathy glanced at me, and then back at Lynn. "Can we come to your house after school today and discuss something?"

Lynn frowned with a confused look on her face. "Discuss what? What is this about? What in the world could the two of you possibly want to discuss with me?"

Kathy didn't raise her voice, but spoke firmly as she looked Lynn dead in the eyes. "If you'll just listen for a moment I'm about to tell you."

Lynn snapped. "Well go on. I'm listening."

"It's pretty private, Lynn, and we would prefer to tell you what this is all about when we come over to your house later," Kathy explained.

"But I never said you could come over." Lynn lifted an eyebrow with confusion still written all over her face.

Kathy nodded, trying to control her emotions to appear more polite toward Lynn. "I know you haven't said yes yet, but we're hoping you'll let us come over after school to talk to you about it?"

Lynn stared at Kathy, frowning, not saying anything, glancing about the cafeteria. No doubt, hoping her crowd wouldn't step back through the door and see her conversing with us.

"Your parents will be home, right?" I asked.

Lynn nodded with her eyes still glued toward the exit door.

"Okay, in that case," Kathy added. "If your folks will be home, there's no way you could possibly think we're up to no good," Kathy said.

Lynn looked at Kathy and frowned. "I wasn't thinking anything like that."

"Well, you're all nervous looking," Kathy muttered a little ruder than she meant to. "But come to think of it, you wouldn't think something like that, that's more how your sidekick would handle things."

"You're referring to Molly as my sidekick?" Lynn shook her head. "Keep saying stuff like that and I'm walking away, okay?"

"I'm sorry, but that was just a slip of the tongue," Kathy apologized. "Plus, we don't have a beef with you anyway."

"Besides, there's no law against hanging out with a stuck up snob like your cousin, Molly. If you want to hangout with someone as arrogant and conceited as your cousin Molly that's your business," I said. "And that wasn't a slip of the tongue."

Lynn raised an eyebrow. "Disrespecting Molly with name calling is not going to get my attention. Pot kettle, to you Mandy," Lynn snapped.

"I beg you pardon," I said and stared at her hard.

"Get over yourself, Mandy. You two can stand here and call Molly arrogant and conceited because her folks are rolling in dough. Look around this room and if there's one among us who's not living the good life, throw the first stone," Lynn bent over laughing.

"Does the name Chase ring a bell," I said politely.

"Okay, Chase or no Chase," she barked at us, pointing toward me and then to Kathy, finally placing her finger on her chest and holding it there. "Our families are loaded," Lynn stated seriously. "Besides, Miss Mandy Clark, who in this town can get any richer than your mother and father; Kathy, your folks are rolling in dough. So, it blows me away how everybody is always calling Molly rich as if the rest of us are living as hobos. So don't stand here and talk like Molly is in a class all by herself?"

"She is in a class to herself, and it has nothing to do with money. It's all about attitude and compassion. Her lack of," Kathy laughed, but stopped herself.

Lynn just stood there staring at Kathy, shaking her head as Kathy continued.

"Furthermore, Lynn," Kathy reminded her. "If my folks are so loaded like yours, why are your parents on their high horse against Kent?"

"They are not against Kent," Lynn fumbled.

"They are against him. Your folks hate my brother and you know it," Kathy stared her in the eyes.

"Where do you hear this stuff," Lynn fumbled with her fingernails.

"Where do you think? Right here on these premises. So don't lie to my face. We both know your folks do not want you dating Kent. The word is as far as your parents are concerned: Kent isn't good enough for you."

"Who cares about that?"

"Kent would if I told him."

"What are you getting at?"

"I'm getting at the fact that your folks think my brother isn't rich enough for their filthy rich little Chase girl?"

"Get over it, Kathy! Why are you bringing this up? Are you trying to pick a fight with me? Who cares what my parents think?"

"You should."

"Well, I don't. I date who I want. Besides, that's how they are. It's not just about Kent," Lynn fussed and stared toward the ceiling with an arrogant look on her face. "As far as they are concerned, no boy is good enough or rich enough for me. It's not because of your family wealth or the lack of. If that was the case they wouldn't want Ricky dating you, but my folks like you. So you can forget the notion that they are against Kent. Believe me when I say no boy is good enough for me in their eyes. That's why I don't pay them any attention. I date who I want."

"Well, if you have all the answers I guess you already know how wonderful Molly is. And we can't fool you by saying she isn't," Kathy said, smiling.

"Okay, that's it. You two can leave now. I get it. You hate Molly and you want me to hate her too. I'm sure you probably call me names when I'm not around, arrogant and conceited behind my back. After all, Molly and I are cut from the same cloth, right? We are two brother's kids. We both have the same last name. And the last I heard our bankbooks are equal."

"Okay, I'm sorry I said that about Molly," Kathy apologized.

"You should be sorry, especially when you have the audacity to ask me to listen to what you have to say. I give you the courteous of listen, and then you act rude and talk to me like that about my cousin. I will not stand here and let you bad mouth my best friend? Whatever you are trying to sell, count me out," Lynn snapped.

"Lynn, just listen for a moment. I said I was sorry. We just need to talk to you for a moment, is that okay?" Kathy held up both arms. "Just listen for a moment."

She narrowed her eyes at Kathy and nodded. "What do you think I have been doing all this time? I have been listening, but I haven't heard anything. What gives? What do you two want from me?"

"We want to pay you a visit after school."

"I can't imagine why either of you would want to visit me. But okay, sure. Pay me a visit after school." She glanced at her gold Gucci watch. "Come around five. Now, is that it?" Lynn asked.

Kathy spoke in a low voice. "No, there's one more thing."

"Okay, I'm still listening. What's the one more thing?"

"Don't mention our visit to Molly or anyone else, please!"

"Sure, fine. Whatever," she uttered with a confused look on her face. "I won't mention it, but you two have me really curious now." She backed away, holding up her arms. "Look, I have to run. See you later, I guess." She rushed away.

Chapter Thirteen

When Lynn Chase answered the doorbell that evening and welcomed us into her big red brick home, she was in a much friendlier mood. She was smiling and didn't seem uptight the way she had appeared at school around her crowd.

"Hey, you two, wow, you're quick." She glanced at her watch.

"Hey, Lynn," Kathy spoke and I nodded. "Why are you surprised? This is the time you told us to arrive."

She smiled. "I know, but I said five to make sure you would arrive somewhere near that time."

"Why didn't you just say the actual time you wanted us here?" Kathy asked.

"It's okay, really. It's just that I have found that most people show up shortly after the time you tell them, that's why I usually say much sooner so they can arrive at the time that I really want them to arrive."

Kathy stared at her with a smirk on her face. "Maybe you should change that method and just say what you mean."

"I agree with you, because you two proved me wrong. I guess you came here straight from school. I just got house myself. Please come in." She stretched out her hand toward the inside of their living room.

I looked at Lynn with humble eyes. "We drove right over because we didn't want to wait too late and interrupt your dinner or anything," I said.

"Mandy, is that your little red mustang out there?" Lynn asked as she closed the front door.

"No, it's mine," Kathy answered.

"It's really nice. It almost looks like mine. Mandy, you have a red mustang don't you?"

I shook my head. "No, my car is midnight blue," I answered.

It was my first time at Lynn's house and my feet seemed to sink as we walked across the thick forest green carpet on their huge living room floor. She led the way and pointed toward the sofa as Kathy and I made our way across the room.

"I feel sort of out of sorts with the two of you visiting me," Lynn said.

"You are not alone." Kathy nodded. "We feel just as out of sorts as you do."

"I'm sure you do, but now that you're here at my house, about to be seated, it might also feel a bit awkward since we are not really close friends and I have no idea why you are both here, but I want you two to know that I'm always polite to my guests," she said with a smile, holding out both hands to us. "Can I get either of you a bottle of water or a can of soda?"

Kathy and I shook our heads as we took a seat next to each other on the long cedar green sofa. My eyes glanced about the room and were especially impressed by the long forest green sheer curtains that hung at all six windows. The enormous room was decorated in expensive elegant style.

Lynn nodded and then took a seat facing us on a matching sofa.

"We won't stay long. We know it's almost dinner time," Kathy said as I sat there beside her, being quiet, waiting to see if Lynn would take the bait.

Lynn nodded and glanced at her watch. "It's not almost dinner time here."

Kathy and I exchanged looks. "Are you sure we are not interrupting your dinner?" Kathy asked.

"Course not, why do you keep bringing up dinner? We never eat this early. I wouldn't have suggested this time if it wasn't okay. Besides, our cook never serves dinner before six. You guys can stay as long as you want. I just want to know what's up." She glanced over her shoulder at the vague voices coming from the dinning area.

"Should we step outside, maybe?" Kathy asked.

"No, we're fine right here," Lynn assured us.

Kathy exchanged looks with me. "But what we have to say is pretty private and we wouldn't want anyone else to overhear our conversation."

Lynn waved her hand. "It's plenty private in here."

"Who's in there?" Kathy pointed toward the dinning area. "Was that Debra?"

"Who's Debra?" I asked.

"That's my mother's name," Lynn answered.

I stared at Kathy and narrowed my eyes. "Why are you calling her Debra and not Mrs. Chase?"

"Whenever Ricky brings me over and I greet her as Mrs. Chase, she tells me to call her Debra. So that's what I call her. I'm not trying to be disrespectful; I'm just greeting her as she asked."

I nodded. "Okay, I didn't know."

"To answer your question," Lynn looked at Kathy. "Yes, that's Momma in there talking to the cook about the dinner menu. There's no one else home to overhear us."

"Your father and Ricky aren't here?" Kathy asked.

Lynn shook her head. "Nope, they're not home yet. We don't expect Daddy and Ricky for at least another hour." She nodded. "Therefore, Kathy, you don't have to wonder if Ricky will catch you here." She exchanged looks with me and Kathy with an assured look in her eyes.

"That didn't cross my mind," Kathy mumbled.

"It probably should cross your mind." Lynn laughed. "If my brother catches you here visiting me, someone you don't even talk to at school. I think he would be curious to know why you are here. He would ask me a lot a questions and I get the sense that you and Mandy do not want me to mention your visit over here to anyone."

"You're right; we don't want you to mention our visit here to anyone at school," Kathy said.

"And you don't want me to mention it to Ricky either, right?"

"You're right again." Kathy waved her hand.

"Okay, now that we are clear about that, you two can relax and tell me what this visit is all about. No one can overhear us and Ricky will not be walking through that door anytime soon." She pointed toward the front door. "So go on and tell me why you're here."

Kathy looked at me. "You want me to tell her?"

I nodded at Kathy. "Sure, go ahead."

Lynn smiled. "I have to admit I'm very curious. We have no associations with each other at school, but for some reason the two of you are sitting in my living room because you need to talk to me about something that seems quite important."

"This is what's up?" Kathy passed her the purse.

"What's this for?" Lynn asked, glancing over her shoulder toward the kitchen where her mother was, holding her voice to a mere mumble as she said. "What are you two up too? What's this all about?" She asked, holding the purse in her hand, staring down at the shiny black purse as if she hadn't seen a new coach purse in her life.

With her huge weekly allowance she could easily purchase anything she desired, but she held on to purse as if she would never see one again. Although she had many designer purses in different colors and sizes, she treated the one Kathy had handed her like a treasure.

"We're giving you this purse for the favor we need," Kathy softly muttered.

"You're giving me this purse for what favor?"

"We need a huge favor from you, Lynn." I nodded at her.

"Okay, but it must be some huge favor if you think I need a new purse to do it."

"Like you said, we are not close friends and Mandy and I realized that we couldn't just drive over here and ask a favor of you empty handed."

Lynn held the purse in her lap as she grabbed her face with both hands for a moment. She stared up at the ceiling for a moment and then shook her head. "Wow, I think I'm getting a bit nervous here. I know you two are not into anything crazy, but I don't even know what you guys want," she stress seriously. "But I'm getting the feeling that it might be something I don't want to be apart of," she said, passing the purse back to Kathy. "I think you should just take your purse until I hear the favor."

Kathy shook her head. "No, keep it."

"You're asking me to keep this purse, but I haven't agreed to anything."

"We know that Lynn, but we're sure you will. This favor we need from you is something you can live with. Believe me."

Lynn hopped out of her seat with a frown on her face. "If it's something I can live with, why are you here pushing a new purse in my face?" she snapped. "I'll tell you why, everybody at school knows how much I love coach purses."

"Calm down, Lynn, please!" Kathy firmly suggested in a low voice, looking toward the archway leading into the dinning area. "This is a private conservation, remember?"

"I know it's private." Lynn took a seat back on the sofa to face them. "But I'm sort of ticked with you two now."

"Why are you ticked, Lynn?" I calmly asked. "You still don't know what the favor is and Kathy just told you it's nothing out of the way."

"I know, Mandy, but I have a bad feeling about this visit. Something in my gut is telling me that you two are up to no good. So, please take your purse back." She threw the purse in

Kathy's lap. "I just think you should keep the purse until I hear what you have to say."

Kathy threw the purse back to Lynn and it landed on the sofa next to Lynn. Lynn held up both arms. "I don't know what you two are thinking, but you can't make me do some favor for you. I'm not a pushover if that's what you thought before you got here."

After a moment of silence, Lynn picked up the purse beside her and examined it. She smiled and exchanged looks with me and Kathy. "Well, what is your favor?"

"Okay, here goes," Kathy uttered softly. "We are here for one reason and one reason only. We want to put a stop to all the lies and non sense about Mandy that's be spread about at school."

Lynn mouth fell open. "So, you're here to shut me up?"

Kathy took a deep breath. "Just hold on a minute I'm not finished. "One of the lies that are being spread paints Mandy as an old fashion big mouth with ancient views about sex."

Lynn held up both hands, shaking her head. "I haven't told anybody that she's an old fashion big mouth with ancient views about sex. Are you here to blame me for that lie? What other lies are you referring to?" Lynn asked.

Kathy looked at me. "There's a lie floating around that I'm a cold fish, pushing garbage in the school paper," I said.

"Its all lies and so is the rubbish floating round that she won't go all the way with a boy," Kathy said.

Lynn shifted in her seat. "Is that also a lie?"

Kathy nodded. "Yes, Lynn, that is also a lie."

"I didn't spread the lie, but I have to admit that I thought that lie was true," Lynn mumbled with surprise in her eyes. "Any numbers of students could have put that one out there." Lynn grinned. "In case you two didn't know, pretty much everyone at school thinks that little piece of information about you, is true, Mandy."

Kathy shook her head, exchanging looks with me. "Listen, Lynn. Everybody at school is in the dark about Mandy. That information is not true is it, Mandy?"

I looked at Kathy and shook my head. It felt weird to lie, but it was necessary.

"They all have the wrong impression about Mandy because she has strong views against premarital sex. That's what it's all about. She writes those articles and now everybody at school has jumped to the wrong conclusion," Kathy explained.

"That's easy to do. Why write so strongly about something if it's not about what you believe in," Lynn mumbled with shock on her face.

"I agree, but in this case, Mandy is not living by those standards that she's writing about. She just thinks those standards are ideal for whoever can abide by them. But everyone thinks she's writing those articles because she's that way."

"Whatever, but that's kind of silly." Lynn looked at me. "That's sort of like if I wrote an article telling everyone to buy a vinyl purse when I hate them myself. It doesn't make sense," Lynn pointed out.

"Okay, maybe it doesn't make sense, but that's what's going on. And everybody at school has put two and two together to come up with four as you have. It's the logical results, but in actuality Mandy is writing those articles but not practicing them."

"Okay, what do you need from me?" Lynn asked.

"We need you to let everyone at school know the truth," Kathy stated.

"What is the truth?" Lynn asked.

"What we just said, Mandy doesn't practice what she preaches. But everybody at school thinks she does. You need to change their perception," Kathy explained. "Once you do that, Mandy won't have to worry about students at school whispering and saying she's pushing garbage."

"What garbage?" She looked at me. "You guys have lost me."

"What do you mean we have lost you? What piece didn't you understand? I thought I made that quite clear?" Kathy stated irritated.

"I know you think I can help change everybody's perception at school about Mandy, but I'm not clear on what."

"Lynn, we think you are clear on what. Think of what everybody thinks of Mandy right now, and reverse it. Is that clear enough?" Kathy snapped.

Lynn looked at me. "Mandy, here's what I know that's being said about you. You're not sleeping with boys and you're writing garbage in the school paper to encourage other teenagers not to sleep with boys. The students are upset that you are writing these articles to push in their faces when they are not interested in what you have to say," Lynn explained politely. "Mandy, that's what everybody thinks of you at school at the moment." She nodded and then exchanged looks with me and Kathy. "But something sounds a bit off with you Mandy."

"What do you mean?" I asked.

"You say you feel strongly about premarital sex and that's why you write about it, but you also are saying that you don't practice what you preach. But my question is, if you are so strongly against premarital sex, why are you doing it yourself? It just doesn't fit that you would write so strongly about something that you don't follow. That's why everybody figured you were not active yet, and figured you were putting yourself above the rest of us because we are active."

I shifted in my seat and felt on the spot by Lynn's reasoning. But Kathy spoke out quickly. "We know that's what the other students think," Kathy stumbled with her words, and then coughed to gather her untrue thoughts. "But believe us, it's a lie, okay? Mandy is no crusader putting down others because of their sexual activities. You got that?" Kathy stated firmly.

"I don't know if I have it or not?" Lynn mumbled.

"Okay, Lynn, think about it like this. You are not a crusader against premarital sex are you?" Kathy asked.

"Well, no, but I'm not writing articles in the school paper and saying it's wrong to engage in sex before marriage."

"But what, we're telling you the truth Lynn, okay?" Kathy tried to sway her.

"I wonder if that's why they are saying you're pushing garbage. Because you're selling something that you're not buying yourself? Or is it because you're pushing something that nobody on campus is interested in hearing?" Lynn smiled.

I nodded and Kathy nodded. If we could get Lynn on board we would nod about anything. Although it was two separate questions, nodding about both statements seemed as good as any.

"That was clear. You both nodded and I'm not sure I know what you nodded about," Lynn mumbled and glanced at her watch.

"That's not important, "Kathy quickly said. "What's important is that you need to be crystal clear about this favor. The bottom line is that we need you to spread this truth around school. And by doing this, students will stop harassing Mandy about those articles she wrote. Do you get us?"

"I can't believe anyone at school is really harassing Mandy about that. I know what everybody is saying and I heard a couple jokes, but nobody is really approaching you and harassing you, are they?" Lynn glanced toward me.

"Why are you looking toward, Mandy?" Kathy snapped. "I just told you that she's being hassled at school, didn't I?"

"Yes, you said it but I don't believe it," Lynn stressed.

"Well whether you believe it or not, believe this. Mandy is no crusader."

Lynn looked at me, smiling. "Mandy, I just got to ask you again. So are you saying, although, you speak out against sex before marriage; it's not what you are really about? You write a good article but you don't walk the walk?"

I shook my head. "Not the least bit," I answered with my fingers crossed.

Lynn started giggling. "This stuff is sort of funny. You guys are nuts. I was wondering all day about your visit and why you two wanted to drop by. It never crossed my mind that it would be about something this weird." She kissed the purse and placed it on the coffee table. "It looks like I'll be keeping this gorgeous black bag after all." She exchanged looks with us both and laughed. "You two have to admit that what's going on here is quite funny. I was so uptight there for awhile when all I have to do is spread around the truth." She glanced at her watch, and then stood up from the sofa and shook her head. "Consider it done."

"Thanks Lynn," I said as she showed us across the room and out the front door.

When we all stepped outside on the porch, Lynn was still grinning. But I could sense that Kathy wasn't please with her overly happy mood. Kathy grabbed her by the arm and held it. Instantly the grin on Lynn's face faded.

"This might seem weird and funny to you," Kathy stated firmly looking her straight in the face. "But it's not weird or funny to us."

"Calm down. I'm not trying to be funny, it just seems funny to me," Lynn said.

"Well, it's not funny to us. Would we give you an expensive purse if this was some silly game?" Kathy kept her irritated voice to a low mumble.

"I'm sure you wouldn't," Lynn said, frowning.

"Okay, remember that and please don't screw this up. Nobody knows better than you that a purse like the one we gave you doesn't grow on trees!" Kathy snapped.

Lynn jerked her arm from Kathy's hold. "Calm down, already," Lynn barked firmly. "I'll do what you asked. I'll get the word out to everybody I know that Mandy is not prudish. If you want everybody at school to think she's loose, pushing articles in the school paper that she doesn't practice herself, I'm the one to convince them."

"Shut your mouth Lynn and just listen." Kathy shook her head. "We said nothing to you about making anyone believe that Mandy is loose. We just need you to spread one bit of news and please don't add to it. If you do add to it, we will know and I'll come looking for you. So please stick to the plan. Just spread around that Mandy isn't the big mouth crusader against premarital sex the way the school campus has painted her out to be. She writes the articles but she's not practicing them. Now, is that clear?"

Lynn nodded. "Yes, it's clear, but what about the next time they read one of your articles in the school paper?" Lynn looked at me.

"Believe me when I say I won't be writing anymore articles on the subject. I'm done speaking out about something that nobody on the school grounds wants to hear."

Lynn looked at me with curious eyes. "Mandy, may I ask, why did you even write that first article? What made you think a bunch of teenagers with raging hormones would want to hear or read about something like that in their school paper?"

I exchanged looks with Kathy and Kathy shook her head. She probably wanted me to just be quiet. But telling Lynn a portion of the truth wouldn't change the rumor that we had asked her to spread. I looked in the eyes.

"Lynn, I'll tell you the truth. I wrote that first article because it seemed like a good idea at the time."

Lynn shook her head. "Although you didn't believe in it, you thought someone else at school would?"

"I guess I did, but I have learned my lesson the hard way. Barrington High will not hear anymore of my opinions on the subject."

"Okay, I got it." Lynn nodded. "Good luck."

"Thanks, I think I'll need it," I mumbled.

"Listen, Lynn." Kathy grabbed her arm again. "Don't, I repeat, don't; tell a soul that we gave you a new purse. And don't tell a soul that we dropped by your house and talked you into spreading this rumor," Kathy said and narrowed her eyes at Lynn. "If you double-cross us, I'll know, and I won't be happy."

Lynn nodded. "I give you my word."

We left Lynn's house in good spirit. We had only her word for it, but since Kathy felt she would not spill on us, I was pretty confident too. And just as Kathy had predicted, Lynn proved to be reliable. By the end of the week before school closed for the holiday break, the word was all over school. One student even told me what was on the Chase party's menu; and shared that Molly parents had given their permission for the party, but they were both out of town on a business trip. And to top it off, before the week ended Brad personally invited me to their party when he ran into me in the hallway at my locker.

"Hi Mandy," he said as he walked up behind me.

I turned around and fall against my locker with my books wrapped in my arms. Seeing his handsome face was a pleasant surprise. "Hi Brad. You startle me."

"I didn't mean to startle you."

"It's okay; I just didn't expect anyone to be standing there when I turned around." I smiled up at him.

"I just wanted to catch you before you headed home."

My heart skipped a beat and I was hoping he was going to ask me out. I stared in his eyes longingly. "Okay, why did you need to catch me?"

"I wanted to invite you to our party." He smiled.

"Your party," I asked, not expecting him to mention the party. "I was so hoping he was going to ask me out, which made his party invitation seem less intriguing.

"Yes, our New Year's party. You did hear about it already, right?"

"Yes, I heard about it."

"I would like for you to come if you don't already have plans for New Year's."

"No, I don't already have plans. I would love to come, but I was wondering if it would be okay to bring a plus one, maybe my friend?"

"You want to bring a friend?" he stumbled with his words and then he was speechless for a moment.

"I was just wondering in case Kathy wanted to come as well."

"Sure, Kathy or whoever you want to bring is welcomed," he assured me.

"That's right, which reminds me. Your party is an open house party."

"Yes, it is; which is really the first time. So, it will probably be packed with wild teenagers all over the place. But I'm hoping it will give us a chance to hangout. Would you like that?"

"Sure, it sounds like fun. But what made you decide on an open house party this time? I haven't attended any of your parties, but they are usually private, right?"

He grinned. "Yes, the parties we give are usually private; and we usually invite a handful of our friends. But this time, the credit goes to our folks."

"What do you mean?"

"Our parents are going to be out of town that evening and when we mentioned that we wanted to have the party. They encouraged us to make it an open house party and invite all the students."

"That was very generous of your folks," I said.

"Yeah, it was. But they set a few ground rules and gave us a budget. But I would have to agree that they are quite generous about stuff like that. It's really the way they are most of the time." He paused. "But they can really be quite including of others around the holidays."

"My father is that way," I said.

"But I guess, not so much your mother?" he asked.

I smiled. "That's correct. They have different viewpoints about life. And when I say different, I mean almost as different as day and night." I grinned.

"But yet, they found their way into each other's lives."

"That's what love does," I said looking into his eyes.

"I guess so," he smiled.

"Brad, I was just wondering about something."

"Okay, what is it?" he asked.

"When I mentioned bringing a friend, you seemed surprised. I guess I want to ask you why that surprised you."

"You caught me. It did surprise me when you mentioned bringing a friend."

"But why that surprised you?"

"It's a man's thing. When you mentioned plus one, I automatically thought of another guy."

I blushed. "So, I take it, the thought of me attending your party with another boy didn't sit well with you?"

He held out both arms. "Mandy, I didn't say that." He grinned. "You are a free woman. I have no claims on you, and I hope I didn't come across as being jealous when I thought you would be attending with another guy."

I grinned because he seemed nervous explaining himself. "No, I didn't think you were being jealous and even if you were, that would have been cute and a compliment to me."

"Okay, so maybe I was being jealous," he admitted.

"Brad, were you really?" I asked and collected myself. "You don't have to answer that. "I'm not trying to put you on the spot. I know we are not dating."

"But maybe we should be dating." He winked at me. "The bottom line is clear to me. It would make matters a lot easier if you just showed up at the party alone. Because honestly, I'm hoping the two of us can hangout together."

"I plan to come alone. I want to hangout with you too," I said, staring longingly in his eyes.

"That's perfect. I can't wait to see you there, Mandy." He glanced at his gold Movado watch. "I need to catch the drycleaners open. But we are good for the party? You'll be there so we can hangout alone, maybe even sneak upstairs to my room?" he said, smiling.

"Sure, I'll be there. I'm looking forward to it," I said, smiling.

"I can't wait to see you there," he said, and then turned on his shiny black shoe heels and hurried down the hallway toward the exit doors.

Although, the Chase party was two weeks away I was beside myself with excitement that he had personally invited me. I stood there against my locker for several minutes replaying in my mind what we had talked about before I finally collected myself and headed toward the exit doors.

Chapter Fourteen

I was flooded with enthusiasm on the evening of the party, which was the last day of 2002. It was a cold, snowy evening, but snowy cold conditions didn't hinder my excitement as I bundled up and headed down the street toward the Chase mansion. I chose to walk and not to drive in the snowy conditions since they lived only three blocks away. Their house was by far the biggest house in the area and by the time I reached it I was quite cold from the wind and snow. But my eyes lit up with a smile when I reached the entrance gate leading into their estate. Suddenly I was filled with anticipated joy, knowing I would be near Brad soon. I walked hurriedly up the long driveway toward their front door and as I got closer to the big house I could faintly hear the music. I looked up at the elegant palace of a house and it seemed every window in the big white house was lit up. I figured it would be standing room only since cars were parked along the street a block away. I walked across the huge porch anxious and nervous about going inside, but before I could ring the bell, I noticed that the front door was slightly cracked. I opened the door and just stepped inside. But just as I stepped into the foyer, a tall older lady dressed in light green maid attire met me and pointed toward the staircase to my right.

"The party is on the lower level," she said and then headed toward the enormous spread of a living room that faced us.

As I headed down the staircase, I slipped out of my coat and draped it across my arm. The white carpet on the steps felt like walking on feathers. When I reached the lower level, standing on the bottom step, the music was loud and several students were dancing, including Todd and Rachel. Five students were standing against the wall with glasses of orange punch up to their lips, drinking it down like water. I spotted Brad right away and he waved his hand over the crowd and beckoned for me. I hurried over to his side and Molly and her gang all gathered around us as well. Surprisingly, they all said hello and welcomed me to the party. They were quite friendly. Their smiles and rare kindness could have been the results of a few alcoholic drinks.

While Brad and I stood next to each other smiling, trying to talk to each other over the loud music, I spotted Ricky Chase standing against the wall staring at us. He didn't seem too balanced as he poured red wine into a glass he was holding. He held on to the bottle in his left hand as he drank the wine from the glass in his right hand. I had never seen him look so intoxicated and wondered what Kathy would think of him boozing it up at a party without her.

Brad tapped my shoulder and broke my fixation with how Ricky was heavily drinking and staring at the both of us.

"What are you looking at?" He asked.

I gestured my head toward the left. "It's your cousin over there boozing it up."

"Oh, yeah, I noticed him to," Brad grinned.

"I didn't think he was that big of a drinker."

"He's not usually, but tonight he's laying it on. Something got him in a mood."

"I'll say. He seems upset and he was staring at us," I said.

"I don't know what he was staring at, but one thing for sure, he's going to feel pretty rotten tomorrow. He hasn't let go of that wine bottle since he arrived."

"Did you know he's Kathy's boyfriend?"

"Who's Kathy?"

"You know Kathy. She's my best friend."

"That's right, Kathy Gross. You two hang out in the cafeteria together."

"Yes, that's her. She's crazy about Ricky."

"So, the two of them are dating?" He asked.

"Yes, they are dating. She's crazy about him and he's crazy about her."

"Where's your friend tonight?"

"She wanted to attend, but couldn't make it due to other family plans."

"That could be why Ricky is so out of sorts with the booze," Brad said.

"That could be it. But Kathy would be here if she could. Like I said, she's pretty crazy about your cousin."

"I think I have heard him mention your friend." He nodded. "I'm sure I have. And based on what I have heard, believe me, he's into her a lot."

"That's good to hear since she's so crazy about him."

"Enough about my cousin," he paused and noticed how I was holding on to my coat. "Do you want to hang up your coat? I can put it away for you." He smiled.

"Thanks, but it's no bother to hold it," I assured him, gripping the coat tightly as if it was my protection in someway.

"Okay that's cool," he said and winked at me. "By the way, you look beautiful. I like your outfit. Blue is your color," he complimented.

"Thank you, you look nice too." I smiled, admiring how handsome he looked in the black outfit he was wearing. He was wearing chic black pants and a silk black shirt.

We continued to stand there; he finished two glasses of punch as I slowly sipped on one. Then not long after I had arrived at the party, long before the count down to the New Year, Brad grabbed my hand and led me upstairs to the main floor, and then up another staircase to the third level where he led me down a long hallway to his bedroom. I had mixed feelings about leaving the party and going to his bedroom. I liked him very much but wasn't sure of his feelings or what he had in mind. I wasn't about to jump into bed with him just to prove a point to a roomful of snobbish drunk teenagers. Therefore, I was a bit nervous and didn't know quite what to say when we made it to his room.

We sat there on the edge of his king size bed for over five minutes without saying a word to each other. Then I thought to myself how silly it all was, and how I just couldn't go through with going to bed with him just because I figured that was what he wanted. But when I stood up to leave, I dropped my coat.

Brad was sitting there with his hands covering his face, as if he was trying to sober up from too much boozed up punch. I figured he wouldn't even notice me leaving, but as I bent over to grab my coat off the floor, he grabbed it first.

"What are you doing?" he asked. "I know you are not trying to sneak out already, are you?"

"Brad, please give me my coat. I have decided to leave."

"But why are you ready to leave so soon?" he asked humbly. "Be good and make me happy. Just sit back down beside me and let's get more acquainted," he said, smiling. "There's so much I don't know about you. You're a knock-out and the finest girl at school, but I don't even know your favorite color or what you like to eat or some of the things you like to do." He looked at me smiling.

"And whose fault is that?" I asked.

"I guess you're trying to say it's my fault."

"Well, what do you think, Brad?"

He nodded. "I think you are right."

"Yes, I'm right. You don't know me better, because you haven't tried to get to know me better," I said.

"I wouldn't say it exactly like that, Mandy. We do hang out sometime."

"Yes, we do hang out sometime on the school grounds. But two people can hardly get to know each other just hanging out on the school grounds." I pointed out.

He nodded, still smiling. "Well, I guess you got a point at that. But I'm sure I can get my act together and do a better job at getting to know you better. Let's start right now." He patted the bed next to him. "Do me a favor and have a seat and before we get into anything else, I'll tell you all about my likes and dislikes and you can do the same," he suggested. "By-the-way, I can tell you right now that my favorite color is black and my favorite food is pizza of any kind."

He seemed more alert and serious, but something inside of me wanted to go home or even leave town. It didn't matter where, as long as it was far away from Barrington, Illinois. So I could try to get Brad Chase out of my head. I wanted to be in his arms, but deep down I knew it was hopeless since he didn't really have feelings for me. He just wanted to get me in bed because most likely he had heard the lie that Kathy and I had encouraged Lynn Chase to spread.

"No, Brad, this isn't the time and place to chit chat. Just give me my coat so I can get out of your room and out of your house. I'd like to go home if you don't mind."

"But I do mind and you haven't said why you're ready to take off. So what's up with you? I thought we were having a good time together this evening."

"You thought right. It has been fun spending time with you. But Brad, it's obvious that you have had too much to drink."

"So what if I have? I'm not out it. I don't seem out of it do I?" he asked.

"No really, but it shows that you have had quite a bit."

"Let me worry about how much I have had." He grinned. "Aren't you having a good time?" He patted the bed next to him again. "Come on, get with it. Have a seat. We just got here," he said, still looking toward the floor.

"Brad, really. Why should I stay and hang around in your room? You may not be totally wasted, but you seem sort of out of it. You guys put too much booze in that orange punch. That's why I couldn't finish my glass. It tasted more like booze than punch. I couldn't stomach it and you had a few glasses."

He glanced up quickly. "I know I did, but I'm okay." He grabbed his face with both hands and then rubbed both hands down his hair. "A few glasses of alcohol can put me to sleep quicker than anything, but I'm not about to fall asleep with a beautiful female like you in my room. So, please be seated right here next to me." He patted the bed next to him again. "Don't you like my room?"

"Yes, no," I mumbled.

"What kind of an answer is that, yes and no?"

"Yes, I like your room, but no, I don't want to sit. I think I should just leave."

"Why do you think you should leave?" He suddenly perked up and stared at me very alertly. "We just got here."

"I know, but you're tired and falling to sleep."

"Don't worry about that. Please be seated."

"No, it's not a good time if you're out of it."

"Mandy, what's with you? We get to my room and before we can relax you're ready to take off." He held out both arms. "Why did we bother walking up all those stairs just for you to get up here and say you're leaving?"

"You seemed more alert when we were downstairs. I didn't know you were this out of it when you led me upstairs," I explained. "Otherwise, I would have insisted on staying downstairs."

"You really know how to break a guy bubble. I guess we could have hung out where we were if I had known my room would scare you away." He held out both arms again. "I know you say you want to take off because I have had too much to drink, but seriously, is that a reason to bale on me in the middle of a party? Who among us haven't had too much drink at this party with the exception of you?" He shook his head. "Did I miss something? What's the matter?" he asked seriously.

"I just think I should go home."

"You keep saying that, but you haven't told me why."

"Brad, I have told you why, you just refuse to listen and hear me."

"Okay, I'm listening, so what's up with you wanting to take off?"

"I just don't feel like hanging around this party any longer," I mumbled, looking away from him.

"You just don't feel like hanging around this party any longer?" he asked. "That's no real reason. Come on, Mandy, you have lost me."

"It's true, Brad. I don't like that you have had too much to drink."

"I'm fine, pretty girl. Are you sure that's all it is to it? Besides, I thought you wanted to come to my party and hang out in my room."

"I did want to come," I said.

"But did you want to hang out in my room?"

"What do you think?"

"I don't know what to think, and for some reason you're not giving me a straight answer," he said.

"I just think I should leave because you have had too much to drink."

"Seriously, Mandy, did I miss something? Was I so off base to assume that you wanted to visit with me in the privacy of my room away from all that noise downstairs?" He paused, staring at me. "And now you stand here and say you want to take off because you think I have had too much to drink sort of kills the moment, not to mention I'm confused. I don't know where you're coming from with that. Jump in anytime and explain yourself. Is it really about those few glasses of punch I drank?" he asked seriously, looking me straight in the eyes.

I looked at him but didn't know what to say.

"So, Mandy, tell me. Are you trying to take off because you think I'm too wasted to be in control of my words and actions?"

"I didn't say that, Brad."

"No, you didn't say it, but is that what you're thinking?"

"Not really."

"Good, because I'm in complete control of my faculties; I have had a few drinks but I haven't over done it." He stood up and pulled me up in his arms.

It felt perfect being in his arms. Overwhelming warmth filled my body: a feeling that made my whole insides feel lighter than a feather. That's when I knew I had to pull away. It felt right, but I knew Brad wasn't in love with me as I him.

"No, Brad, that's enough."

He narrowed his eyes, staring at me with a puzzled look on his face. "Mandy, I guess I should ask you, what's the problem now? You have admitted that you don't think I'm wasted. But something is still bothering you. Is it being alone with me in my room that freaking you out, because you are acting a bit weird."

"I'm not acting weird," I pouted.

He smiled. "You're right, weird isn't the right word for your behavior, but standoffish is. You won't even let me touch you. I thought being alone and making out was the whole purpose of coming to my room."

"So, I'm just some girl that you brought to your room to sleep with?" I stared at him. "Is that how you see me?" I snapped.

"Wait a minute, Mandy. Where is this attitude coming from? Of course, I don't see you like that. I could never see you in that way."

"But you still want me to hop in bed with you?"

"Well, it did cross my mind," he admitted. "But I was under the impression that our feelings were mutual. If you're not really into me, I get it."

"Brad, it's not that I'm not into you."

"Okay, so you are into me? Is that what you are saying?"

"Maybe I am saying that." I took a seat on the bed and stared at the floor.

He took a seat beside me and started rubbing my back. "Okay, if you're into me, what's up with you? You certainly don't act like you're into me."

"You wouldn't understand," I cried.

"Try me, I might. Guys are not as unfeeling as our reputation states," he teased.

I shook my head. "It's a big mess."

"What's a big mess? Just tell me. Anything but tears; it really bothers me to see a girl cry. It makes me sad. Besides, no girl should ever cry over a guy." He paused with a serious look on his face and then smiled. "But seriously, Mandy, if you are upset because you think I'm pressuring you or trying to persuade you to do something that you're not into, please don't worry about it. I would never do that. You don't have to do anything you don't want to do. If you are not comfortable with me touching you, I won't. I'm not going to do anything you don't want me to. It's up to you, Mandy."

Still staring down at the thick cedar green carpet on his bedroom floor, it pleased me what he had said, but I still didn't reply.

"Come on, beautiful, dry your eyes."

I took my fingers and dried my eyes and looked at him. "I'm sorry about that but I felt overwhelmed for a moment."

"So, you're not afraid to be here in my room, and you understand that I'm not expecting anything of you that you're not ready for?"

I nodded. "I trust you Brad. My tears were not because of you."

"Okay, I'm glad to hear that, and if you don't want to share I won't pry, but since you are not afraid to be here in my room with me. Let's spend a little time making out." He grabbed my face and hungrily pressed his lips against mine.

We fell over on his bed wrapped in each other's arms and two pillows from his bed fell to the floor. He kissed me tenderly for a few moments and then we just laid there next to each other in silent. He was lying on his back with one hand under his head, staring up at the ceiling; and I was lying on my back with one hand under my head, staring up at the ceiling. The only sound that I could hear other than the beat of my own heart was a slight wind blowing against his bedroom windows.

Chapter Fifteen

The lamp on his bedside table was dimly shining casting a cozy ambiance to his large room as we laid there on his king size bed. His right hand held my left hand tightly as we laid there looking up at his tall white ceiling. While he wasn't looking toward me, silent tears poured down the sides of my eyes that I quickly dried with my fingers. I told myself how silly I was to cry for someone who had never actually asked me out. And after lying there on the bed next to him for awhile, something warm touched my neck. It was his warm fingers touching my neck. He pushed my hair aside and brought his face closer and kissed the side of my neck.

"Mandy, are you okay lying here on my bed next to me like this? If you don't feel comfortable, let me know." He pulled my hair aside and kissed my neck again. "I'm very pleased. It's incredible to have you lying here on my bed next to me like this. And I don't want this to sound corny, but for some reason, seeing you lying here next to me makes you appear even more beautiful than you are, if that's even possible," he whispered against my neck.

My overwhelming excitement made me momentarily speechless and as I went to sit up, his strong smooth hand rested on my chest and stopped my rise, as he sat up in bed and looked down at me. He looked me straight in the eyes with a deep desire in his eyes. I looked at him speechless. I felt like I was wide awake in a dream. It seemed like a dream and I was concentrating heavy to make sure it wasn't a dream. But it felt dreamlike and I suddenly felt spellbound and didn't want to awaken to face reality since my face was just inches from one of the best looking boys alive. He called my name and brought me back to actuality.

"Mandy, I'm so glad you're here in my room. You look so beautiful lying there," he whispered as he smiled, bringing his face closer to mine, then he covered my mouth with his in a tender kiss.

I still hadn't managed a word as I laid there on his bed filled up with love for him. Overwhelming sensations consumed me with out of control warmth from the mere thought of him; and as I struggled to breathe, he covered my mouth completely with the urgency of his kiss. He took both hands and grabbed my face; and then wrapped his arms around my head and made me literally scream inside with passion as he kissed me hungrily. I was like a rag doll in his strong arms. It took all my strength to breathe. I couldn't move an inch or utter a word.

He held my neck with both hands and kissed my neck and then journed to my chest, which he held and kissed through my blue lace top. His hands were warm as he rubbed them tenderly across my stomach through the fabric of my skirt. He then pulled my blouse out of my skirt, pushed it up near my chest to reveal my bare stomach, which he smoothed his hands across and before I could catch my breath, he had put his warm lips against my stomach and kissed me there. He rubbed his nose across my stomach and it was slightly cool against my skin.

"Mandy, everything is fine. Nothing is going to happen that you're not ready for. We're just having fun. I'm not trying to go any further."

His words were spoken in a soft, passionate manner as I felt out of control desire for him building in me. His touch was too unbearably thrilling as he gently kept rubbing his nose across my stomach, as he took his hands and slowly, inch by inch pulled down on my elastic-waist skirt, bringing his face down inch by inch with every revealing inch of bare skin and just when his face reached the bottom of my stomach, I was afraid our adventure in his bed may go to far.

"Brad, I think we should stop," I uttered firmly.

I managed to push him away and rolled out of his bed. I stood there beside the bed pulling up my long blue skirt, tucking my blouse back in. Tears were falling down my face. I couldn't look at him. I saw him out of the corner of my eye as he hopped out of bed and was standing there across from me, straightening his clothes. Then he stepped near me and faced me. He reached out and lifted up my face to look at him. He had a confused expression on his face. His hands were still warm as he held up my face toward his. My body tingled and ached from his touch. I wanted him to place me back on the bed and wrap me in his arms again, but I couldn't allow my hopeless love to blind me of my good sense. I knew he wasn't in love with me. Plus, I had to remember the promise that I had made to myself to wait until marriage. I couldn't allow myself to make the same mistake that my mother had made so many years ago.

He looked into my eyes long and hard and I'm sure he could feel my passion. He slightly smiled, as he brought his mouth closer to mine. "Mandy, don't push me away. I want to kiss you again."

With those words, I was back under his spell as he pushed his mouth against mine and swallowed me up, pushing me against the wall, pressing his body against me, sliding his hands up and down my back.

With every bit of strength I could manage, I tore from his arms. "No, Brad, I can't go all the way with you," I blurted out and paused. "I'm not saying you are trying to go all the way, but I think we should stop before things go too far."

"Mandy, don't worry about that," he suggested. "We are not going to let that happen. We are just hanging out having fun. You are having fun, aren't you?"

"Yes, of course. I just think we should slow down. I really get the sense that you are nowhere near ready to slow down right now; and that sort of makes me uneasy."

"Mandy, you have no reason to be uneasy. Just let yourself relax."

"It's not easy to relax when you are doing what you are doing."

"What am I doing?"

"You are touching me."

"I just have my arms around you."

"I know, but touching me anywhere makes it hard for me to concentrate."

"I get that. But that's a good thing. It's the same for me. It just means that we really like each other," he said. "Besides, I get that you might be a bit uneasy and you don't want things to get out of hand, but I promise you that will not happen."

"Brad, how can I take your word that nothing will happen, when I know you don't really have any feelings for me?" I mumbled sadly.

He smiled, looked away, and then turned his back to me. He faced me with a serious expression. "Mandy, can't you see there is something between us." He touched his chest and then mine. "So, yes, I think you should take my word for it."

"I think there's something between us too." I looked in his eyes. "But that doesn't mean you have feelings for me. Brad you have never asked me out, so I know you couldn't possibly have any feelings for me."

"Mandy, you are such a pretty young lady. Why would you say I couldn't possibly have any feelings for you?"

"Well, do you have any feelings for me, Brad?"

He smiled at me, but did not answer.

"So, I was right. You don't have any feelings for me; and I'm sure its not a surprise to you that I like you."

"Look, Mandy, lighten up. Just enjoy this time that we have with each other. We both just agreed that there's something between us."

He tenderly grabbed my shoulders, bringing his mouth closer and closer to my neck as I stood against the wall shaky from his touch. My whole, entire being wanted to be in his arms again kissing him.

"Mandy, you are very special," he whispered in my ear.

"But do you have real feelings for me, Brad? I need to know if you are in love with me. We are in your room like this and I would feel a lot more comfortable if I knew you had real feelings for me. So just tell me, do you care anything for me?"

"Of course, I care something for you."

"What is that something, just a pretty girl to have in your room tonight?"

"Mandy, you know that's not what I think of you."

"What do you think of me? I probably shouldn't even ask you that question because I already know the answer. If you loved me, I'm sure you would have asked me out by now. So that's my answer right there," I sniffered in his arms.

"Come on, Mandy. How did our conversation go from you wanting to leave to us having fun to you wanting to know if I'm in love?"

"It just did, but you don't have to worry about answering the question because remember I just figured it out for myself."

"I don't think you have figured out anything. How can you know my mind? You don't know how I feel or what I'm feeling," he whispered in my ear.

"Maybe you're right, that's why I asked you."

"What would you say if I told you I adored your eyes and your laugh?" He held me tigther, as his breathing became rapid and I could sense his desire getting stronger.

"But do you love me? Just answer yes or not," I insisted.

"I love your slender figure and how easy I can wrap you in my arms. I also love your nose and your beautiful thick curls hanging on your shoulders. I love grabbing a handful of your hair like this. I love the feel of your hair against my face," he whispered in my ear as he gripped my hair, pulling my head back, placing his warm lips against my neck once more, and by now I was lost in his arms.

My insides had become even weaker than before. A constant build up of excitement had robbed me of my collected thoughts and strength, but I managed to utter once more as he lowered me back down to the bed. "But are you in love with me, Brad?" I uttered in a low voice.

He laid me back on the bed and placed one finger against my lips. "Mandy, don't talk. I'm going to answer your question. All this time I was thinking about what you were asking me. I didn't answer before because I didn't want to answer untruthful. So here's my answer to the best of my knowledge," he whispered softly. "I honestly think that the only straight answer I can candidly give you, is no. I respect you too much to lie here next to you and say what I think you want to hear. That would be deceitful in an effort to make you more vulnerable and I'm not that guy to trick you in that way. So the truth is, I'm not in love with you, Mandy, and I'm sure you are not in love with me. We haven't known each other long enough to be in love. This is our first night together so how could we be in love?" he whispered against my neck. "But we both have to admit that we like each other and there's something between us."

"Yes, I do like you," I softly uttered.

"And I like you," he assured me. "And better yet, I love the feelings you are stirring in me and I love being with you, Mandy," he whispered softly.

After his explanation that we hadn't known each other long enough to be in love, I opened my eyes, but quickly closed them. The fact that he wasn't in love with me gave me no desire to push him away. It was no use. I felt like a leaf beneath a stone.

I had no strength to push him away and I didn't want to push him away. And as he pulled me tighter and tighter against him, I felt myself fading into another existence, a world unknown to me, a world of absolute unbelievable happiness.

"Mandy," he uttered softly against my lips. "Now that I have answered your question, and you know I'm not in love with you, do you want me to stop holding and kissing you? Tell me what you want. I know you said you didn't want to go all the way if I wasn't in love with you. So I'm not going to take advantage of this situation. I have too much respect for you to go any further, knowing your heart and soul is not in it. So it's up to you, Mandy. I would love to spend hours on this bed with you, enjoying the pleasure of you lying here next to me, but it's your call. What do you want, Mandy? We can stop kissing and sat up and talk if that's what you want."

I found the strength to touch his handsome face. I had to reach out and touch him to bring myself back to reality. The evening had turned out so dreamlike and wonderful. I had hoped to spend some time with Brad, but not in my wildest dreams had I expected to be lying in his bed next to him, wrapped in his arms. It just seemed too precious to be true. I felt so blessed to be with him until all that mattered was the fact that I was finally alone with him. Even knowing he wasn't in love with me, and had never asked me out, didn't discourage me from wanting to be with him.

"I think it's okay if we lie here a bit longer," I said.

"I'm glad you said that," he whispered. "Lying here with you is a lot more fun than spending time at that party downstairs," he said softly, laughing. He seemed more alert than ever as he wrapped me in his arms. I wrapped my arms around him and gripped him tight as if I was hanging over the edge of a mountain, holding on for my life. He brought his mouth down on mine and swallowed me up in a loving kiss that was unlike anything I could have ever imagined. I was lost in his embrace and kisses until it dawned on me that I was completely losing myself in his arms.

"Mandy, I know I keep saying this, but holding you close is out of this world. I could get real use to holding you like this. This can become a habit if we're not careful," he said kissing my neck.

"Brad, I really do think…"

"You really do think what?" he asked. "Were you going to say, you really do think this is great?"

I was glad he hadn't figured out that I was going to say I really do think I'm in love. Maybe he wasn't in love and felt I wasn't in love, but my heart was telling me something different. It was telling me that I was in love.

"So what were you going to say?" he asked.

"I was going to say I really do think we should stop," I mumbled, pushed him away and sat on the edge of the bed.

"That was fun wasn't it?" He smiled and kissed the side of my face as he took a seat on the edge of the bed beside me. "Why did you stop? You had said we could lie there a bit longer."

"I know, but a bit longer had gone by and it was time to stop," I mumbled.

"It's still not that late, Mandy." He looked at me. "I get the feeling that you wanted to stop because you got sort of nervous." He touched my cheek. "Am I right? Is that the reason? Because you know nothing was going to happen that you didn't want."

"I just figured we should stop before things got out of hand," I muttered.

"But nothing was going to get out of hand if it wasn't what you wanted."

"Brad, I do trust you. But I just think we should stay out of your bed."

"We were just kissing. It was fun wasn't it?" he asked.

I nodded, looking in his eyes. "Yes, it was fun, but fun has a way of taking control of someone's willpower and I really think we shouldn't."

"Shouldn't what? I know you're not afraid, are you? I heard you're not crusading against it anymore. So, I assume you're down with it."

"Down with what, Brad?"

"You know what I'm referring to." He stared at me, smiling. "Are you really going to make me spell it out?"

"Maybe you do need to spell it out."

"Okay, I'm referring to sex," he said humbly. "I just figured you knew what I was referring to. Besides, being here in my room alone with you like this, what else would a young man with raging hormones be referring to?"

"Nothing else, I guess."

"So what's the deal, Mandy? Are you down with it? It's not that I'm trying to pressure you into anything. I'm just trying to figure you out. We both agreed there's something between us. And you say you're into me and I believe you are, but you're giving me mixed signals. We were enjoying each other, kissing on my bed; then suddenly you pushed me away and now I can't touch you anymore."

"I didn't say you can't touch me anymore. I just figured it was time to put the brakes on our adventure in your big bed."

"Tell me one good reason why you wanted to stop when we were both having fun and there were no risk of me taking advantage of you?" he asked curiously.

"Brad, I just felt we should stop, isn't that a good enough reason."

"It would be if I didn't know you were into me." He touched my face and smiled. "Do I need to wonder that maybe you are not into me?"

"No, you don't have to wonder about that. That much I can be clear on. I am into you but it doesn't mean I'm ready to sleep with you."

"Okay, you're not ready. That's all you had to say." He patted my knee as if to say he understood. "But Mandy, you didn't answer my question."

"What question are you referring to?"

"I asked if you are still crusading on the school grounds against premarital sex."

I felt a bit embarrassed that he had asked me the question. "Brad, why are you asking me that, it's not something I'm comfortable discussing with you?"

"I don't mean to make you uncomfortable but with the situation at hand."

"What situation at hand?" I snapped. "The fact that I didn't want to keep lying in your bed like that, is that the situation at hand that you are referring to?"

"Mandy, I'm curious because last week I heard otherwise that you are no longer speaking out against the subject."

I threw up both hands. "I can't believe you are bringing that up. What does that have to do with you pressuring me now?" I snapped.

He stared. "Correction, I'm not pressuring you. I just wanted hold and kiss you, which we were doing just fine; and if it had gone further that would have been great, but it's not like I was expecting that. So, could you just answer the question? Was all that talk at school about you changing your viewpoint a rumor or the truth? Are you still crusading against premarital sex or not?"

"What difference does it make? You still shouldn't be pressuring me like this."

"Mandy, stop saying I'm pressuring you? You know that's not what's going on." He glanced up at the ceiling.

After a long silence between us, he looked at me and touched my face.

"Okay, Mandy, maybe you're right. Maybe I am being a jerk and somewhat pressuring you. But that's not my intentions."

"Brad, thank you for understanding," I mumbled softly, looking him straight in the face as I wiped tears from my eyes.

"Come on, no more tears in this room," he said, smiling. "Can you promise me that?" He teased to lighten up the moment.

"Mandy, I know I said I'm not in love with you, and I hope it didn't come out sounding as if you didn't mean anything to me. When I said I wasn't in love with you I was trying to be honorable. It's a trait I got from my father. He tried to instill in me and my brother to always be truthful with a girl and never lead someone on no matter what the cost. It would have been real easy for me to just say I was in love with you just to take advantage of you, but that's not me. I hope you know I'm better than that."

"I couldn't feel this way about you if I thought you weren't better than that," I said looking in his eyes.

"I'm glad to hear that, but I also want to mention that you are right about something," he said and paused in my eyes.

"What is it that you think I'm right about?" I asked.

"You are right that I haven't asked you out."

"But I don't want you to ask me out just because I said you haven't asked me out. I wouldn't mean the same. It would be a pity date. Because if you wanted to ask me out, you would; however, on the other hand, if you do really want to ask me out then that would be a different story." I realized I was nervously going on and on about him asking me out and quickly stop talking.

"Can I talk now," he teased.

"Sure, go ahead. I'm sorry I got carried away like that."

He caressed the side of my neck with his right hand as he looked at me. "Mandy, what I would like to say is I really like you a lot, and I think you know that. I'm sure you have noticed how I always stare at your table when you're in the cafeteria with your friend Kathy."

I looked at him with surprise in my eyes. "No, I hadn't noticed you looking at me in the lunchroom, but Kathy has mentioned it. But frankly, I didn't believe her."

"Believe it, it's true. So, with that in mind, that should let you know that I'm not trying to lose your respect or scare you away."

"Brad, I might could wholeheartedly believe that if you hadn't ask me to hop in bed with you the first time we are alone together?"

"Actually, you are right and you are wrong," he mumbled staring straight ahead.

"What do you mean, how can I be right and wrong?"

"I'll spell it out for you, Mandy. Yes, I wanted you in my bed but it wasn't about expecting you to have sex with me. So that's why you are right and wrong. Right that I wanted you in my bed, but wrong that I wanted to sleep with you," he explained.

"So, if I had been willing, you would've put the brakes on?" I asked, smiling.

"Hey, that's a trick question." He laughed.

"What's tricky about it? Would you have gone further or not?" I teased him.

"I'm not going to answer that question because I don't want to step into your trap. But don't hold that against me that I didn't answer. Besides, you can't blame a guy for trying, can you?"

"The jury is still out on that one." I nodded and smiled at him.

"Okay, the jury is still out, I hope you bear in mind that I have had a lot to drink." He held up one finger and turned my cheek to face him. "On top of that, you are alone with me here in my room; and you look so beautiful."

"You think I'm beautiful?"

"I don't think you're beautiful. You are so beautiful, Mandy. I'll take it a bit further. You are the most beautiful girl I have ever laid eyes on."

I grabbed my cheeks with both hands. "Brad, I know you have had a lot to drink and it's rumored that when a man drinks too much, all females look beautiful in his eyes. But I'm going to hold on to what you just said to me. I will treasure your compliment and keep it in my heart always."

"Please do, because I meant it."

"I don't know how much is booze and how much is you, but I'll cherish it."

"Good, so am I forgiven for coming on too strong?" He grabbed his face and collected himself. "Besides, that's water under the bridge. I have my wits about myself now; and I'm hoping you'll give me your number."

"I can't believe it; did you just ask for my number?" I teased.

"Yes, I did." He smiled. "I'm catching on. Who knows before this night is over I might even ask you out," he teased.

"Now that would be a miracle." I hit his shoulder in a playful way.

"Seriously, Mandy, I do want your number. I can't believe I haven't asked for it before now." He paused, looking in my eyes with a big smile on his face. "Just maybe we can start seeing each other," he said seriously. "And if that happen, you won't be able to throw in my face that I never asked you out." He grinned.

Brad spoke sincerely and his words and honestly had given me courage to open up to him. "Brad, there's something you should know and I'm just going to tell you," I mumbled in a low voice, staring in his eyes.

"Okay, what is it?"

"The whole truth is. I have been acting a bit weird and standoffish toward you. And I have been giving you mixed signals," I admitted.

He nodded compassionately. "And you're going to tell me the reason for that?"

"Yes, I am. It's because I'm just not completely comfortable being alone with you in your room like this, Brad. To be completely honest, it wasn't about you coming on too strong that made me push you away."

"Okay, what was your reason for pushing me away?" He asked curiously.

"I'm just not ready yet."

"You're not ready yet?" He repeated.

"That's right, I'm not ready."

"So, you had no intentions of going any further with me this evening, not at any point while we were on my bed?" He narrowed his eyes at me. "Not that I had already counted my chickens."

"That's true; I had no intentions of ending up in your bedroom." I shook my head. "It was all a big misunderstanding or some trap that I stepped into."

"What do you mean about a misunderstanding? You knew I was bringing you to my room when I asked if you wanted to come upstairs with me. And yes, I was hoping to be with you in that way, but it's not like it was written in stone and something that I absolutely expected from you. So, I don't get what you are saying about a misunderstanding and stepping into some trap?"

I shook my head. "I wasn't referring to anything you did or said. You haven't done anything wrong. Besides, none of that really matters right now. What matters is my honesty with you. Isn't that what matters to you?" I stated sincerely.

"Of course that's what counts. So what are you getting at, Mandy? What honesty are you trying to share?"

"That I had no intentions of going all the way with you, since I haven't decided to go all the way with anyone yet."

He gave me a long stare and grinned. "Okay, so you haven't? What's the big deal?" He paused and grinned. "Although, there is that rumor that I mentioned before that you don't care to discuss."

I shook my head. "I know, my crusade against premarital. What a mistake to think I could get through to any of those teenagers at Barrington High."

"So, now that you have mentioned it, is it safe to get into this discussion?"

"Brad, you are right. I don't care to discuss it, but I might as well. It's a situation that I put myself in. If I had only kept my opinions to myself I could have saved myself a lot of grief from a boatload of kids."

"Okay, I take it; you wish you hadn't voiced your objections on the subject?"

"That's correct. We live and learn. I learned my lesson to think twice before I try to impose my values and views on someone else."

"Mandy, from where I'm sitting, your values and views are perfect. But the latest rumor going around school says you have a strong viewpoint against premarital sex, but you don't practice what you preach, since you are also sexually active. That's what I heard before school closed for the holiday break," he shared.

"Yeah, I know about the rumor," I mumbled.

"So what's going on with that? Why would someone purposely start a rumor about you and say you are sexually active if you're not?"

I remained silent, staring at him.

"And I'm assuming it's a rumor, because from what I can tell your viewpoint has not changed. Besides, you have just shared with me that you haven't been active."

"That is correct. That rumor is just a lie and the worse part is that I started it."

"Hold on, Mandy, you have lost me. You started the rumor about yourself?"

"Yes, you heard me correctly. I'm not proud to admit this, but yes, I did."

"That's incredible that you would start a rumor about yourself." He grabbed his face and took a deep breath. "You need to make me understand this one. I can't picture you out on the school ground spreading lies about yourself."

"Brad, it's a big mess. I didn't actually spread the lies myself, but I encouraged someone else to spread them. I'm so ashamed of myself for having someone spread lies about me. But I was so desperate and needed to keep certain people off my back."

"Mandy, none of this makes any sense to me. I'm still not hearing why you felt you needed to have a lie put out there about you."

"Look, Brad, when I started writing my articles and speaking out in the school paper against premarital sex, a lot of the female students started giving me a hard time because they felt that I felt that I was putting myself above them. Some of them were downright rude. And believe me; I'm not proud of what I did. But it was proposed that if the students at school thought it was just a viewpoint that I wasn't really practicing, then maybe they would get off my back and let me breathe."

He raised an eyebrow and stared with less confused eyes. "Mandy, this too should pass. You got yourself caught up in a peer pressure pool."

"You're right, but it won't happen again."

"So, I take it, certain students were ruder to you than others?"

"That is correct. Some were rude, but a handful was ruder. I had to do what I could to keep certain individuals off my back." I explained. "And the results ended up being that rumor lie."

"Can you share who those certain individuals are? Why would anyone be so overly rude to you about what you wrote in the school paper? People don't have to share your opinion and views, but to be downright nasty is juvenile."

"Nasty is the right word to use for how one person in particular treated me."

"Are you going to share who that person is? I can't imagine someone would cause you that much hassle over your own viewpoint. Afterall, this is a free country and we are all entitled to our own views." He touched my face and looked in my eyes with care. "So, Mandy, who is this rude person that caused you so much grief?"

I gave him a ten second stare, but dared to mention that it was his sister who had caused me the most hassle over my articles on the subject.

"I would prefer not to mention any names. I just want all of this to fade away from everybody memory," I explained.

He nodded. "Sure, I get that."

"Besides, I know it sounds silly, but I get that some of the students just didn't want to hear my views against premarital sex. They just felt that I should have kept my opinions to myself."

"Maybe, but who cares about what those spoil brats at Barrington High thought or didn't think about you?"

"I do. Believe me. I know I shouldn't but I do."

"Why should you." He gripped my shoulders. "Mandy, you can't live your life according to how someone else may think of you. Stick to your bones and be yourself."

"I know that, Brad. It's just easier this way."

"Okay, if you say so, but I have no idea what you're getting at that it's easier just to give in to those big mouths who want to be rude to you about your views."

"I'm sure you don't because you are a guy afterall."

He narrowed his eyes at me. "Okay, I'm a guy, and what does that have to do with not giving a damn about what the gossip is at Barrington High?"

"I just mean, it's a little different with guys because you don't have other guys ragging on you about stuff. For an example, if you were to write an article in the school paper about the same subject with my same viewpoint, I doubt if any guys at school would be rude to you; and all the girls would probably praise you."

He nodded and smiled. "You could be right at that."

"Well, the female population at school is quite different. Some of them have been very hard to take, as I pointed out, because of my platform of standing up against premarital sex. But if they think I have backed down and no longer think that way, the better for me." I took a deep breath. "Believe me; it has really made my life at school a lot more bearable since they think it's no longer my view. But I didn't want to be dishonest with you and that's why I told you the whole truth."

"I feel honored that you felt you could be open and completely honest with me about all that non-sense at school. Not non-sense from your part, but non-sense from those who made you felt you needed to lie just to get them off your back."

"I'm glad I shared it all with you as well. I confided in you because I trust you and know you won't breathe a word to anyone about what I told you."

He smiled and grabbed one of my curls and shook it in a playful way. "Wow, Mandy, I knew something here didn't wash. But thanks for filling me in. It completes the puzzle and it all adds up." He stood to his feet.

I stood up with him and searched his face, trying to figure out his reaction to what I had just shared. I couldn't make out what he was thinking.

He glanced at his watch. "I think it's about time to get you back downstairs."

I nodded. "Yes, I think you are right. We don't want the search crew to come looking for us," I joked.

"No worry of that, I think everybody downstairs is probably trying to stay coherent." He laughed. "They probably haven't even missed that we left the room."

When we walked over to the door to leave, he leaned down and kissed me on the side of the face. Then he stood there with his back against the door looking at me.

I looked in his eyes and realized at that moment that I had never seen such a handsome fellow. He was all I had ever dreamed of and now I was so hopeful of finally being his girlfriend.

"Why are you standing against the door?" I asked, smiling. "Have you changed your mind about going back downstairs right now?"

"No, I haven't changed my mind." He smiled. "But I think we should probably head back because the party is about to end in the next thirty minutes. But before we leave my room, you can rest assured that your classmates won't hear a word about what you have confided in me." He winked at me.

"Thank you, Brad, but I already knew you wouldn't say a word."

"I should be thanking you for giving me your number. Now, maybe, we'll be able to find out what it is between us."

Chapter Sixteen

Brad and I were standing on his front porch after the party had thinned out. It was twelve-fifteen and everybody had started to head home.

"I had a really nice time tonight," he said with his back against the frame of the house trying to shield his coatless body from the cold wind. "It's not really that late." He glanced toward a group of students leaving. "I know everybody is starting to head home, but it doesn't mean you have to."

I smiled up at him with both hands in my coat pockets. "I would love to stay longer but I think I should take off. My curfew is one o'clock for this evening but it's snowing rather steady. I told Mom I would try and get home sooner."

He nodded and smiled. "Okay, but let me grab my coat and walk you."

"Thanks, but I'll be okay. The street lights are bright and there's a host of other students walking down the street as well."

"Okay, if you insist." He pulled me next to him and kissed me.

I was glad he had shown interest and offered to walk me home, but I wanted to walk alone. I had a lot to think about. The evening had really taken me by surprise. Brad had asked for my phone number, and confessed he really liked me. I was filled with excitement. The only boy I had ever liked would finally be my boyfriend. I just wanted to get home and dream about him all night.

After walking halfway home, I was startled when tall, skinny, eighteen-year-old, Ricky Chase, ran up behind me and grabbed me by the arm. He was handsome like the rest of the Chase guys and wore long black braids hanging down his back; and rather on the quiet side compared to his cousins.

"Hey, wait up Mandy," he said.

"Ricky, what are you doing? You startled me."

"I wasn't trying to startle you. I just wanted to catch you before you made it home." He kept his grip on my arm.

"Let go of my arm." I jerked my arm away and stared in his face. "It's obvious you have had one too many. You are falling down drunk, which I'm surprised."

"Everybody at the party had too much to drink, why is that a surprise to you?"

"It's a surprise because it's out of character for you from what I know."

"Just what do you know about me anyways?"

"I know you are usually well-mannered and polite."

"Well, who says I'm not well-mannered and polite at the moment?"

"I say it. If you were you wouldn't have sneaked up behind me and grabbed me by the arm as you did," I snapped. "But being intoxicated as you are, I'll excuse your drunken behavior."

"Did you excuse my cousin's drunken behavior?" he asked rudely.

"This isn't about Brad, this is about you. When I first arrived at the party, I noticed how you were standing against the wall drinking all that wine."

"What does it matter how much wine I drank? I didn't chase you down in the snow to stand here and chit chat about my drinking habit."

"Why did you chase me down?" I curiously asked.

He grabbed my arm again. "Come with me and you'll find out."

"Let go of me," I jerked my arm away in a heat.

He looked at me like I was being a snob. "Well, excuse me, Miss Mandy Clark," he shouted rudely. "But I don't know why I'm saying excuse me, when you're no better than the rest of those snobbish tramps at school," he said and stared at me and grinned. "You know I'm right, don't you. You're a little slut just like those cheerleaders Molly hang out with, aren't you?" He kept grinning.

"What are you talking about, Ricky?" I shouted angrily. "I don't care how much wine you have drank, you are being a real jerk right now to say something like that to me. I have to keep reminding myself that you are wasted."

"Think whatever you want, but I'm not wasted. I had my share of wine but I can hold my liquid," he said calmly. "So, tell me, Mandy, where are you headed?" He asked.

"Where do you think I'm headed? I'm headed home?" I wiped the snow from my face with my coat sleeve.

"It's New Year's, the dawn of 2003, let's hang out some more," he suggested.

"Ricky, I have to go." I headed down the sidewalk.

"Wait up, where are you headed?" he asked.

"Ricky, get a grip please and stop asking me silly questions. Can't you see through your drunken eyes that I'm only a block from home?" I stopped in my tracks, stared at him and shook my head. "You need to head straight home. You are in bad shape. You drank a lot at the party and you're standing here on the sidewalk in the snow, still drinking! So please go on home and stop following me." I took both hands and shoveled him away from me.

"Why did you shovel me like that? I just thought you might like to come to my house for awhile." He lifted his wine bottle up to his mouth and took a big gulp.

"Ricky, you are with my best friend, so I know you didn't just ask me to your house. Are you trying to come on to me?"

"What if I am? We are both young and single." He lifted his wine bottle and gulped down more red wine.

"That's your booze telling you that because that's only half true. We are both young but we are not both single. You are dating Kathy and if she knew you were behaving out of line with me, she would not be happy with you."

"But Kathy isn't around. She didn't come to the party with me. She chose to go to some old stuffy bash with her folks. She left me high and dry when she knew I wanted her to come to this party, so why should I think of her?"

"You should think of her because she couldn't get out of that party with her folks, okay. She wanted to but just couldn't."

"Enough about Kathy just come over for a little while. I'm too alert to go home and fall asleep."

"Ricky, it's cold out here. I need to get home. I'm not going to your house so stop asking," I shouted loudly. "I can't believe you're trying to get me to go home with you. Does all that wine in your stomach possess you to behave in this way? The Ricky Chase I know is quiet in class and doesn't behave the way you are right now. You have always been respectful of me, polite with good manners. Now you are standing here drunk in the middle of the night asking me to go home with you."

"Calm down, Mandy, is that a crime?"

"No, it's not a crime, but why would you ask me to go home with you in the middle of the night? I doubt if you have an honorable intention. So Ricky, do me a favor and get out of my face." I shoveled him again. "I can't believe you are acting this way, asking me to come to your house this time of night," I snapped.

He turned his wine bottle up to his mouth and took another gulp. "I know you can't believe it. You just said that."

"So, other than the lame excuse about being too alert to go home and fall asleep, why are you asking me to go home with you." I gave him a hard stare.

He gave me a hard stare and narrowed his eyes at me as if he knew some secret on me. "Why are you playing hard to get? I know better." He grinned.

"What are you getting at, Ricky? You don't know what you are doing or saying right now. Kathy would be very upset and disappointed in you if she found out how you are carrying on with me. You know how crazy you are about her."

"I'm sure you got your information from Kathy, right?"

"What if I did?"

He grinned. "Well, you were misinformed if that's what she told you."

"It's not what she told me," I said firmly. "It's what the whole school knows. You are her shadow, remember?"

"I'm nobody's shadow!"

"I see, well, if that's so, why is your little red sports car parked in her driveway all the time?"

He raised both hands. "I'm just hanging out over there to talk to Justin, not your know-it-all big mouth friend. Why can't she keep my business to herself?"

"If it's not true, why do you care?" I paused and then shouted. "You don't have to answer that because I happen to think you're lying through your teeth! Just admit you love the girl."

"I'm not admitting it because it's not true," he barked.

"Stop lying Ricky. Everybody at school knows how crazy you are about Kathy and how crazy she is about you."

"I'm not crazy into any female!" he stumbled with his words.

"I'm going to excuse your dishonesty about your feelings for Kathy since you are so falling down drunk."

"You don't have to excuse my dishonesty." His eyes turned stone cold. "Just stop trying to change the subject to me and

Kathy. I would appreciate an answer to my question. Are you going home with me or not?"

"Not! I have told you over and over that I'm not," I said sharply.

He frowned and rubbed his chin, standing there with his bottle of wine swinging at this side. Then with the blink of an eye, I saw an array of blue and black stars as Ricky's elbow accidentally hit me across the face when he turned the wine bottle up to his mouth.

"Watch it," I screamed and tumbled about.

And just as he lowered his bottle, before we could step aside a group of rushing students from the party came hurrying by and accidentally caused me and Ricky to slip down to the snowy ground. Ricky grabbed me and held me down and sat on top of me.

"What are you doing? Instead of you helping me up, you think it's a good idea to sit on top of me on this cold snowy ground?" I shouted angrily. "If you don't get off of me, breathing hard and acting wild and disrespectful I'm going to scream and cause a commotion," I snapped as I lay in the snow trembling with anxiousness.

"Why did you go upstairs with Brad? Everybody at the party knows you went upstairs to his room."

"So what if I did. It's my business what I do. So will you please get up off of me, Ricky," I yelled. "I know you are stinking drunk out of your mind and don't know what you are doing, but this is ridiculous and need to stop!"

"I will let you up when I'm good and ready. Do I make myself clear?"

"Why are you doing this, Ricky? This is not who you are and I know it's all that boozed up punch and wine from the party that has you acting like some fool," I yelled. "That's why I'm not going to tell anyone about this, but you need to stop now."

"Who would you tell anyway; and what would you tell?"

"Listen, Ricky, if I wanted to get you in trouble I could make a fuss about you sitting on top of me like this. I could tell plenty how you won't let me off of this cold ground. So just stop fooling around and get off of me."

"Why should I? I'm disappointed in your phony behavior, Mandy."

"You are disappointed in my behavior? Don't make me laugh. You are the one who's falling down drunk and sitting on top of me like a wild person. So, if anybody is disappointed in anyone's behavior, I'm disappointed in yours, hands down."

"Whatever, Miss Mandy Clark, just hear this! I think you are the biggest hypocrite at school. You are crusading on the school grounds and writing all that garbage in the school paper about your objections to premarital sex."

"Ricky, why are you bringing that up? Just get off of me already."

"I'm bringing it up because you are acting as if we are all sinners and you are a saint? You made it sound as if you were practicing what you preach. But obviously you had us all fooled. I definitely had my head in the clouds about you. I read a couple of your articles, but I was dead wrong about you, Mandy. You are no different than the rest of those high hat bitches. So just admit it."

"I don't have to admit anything to you, Ricky Chase. Just please let me up," I yelled in his face.

"No, I'm not letting you up until you admit how you're a hypocrite. Go on and admit that you are a fraud, writing those articles when you don't even believe what you are writing. Otherwise, you wouldn't have disappeared off to Brad's room and engaged in what you are telling everybody in your articles not to do."

"What are you getting at Ricky?"

"I think you know what I'm getting at. You didn't disappear off to my cousin's room for all that time to chit chat."

"Ricky, it's none of your business what happened between me and Brad. But just to set you straight, you have the wrong understanding. Nothing happened upstairs between me and Brad, okay?"

"It sure looked like something happened. You two disappeared upstairs for a long time. The party had just started when you sneaked upstairs, and it was almost over when you two finally came back down."

"So what, nothing happened."

"Are you telling me, he didn't kiss you or get to first base with you upstairs? Knowing how Brad is into you, he probably had his hands all over you; and as much as you are into him, I'm sure you had no problem with that."

"What if I did kiss Brad, it's none of your business, Ricky. Why should it matter to you? You are dating my best friend, remember?" I reminded him. "I don't think she would be too pleased to hear about your little stunt here," I shouted. "Now stop acting like a fool and get off of me, will you please?"

"Stop yelling, I'm not hurting you or anything."

"Maybe not physically but mentally you are drunk and full of attitude. I'm lying here praying you won't flip out and really do something stupid that could hurt me and land you in a lot of trouble. You're sitting on top of my thighs making it impossible for me to move an inch," I said disappointedly. "We just left a fun party and now I'm freezing laying here on this cold snowy ground."

"Laying here on a little snow is not going to hurt you." He pulled off his gloves and threw them aside and then took both of his cold hands and grabbed my face.

"Your hands are too cold to touch me," I shouted. "Besides, your entire body smells like wine. Don't touch me; just get off of me right now!" I couldn't take his out of control behavior anymore. The feel of his cold hands made my face sting. I was already trembling lying on the cold snow and that made me extremely angry with him. I clenched both fists, and quickly bit down on the palm of his right hand. I knew biting him would make him crazier, but I had to make him get off of me.

"Damn you, Mandy!" He yelled. "You shouldn't have done that!" He jumped off me and grabbed his arm, tripped over his wine bottle, and then picked it up and threw it down the street.

I hopped up to run, but he grabbed me by the arm and I slipped and fell back down in the snow. Then finally, I managed to pull away from his grip. He looked at me and shook his head, picked up his gloves out of the snow and headed down the street toward his big house.

My weak legs managed to get me the one block I had left to walk home. I held my face and cried all the way. The moment I unlocked the front door, all wet and muddy from the wet snow, I bumped against a stand in the foyer and knocked a tall vase to the floor. It hit the floor and made a loud crashing sound. Mom heard the noise and came hurrying down the staircase.

"Mandy, what happened?" Mom asked, holding her blue robe together as she found me in the foyer removing my coat.

"I'm sorry I woke you with all that noise." I hung my soil coat on the coat stand in the corner of the foyer. "I broke that tall green vase." I looked at Mom with regretful eyes. "I'm sorry but I think it cracked in too many pieces to be repaired." I took a seat on the bench in the foyer and slowly removed my boots.

"I don't care about that vase, sweetheart. I'm just glad you are okay." She glanced at my wet, muddy coat. "But you don't really look okay."

I didn't comment as I slowly stood up from the bench.

"Sweetheart, how did you get your coat all wet and muddy? Did something happen at that party? You haven't answered me if you're okay?"

"Mom, I'm not really okay," I admitted, headed toward the staircase.

"What happened, dear?"

"I'm sore and exhausted from falling in the snow."

"You're sore and exhausted from falling in the snow?" Mom asked and glanced toward the snow. "I know it snowing quite heavy out there. Did you slip and fall in the snow on your way home from the party?"

I nodded.

"So, I guess that's what happened to your coat? It needs a visit with the cleaners." She headed up the staircase behind me.

"Yes, that's what happened."

"You didn't hurt yourself did you?"

"No, I'm not hurt but I bruised one of my knees."

I didn't mention Ricky's stunt. Afterall, he was upset with me because of an untrue rumor that I had started about myself. I figured he deserved a second chance to sober up and never act like an out of control jerk again.

Chapter Seventeen

Sitting at the kitchen table at Mandy Manor, Kathy and I were so excited that we had attended our high school graduation at noon and now three hours later, Mrs. Lawson had surprised us with my favorite dessert, her homemade lemon pie.

Kathy looked beautiful with her hair pulled back in a French roll with two long curls hanging on either side of her face. It complimented her oval face and I hoped it complimented my face as well since we had both gotten the same hair style. We were also both dressed in a similar but not identical fashionable two piece beige dress for our evening out together at the graduation party. The school was throwing the event at a facility uptown at five o'clock for all graduates.

"This day is one for the history books," she said, slicing a piece of pie.

"Yes, it is; we have officially graduated from Barrington High on this warm sunny day," I said excitedly. "This is the day we start our new lives after high school."

"Remember what the principal said to all of us? This day marks your journey into adulthood. This clear Wednesday afternoon on June 18, 2003, is the beginning of your future. The direction you take after this day will define your history."

"Yes, Kathy, he made a good speech. He said this is our time to go out into the world and shine. He said we need to be cautious about the choices we make."

"I know, he said we need to be honorable and be respectful and if something feels wrong, it probably is." She smiled and nodded.

I glanced at her and quickly looked away as something stung the inside of me when she repeated the principal words. I shifted in my chair and lowered my eyes to the slice of pie in front of me.

"Wow, what was that look for," she narrowed her eyes at me.

"What look?" I asked.

"You just flashed me a weird look," Kathy said.

"What are you talking about a weird look?"

"I don't know, you had regret or guilt in your eyes," she said casually. "This is a happy day and not one for regret or guilt. Although I'm sure it's still hard to get through a day without bombing out about your folks pending divorce."

I nodded. "Yes, it's very hard." I lifted my water glass and my hand shook as I brought the rim up to my mouth and took a quick sip.

"Mandy, I'm so sorry, but the divorce is final very soon, right? Maybe that will be for the best and you and your mom can try to get over this."

"My parents' divorce is something I'll never get over," I mumbled.

"Well, you'll have to get over it. You got your own life to look forward to, remember what the principal said?"

I stared at her with tears falling down my face. "Yes, I remember what the principal said and that's why my conscience is bothering me now."

"Well, you need to dry your tears because it shouldn't bother you. It's not your fault. You can't change your parent's mind and put their marriage back together. "

"Kathy, my conscience isn't bothering me because of the divorce; it's bothering me because of something that happened at the New Years party or to be precise, it happened after the party."

"Well, whatever took place six months ago, Mandy, you just need to get over it. This is our big day." Kathy waved a hand. "I'm not trying to be unfeeling about whatever it is that you are referring to, but you need to enjoy this day. We just graduated from high school and we have a big bash to attend in a couple hours. You need to cheer up fast," she suggested.

"I can't cheer up until I get this off of my chest. My conscience will no longer let me keep what happened inside without sharing it with you," I stated firmly and stared across the table at her. "Kathy, there's nothing I need to tell you."

"Okay, what's up?" she said casually as she stuck a fork of pie into her mouth. "If you need to unburden yourself so you can feel better, please go ahead. But I can't imagine what have you twisted so tight all of a sudden."

"I didn't want to tell you this," I said regretfully.

"You didn't want to tell me what?" she asked with a concerned look in her eyes.

"It's about Ricky." I lifted my glass and took another sip of ice water and tried to collect myself to get the words out that I needed to say.

"Okay, let's have it, what did you hear?" she smiled.

"It's not something I heard about Ricky, it's something I know."

"Something you know?" she pushed her dish aside and placed both elbows on the table and leaned in toward me. "Mandy, you are starting to worry me now. "What are you trying to tell me about Ricky?"

I took my napkin and wiped the tears from my face. "I didn't want to hurt you by telling you about his drunken behavior," I mumbled sadly.

"You didn't want to tell me about Ricky's drunken behavior? He's never drunk, what are you talking about?"

"Ricky got wasted at the Chase party and he followed me halfway home and carried on inappropriate with me."

Kathy shook her head with stunned eyes. "Mandy, do you hear what you are saying?" She grabbed her cheeks with both hands and her mouth fell open. "I hope you are kidding me, right? Not my Ricky."

I shook my head. "I'm not kidding. I wouldn't kid about something like this. He was so drunk and he did and said some really awful stuff."

"What did he do that was so awful?" she demanded.

"As I said, he was carrying on inappropriate with me," I mumbled.

"You need to spell it out! I want to know what you consider inappropriate."

"He kept asking me to go to his house."

"Did he explain why?"

I nodded. "Yes, he gave me some lame excuse."

"What was it?"

"He said he was too alert to go home and fall to sleep."

"Did you think he meant something else other than that?"

"Come on, Kathy, I know you don't want to believe the worse about Ricky, but he was out of line to ask me to go home with him in the middle of the night."

"Of course he was out of line and his behavior was inappropriate to ask you that." She hopped out of her seat with both hands holding her cheeks. "Mandy, why did you wait so long to tell me this?" she asked with deep hurt in her eyes.

"I didn't want to see you upset like this." I held out both hands. "Besides, we both know he's not a big drinker. He had drunk too much and he was so drunk and out of his mind until he probably wasn't aware of his actions and words."

"If that's how you felt why are you telling me now?"

"I had to tell you."

"No, Mandy, you didn't have to tell me something like this if you are so sure he didn't know what he was saying."

"Kathy, I'm sorry you are upset, but this happened six months ago and I'm sure Ricky will probably never allow himself to drink that much again."

"I'm still waiting to hear why you felt you needed to tell me this to upset our special day. You have kept this to yourself for the past six months then you wait until the day of our graduation to tell me," she snapped. "I can't get that image out of my mind of him asking you to his house; and why he was asking you in the first place."

"I didn't know I was going to tell you today, I had planned to keep his drunken behavior to myself."

"Why didn't you, Mandy, why didn't you?" She wiped a tear from her eye.

"What the principal said about if it feels wrong, it probably is. It felt wrong to keep this from you and I needed to tell you. But not because I wanted you to be upset with Ricky or break up with him, but because you are my best friend and I just didn't feel right keeping this from you. I didn't want to go off to college with this secret between us."

She took her seat back at the table and stared out into space. "Well, you freed your conscience but you didn't do me any favors by telling me, especially today. You picked the worse possible time to unburden yourself. Now, we both are upset on what is supposed to be one of the happiest days of our lives."

I got out of my seat and mumbled. "I guess we should head upstairs and freshen up before we head to the party.

She glanced at her watch. "We still have plenty of time."

"Not really, I need to change into something else. I spilled a piece of pie on my outfit."

"Okay, sure. Go up and change. I'll stay down here."

When we arrived at the party, Ricky was standing near the refreshment stand talking to Kathy's brother Justin. They both looked handsome in their off white tuxedos. Kathy dashed across the room in their direction and I followed. I managed to grab her arm before we reached them.

"Kathy, what are you going to say to Ricky? Can this wait until later?" I asked, "This is a party, remember?"

"Mandy, I'm not sure what I'm going to say, but no, it can't wait until later," she snapped. "I know it's a party but you should have thought about that before you decided to unburden yourself of such a secret just hours before the party." She rushed away from me in Ricky's direction.

"Hello beautiful," Ricky said to her as she walked up to face him. "You both look nice."

"Yes, you both do," Justin exchanged looks with me and smiled and then he headed across the event hall in Molly's direction.

Kathy stood there staring at Ricky and then exchanged looks with me and I shook my head, hoping she wouldn't say anything until after the party.

"What's going on with you two?" he asked.

"I'll tell you what's going on and it's not good," she snapped angrily. "Mandy just told me about your drunken rampage."

He stared at her confused for a moment and then swallowed hard and glanced up at the ceiling before he looked at me with apologetic eyes. "Mandy."

"Ricky, yes, I told her. I know I said I wouldn't mention it and kept it inside all this time, but I just couldn't keep it inside any longer."

"Mandy, I'm sorry about my behavior and how I carried on, but you know I was wasted and out of it. I hope you can forgive me."

I nodded. "Yes, Ricky, I forgive you. I know you were acting from the booze."

"But I don't know you were acting from the booze," Kathy snapped.

"Kathy, I had drunk so much I shouldn't have been walking the street. I was so messed up until I can't even remember most of the events. I know I was out of control and behaving like a wild fool, but I can't remember any of it in clear details."

"I'm just concerned with what you asked Mandy that evening," Kathy said.

"What do you mean what I asked Mandy?"

"You asked her to go home with you, and I want to know why did your drunken mind ask her that?"

"Kathy, it's hazy to me, but I can't imagine why I would have asked Mandy to my house," he said humbly.

"Well, you did ask her. I read somewhere that a drunken person says what a sober person thinks."

"Kathy, what are you implying?" he asked.

"I'm not implying anything. I'm just trying to get to the bottom of what happened and why you asked Mandy to your house."

"How do you expect to get to the bottom of something that I don't completely remember and would never do if I hadn't been controlled by a stomach filled with red wine," Ricky stressed.

"Mandy said you gave her some lame excuse that you were too alert to go home and fall asleep. Do you recall saying that to Mandy?"

He shook his head. "I don't recall saying it, but I'm sure I said it if she said I said it. I don't dispute it, I just don't remember it." He held out both arms. "We are at our graduation party, can we drop this and pick it up at some other time?" he asked Kathy.

"No, we can not drop it until I say we can drop it. I'm extremely upset and disappointed about your behavior with my best friend. You get so wasted and say inappropriate stuff to her," Kathy argued. "I don't know how to get past this. You were so out of it until you don't recall everything, but it happened just the same."

"Kathy, I'm sorry. I'll never let something like that happen again. You know I'm not a drinker and I'll never drink that much again. I made a stupid mistake that I feel pretty rotten about," he assured her.

"You should feel pretty rotten," Kathy fussed.

"If my intoxicated mind was asking Mandy to go home with me, it was due to a sheer drunken request. I like Mandy as a friend but the thought of being romantic with your best friend is revolting to me," he said firmly.

"But why else would you ask her to your house in the middle of the night?"

"Kathy, I don't know the answer to that."

"You need to find the answer if you expect for this relationship to continue."

He gripped her shoulders and stared down in her eyes. "Kathy, I love you," he blurted out. "There I said it. I love you."

Kathy was speechless and motionless for a moment as she looked longingly into Ricky's eyes. "You have never said that to me before." She grabbed her stomach in pleasant surprise of his confession of love. "As much as it means to hear you say those words to me, how do I know you are not just saying them to stop me from questioning you about your behavior on New Years?"

"You can look in my eyes and tell I meant what I just said. Miss Kathy Gross, I love you a lot. I'm sorry I behaved like a drunken fool with inappropriate behavior toward Mandy and said what I said, but you are the only girl I want to take home with me ever." He leaned down and kissed the side of her face. "Now, is all forgiven? Can I fetch you two a cup of punch?" he asked humbly.

"A cup of punch sounds great to me," I said, smiling to knock Kathy out of her sad mood.

She nodded. "Sure, I'll take a cup of punch."

Ricky stepped a couple feet to the refreshment table, lifted the long stemmed metal dipper and dipped it into the large punch bowl and filled three cups. He appeared anxious as he passed us both cups of punch at the same time. "Here you are," he said. We took our drinks and we both sipped them right away. He then reached down and lifted his cup from the refreshment table and took a sip. He seemed anxious as if he didn't know what to expect from Kathy. "That's one of your favorite songs, You Rock My World by Michael Jackson, would you like to dance?" Ricky asked Kathy.

Kathy shook her head. "No, I do not; I just want to get through this party because I'm not having an ounce of fun. I just want to scream about what Mandy told me and about how you behaved toward her at the beginning of the year."

"So, you're still upset?" he asked.

"Yes, of course, I'm still upset. This is all fresh in my mind. It may have happened six months ago, but I haven't had six months to soak over it as you two have," Kathy stated in a heat. "The both of you kept me in the dark. Now I have to process this mess in the best way I can."

"I understand that much." Ricky nodded. "But what do you have in mind?"

"I have in mind that we should probably take a break."

"Take a break?" Ricky quickly asked.

"Yes, while I'm trying to process this mayhem in my brain where it will fit and not drive me batty just thinking about it."

"Take a break as in break up, I assume?" he asked.

Kathy nodded. "Yes, I think so, until I can deal with the thought of you asking my best friend to your house in the middle of the night." She wiped her tears with her fingers. "I can't believe your motives were honorable at that late hour no matter how drunk you were."

"So you want to break up with me for something stupid I said six months ago?"

"It's not just something stupid you said, it something stupid you said to my best friend."

"Kathy, I said I'm sorry. It was a drunken mistake. Can you just please forgive me and forget I acted like a fool. Mandy forgave me, why can't you?" He pointed to me.

"I'm sorry, but at this moment I can't forgive and forgot," Kathy cried.

"But Kathy, that was six months ago and I have explained that it's hazy and I didn't know what I was saying," he stressed desperate for her forgiveness.

"Maybe you didn't, but I know what I'm feeling and right now I can't deal with the thought of you saying something like that to my best friend."

Ricky raised both arms and shook his head with a broken look on his face. He had water in his eyes and was clearly crushed as he rushed out of the event hall. Kathy and I exchanged looks, grabbed hands and rushed out behind him. When we rushed through the double doors of the building, Ricky was walking quickly toward his car in the parking lot. He never looked back as he hopped in his car, started the engine and speeded away from the facility.

Kathy wouldn't go back inside to the party. She stood outside and cried until I grabbed her hand and led her to my car and drove her home. She was sad about telling Ricky that they needed a break, but she didn't take back her words. Therefore, I was so crushed that she was miserable over breaking up Ricky and by the time we all left for different universities that fall, she and Ricky still hadn't gotten back together.

On top of my crushed heart that Kathy and Ricky couldn't seem to find their way back to each other, I was also miserable that my parent's divorce had just finalized. Mom ended up with the house, half of all the other properties, a double suite at our disposable year round, at the Country Club Inn Resort on the outskirts of Barrington, full custody of me and thirty thousand dollars a month.

Chapter Eighteen

Traveling home from Yale University on Amtrak was an overnight train ride during the late summer of my third year at college. I was seated at a window seat looking out in thought of all the events that had occurred during my time away at college. My father had recently remarried and he had recently gotten elected mayor of Chicago. Our lives had changed tremulously but I looked to my future with new eyes.

Mom was standing inside the train station waiting with two cups of coffee in her hands. It was only eight-thirty in the morning and the coffee in her hands looked good. I placed my small luggage on the floor and she handed me a cup and then we hugged and cried, so pleased to see each other.

By the time we walked the two blocks to where Mom had parked, she had finished drinking her coffee and placed the empty cup in a trashcan we passed along the street.

"We are headed straight to the country club from here and can have breakfast there if you like," she said, took her keys and unlocked the doors of a shiny red Mercedes just a few feet away.

"That's fine." I took a sip of coffee in awe of the fine new car. "Mom, this is a nice surprise." I opened the passenger's door and placed my coffee in the cup holder. "Your new car looks priceless."

"I bought it last week," she said, smiling as she unlocked the trunk.

"I really like it. Did Aunt Bonne buy a new car too?" I said in a joking manner, placed my small piece of luggage in the trunk and then shut the trunk.

"What was that, Mandy?" Mom asked as she got inside.

"It wasn't important," I said and I hopped in the car and closed the door.

Mom gave me a solemn look as she started up the engine. "I needed to buy myself a cheer up gift after I read about your father's new marriage." Mom smiled and headed toward the highway.

"Mom, thanks for driving down to pick me up."

"Of course, are you kidding? I have missed you like crazy and wasn't about to have any of the staff drive down here for you."

"I miss the staff too, but I have to admit that I'm glad we are not stopping at Mandy Manor."

"Why is that, dear?"

"I just don't want to run into any of my friends or the neighbors," I uttered lightheartedly. "I don't have the stomach to hear all the talk about town that involves Dad and his new wife or his new career."

"I understand, because I'm tired of hearing about it myself. I'm sure there'll be no talk about Daniel at the resort. We are headed straight there and our suite is booked for your entire summer break."

"That's great." I laughed.

"Sweetheart, are you excited?" Mom asked. "You will have the opportunity to meet a host of interesting people at the country club."

"Mom, I'm happy to spend the time with you and I love the amenities at the country club."

"But what, I hear one coming," Mom said.

"But I know most of the interesting people you are referring to, and they are not that interesting to me," I admitted. "They are sort of stiff."

"They are what?" she asked.

"They are sort of stiff."

"Mandy, what are you saying?"

"I'm saying, they are all rich and some very rich, but."

"Go on and finished what you were about to say." Mom threw me a quick glance and then placed her eyes back on the highway ahead. "They are rich but what, sweetheart, nothing you say is going to offend me. I will most likely agree with it?" Mom laughed.

"In that case, what I was going to say is that a lot of those country club regulars just seem too arrogant, uptight and sometime unsociable."

Mom nodded. "Some are that way, but many are quite interesting and those are the ones you will enjoy meeting. But always be polite, sweetheart."

"Mom, I'm always polite but I just don't feel much compassion floating from the regulars at the country club."

Looking out the passenger's window at all the familiar scenery of being back in the state, I mumbled. "Mom, I feel like I don't really know Dad anymore. He seems almost like a complete different person from who raised me," I explained. "It seems he has been extremely busy remaking himself from the father I knew to someone I don't recognize. First he moved out of the house and in with his secretary. That came to me as a complete shock. Then he divorced you and got into polities; and now he's the mayor of Chicago."

"Aren't you forgetting something from that list?"

"Oh yes, now he just recently remarried."

"I can't believe this is the father who tried to instill all those good values in me."

"We have to look at it this way, Mandy. Your father is still a good man who has made some mistakes."

"Everything about Dad has surprised me lately. I know I was surprised to hear that he had gotten into politics. It was during his campaign for mayor, when I noticed his picture in the local paper regularly."

"You have the local paper delivered to you at the university?"

"Yes, so I can keep up on the local news and it makes me feel closer to home to read the paper from home."

"I'm sure it does. You are quite far from home out there in New Haven, Connecticut. But we can be pleased that you are attending one of the most prestigious schools in the world."

"Mom, after I noticed Dad picture in the paper, I caught one of his campaign ads on TV; and watching him on the television made me feel like I was looking at a stranger," I mumbled disappointedly.

"Why do you feel so distanced from your father?"

"Since I have been away at the university, Dad and I haven't kept in close touch. I email him but he doesn't reply to emails I guess."

"Has Daniel visited you at school at all?" Mom asked.

I shook my head. "No, Dad has not visited me. He hasn't made any time to come visit me there. And in my mind, I gave him excuses and kept telling myself that he was too busy to take the trip. I just didn't want to acknowledge that he was happy with his new life away from us."

"There is no excuse, Mandy, for your father not to try to spend some time with his only child."

"That's how I feel too, but I guess Dad is too busy being a new husband and a new mayor." I lifted my coffee cup from the holder and took a sip and then placed it back in the holder. "It surprises me that he is now into politics, which is something I never knew he was interested in. Growing up at Mandy Manor before the divorce and he moved out of the house, I can not recall Dad ever mentioning an interest in politics."

"During your first year at the university, we had a discussion over the phone about his interest in politics," Mom reminded me.

"I know you mentioned that he was interested in the field or entertaining the idea of jumping into politics. But when you mentioned that to me, Mom, I didn't think it was a serious career choice that Dad was going to actually embark upon. But last November when I was sitting alone in my dorm room watching him on TV giving a campaign speech about why he would make the best mayor for Chicago, I was so stunned to see him in the race. And although I'm still bitter and disappointed in him for breaking up our home, the night of the election while listening to the returns I was happy that he won."

"You were glad he won because he's your father and no matter what, you love him. And if I'm being honest, I still love your father inspite of everything."

"Mom, I knew you still loved Dad and with all my disappointment in him I keep holding out hope in the back of my mind that the two of you will find your way back to each other. That would be the one thing that would make me completely happy."

"Mandy, you are twenty years old, an adult and much too old to fantasize about your parents getting back together."

"Mom, I know you are right, but I almost feel lost inside with the two of you divorced from each other and living separate lives."

"In time you'll get used to it, sweetheart," she assured me.

"I haven't gotten use to it yet. Your divorce finalized during the summer of 2003 and now it's August of 2005 and I still haven't gotten used to your separation."

"Mandy, it's more than a separation. Your father has moved on and remarried."

"I know he has, but I don't have to like it."

"No, you don't have to like it, but you need to try to let go of the bitterness and accept it, Mandy," Mom suggested.

"I'm trying, but he has shut me out it appears. He didn't personally tell me about his upcoming marriage. I had to read about it in the local paper. That day after class I had plans to go to a movie with some friends who cancelled and I grabbed the paper and decided to read through it just to pass the time away, but when I stared at the front cover story; my heart raced when I saw a picture of Dad with Doris standing next to him holding his hand. The headline read: "Mayor Daniel Clark and his charming wife, Doris, attend the opening of the new city library."

"Sweetheart, I'm sorry. That was very inconsiderate of your father to have you to find out that way. Although, he knows how you feel about his choice to be with Doris, therefore he also knew that calling you up and informing you wouldn't have gone over well either."

"Mom, it was so painful to read that he had gotten married to the woman who broke the two of you up. Seeing that picture and reading that headline stunned me so much until it felt like something sharp turned in my stomach and broke off a piece of me that couldn't be pasted back together."

"Does it still hurt that much?" Mom asked.

"No as much as it used to, but reading about his marriage last month seemed to reopen some of my wounds. I had always secretly hoped that you and Dad would find your way back to each other, and now with a new marriage to someone else, my dream for your reunion seems almost impossible."

"Mandy, I still love Daniel, but he has moved on. Before he married Doris I would think about that possibility some time, but now I have to erase that thought from my mind and move on as he has done."

"Mom, when did you first hear about Dad's marriage to that woman?"

"I didn't read about it, one of my friends read it and told me. I didn't let on but the news crushed me greatly. If I had known about the engagement I could have mentioned it and that would have softened the blow when you found out. But I never saw an announcement or read about one, the public read about the marriage after he and she had already married," Mom explained.

"Mom, I'm sorry about Dad's marriage to that woman."

"No need to be sorry, Mandy. Deep down we both knew it was coming. Your father is a determined man if nothing else. And now, he's no longer my husband. He's married to his secretary." Mom shook her head. "Although I doubt she'll remain his secretary much longer now that she has snagged him. She'll probably hire someone else to handle his paperwork and her secretarial duties, and then she can worry about that person stealing him away from her," Mom stated seriously.

"Mom, did you know Dad was interested in running for mayor?"

Mom laughed. "He never mentioned to me that he was interested in running for mayor. Although, when he likely made that decision, he and I weren't keeping each other abreast on each other's business. He only had the one conversation with me about politics and that was during your first year at the university. At that time, he did seem quite motivated toward politics. But to embark on a huge responsibility like the mayor of a large city like Chicago." Mom shook her head. "I never saw that coming. I never thought he was serious enough to actually run for office."

"Mom, it's a complete surprise to me as well. Dad never mentioned an interest in running for public office. I can remember back when we had our weekly walks in town and he would tell me lots of stuff, but he never mentioned politics."

"Well, a few years ago when your father mentioned it to me I just never took him serious." Mom paused. "Looking back, I guess that was one of my mistakes with Daniel. I just didn't listen or show enough interest in his interests," Mom humbly admitted.

"Mom, don't blame yourself for Dad's choice to leave home and move in with his secretary. He took a vow with you and he could have chosen not to break it no matter how bad things seemed at home with the two of you."

Mom patted my shoulder. "Thanks for the support, sweetheart, but I have to face my shortcomings that led to your father walking out of the door. I practically pushed him into that woman's arms with my bitter rudeness toward him. Hindsight is clear, and I'm sure Doris was his shoulder to cry on with the deep understanding that he couldn't get from me. Therefore, sweetheart, I would like to apology to you for the part I played in destroying your home."

"Mom, thank you, but Dad chose to have an affair. With all your shortcomings you were never unfaithful to Dad."

Mom shook her head. "No, I wasn't, not while we were married. But in Daniel's heart, I was unfaithful to him before the wedding."

"Mom, what do you mean?"

"It's a long story about something that occurred before you were born. I had two boyfriends, your father and another boy named Robert Dieringer. I chose to marry your father, but broke up with Daniel for three weeks and started dating Robert again for two of those weeks and during those two weeks with Robert I broke a promise to Daniel when I allowed Robert to be my first," Mom explained regretfully. "Your father and I got back together and eventually married but he continued to throw that broken promise back in my face."

For a moment, my mind flashed back to the argument I had overheard between them about her broken promise, but couldn't see how it compared to his betrayal. "Mom, your broken promise took place when you and Dad had broken up and were not dating at the time. I don't know all the details, I just know that a broken promise to a boyfriend is not as big of a betrayal as a broken marriage vow; and that's what Dad did when he moved in with that woman when he was still married to you," I stated seriously. "So much for his high morals and principles and now we can add abandonment to the list."

Mom glanced at me but didn't comment and I continued.

"Yes, Mom, the wonderful thoughtful father that I grew up with has abandoned me in my eyes."

"Mandy, you know your father still loves," she quickly said.

"I'm sure he does, but he has changed so much and I never hear from him."

"There's no excuse, but Daniel has a new demanding life right now."

"I know he has a new demanding life, but I'm still his daughter. He doesn't even try to go out of his way to see me or spend any time with me anymore. His priorities seem much different from when he was with us."

"Very different," Mom agreed. "But from what I have read and the way it appears, your father is very busy but also quite content with his new life."

"Maybe he is, but what about us. I still haven't gotten over my resentment toward him for breaking up our home," I sadly mumbled.

"I'm still resentful to, sweetheart, but we need to let it go I suppose because your father isn't losing any sleep over us," Mom said. "So let's change the subject. It's great to have you home for awhile."

"I'm glad to be here for awhile and spend my summer break with you. I have missed you, Mom. Being away at college all this time is our first long separation apart from each other," I said.

While Mom drove down the highway headed toward Barrington, we kept glancing smiles at each other. She had only changed slightly. She was still young at 44, and she was taking very good care of herself with no noticeable lines or wrinkles about her face or near her eyes. Conscious of barely any change in her, I asked abruptly.

"Mom, have my looks changed that much?"

"Have your looks changed?" she laughed softly. "I would think so. You are all grown up now, young lady."

"But do I," I said.

She finished my sentence. "You look beautiful as ever, sweetheart." She held up one finger at me but kept her eyes looking straight ahead at the stretch of highway in front of us. "But there is one thing we need to do for you as soon as we can clear our schedules."

"What's that, Mom?"

"We need to go shopping and buy you a closet of new clothes."

I glanced at her and smiled. "A closet of new clothes; what's wrong with the closet of new clothes I just recently bought?"

"I'm sure they are all wonderful pieces," she said excitedly. "But look at you. You are all grown up now and we have to dress you accordingly." She gave me a quick glance and back at the road. "You are not turning down a new wardrobe, are you?" She threw me a quick glance and winked.

"Of course not," I smiled. "I just don't see the need."

"That's because you are still so young. However you're no longer a youngster. You have grown into a lovely young woman, and I want to show you off to all my friends, and of course their rich sons. Sweetheart just wait, you're going to be the talk of the Country Club Inn this summer with lots of prospective young men hanging around you, I'm sure; and that reminds me," she said and paused, flashing me a smile as if she shared some kind of secret that I didn't know but she couldn't wait to tell me.

"That reminds you of what, Mom? What are you up to? No matchmaking, please. I have always told you that I'm not interested in Wesley Jr. You have always tried to push me toward him, but Kathy and I both tried to tell you that it wasn't her brother, Wesley, that I was hung up on back in high school."

"I don't see why not? Wesley is a fine young man, and smart to boot."

"I know that and he happens to be the son of your two best friends," I stressed laughingly. "So you might be somewhat partial where Wesley is concerned," I teased. "Plus, Mom, you don't have to convince me. I already know how wonderful Wesley Gross is, but I have never liked him as more than a friend."

"If you are not interested in the young man, why are you getting so worked up over the possibility of going out with him?"

"Mom, I'm not getting worked up. I'm just trying to make a point so you know I'm not interested in Wesley Jr. I wasn't interested in him in high school and I'm not interested in him now."

"But dear, a lot of time has passed since high school. How do you know you're not interested in Wesley Jr. now? He's in medical school studying to be a doctor you know?"

"Everybody at school knew he wanted to be a doctor; and yes, Kathy wrote and told me that he's in medical school, studying to be some kind of surgeon. A brain surgeon, I think; and I'm really proud of Wesley and I like him a lot, but I'm still not interested in him to be my boyfriend," I assured her.

Mom nodded and smiled. "It pleases me that you're not stuck on Wesley Jr. If you had been that would have been okay, but since you are not, that's even better. Yes, I agree. Wesley Gross, Jr., is a fine young man but to be completely honest, I'm stuck on those Chase boys for you," Mom said seriously.

"What did you say?" I asked. She had caught me off guard by mentioning the Chase name. Hearing the Chase name somehow made a plain conversation seem exciting.

"When I said that reminds me, I was referring to the fact that the Chase boys have suites at the resort this summer," Mom casually relayed.

She had no idea I was deeply in love with Brad Chase. During my high school days she knew I had a crush on some boy, but she probably thought it was Wesley Jr. She never knew it was

Brad because I never confided in her that I liked him. After-all, he never dropped by asking to take me out. Therefore, I figured what was the use of telling her I had a crush on some boy who didn't even like me enough to drop by my home and spend time with me or take me out.

"I said those popular Chase boys, because regardless to how smart and well educated Wesley Jr. is, and as you mentioned with his folks being my best friends, he could never measure up to a Chase. Only a Chase boy is good enough for my daughter," Mom continued her talk about the Chase clan.

When Mom first picked me up from the train station I was rather sad thinking about my father's new life. Therefore, I was listening to her, but sort of half listening, but when she mentioned the Chase boys. I was hanging on her every word.

"The Chase boys?" I asked curiously, but I meant more as a statement.

Mom nodded. "Yes, the Chase boys, those extremely rich bank people."

I grabbed my chest without her being the wiser. "You mean...?"

She threw me a quick glance and nodded. "Yes, Brad Chase and his brother Todd. They have a suite at the resort for the summer."

"Mom, are you sure? How did you find out?"

"I'm quite sure. I read it in the society page. You could find these things out as well if you took the time to read the society page once in awhile."

I smiled and said excitedly. "You are right, Mom. I guess I should glance at it sometime. I just figured the news would never interest me."

"Never say never, sweetheart. It's apparent that bit of information has cheered you up. After-all, those two young men are basically considered royalty in this part of the world; and you do know them right?"

"Yes, Mom, I know them both, but I haven't seen them since high school."

"Well, get ready to get to know them better," she said excitedly.

I didn't comment, thinking how Brad never followed through on his interest for me back in high school.

"Get ready to be dazzled, sweetheart. This summer you will rub shoulders with the filthy rich. Their mother, Connie Chase, is President of the downtown branch," Mom continued excitedly. "Did you now that?"

I was thinking to myself how I didn't know that and how that piece of news really didn't matter to me. I was only interested in hearing about Brad and Todd.

Mom continued. "Of course their mother will not be at the resort tonight, but her daughter, Molly, and her sons, Brad and Todd will. From what I hear, Connie will arrive tomorrow; and apparently she's giving some kind of talk. But in the meantime, her two handsome, very rich sons will be around to dazzle all the young ladies. And no doubt their sister, Molly, will keep all the young men busy asking for her hand on the dance floor. That is quite alright since you'll have the attention of the two kings of the ball," Mom said seriously.

"Mom, they are not kings."

"They might as well be. They live in a palace and own as much gold." Mom smiled. "Yes, Mandy, the Chase clan is the family everybody wants to connect with."

"If that's the case, where is Mr. Chase?" I asked, as we turned into the beautiful redbrick driveway of the lovely Country Club Inn Resort.

Mom's shoulders arched awkwardly. "Ron Chase won't be at the resort this summer as far as I know. He moved away."

"Moved away to where?" I asked.

"He moved back to his hometown of Springfield."

"That's right; Mr. Chase is from the same hometown as Dad."

"But why would Mr. Chase want to move back to Springfield? He has so many banks in this area," I asked.

"I can't really answer that except to say, he has so many banks down there as well," Mom pointed out.

"But still, Mom, Springfield is no Chicago."

"That's for sure, but it is where he was born and raised. Besides, I heard that he decided to move back after he said I do to the second Mrs. Chase."

"I guess he didn't want to run into the first Mrs. Chase," I mumbled.

"That could be it. But after their divorce a couple years ago, and he remarried. I read in the society page that he decided to move downstate to manage his other branches. The man has more money than he knows what to do with."

"Sort of like you, Mom," I teased.

"What was that, Mandy?" Mom asked.

I changed the subject. "I was just wondering why nobody stays married it seems."

"Mandy, sweetheart, don't think that way," Mom seriously replied. "There are plenty of couples who stay married until death does them part," she said assuredly. "It's just the few of us who can't seem to make it work that makes it appear hopeless for everyone else."

I shook my head. "I don't know what to think about marriage anymore. I always thought you and Dad had a perfect marriage until I realized you didn't. Then just like that it was over. You and Dad couldn't make it work. Now I learn that Todd and Brad parents couldn't make it work; and come to think of it, most of your friends are divorced."

"Not all of my friends are divorced," Mom corrected me.

"Maybe not all, but most of them that I know, except for Kathy's parents."

"That's about true Wesley and Deanna are the exception. They met at the university during the same time that your father and I started dating. The four of us were good friends and we would often double date. But they became a marriage couple three years before Daniel and me. They announced their engagement during our first semester and at the end of our first college year, Deanna and Wesley were united in matrimony. But they never missed any classes. Not even when Deanna was pregnant with Wesley Jr. and delivered before graduation. They were college sweethearts, married young and they are still together. They are the couple who knew how to make it work."

"Mom, that's a great story about Mr. and Mrs. Gross, but those are really depressing odds considering how many of your friends are now divorced."

"Mandy, this is true, but don't let my sour grapes and those of others sway your romantic side. You are still very young with a lot to learn about life and love. Please hold on to your positive outlook on life and dreams of true romance."

Chapter Nineteen

At the Country Club Inn dance that evening, my eyes did a double take when I spotted the grown up Todd and Brad Chase. They walked through the side entrance together and as they headed across the ballroom floor toward a group of people who were waving their arms and beckoning for them, they strolled across the thick red carpet and through the crowd as if they owned the place. They both looked strikingly handsome like they belonged on the cover of a fashion magazine. They were both taller than I remembered back in high school, about six foot, slender, bronze smooth skin and almost too attractive for words. Todd's presence beamed the room, dressed in light grey sporting a thin silver tie. He looked divinely handsome and refine with sleepy looking deep brown eyes that sparkled from the lighting. Standing beside him was his super good looking brother, dressed in all white, sporting a thin blue tie. Brad radiant light brown eyes and invisible pores highlighted a face that was almost gorgeous.

Mom was standing toward the front of the ballroom and she looked stunning wearing a long black open back dress that draped off her body beautifully. She looked in my direction and waved. She was smiling and pointing both hands toward Brad and Todd who were standing midways the room mingling with a group of people. She obviously believed that both of the Chase boys were personally designed for me. From the moment they had walked into the room all female eyes, including mine were on the two of them. I could not take my eyes from their sight. I kept glancing between where they were standing and my mother's direction. They hadn't noticed me since they were both engaged in conversation with friends. Then all at once they both glanced about the room at the same time and spotted me.

Luckily, to save me from embarrassment, they didn't notice Mom staring and pointing toward them as they both headed across the room in my direction. When they reached me, they both smiled and said hello, appearing to be pleased to see me. But they didn't mingle in my presence long before they excused themselves and stepped away. I glanced across the room at Mom and she was motioning for me to follow them. I glanced around to see where they were and noticed that they were standing nearby mingling with some friends. Then I glanced over at Mom and shook my head. "No." I wasn't about to tail in behind them. It would be in poor taste and unladylike to follow them around. If they were interested in holding a conversation with me, they would approach me later. I would wait patiently like a real lady.

But within seconds of shaking my head, Mom made her way back over to my side. "Mandy, don't let those two get too far out of your reach this evening."

"Mom what is that supposed to mean?" I asked.

"It means you need to keep in mind how Todd and Brad both have great futures ahead of them," Mom explained.

"The same way you want me to keep in mind that Wesley Gross has a great future ahead of him?" I smiled.

"No, not the same way," Mom mumbled, taking the last sip from the glass of champagne in her hand. "There's a difference between Wesley Jr. and the Chase boys." Mom stopped a server and took a glass of champagne from his silver tray.

She handed him her empty glass and turned to me as she sipped the champagne. "Now, refresh my memory. What was I about to tell you?"

"You said there's a difference between…"

She finished the sentence. "Yes, a significant difference between Wesley Jr. and the Chase boys."

"We all are different, but how can there be a significant difference between Wesley, Brad and Todd? They are all rich and good looking with great futures ahead of them," I pointed out.

"Yes, that's true, but the significant difference is that Wesley Gross, Jr. is not the object of your affection."

"Mom, what are you saying?"

"I'm saying I finally have somewhat of a clue."

"You have somewhat of a clue about what?" I asked.

"I used to be your age Mandy, and it just dawned on me that you are quite taken with those Chase boys." She touched my nose in a playful way. "You like one of them, but I'm not sure which one." She smiled. "But before this evening is over, I'll probably know. Todd or Brad, either would suit me. After all, they both just graduated from college this month." She held up one finger to another passing waiter.

"No more champagne for me. I'll take a glass of ginger ale." She looked at me. "Do you want anything, dear?"

"I'll take a glass of ginger ale with lime juice." I nodded.

"Lime juice in ginger ale, I haven't tried that," Mom said laughingly and continued about the Chase boys. "Did I tell you that they are both working in the family business?"

"I'm not surprise, Mom." I smiled. "Born in money, work in money," I teased.

"They are both vice presidents of the downtown branch," Mom relayed kindly as the waiter handed her a glass of ginger ale and passed me a glass of ginger ale with a slice of lime. Mom took a quick sip from her drink and continued. "Those young men are both well-mannered and polite, not to mention such fine-looking young men; and it doesn't hurt that they are both filthy rich just like the rest of the Chases." Mom took another sip from her glass, looking toward Todd and Brad.

"Mom, you don't have to convince me how wonderful they are. I'm sure you can tell that I think they are both wonderful."

"Well, that's good to hear because only the best young man will do for my daughter." Mom kept smiling. "Those Chase boys are the best around."

I stood there listening to Mom, but what she didn't know was that I was carrying a torch for Brad. A torch that was lit during high school and years later had not dimmed its flame. High school seemed like another life time ago, but that first kiss from Brad was still on my lips and in my heart. I had loved him deeply back then, yet he and I had never gone on one single real date. He had never asked me out or visited me at Mandy Manor. We only socialized and hung out together on the school grounds.

"Mandy, time has served you well. You look just as beautiful as the last time I saw you," Brad stepped up and tapped my shoulder. "It's really good to see you here."

"Thank you, it's really good to see you too; and you look strikingly handsome yourself," I said, smiling up at him.

He smiled and winked at me. "We are getting off to a good start. I do believe. Do you care to join me at that table?" He pointed to the table just a few feet away.

Smiling and feeling anxious, I said quickly, "I would love to." I headed toward the little round table that seated two and he followed me.

We took a seat at the little round table that was draped with a white linen cloth with a dim lit candle in the center of it. Sitting at a table alone with him was just what I had hoped for. But after graduation and moving away to college, I always wondered what I would say to Brad if we were to ever meet face to face again. Now I was in his presence and all the things I thought I would say to him seemed lost to me. I had loved him for so long and so deeply, but his feelings had never appeared to be in that special way what my feelings were for him. It suddenly made me feel very vulnerable and very happy that his presence still brought such happiness to my heart.

After we were seated for a few minutes, just long enough to get comfortable in our seats, Brad stood from his seat, took the candle that sat in the middle of the little table and placed it on another near by table. And after he was seated back at the table, he leaned forward with both elbows, holding his chin in his hands. "Mandy, it's really great to see you here. I know I already said that, but I can't help for repeating myself. I just want to look at you for a moment. I can't get over how lovely you look tonight."

"Compared to my high school days?" I teased.

He held up both arms. "No that's not what I meant. You were just as lovely back then, but now even more." He glanced about the room and spotted my mother. "Do you and your mother plan to stay here at the resort for the entire summer?"

I looked in his eyes and nodded. "Yes, that would be so, just as always. What about you? Are you here for the summer as well?"

He shook his head while tapping his right hand on the table. "I wish I could answer yes to your question, especially since you'll be here," he said with warmth in his voice. "But I'm a working man now and duty calls. I'll only be hanging out here for a couple weeks." He stared deeply into my eyes as he spoke; and what could have been wishful thinking on my part seemed like glitters of warmth and desire in his eyes for me. "And I'm hoping we can hook up and get reacquainted with each other during some of that time. That is, if you would like to get together some time."

I nodded, smiling with my eyes glued to his. "I would love too."

"You would love too," he repeated with a small smile. "That's a great start."

I nodded. "I think it's a great start too."

"And to think I almost declined when Mom booked our suites this year. With my new position and all, I wasn't sure if I wanted to take the time off." He winked. "This is one time I'm glad I allowed my mother to twist my arm, as you can see how delighted I am that we ran into each other here."

"Me too, Brad. It's been three years, you know."

"Three years, really; I guess it has." He nodded. "Where did the time go? Sitting here with you, it seems like yesterday. You are just as gorgeous as if no time at all has gone by." He touched his chest and pointed to me. "Just can't believe it's been that long since we last saw each other."

"It was during that New Year's Eve party that you, Todd and Molly threw at your house. Your parents were out of town and you guys threw this big bash and invited whoever wanted to show up. That party was the last time, remember?"

"How could I ever forget that silly party?" He smiled with a serious warm look in his eyes. "You were the best memory from that evening. That's for sure."

Mentioning the past caused my heart to race faster than what it was already pounding from just being in Brad's presence.

"I'm glad you remember that night, Brad."

He smiled and winked at me. "Like I said, how could I forget? We were just kids at the time, but being alone with you in my room was the highlight of that evening. I enjoyed our time together all those years ago," he assured me.

I nodded. "Yes, it was fun." I glanced down toward the carpet in deep thought about how I had such a huge crush on him back then.

He reached across the table and touched my hand to get my attention. "Where did you go?" He asked, teasingly. "Do you like the music the band is playing?"

"Sure, I think it's great."

"I thought you would say that. I like it too." He stood up and reached out his hand to me. "May I have this dance?"

"Sure, I would love to dance." I stood and placed my hand in his as he led me toward the dance floor.

"I might be a little rusty on the dance floor. It's been awhile," he whispered.

"For me too, but I thought you would never ask," I said, teasingly."

Brad held me tenderly close on that crowded dance floor as we danced to live band performance of Whitney Houston's song, I'll Always Love You. It felt as natural as breathing to be in his arms close enough to feel his heartbeat.

"Mandy, having you in my arms like this feels right. If only my brain had been screwed on right back in high school I wouldn't have allowed you to slip between my fingers. I was too full of myself to see what a treasure I had in front of me. I hope tonight will be a second chance for us. Maybe we can start over," he said in a whisper against my hair as I felt light as a feather in his arms.

"Start what over?" I asked.

"Start over what never really got off the ground when we were in high school," he whispered against my hair. "I don't plan to let you get away again. What do you think? Would you like to start over? It would make me pretty happy if you said yes, although, if you need to think about it I can be patient for someone like you."

My heart was in my throat listening to Brad, but something inside of me froze up with anxiousness. And although the dance floor was slightly crowded with other couples bumping up against us, it felt wonderful to be in Brad's arms as he held me close and we danced to the soft music of the band playing. However, after the second dance with him, I decided I was too emotionally attached to him. I didn't know if he was still stuck on himself and too much of a playboy as back in high school. He had mentioned that he wanted to start over, but I didn't want to wear my heart on my sleeve for him as I had years before. I was older and wiser and didn't want to repeat the same mistake, and his brother, Todd was quickly growing in my thoughts as the safer choice for me to hang out with. Therefore, when the music stopped I was thinking in the back of my mind how would I walk away from him. I didn't want to walk away but I needed to walk away just to catch my breath. I didn't want him to know how magically his presence still affected me.

And as we stood at the edge of the dance floor, he looked at me and smiled.

"I noticed you didn't answer my question about the two of us starting over and getting reacquainted. Do you want to?" He gave me a serious stare.

"What does starting over and getting reacquainted mean in your book, Brad?"

"Mandy, what do you mean what does it mean?" He smiled and touched the side of my face. "It means I'm into you and would like to hang out with you more."

"Hang out with me?" I asked, unclear about what he meant by hanging out.

"Yes, hang out; as in spend some time together while we're both here at the resort," he said casually and held up one finger. "I'm going to grab a glass of red wine, what can I get you? What was that drink you had at the table? I'll get you a fresh one."

"That was just ginger ale," I answered.

"Would you like another one?" he asked.

"No, I'll take a glass of red wine, thanks," I said, smiling.

"Okay, wait right here. Two glasses of red wine coming up," he said and headed toward the bar. He glanced over his shoulder, smiling. "Should you be drinking?" He made a fist with his hand, held his head back and placed the fist against his mouth. "Are you legal now?"

"Close enough." I smiled back at him.

I watched his back as he walked away. He was gorgeous and made my heart race, but I couldn't help but think back to our high school days. He had given me hope and made me think he wanted to date me back then, but he never followed through on going steady or spending any time outside of school time with me. Walks together on the school grounds didn't count; either lunch together in the school cafeteria. The only time we spent together that counted as somewhat of a real date was the night of the New Year Eve's party when we were alone together in his bedroom. That night we kissed for the first and only time; and we had a long talk that evening that made me feel so close to him; and he seemed to understand me. However, spending that time alone in his room talking and all the headway I thought we had made toward a real courtship went nowhere. Even though, he had asked for my phone number that I gave him excitedly, he never called and asked me out after that night. He wasn't interested in me at that time and no matter how charming he seemed now, all grown up wanting to start over; he was probably still not interested in me in the way I wanted him to be.

Therefore, while I waited for Brad to return with the drinks, my negative thoughts and theories got the better of me and threw many red flags flashing in my brain and they all read: stay away from Brad. Nevermind the fact that we were both grown up now and I actually had no idea of his true feelings — but the thought of him not being interested was too painful to bear. I tried to collect myself, glancing about the room when I spotted his brother, Todd. He was looking in my direction and he smiled at me. I smiled back and suddenly I saw him with new eyes. Looking at him now, somehow he seemed friendly and safe. His presence didn't fan the flames in my heart as Brad. His presence seemed calming and at ease. But as I glanced back and forth at him from a distance, he was busy talking to a group of people, but he kept looking back and forth at me as I looked back and forth at him. He was quite handsome as well, but he didn't set my heart on fire as Brad.

Then as I stood there with my thoughts, a swift scent of expensive cologne grabbed my attention when Brad stepped up with two drinks in his hand. He placed the drinks on a nearby empty table and said, "Would you like to sit here or back at the other table?"

I shook my head. "Not right now." I stared toward the side entrance.

His eyes followed my stare and he quickly said. "How about a walk in the moonlight, Mandy?" he asked. "Would you like to get out of here for awhile and take a short walk? It's a perfect night for it." He smiled.

My heart wanted to say yes. I wanted to be alone with him more than anything, but my words said something different. "It's a perfect night for it, but maybe we should stay inside."

"Let's take that walk. The weather couldn't be nicer," he insisted.

I shook my head, looking down toward the floor. "I think I'll pass."

"Okay, sure, be like that," he teased. "Besides, walking in the moonlight with a pretty girl like you would be fun, but just standing here, spending time with you anywhere is just fine with me." He gathered our drinks from the little table and handed me mine. Then he pointed toward our little table in the corner. "Would you like to take our drinks back over to that table?"

I took a sip of the wine, holding it with both hands. I knew I had to find the courage to say no and distant myself from his company. "I think I would rather just stand here."

"Stand here at the edge of the dance floor?" he asked, staring me in the eyes. "Is that a brush off?" He smiled lightly, holding out both arms. "What happened? I thought we were having a good time. Was it something I said? I'm sorry if I offended you in some way. Tell me, what's up, so I can fix it," he said in a sincere voice.

"You didn't do anything. Don't even think that. You didn't offend me, Brad. It's nothing like that," I assured him. My heart was crushed that he thought so.

"If it's nothing like that, can you tell me what's going on? Because it's not my imagination that something has changed between before I stepped away for the drinks and now."

My nerves tightened and I couldn't tell him the truth that I was still carrying a torch for him and that I was too afraid to spend time with him in fear of his rejection. "Brad, it is your imagination because it's nothing really. I just don't want to take a walk or sit at that table."

"At least not with me it seems, but just moments ago it seemed being in my company was fine. I don't know what happened between the time we stop dancing and I walked over to the bar to get our drinks. You say nothing has changed, but you somehow seem distant all of a sudden."

"Brad, just let it go. Everything is okay," I mumbled unconvincingly.

"I'll let it go, but everything is not okay. It's clear you have given me the boot, Mandy. I guess I'm a little confused since we seemed to have been getting along so well. Then just like that, a cold shoulder straight from nowhere." He stared at me with warmth in his clear brown eyes. "It's a bit too warm outside for a cold shoulder, don't you think?" He smiled, lovingly.

My heart raced faster as heat flooded my face. "It's never too warm for a touch of cold weather to rush in," I smiled, teasingly looking in his eyes as I drew away from the soft electrifying touch of his hand on my shoulder.

We stood there gazing lovingly into each other eyes, and I so wanted him to pull me into his arms and kiss me; and then suddenly at that moment Todd walked over and tapped me on the shoulder.

I glanced around and smiled at him.

"Do I finally get a chance to dance with you now?" He asked, smiling.

I nodded and rushed ahead of him toward the dance floor. I didn't want to leave Brad, but deep down I felt it was probably for the best since deep down inside of my fragile heart I felt he wasn't serious about getting to know me. And if he was, I didn't trust myself to give him a chance since I didn't want to take a chance and be rejected again as I was before. I glanced over my shoulder and Brad was standing there with his arms folded, looking toward us shaking his head. He had just gotten drinks for us both and probably thought we would take a seat at the little table and continue our visit and converse with each other, but I completely turned on him after he left to get the drinks, as thoughts of the past haunted me. Unbeknownst to him, when he returned with the glasses of wine, I knew I had to somehow get out of his company. When Todd asked me to dance, it was my chance to walk away from Brad.

"Thanks for the dance," Todd said, as he held me close.

"You are welcomed," I mumbled.

"For a while there, I thought Brad was going to keep you to himself all night, but figured he would give you a break soon or later."

"What did you mean by that?" I asked.

"My brother isn't known to stay in one spot for too long," he said.

"Okay, I'm not sure what that means and how it refers to dancing, but I'll play along. So in other words, you are known for staying in one spot?" I said looking up at him, smiling; and suddenly a flash from the past entertained my thoughts for a brief moment. I saw a snapshot of my father dancing with his new wife, who was his secretary at the time. I tumbled and missed a step from that hurtful thought. After-all, that evening was the beginning of the end for my parents' marriage.

Todd glanced over his shoulder and then a quick glance toward the floor. "Did you trip on something or get stepped on?" He asked.

I shook my head. "I didn't trip on anything or get stepped on. I'm just clumsy and still troubled by some old memories that just will not vanish from my mind," I said, laughingly.

"The dance floor isn't a place for old troubled memories," he teased. "This is where you make new exciting memories. Besides, I don't think you should allow those kinds of thoughts to divert you when you're out trying to have fun." He grinned. "So, this is an order to keep all old memories tucked away until the music stops," he joked.

"I think you are right, Sir. Your order has been accepted." I laughed.

"We are joking here, but on the serious side, any old memory of yours is more blessed than I am," he whispered sincerely against my neck.

"I don't follow," I said.

"They have had a chance to hang out with you a lot longer, of course."

When he said the words "hang out," it made me think of what Brad had said about wanting to hang out with me.

"I guess the saying: "hang out" is a pretty popular line, is it not? Is it something you and your buddies use a lot?" I curiously asked.

"I guess," he said, and then after a long pause he continued. "I think Brad uses it from time to time?" He grinned. "But of course, Brad is no buddy of mine."

"You two seem to be glued to the hip. I thought you were buddies."

"No way, he's just my brother." Then he added, "Plus, I would advise you to take whatever he says with a grain of salt. If you haven't noticed, Casanova is way too conceited and stuck on himself."

"No I haven't noticed that about him."

"Well, it's true. You can be quite sure of it," he assured me.

"You wouldn't say that because you're in competition with your brother, would you?" I laughed.

He smiled. "You got me. That could be my reason for throwing him under the bus and trying to dirty up his reputation a bit."

"Well, I guessed as much, but it doesn't matter. Because spotless reputation or not, I don't think your brother is right for me," I said seriously.

"Mandy, I must say, this evening is turning out better than I thought it would."

"Why is that?"

"For one, you seem to be on the same page with me that Brad isn't right for you." He touched my face with a big smile on his face as if he had just gotten a special toy for Christmas. "And I must admit that it surprises me a lot that you are here spending time with me instead of him. But I'm not complaining."

"And why does it surprise you?"

"Do I have to spell it out?" He teased. "You were into Brad back in high school and you were never into me back then. Actually, you wouldn't even talk to me."

"That's not true," I said as the music stopped.

"I think it is true," Todd smiled, as we walked off the dance.

He followed me outside onto the back lawn near the pool and we both took a seat on a poolside bench. We looked at each other and smiled. It felt soothing to be in the fresh outdoors away from the crowd, the chatter, and the music.

Sitting there beside him; I looked at him and slapped his arm in a playful way. "I get it; are you referring to the day you asked to carry my books and I shook my head and barely said two words to you?"

He stared and smiled as if he didn't follow.

"You just said a minute ago that I didn't talk to you in school."

He nodded. "Yes, I said that."

"Well, I'm just saying, I get it, because you were probably thinking of the time when you asked to carry my book."

"That would be the time?" He grinned.

"I was having an awful day and it wasn't your fault. It was just a couple weeks after that New Year Eve's party and I was still upset with Brad for not calling me as he had promised."

"So, you were upset with my brother, but you took it out on me?" he teased, as he playfully poked me in the side with his elbow.

"It wasn't like that; I just didn't think it would be too cool to let you carry my books when I was hoping Brad would carry them. Besides, how would it have looked for me to talk to you when I was so crazy about Brad and pinning away for him at the time? I thought if Brad saw us talking it would have messed up my chances with him. Not realizing I didn't have to worry about that since Brad really wasn't serious about a relationship with me."

"That's not the impression I got," Todd mumbled.

"What was that?" I asked, in case I had heard him incorrectly.

"Just saying, he seemed into you at that time. Why wouldn't he be?"

"I'm just saying that's how it seemed," I answered. "My memory serves me well and at the time, other than the time we spent together at the New Year's party, he halfway ignored me." I paused as the thought of Brad's disinterest stung my insides. "Besides, I didn't realize he wouldn't be back to school. Of course, he didn't mention that bit of information to me when we were together in his room at the party. So I had limited incorrect knowledge, thinking that the two of you would still be on campus after the holidays, until at least my graduation in June, which would have given me at least six more months to see him at school before you two would ship out to college. I only discovered the day after I ran into you at school that you and Brad had ended your school program and had been accepted into the university."

"Mandy, I ran into you that day because I had dropped by the school to pick up some things I had left in my old locker. Otherwise, you wouldn't have seen me on campus anymore either."

"I'm sorry Brad didn't mention it to you, but we told all our friends that we were not returning after the holidays. I'm surprised he didn't mention it to you at the New Years party. You two seemed quite friendly at the party."

"We were quite friendly at the party, but Brad didn't mention anything about not returning to school after the holidays. In his defense, we were busy talking about other things that seemed pressing at the time."

"Okay, Mandy, I'll tell you about the program that Brad and I attended at Barrington High. As you know, Brad and I officially graduated from school in 2001, two years before you, but we remained on campus in that special financial business program until the end of 2002."

"I guess I never really understood that program the two of you were in because it never came up in conversation when Brad and I talked during that time."

"It was and still is a special financial business program that my father actually spearheaded and organized at Barrington High. It was started in 2000 and it's sponsored by the University of Illinois," Todd explained.

"Your father organized it?"

He nodded. "Yes, Dad started that program back in the hope of turning out top notched financial business candidates for his banks."

"That was thoughtful of your Dad, it doesn't just help his bank it also helps some smart financial minds get an in-depth head start in the financial world."

"That's true, but to qualify the senior needs to have carried a 4.0 throughout their junior and senior year," he explained.

"I see, but it was all over school that you and Brad got straight-A's all through high school." I hit his arm in a playful way. "Good work."

He smiled. "We did at that, and it wasn't tough for us to be accepted, but some struggle to maintain that kind of average."

"Yes, some like me," I laughed. "I'm holding on with a 4.0 but it's not easy."

"It was easier for me than it was for Brad; some of us are smarter than others and I guess I was just born smart," he said conceitedly.

"Okay, great, but aren't you being a bit arrogant right now?" I asked.

He laughed. "I was just kidding."

"I'm glad you are kidding, but what are you kidding about? Are you kidding about being smarter than others or how arrogantly you said it?"

"How arrogantly I said it, of course."

"That's good, but did you enjoy the program?" I asked.

"I especially enjoyed it because it allowed us to remain on campus and close to home at Barrington High under the guidance of a super sharp finance professor."

"What's the benefit of the program? You and Brad could have easily gone to the university and had the same professor teach you there."

"The benefit of the program was and still quite unique because it only accepts six students for the two year term. The professor dedicates all this skills and training to six students instead of a roomful at the university."

"That's a great benefit, for sure," I said.

"Plus, we loved being able to hang out at the high school for another two years while studying and receiving college credits. At the start of 2003 when we started at the university, we walked on campus with two years under our belts. We graduated from the university at the beginning of January of this year."

"Thanks for explaining. I never knew how that program worked."

"Now you do, and to think you found out all that information because I mentioned you didn't talk to me at school."

"You mentioned that, but you know that wasn't true. I just didn't feel comfortable talking to you because of my crush on Brad," I uttered sincerely.

Todd swallowed hard and stared up at the star-filled sky for a moment and then narrowed his eyes at me. "Okay, but things are not that different now."

"What do you mean by that, Todd?"

"I mean, you didn't feel comfortable talking to me back in high school because of your crush on Brad." He stared seriously and rubbed his chin. "Has that changed?"

I stared at him and couldn't believe he had put me on the spot. I pushed back my emotions and lied in his face. "Of course, it has changed. We were just kids at that time." I waved my hand. "Now, could we please change the subject and talk about something else other than my high school crush on your brother?"

"Of course, we can change the subject, consider it dropped." He pointed toward the entrance door. "I'm going to run inside and grab us a glass of punch," he said and caught himself. "Or would you prefer something else?"

"No, punch is fine. I'll wait here," I said looking in his eyes.

"I'll just be a moment," he said looking me warmly in my eyes for a moment, and then he stood to his feet and headed across the grounds toward the entrance.

No more than a couple minutes after he left me sitting there, Brad stepped over to where I was seated. He had a glass of champagne in his hand and offered me a sip.

"You want a sip of this?" He extended the glass to me.

"Sure, why not?" I took a sip and handed the glass back to him. I felt I needed a sip to calm my nerves since I didn't know what I was doing. I was spending time with Todd when I really wanted to spend time with Brad.

He glanced about, probably checking to see if Todd was heading back. "I was waiting for this opportunity to step out here and talk to you again. I was keeping my eyes on you and Todd waiting to see when he was going to give you a chance to breathe and mingle with someone else." He turned his glass up to his mouth and took a swallow of his drink. "I have also been racking my brain trying to figure out what happened to us?" He held out both arms. "We were getting along so well; and then it all went wrong somehow and you got swept away by my brother. I guess I'm losing my touch," he teased.

"Brad, it's not you. It's me. I'm just out of sorts. I don't know what I'm doing," I mumbled in a low voice.

"I can enlighten you on that," he replied. "You are spending time with my brother and not me," he said seriously with a smile.

"That much I know. But I don't know why I'm spending time with Todd and not you," I stumbled with my words.

"I can answer that. My brother doesn't know how to let someone breathe. That's why when I saw Todd walk away; I figured it was my chance to reclaim your company." He turned his drink up to his mouth and took another swallow from his champagne glass and then offered me another sip.

"No thanks, Todd just stepped inside to get us a glass of punch. He'll be back shortly."

"Is that my queue to leave?" Brad asked.

"I didn't say that."

"Okay, let me ask you another question," he said and then paused before he continued. "I really would like to know the answer to this one. Are you spending all this time with Todd because he's like glue and won't leave your side?" He asked teasingly and paused. "Or maybe you're spending time with him because you want to. Is that it, Mandy? Are you hanging out with my brother because you want too?" he asked with a serious tone to his voice.

I didn't answer.

"Does your silence mean you want to spend time with my brother, maybe you prefer his company to mine? "

"I didn't say that, Brad." I looked straight ahead and not at him.

"Okay, then what are you saying? I thought we would get a chance to talk and spend a little more time together before this night is through. What do you say? You want to come back inside with me and dance some more?"

"I can't do that, Todd will be back with drinks and I told him I would wait here."

"What's the big deal, Mandy? We'll see him inside and he'll see we're dancing. Come on." He smiled and reached out his hand for mine.

But just as he did, we noticed Todd headed across the grounds toward us. He spoke as he walked toward us. "I can't leave Mandy alone for five minutes before you-know-who shows up trying to steal another dance from her," Todd said, smiling.

Brad smiled at him. "You got that right. Sounds familiar, doesn't it? You stole her from the dance floor first."

Todd nodded as he handed me a glass of the fruity drink, and then looked at Brad and said, "I did at that, didn't I? Beat you to the punch." He laughed and held up one finger. "But there's one big difference between the two incidents."

"And what's that?" Brad asked.

"Mandy prefers my company to yours," he said jokingly.

"Whatever, I'm out of here," Brad snapped, and then glanced over his shoulder at me as he walked away. He had disappointment in his eyes.

My eyes followed Brad as he strolled across the grounds toward the entrance. My heart sunk into my chest with screaming silent pain. He had expected me to spend more time with him. What he didn't know was how I was trying to push my feelings for him aside. I was trying to pretend they didn't exist so I wouldn't have to face the pain of possible rejection again. I asked myself was it childish to let the fears of the past cloud my judgment about the present; or allow it to act as a hindrance to stand in the way of a possible future together for Brad and I.

"What's eating him?" Todd joked. "I think his ego is bruised because you wouldn't give him one last dance," Todd joked as he took a seat beside me.

I stumbled with my words as they poured out sadder than I meant them to. Discomfort still stabbed at my insides from the whole charade of my childish pretense. "I don't think anything is eating him. I'm sure he's okay."

"He didn't seem okay to me." Todd grinned. "He was anything but okay. I'm telling you, he's ticked that you're spending time with me instead of him."

I smiled and made light of it for Todd's benefit. "I'm sure it's not that."

"Well, what else could it be? He hasn't seen you in three years and just because the two of you hit it off back in high school, he thinks he can pick up where he left off." Todd shook his head. "He needs a reality check and to think again because that ship has sailed, right? You are now with the smarter, best looking brother."

"Someone is being a little conceited and arrogant," I said.

"I'm just kidding around, but I'm not kidding about that ship has sailed."

"Todd, what do you mean by that?" I sipped the punch, holding it with both hands, staring straight ahead.

"I'm just repeating what you told me earlier. You no longer have a crush on Casanova."

"Oh, that. That's true," I lied.

"That's rotten luck for Brad, but not for me. This time I get the girl." He smiled.

My stomach was still tight as a knot. I felt awful about how Brad probably felt and I felt even worse with how Todd was starting to feel. But I was trying to convince myself that I was doing the right thing and making the right choice to start a relationship with Todd instead of Brad.

"Sure, maybe it is rotten luck for Brad, but we need to change the subject and talk about something other than your brother?" I quickly hopped off the bench.

"Of course, I'm all for changing the subject and never bringing up Brad's name if I don't have too." Todd stood up from the bench with his glass of punch in one hand and reached for my hand with the other one.

"Let's take a walk over near those evergreens." He pointed toward the trees.

I nodded. "Okay." But I noticed how I seemed quieter with less excitement since our encounter with Brad.

Walking along the well-lit grounds, we stopped and Todd leaned against a tall tree. We talked a bit more about high school, and then the university, as well as his and my past studies and my present studies. Then he asked.

"Isn't your father the new Mayor of Chicago, Mayor Daniel Clark?"

"Yes, that's my Dad, but you knew that didn't you?"

He nodded. "Yes, I was ninety-nine percent sure that it was your father," Todd said. "I hear he's a no non-sense, straightforward kind of person."

"Straightforward?" I repeated sharply. "Oh, you probably mean my father is straightforward in his professional life?"

"I beg you pardon," Todd smiled. "I don't follow."

I waved a hand. "Nevermind me, I'm just thinking out loud."

"Okay," he smiled as he stepped closer to me. But as he stepped closer, I stepped back. There was a moment of silence. Then he looked me in the eyes. "Don't tell me you're still…?"

"What did you just ask me, if I'm still what?" I asked.

"You know, Mandy."

He caught me off guard with what he was referring to, which was none of his business, and I stumbled with my words, "I beg you pardon?"

"Mandy, I hope I didn't offend you by asking you that."

"Why did you ask?" I slightly snapped.

"Just sort of kidding in a way, but remember that rumor that spread all over about you at Barrington High."

"You still remember that? I can't believe you're bringing that up," I said firmly.

"It was just a joke. I didn't mean to upset you."

"Well, you sort of did. Besides, what took place at Barrington High was a long time ago and I don't want to be reminded of such things that I'm not proud of."

"You are right, Mandy. It was a long time ago, three years ago and we're all grown up now." He paused, looking in my eyes for a second. "So, I take it, your maiden days are long gone by now, are they?"

"You just did it again," I snapped.

"Did what?" He asked.

I glanced up at him, startled that he didn't seem to realize how he was offending me with his loose talk, but then I had to realize it was coming from the champagne that he had drank earlier.

"Nevermind, could we change the subject again?" I looked up at him.

"Of course, whatever you want." He smiled, walked up to me and pulled me close to him, with one hand moving quickly and caressing my waist, and then up and down my back and shoulders, while his mouth covered mine, hard, forceful and demanding. But with the strength of my convictions not to jump into a serious relationship that would most likely end up in divorce, I took both hands and pushed him in the chest away from me.

Todd leaped back. "What's the matter?"

"Do I need to paint you a picture," I snapped. "I thought I needed to worry about Brad getting fresh," I shouted. "Remember, your Casanova brother. The one you said is conceited and stuck on himself. But you are the one who seems conceited and arrogant! You make all of these inappropriate remarks, and then say you are kidding when maybe you are not kidding."

"Mandy, lighten up."

"Why should I. You said Brad is a Casanova, but you seem to be a smooth operator yourself."

"Mandy, what's the big deal. I only wanted to kiss you again."

"The kiss was alright earlier. But earlier was then and this is now; and now I didn't want to kiss you." I walked away from him and hurried across the grounds to the side entrance. I didn't head back to the ballroom, I ran down the hallway to the elevators.

Chapter Twenty

In my hotel room, I took a shower and dropped into bed. I was so disappointed in the evening regarding how I behaved childish and untruthful in an effort to pretend I was interested in Todd and not Brad. If my pretense act didn't upset me enough, I felt just awful and disappointed in how the night ended with Todd's fresh behavior. My brain danced around the thought of how great it was to be home for the summer away from the constant chatter and commotion of the university crowd, but no rest and relaxation would be coming my way since Mom had encouraged me to spend the entire summer with her at the Country Club Inn Resort. Now I would have to spend my summer surrounded by fresh entitled behavior of poor rich boys. It would have been better to just stay on campus all summer than to mingle with people that frequent the Country Club Inn. Men you couldn't trust for a simple dance or a ten minute talk; and apparently my judgment of what a decent man consisted of wasn't on track. Todd had seemed quite polite and a safe choice to help me take my focus off of his brother. Pretending to like one brother when I was really in love with the other wasn't pure on my part, but I was desperately trying to protect my heart by not repeating history with a man who had once tried to get me in his bed and when it didn't work out, promised to call and take me out, but never followed through. In a sudden burst of unhappiness, I cried myself to sleep.

In the light of day the next morning, I figured all chances of finding love with a Chase man was gone completely, but right after breakfast, the soft knock on our hotel door was Todd. I had just dressed and was sitting on the sofa reading a magazine and drifting back off to sleep when I was startled awake by the unexpected three soft knocks on the door. I hopped off the sofa and hurried across the room to answer the door. I thought the knocker was room service to pick up the breakfast trays, but it was Todd standing there with a serious look on his face. He was dressed in a pair of jeans that looked like they had been hand pressed to perfection and a light blue designer shirt that looked priceless.

"Hi Mandy, I apology for knocking on your door at this early hour, but I'm glad you answered instead of your mother."

"Todd, what can I do for you?" I said sandwich between the door and the frame, still thinking about his fresh behavior from last night.

"Listen, Mandy." He held up one finger and smiled. "Please don't shut the door in my face. I know I was a jerk last night and I'm not pleased with myself. I'm here to apology. I couldn't sleep a wink last night for thinking about how I messed things up for us with my stupid behavior." He hit his forehead. "I know better, but I just got caught up in the moment and the booze."

Deep down I was glad he had shown up to apology, and I was letting him off the hook easy because he hadn't been that big of a jerk. I had been too sensitive and touchy because of my emotions toward Brad. The least thing Todd could have said out of the way would have been an excuse for me to have walked away from him last night. "Well, it is quite early for an apology," I mumbled. "Couldn't this have waited until most people are out of bed?"

He glanced at his diamond Rolex watch. "I didn't get you out of bed, did I?"

"Do I look like I just got out of bed? I'm standing here fully dressed," I snapped.

"I see you are dressed," he uttered softly, trying to be polite. "But I asked anyway since you made the comment about giving people a chance to get out of bed."

"I know what I said, but I said it to make a point about how early it is. For goodness sake, it's only ten o'clock in the morning."

"I know it's early, Mandy, and I apology for the timing, but as I said, I didn't get any sleep last night and my day is not going to be worth much until I can clear the air with you." He held out both arms. "So what is it going to be, do you accept my apology?" He smiled.

I nodded. "Of course I do."

He grabbed my hand and held it gently. "Come with me."

"Where are we going?" I glanced over my shoulder but didn't see my mother stirring about.

"It's a beautiful morning. Let's take a walk and talk, so we can erase that conversation we had last night," he suggested with a smile.

I stepped out into the hallway and shut the door behind me. "Okay sure, but I don't think there's anything about last night that we need to erase," I said sincerely, looking in his eyes.

"Is that so, you wouldn't erase a thing?" he asked, as we held hands walking down the hallway toward the elevators.

"That is so, I wouldn't erase any of it," I said.

"I lost sleep over it, but you wouldn't erase any of it?" He stopped in his tracks and stared at me. "But I thought you hated me for my behavior last night."

"No, I enjoyed our time together mostly. It wasn't entirely your fault. I was dealing with a lot of emotions last night regarding my father and some other things; and on top of that, I just thought you came on a tad too strong with me too soon."

"I see, I'll wait a bit longer before I come on too strong with you next time," he teased.

"So you will, will you," I smiled.

"This is so cool, Mandy, that you and I are on the same page again enjoying each other's company. So I'm really forgiven for being too fresh with you last night?"

"Yes, sir, you are."

"Well, just so you know. I realize I had that hard push in the chest coming to me last night. I'm really sorry about the way I behaved and the night couldn't end soon enough for me. I kept waking up staring at my bedside clock, rushing the hours by so I could rush to your room and see if you were still talking to me."

"Well, looks like I am still talking to you," I laughed.

"That's not enough," he said as we stopped and took a seat on one of the many white iron benches spotted about the grounds. The bench was surrounded by an array of colorful flowers a beneath a tall shade tree on the far east corner of the grounds. "I want to be friends, and I mean close friends."

I stared at him and smiled. "Close friends, like best friends?"

"Yes, all the above," he whispered and nodded; and then paused in my eyes for a moment. "But actually, I like you, Mandy. I'm very much attractive to you," he said in a whisper. "And I realized just how much last night when you walked away from me," he said sincerely. "I need someone like you in my life. But what I'm really trying to ask you is would you consider going steady with me?"

I nodded. "Okay, do you mean going steady, as in like best friends hanging out or going steady as a couple?"

"Whatever you are comfortable with of course, but I like the sound of best friends going steady," he said.

I looked at him. His clear eyes had a sincere look to them. My heart pounded with nervousness as I nodded. "Sure, I like the sound of it also. Therefore, of course, we can try," I said, smiling.

He smiled at me. "Are you sure you're okay with dating me?"

"Yes, I'm sure, why wouldn't I be?"

"I'm just asking because of Brad."

"What does your brother have to do with it?"

"Well, he's still into you, and you were into him at one time. You going out with me may not sit too well with him. I will probably constantly get an earful of disapproval from him once he finds out, which is needless hassle if you still want to be with him instead of me." He paused for a moment before he continued. "But if you're sure you want to give us a try, I could care less whether he's on board with our new relationship or not. That's why I'm asking if you're sure."

I was silent for a moment, thinking about how much I really wanted to be with Brad. But pushed those feelings aside and accepted Todd's proposal to go steady.

"Yes, I'm sure I want to give us a try. I would like that, being best friends with you."

"Will you start by having dinner with me tonight?" Todd asked.

"Of course, Mr. Chase, I would love to have dinner with you." I accepted.

"Great, the lady said yes." He smiled. "I was thinking of maybe a quiet dinner in some chic restaurant downtown," he said.

"When you say downtown, do you mean…?"

"Yes, I mean downtown Chicago. Is that okay?"

"Of course, it's okay. It's better than okay. It's perfect. I love dinning downtown. What time should I be ready?"

"What about right now?"

"Right now, it's only ten something in the morning," I said, grinning.

"That I know, but let's head downtown and make a day of it. We can dine at the restaurant of your choice this evening," he promised

"Okay, that's a date. Let's do it," I said excitedly.

Chapter Twenty-One

As that week passed, Todd and I became closer, spending as much time together as we could. Todd was not into the Country Club Inn crowd either, and except for the swimming and the Saturday night formal dances, for the next week we found our fun and entertainment in downtown Chicago. But best of all, our friendship started to grow on me and I found myself looking forward to seeing him. My nervousness with him subsided as I began to feel more at ease in his presence.

We would drive downtown and park near the lakeside and walk around talking about different things. It was easy and comfortable talking to him. Gradually, he told me all about his life and how unhappy he was growing up in a very wealthy, yet unhappy home. It was easy to converse and confide in him since his childhood had been similar to my own; the disappointment in his father for divorcing his mother and remarrying; his irritation with his sometime self-centered mother.

"What would make you happy? What do you want out of life?" I asked him that Thursday evening while we were out to dinner.

"What I want," he confided while we were seated at a private round table in an upscale Barrington restaurant, "Is the love and devotion of a good woman who is not going to seek a divorce at the first sign of trouble; and I want a good career that moves me to the top of the banking industry. I want to one day follow in my father's footsteps. There's plenty of work at the branch that I manage. But my Uncle Brandon, my father's brother, has also offered me a vice president position at another branch."

"Brandon Chase, he's Lynn and Ricky's father?" I asked.

"That's correct." Todd nodded. "Do you know Uncle Brandon and Aunt Pearl?" he asked, smiling.

"Not really, but I have seen them at the bank. I just know of them because I was in class with your cousin."

"Which one," Todd asked.

"I was in class with both, Lynn and Ricky."

"That's right, Lynn and Ricky graduated the same year as you, two years behind Brad and I." He paused, "Actually, Ricky was supposed to have graduated a year after Brad and me, but because of some sickness when he was younger, he missed too many days and repeated the sixth grade. Otherwise he would have graduated in 2002 instead of 2003," he explained.

"How did that happen?" I asked.

"How did what happen?" he asked.

"How did you and Brad graduate the same year? You are one year older than him, right?"

Todd shook his head and smiled. "I'm only nine months older than Brad. And because of how his birthday fell, we started school at the same time."

"Okay, I see." I nodded. "I just wondered about that."

He smiled. "A lot of people do. Some people think we are twins."

"I can see how some would think that. You clearly could pass for twins. But not identical."

He winked. "Are you trying to tell me I'm not as handsome as my little brother?"

"Don't be silly, that thought never crossed my mind."

"Loosen up, I was just kidding, of course. The only thing I'm rattled about is my Uncle Brandon's offer. I might consider it." He nodded.

"It sounds like you are not too sure. Besides, I'm a bit curious as to why you are considering your uncle's bank over your father's, especially since your father's bank will one day be yours anyway."

He smiled. "You have a good point. But someday is not now. That's why I'm sort of on the fence about my Uncle Brandon's offer."

"Is there any particular reason why you're considering his offer, but still hesitant about the decision?" I asked.

"For one, I feel he'll give me more leeway at being in charge than my father will." He paused. "But I also know how Uncle Brandon has a control issue. He needs his hand in everything just like my father. So it really isn't much difference. I'm sure I'll be under his control at that particular branch if I take the position he's offering." He lifted his wine glass and took a sip. "But the upside, Uncle Brandon and I have become closer friends since my father left town."

"Your father left town?"

"Yes, he's living in Springfield with his new wife. I thought you knew that."

"Of course, I do know that. I was caught off guard when you said he left town. But as soon as the words came out of my mouth, it dawned on me that Mr. Chase was no longer living in Barrington. I'm really sorry he moved away, but I'm glad you're close with your Uncle Brandon. It will no doubt help working matters if you take his offer."

"I'm sure it will since Uncle Brandon and I have more of a best friend relationship these days."

"You have a best friend relationship with your Uncle?"

He nodded. "That's what it's turning out to be. We have gotten quite close since my father remarried and moved downstate."

"How often do you, Brad and Molly get the opportunity to see your father?"

"Molly gets to see him all the time, since she moved downstate. She's staying with my father in Springfield."

"I didn't know Molly was in Springfield. Isn't she still in college?"

"Yes, in Springfield. She attends UIS, the University of Illinois in Springfield."

"I see, she attends school there and lives with your father while in college."

"That's true and she also works part-time after classes at one of the branches."

"Is Molly in town? I read Molly was going to spend time here at the resort with you and Brad."

"It was printed that way in that article, but my mother and Molly ended up cancelling at the last minute. That's why Brad and I ended up with two suites and a penthouse at our disposal," he explained. "But back to your question, Brad and I only get a chance to see our father a couple times a month. But to my father's defense, he loves the phone and calling every other day; mostly, to put the pressure on Brad and myself to relocate to Springfield," he laughed.

"He wants you two to move there?"

"Yes, he does, to head some of his branches there."

"How do you feel about relocating to Springfield to manage those branches?"

"I won't make the move and I'm sure Brad would never do it either."

"But Molly is there you just said."

"Yes, she is there, but only because she's attending the university there. She has no real desire to hangout in Springfield and work at those branches. Father knows she's only there until she gets out of school."

"But she is working at one of the branches?"

"Yes, part-time; but believe me; Molly is not planning to live in Springfield after she finishes up at the university. She is seriously dating Justin Gross and I can't see her remaining in Springfield while he is still in this town."

"Wow, they are still together? That's great, I remember she was dating Justin during high school," I said, smiling.

"Yes, those two are still into each other just as much," he assured me.

"But she's in college in Springfield and also working for your father there."

"That is correct, many miles from Michigan State where Justin is attending. Ricky is at Michigan State as well."

"Where's your friend, Kathy, attending school?"

"She's at OSU, Ohio State in Columbus."

"I see, didn't she used to date Ricky?"

"Yes, but they broke up right before we all left for college."

"That's too bad. He was really into her. I guess something went wrong." He lifted his glass of white wine and took a sip.

"Yes, something did," I mumbled, thinking about the incident that broke them up and how I felt somewhat responsible.

"How is your meal?" he asked.

"It's delicious," I lifted my iced-tea and took a sip. "This is the best white fish and roasted potatoes ever," I said, smiling. "How is yours?"

He nodding, smiling as he forked a piece of fish in his mouth. He chewed his food and then lifted his glass of water and took a swallow. "Super tasty," he said. "The food here is always great. This happens to be my father favorite restaurant."

"Your father has good taste in restaurants," I said, smiling.

"That's one of his better traits; and in all honesty, he has many," he said, smiling. "I think his better traits probably overshadow his very controlling side. If not, it's a close tie." He shook his head. "But he can be quite controlling when it comes to work."

"It sounds like your father is extremely demanding and controlling when it comes to work, especially if he just expects you and Brad to just pick up and relocate to Springfield at his demand."

"He wants that, but he knows it's not going to happen." He nodded. "But yes, my father can be quite demanding and controlling." He took his knife and fork and chopped the tomato on his dish in four quarters and then took his fork and placed a quarter in his mouth. "But so can his brother. Listen to this," he laughed. "Uncle Brandon likes to give marriage advice. If he could, he would control when Brad, Ricky, Lynn and I marry. Uncle Brandon thinks none of us should think of marriage until very late in life."

"Why does he give out that kind of advice?"

"Who knows, maybe he felt he should have waited and now want us to do what he felt he should have done," Todd explained. "But Brad and I don't really pay him any attention when it comes to marriage advice since our own father gave us a good example of how a marriage can seem just fine and then suddenly spin out of control toward divorce court."

I nodded, thinking how he had just described my exact thoughts about what happened to my parents' marriage. I thought their marriage was prefect until one day I realized it wasn't.

"Therefore, Uncle Brandon doesn't need to discourage us in that area. Our guards are already up."

Suddenly my mind wasn't on his Uncle Brandon's advice. I wanted to know how he really felt deep down about marriage.

"And you," I asked, "How do you feel about waiting until late in life to marry?"

Todd laughed sharply and stared at me for a moment before he answered as if I had caught him off guard with my question. "It suits me just fine. From what I have seen of it, how my father divorced my mother and now she's bitter; and he's remarried. I think being single is a good fit for me. Marriage seems to cause more headaches than I'm ready for."

I nodded. "I agree with what you are saying. Marriage isn't for me either," I assured him, "I decided a long time ago that I wouldn't take that step."

Todd smiled at me and winked. "Well I hate to be the bearer of bad news."

"What do you mean?" I asked.

"If you think you are going to stay single I'm here to tell you that the odds are against that."

"The odds might be against it, but it's the way I feel," I said seriously.

"I'm sure you feel the way you do with good reason. However, you might as well face the facts that your fate is destined to be the bride of some lucky guy who will one day steal your heart."

"I'm not so sure of that considering my dark thoughts about marriage."

"I'm sure of it. Mandy, do you actually think that someone as gorgeous as you will somehow stroll through life without some fortunate fellow making you his bride?" he stated seriously.

"It could happen." I smiled, looking in his eyes.

"It could happen, yes. But the odds are stacked against it. Believe me; you will end up being some very lucky man's wife."

"You sound so sure of some Prince sweeping me off my feet and luring me away into marriage; do you have any idea who that lucky man will be?" I teased.

"I'm sure it will happen." He narrowed his eyes at me. "But as far as that lucky fellow goes, I have no idea who he will be. But I know what I can tell you."

"What's that?"

"I hope he doesn't steal you away too soon," he smiled.

"No worry of that." I shook my head, lifted my glass and took a sip of iced-tea.

"Okay, if you say so, but I think some lucky fellow will walk you down the aisle even if he has to mesmerize you and put you under a spell," he said, smiling.

"Maybe some lucky lady will mesmerize you and put you under a spell," I said.

"That's not likely."

"Oh, it's not likely for you but it is for me?" I smiled.

He nodded. "For a guy, it's altogether different."

"How is it different?"

"It's quite simple, since the man most likely does the proposing, if he wants to stay single we will."

Chapter Twenty-Two

Spending my summer break with Mom turned out to be my most memorable summer, but it passed with unbelievable speed and before I realized it, August had ended and we were celebrating Labor Day. It was a very busy weekend before Mom and I checked out, the Country Club Inn hotel was crowded with more people than I had ever seen at the resort hotel. Every stall in the parking lot was filled with cars for the Labor Day events and picnics. A dinner dance was scheduled for both Friday and Saturday evenings. The official summer season was closing in the elegant style that the Country Club Inn was known for, and although Mom and I had originally made plans to check out, I had convinced her to stay until the following weekend when I would head back to the university. I didn't have the stomach to go back home to Mandy Manor and wallow in the sad memories of a house without my father. I needed more time to get used to his new wife and his new life away from us. However, to put my father on the backburner of my mind would not be easy, since I woke up the next morning thinking of how we were all together as a family many summers before. But for awhile I was able to take my thoughts off of Dad that Friday morning at nine o'clock when Todd joined Mom and me for breakfast in our suite. After which, he left the resort to met up with his Uncle Brandon in Chicago.

An overwhelming loneliness wrapped around me, which grew as the day faded into evening. Then around seven-thirty with no other plans on my agenda, I reluctantly joined Mom and some of her friends in the dinning room. Dinner with Mom and four of her friends was noisy and boring; and to my surprise her doctor, Claude Horton, was one of the dinner guests. Then a couple hours later while still seated at the table with Mom and her friends having iced-tea to their cocktails, I saw Todd step into the dinning room, tall, tan and smiling, dressed in an expensive black shirt and black slacks, finished off with a stylish silver belt. He was such a good looking man, but I still couldn't seem to shake my feelings for his brother.

Although Mom was engaged in conversations with her friends, she spotted Todd when he stepped into the dinning area. She discreetly touched my hand and motioned me to leave the table to greet him. I excused myself and hopped out of my seat. I was more than ready to leave my mother and her friends. And a moment later, Todd and I were outside. He held my hand and swept me down the beautiful walkway toward the edge of the manicure grounds.

"It's packed in there," Todd smiled, as we took a seat on a bench, "This place is always way too crowded, especially for young people like us who wants to have some privacy away from all those old heads."

"There doesn't seem to be any privacy around this place," I smiled.

"I'm sure we can find some," he whispered. "I couldn't wait to get back here to see you, Mandy." He smiled at me. "And was actually thinking of you the whole time."

"I was thinking of you also; and hoping you would return soon. Before you arrived I was going stir crazy spending time with Mom and her friends," I said, smiling.

"I guess we both missed each other." He grabbed my hand and we stood up from the bench.

We stood facing each other and as we stared at each other for a moment, he searched my face for approval before he pulled me in his arms and brought his face down to kiss me. It was a gentle passionate kiss that lingered longer than I had expected; and although it didn't give me butterflies, it made me feel safe and secure.

When Todd pulled his lips from mine, he stared at me with sincere eyes. "Mandy, as I mentioned, I have been thinking about you all day. I wanted to get back here so I could hold you like this. A lot happened today, too."

"Oh, yes, tell me about your meeting with your uncle. How did it go?"

"It turns out fine. Uncle Brandon was quite impressed with me, of course."

"That's great, right?"

"Yes, it's good, but there's one downside," he said.

"What's the downside?" I asked.

"I'll be leaving the resort on Monday," he announced.

"Why do you have to leave on Monday?"

"After meeting with Uncle Brandon I have decided to take his offer."

"And he needs you to start on Monday?"

"Yes, I'll start on Monday, but the job isn't official. We both agreed it's just a two-week trial and if I decide it's not a good fit, I can resume back at my father's branch where I am now."

"That sounds like a safe bet," I smiled.

"Yes, I think so," he nodded. "But as I said, the downside is leaving the club. He wants me in his office early on Monday to start the two-week trial right away."

"Wow, he wants you there as soon as possible," I mumbled.

"Yes he does, because if it doesn't work out with me, he'll need to recruit someone from the outside to fill the position."

I tried not to show it but with Todd announcement that he would be leaving the resort on Monday weighed strongly on me. And although Mom and I would be leaving the following weekend, I still couldn't shake the sudden heaviness against my heart that he was leaving. It all stemmed back to that awful feeling that came over me when my father left home.

"I hope you know that I'm not thrilled about leaving so early on Monday or leaving here at all." He winked at me in a warm way. "It's been such a splendid summer, but I guess you'll be busy anyway."

"What do you mean I'll be busy anyway?"

"Well, won't you be busy getting ready to head back to the university?"

I was suddenly aware of his soft hand holding on to mine. "You're right; I will be busy getting my things together to head back to college."

"I have an idea." He grinned at me. "Since this is our last weekend together for awhile, couldn't we celebrate and have a late snack to ourselves? I have the keys to our penthouse, Brad won't be using it. He used it earlier in the day, but he has a couple friends in town and they are rooming in the city for the weekend; Brad is going downtown to spend the evening there with his friends. We could sneak off to our castle in the sky right around seven and spend the rest of the evening there. How does that sound? Are you up for spending some time in our penthouse?"

"Yes, I'm up for it. That sounds like fun," I said, smiling.

"That's what I thought." Todd smiled and kissed me again.

Now standing right outside the entrance of the Country Club Inn lobby, Todd kissed me in a soft passionate way. But I found myself comparing his kiss to Brad's. And had decided that no other man's kiss would ever measure up to Brad's and I would just have to accept my fate of not being with the man I truly wanted to be with.

After the kiss, we stepped inside the lobby and smiled at each other for a moment before Todd headed down the hallway in one direction toward his suite and I headed in another different. I was smiling as I headed toward the elevator, thinking of my plans with Todd. We had made arrangements to meet downstairs in the lobby at ten-thirty and head to his penthouse. But my heart raced when I spotted Brad at the other end of the hallway heading in my direction. I was always too emotional in his presence and didn't want him to notice. And as I walked down the long hallway toward the elevator, I had almost reached the elevator when Brad met up with me. He looked spectacular dressed in a silk burgundy shirt and neat black slacks and black shoes that shined from the overhead crystal light. I wanted to run into his arms and pour out my feelings. But something inside of me wouldn't let me share my true feelings with him. I was more afraid of how his rejection would crush me than I was of anything else I could imagine. He was holding a glass of champagne in one hand, which didn't seem to be his only drink of the evening. He appeared a little unsteady. His face seemed slightly flushed. And when we met up, he reached for my hand and held it gently.

"Hi Mandy, I just saw you with Todd. The two of you seemed quite cozy," he said in a playful way, "I saw the two of you walking around outside and I guess the joke is on me. I was so full of myself to think it was me you wanted. But from the looks of things it's my brother you are into." He paused with a warm glow in his eyes. "How could I have been so off base about that? How could I have misread your feelings? Anyway, when I saw Todd leave you in the lobby and you both headed in opposite directions I came around the other way so I could meet up with you. I wanted a goodnight kiss too."

The fact that he was being fresh in a rude manner surprised me, but I realized he had had too much champagne so I managed a smile. "Not this evening, Brad," I said. "It's clear that you have had too much to drink."

His arms tightened around me, but his tone was soft. "One kiss can't hurt anything, can it?"

I looked in his eyes lost for words because all my strength was draining away since I wanted him desperately. Although whatever I felt for him, I pushed it out of my mind. I had decided to be with his brother and not him. So, no way was I going to surrender a kiss to him, especially in his somewhat drunken state. But before I could say another word, I saw Todd's hand pushed Brad's shoulder. Brad was caught by surprise and slightly stumbled back.

The surprise shovel seemed to sober Brad up as he shook his head and straightened his clothes. "Hey, watch it. Shovel me again and I might just shovel you back. Don't be so smothering. Why are you so bent out of shape anyway?" Brad held up both arms. "This is a free country isn't it?" Brad asked with a sharp edge to his voice. "I was just asking Mandy a question, which she didn't answer I might add."

"It didn't look like that from where I was standing. So just keep your hands to yourself, okay; and go drink some coffee," Todd snapped. "Walking around here with a glass of champagne in your hand is bad for business."

"You think some of the customers will care that the vice president had one too many glasses of champagne, trying to have a little fun?" Brad grinned.

"Who knows, they might," Todd stressed, trying to control his emotions in my presence.

Brad nodded. "Yes, I agree that they might. You could be on to something."

"But on the other hand, I seriously doubt if any of our customers are actually rooming here at this resort?" Todd said arrogantly.

"Don't be so arrogant, brother of mine. Just because you have deep pockets doesn't mean others don't," Brad remarked.

Todd seemed quite upset with Brad and didn't wait to listen to anything else that he was saying. He grabbed me by hand almost pulling me, walking quickly down the hallway toward the elevators.

"Sure, go on and walk away but you know I'm right," Brad hollered toward us. "I'm also right about Mandy."

Todd and I exchanged looks as he continued.

"Mandy, you can't hide from your feelings," Brad said calmly. "I could see it in your eyes, young lady. You might be with my brother, but you have feelings for me."

Brad's words faded away as Todd and I quickly stepped inside the elevator and the doors shut. We were both quiet and shaken as Todd punched the 30th floor button so hard as if he would push it out of its socket. However, he didn't justify Brad's words by asking me if he was right. He stepped off the elevator with me and walked me to my suite 3005. He kissed me on the cheek, and said, "Let's do a rain check on that late snack. Suddenly my appetite has vanished."

"I know the feeling. My appetite is dead as well," I mumbled.

He backed away from the door, waved me goodbye and then he was gone. I stood at the door for a moment shaking with confusion. With nervous fingers, I opened the door and rushed inside to find Mom waiting in the middle of the room with an upset look on her face.

"Mandy, I was looking for you," she said quickly, and there was no mistaking the disturbance in her voice. "I dialed your cell and heard it ringing in your room. So I couldn't reach you by phone."

"Mom, I'm sorry you couldn't reach me, what's the matter?"

"Everything since your father and his wife has a room here."

I grabbed my face with both hands. "When you say here, do you mean he knocked on our suite door?"

"That would be correct." Mom shook her head in discuss. "Daniel has some nerve to show up here and spoil our retreat together. I'm sure his excuse is that he wanted to see you before you head back to the university, but why during our retreat? He can visit you at school, if he would. Anyway, he was here earlier looking for you."

"Did he drop by to see me alone, or was Doris with him?"

Mom swallowed hard. "It surprised me, the nerve of them, but actually your father and Doris both dropped by."

"I can't believe he had the nerve to bring that woman to our room."

"It was hard to take and I know it's hurtful for you to hear. But we have to keep in mind that she is his wife now, sweetheart," Mom reminded me.

I drew a deep breath and sort of crumpled onto the sofa. "I'm not interested in seeing Dad and his new wife. I'm just not ready. I miss him, but it would be awkward and I wouldn't know what to say to them," I mumbled sadly. "I hope he doesn't come back this evening looking for me. I'm just not ready to see him."

"I'm sure he won't be back this late in the evening to disturb your rest."

"I don't plan to hop in bed right away. I plan to stay up for awhile, but I still don't want to visit with Dad and his new wife."

Mom smiled and suddenly seemed less troubled as she patted my shoulder. "I understand, sweetheart. He can not force you to see him and that lady," Mom said, probably pleased that my days of blindly worshipping my father had long ceased. Plus, I was twenty and her period of full custody and guardianship had ended. But yet I hadn't forgiven Dad and had chosen to stay on with her. And I had no intentions of ever living with my father and Doris.

I stood up and gave Mom a hug. She kissed me on the cheek and then turned and headed back to her room. I watched her back as she watched away. I felt empathy for her, knowing how much she still loved my father. But I took a deep breath and collected myself of the entire evening: running into Brad and then finding out that my father had visited while I was out. It was a lot to take in and I needed someone to talk to other than my mother and felt it was a perfect time to sit back and give Kathy a call. I rushed in my room, grabbed my cell phone and plopped back down on the sofa in the sitting room. After I was comfortable with both feet beneath me on the sofa,

I picked up the remote from the coffee table and clicked on the TV to a movie channel. Some movie was already in progress but it didn't matter. I just need the distraction to take my mind off of other things. I took the remote and lowered the volume and then dialed Kathy's cell number. She picked up on the first ring.

"Hey stranger, were you waiting for my call?" I laughed.

"I was sort of hoping to get a call from you," Kathy admitted. "But frankly I didn't think you would be calling me while you and your Mom are retreating at the Country Club Inn. How is it going?" She asked.

"We are having a good time. But I have some news for you."

"Some news, like in romantic news I hope," Kathy laughed through the receiver.

"Yes, it is romantic news and you won't believe who I met here and now dating."

"You sound pretty excited so it must be Brad."

"No, it's not Brad. It's Todd."

"Todd Chase, what for? He's super fine but he's not who you always daydreamed about at school. It was always Brad. So you need to explain yourself quick to make sense of this new development. Otherwise, I'll never buy that you're suddenly into Todd now and not Brad."

"You're right. I'm still just as into Brad. But I'm dating his brother because of my silly fear of being hurt by him. I have somehow convinced myself that I'll be better off and happier with Todd. I can't believe I have settled for Todd when I'm really in love with Brad."

"You say you can't believe it. I know I can't believe it. But yet, you seem okay to go through with this pretending. I know it's all about high school and how he rejected you back then. You are afraid of that same kind of rejection that you dealt with during our high school days when Brad didn't return your affection."

"That's true. I wouldn't be okay with going out with his brother if Brad would have shown me the slightest interest back then. I know we are all grown up now, but it still hurts that I carried a torch for him all through high school and he showed minimum interest. I have loved him for so many years and I have hoped upon hope that he and I would find our way to each other." I paused to collect my emotions. "Here I am pouting because we are not together; and on top of that I'm now dating his brother. Therefore, I know it's my fault and not his that I chose to be with Todd and not him. When we met here after all those years since high school, I could have given us a chance and taken the leap with Brad even with my heart at stake. But I was too afraid to give the two of us a chance and that's the bottom line to why I'm now dating Todd. The both of them were trying for my attention and I chose Todd to protect my heart from the man I really wanted to be with. But like I said, maybe I should have given Brad and myself a chance."

"Yes, you should have. Because if you ask me. No matter how you date Todd and try to push Brad out of your mind and out of your heart, at the end of each day, Brad will still be the one in your heart. The way you feel about that guy is not about to die just because you go out with his brother. Try if you may to push him out of your system, but I know and you know that your happiness will never be complete without Brad Chase being a part of your life."

The ringing of the hotel phone startled me and interrupted my phone conversation to Kathy. "The other phone is ringing. We'll talk later." I ended my call to Kathy and placed my cell phone on the sofa beside me; picked up the remote from my lap, clicked off the television and grabbed the phone sitting on the table at the end of the sofa.

Todd's manly voice came through the receiver strong and polite, "Mandy, I'm glad you answered. What are you doing right now?"

"I just got off the phone with Kathy and I'm about fifteen minutes into a movie, why?"

"Well, I was just thinking and it's not dreadfully late," he said cautiously.

"No it's not dreadfully late, but it's getting there," I reminded him.

"I agree that it is getting late, but it's not even the bewitching hour yet."

"Why Todd, what did you have in mind?"

"I need to see your beautiful face again, I'm sort of bombed out that we didn't get to meet and have that late snack together as we had planned. So what about sneaking out to the pool house? I promise we won't run into Brad again. For your information, he has retired for the evening. He was in no shape to head downtown, so he's in the penthouse. I just saw him hop in bed. Besides, I want you all to myself for awhile and I think we need to discuss the non sense he was saying earlier."

"Yes, I would love to be alone with you too," I assured him. "And I agree that we do need to talk about what Brad said earlier."

I hung up the phone, slipped into my shoes and threw on a sweater. Then grabbed my purse and phone, and with a quick comb through my hair and a bit of press powder on my face, I hesitated in the bathroom mirror on whether I should knock on Mom's door and let her know I was leaving the room. I glanced at my watch and it was almost eleven. I chose not to disturb her and eased out of the suite.

When I made it outside, Todd was standing outside of the pool house with a blue blanket in his left arm. When he spotted me headed toward him, he stretched the pool house door open and held it open until I reached him and then we both stepped inside together. The moment we were inside the cozy little pool house, Todd quickly took the blanket he was carrying and spread it out on the floor. After he was done he looked at me and smiled, pointing both arms toward the blanket.

"Please be seated," he said, smiling.

We both dropped down to the floor and sat on the blanket at the same time. He looked at me smiling. "Are you cozy and comfortable and glad to be alone with me?" Todd asked, teasingly as we sat nervously looking at each other. "Sneaking out here at this late hour is exciting and cool, don't you think?"

"Yes it's exciting and cool," I agreed, but the coolness had faded out of our relationship. Things could only be cool when they were carefree and I had a feeling that things had changed and Todd cared more than I wanted him too, which meant I would have to face how I really felt about him.

Deep in thought with my mind racing, I fell back on the blanket and stared up at the ceiling, and then looked toward the wall and started to count the tiny blue flowers on the wallpaper. Todd was watching me, as he leaned on his elbow. I turned to him and flashed him a smile and could see deep emotion in his eyes. Something about the expression on his face touched me and held me motionless. Then quickly he leaned over and brought his mouth down on mine and kissed me demanding with overwhelming passionate as if he had never kissed me before. I didn't push him away.

My arms closed around his back, holding him tight. All the intense love I thought I felt for him flooded throughout me. Then slowly Todd pulled away from my lips and smiled at me.

"I know we haven't been out here that long, and I could stay out here with you for hours, but I'm thinking we should get you back to your hotel suite."

"Why are you thinking that?"

"Don't you hear that thunder? I think a storm is coming," he said with an anxious seriousness to his voice.

"What difference does it make? I think this pool house is good shelter from a storm. Besides, we just got out here," I said.

He nodded. "I like the way you think. We did just get here," he said. "But are you sure you want to stay all night with me in this pool house?" He touched my face.

"Maybe I do."

"Maybe isn't a yes," he said. "I only want you to stay if you are sure."

"Why is affirmative so important?"

"It's important, Mandy, because I have fallen in love with you."

I looked at him, stunned by his confession. For a moment I couldn't speak and then I nodded. "Yes, I'm sure, Todd," I said.

"Yes, you are sure, what?" he asked.

"I'm sure that I would like to stay out here with you." I touched his face. "I have wonderful feelings for you also. They are so unique. It must be love."

Immediately, Todd pulled me in his arms again. His voice was soft and romantic. He reached out and touched my face with deep emotions showing in his eyes. It was clear he had developed deep feelings for me. He nodded and smiled at me. "Okay, the girl has spoken. It must be love," he said, placed one finger on my lips and then touched his chest. "From your lips to my heart," he said in a whisper, looking longingly in my eyes. "Mandy, I hope you really mean that," he said, smiling with a serious look in his eyes. "Only say you love me if you mean it; and not because I just said it to you."

"I'm not saying it because you just said it to me. What I feel for you must be love. It feels too wonderful to be anything else."

"It warms my heart to hear you say that. But you're sure you're not just saying it because you feel the need to be polite and say it back to me."

"I'm not just being polite. I meant what I just said; I have wonderful feelings for you," I assured him.

He pressed his lips tenderly against mine and gave me a quick kiss. "Okay, beautiful lady, if you're certain that's good enough for me," he whispered. "But are you also certain about this step we are about to take?" he asked seriously.

"Yes, I'm sure, but I always pictured it different in my mind," I paused and then continued. "I know we care for each other and staying the night together is okay because of how we feel about each other. But if only we were married to each other, I would probably feel more secure about it," I mumbled breathless.

"Mandy, we are in love with each other and that makes it special. We love each other now, tonight, this hour. It's real and honest," he said lovingly.

"You are right; only this hour is our," I said, as I lifted my lips to his, and words were lost as he urgently covered my lips in a passionate kiss. Then he pulled away and looked at me lovingly for a long moment. "Mandy, I'm sure you pictured your first time differently and not on the floor of some pool house," he said heartfelt and paused. "Believe me, I want you to stay the night out here with me, but nothing more will happen this evening. Our special time will come and it will feel right for you when it does; and it won't be on the floor of some pool house."

Peacefully we slept on the thick blue carpet floor of the pool house but I was constant awakened by the loud thunder and lightning and the heavy down pour against the windows. It frightened me a bit and I snuggled closer to Todd. He held me close and made me feel safe. But laying awake beside him on the floor as we listened to the storm, we had no words. We had kissed passionately and confessed our feelings for each other. But on this stormy night, I accepted the fact that I couldn't make Brad love me, but I could accept Todd's love. The past would be left in the past and the fact that Todd and I had confessed that we cared for each other meant it would be no going back. Todd and I had found each other.

Chapter Twenty-Three

In the fall of 2007, at age twenty-two, I received my Bachelor of Science Nursing degree from Yale University. And Kathy received her Bachelor of Science Nursing degree from Ohio State University. That same fall, Kathy and I were hired as registered nurses at Barrington Medical Clinic. Then surprisingly within one year, my position was upgraded to supervisor where I was in charge of a total of ten other nurses. I was very content with my job, but my social life was still in chaos. Todd and I were still dating, but I wasn't sure of my feelings for him. I knew I cared a lot but wasn't sure if I cared enough to build a future with him. Then he decided for me when he proposed to me at the end of 2009. But by the end of three Thanksgivings later he was still waiting for me to decide on a wedding date.

He seemed content, but something in his eyes told me that he wasn't. He had just had Thanksgiving dinner with me and Mom at Mandy Manor. Mom had finished her meal and left the dinning room. Todd and I were still seated at the dinner table finishing up our desserts when he reached out and touched my hand.

"Thanks for inviting me over for such a nice meal this evening," he said, smiling at me. "And some of my favorites were on the menu. Could this be that special occasion I have waited for?" He gave me a long loving stare as he forked a piece of apple pie into his mouth.

I replied awkwardly. "Todd, can I just invite you over for Thanksgiving dinner without it being a special occasion? Why do you need an explanation for every little thing?" I replied with a heated edge.

"Mandy, lighten up. What's the attitude about?"

"It's about how you expect every occasion to be an occasion for me to decide on a wedding date. When the time is right, I'll know it."

He nodded. "I'm not sure that time will ever come."

"What do you mean by that?" I snapped.

"I just don't think you'll ever think the time is right," he admitted.

"I didn't say that. I just want you to stop pressuring me and expecting me to pick a wedding date when I'm not ready."

"It seems to me when you accepted my ring three years ago that you should not have accepted it if you wasn't ready to be my wife," he said firmly.

"People have long engagement all the time," I mumbled.

"Mandy, I know that, but I think three years is pushing it. If you have changed your mind and no longer want to marry me, you need to let me know," he stressed.

I stared at Todd and shook my head. "I'm not having this conversation."

"What do you mean you're not having this conversation?" he said with a heated edge to his voice. "Has it come to this? I can't even ask you a simple question anymore? You draw an attitude and you don't want to talk about it!" He wiped his mouth and threw the cloth napkin on top of his dish of half eaten apple pie and sprung from the kitchen table, and then the chair he was seated in fell over from his abrupt stand and made a loud slamming noise against the hardwood floor.

I frowned at Todd with a confused look on my face. "What's your problem, Todd?" I asked, still seated, poking my fork in my uneaten slice of pie.

Todd had his back to me with both hands on his head, staring up at the ceiling. "Mandy, do you really need to ask me that question? I'm sure you already know that my problem is you," he said with his back still toward me.

My mouth fell open. "I'm the problem? What an insult."

"It's not meant as an insult." He turned toward me with sad eyes. "But seriously, just think about it for a moment."

"Think about what? What are you getting at?"

"Mandy, I'm not trying to insult you or be disrespectful or hurtful, but what I'm trying to say needs to be said."

I quickly snapped. "And what you're trying to say is that I'm the problem?"

"You are the problem, Mandy, but let me explain why."

I held up both arms. "Okay, you have the floor. Enlighten me on why I'm the problem. I know it has to do with the fact that I'm not ready to set a wedding date."

"Yes, that too; but for starters, Mandy, you are not happy in this relationship and never has been," he said sadly, lifting the chair from the floor. "Yes, in the beginning you were somewhat happy, but never really happy. Your resentment has continued to grow over the years." He held up both arms. "And now you are just miserable."

"How do you know how I feel? How dare you get inside of my head and try to tell me how I feel? You don't know my mind," I protested.

"I think I do know how you feel, and you know I'm right, Mandy. Why not admit it?" he stressed as if the thought tore at his heart.

"Admit what, that I'm not happy in this relationship just because you say I'm not happy?"

"Mandy, please, drop the attitude. I think I deserve the truth from you. I just want the truth about your feelings for me and this relationship. It's plain as day to me that this relationship is headed nowhere and your feelings are lacking in my department. But I'm not totally blaming you for our situation."

"So, if you're not totally blaming me, who else are you blaming?"

"I'm also blaming myself. After all, it's partly my fault just as it is yours."

"Please enlighten me to your revelation," I suggested.

"Sure, I'll spell it all out to you. It's just as I said, you are just not happy in this relationship. It's simple as that," he said calmly, taking a seat back at the table. He propped both elbows on the table and gave me a serious stare. "Look, Mandy, I'm not trying to distress you. I just think it's time we stop beating around the bush about us. The bottom line is quite clear to me," he paused staring down at the table for a moment. Then he looked across the table at me. "I know you are not in love with me."

"You know I'm not in love with you? How do you assume to know how I feel?" I grabbed my face with both hands and held my cheeks, speechless for a moment.

"Mandy, give me credit for having a brain. It's pretty obvious that you're not. You don't act like a woman in love, at least not with me."

"Todd, how can you sit here and say something like this to me?"

"I can say it because I know you are not in love with me; and I have known all along," he admitted sadly, yet firmly.

"But you asked me to marry you anyway?" I mumbled, sadly looking down at the uneaten apple pie on my plate. I pushed the plate aside and held my face up with both elbows on the table. His outspokenness had stunned me.

"Yes, Mandy, I asked you to marry me anyway because I was so crazy in love with you and I still am. But back then I told myself at that time, it didn't matter. I thought you would come to love me back," he said sincerely. "And if I'm being completely honest, my pride wouldn't let me walk away and look like a failure. But frankly, I'm just fed up with being with a woman that is not all there."

"What do you mean not all there?"

"You're with me but you're not. Your mind is always preoccupied on something or someone else," he relayed. "And I'm just not interested in continuing a relationship with someone who isn't into me."

I wiped a tear that dripped from my left eye as I sat there very still and quiet listening; now looking in his eyes.

"Todd, I am really offended that we are having this conversation," I cried. "You are sitting here showing me little or no respect by telling me how I feel. I think I know how I feel."

"Mandy, I'm not trying to offend you. I'm just trying to get a straight answer from you and see where you are coming from. If I'm so far off base with what I have just said about how I think you feel, then please speak out and call me a liar. Tell me how you love me deeply and can't wait to set a wedding date. Better yet, let's set one right now. Can you do that and put an end to my doubt?"

"Todd, I do not want to get into a discussion about setting a wedding date when we haven't finished our first discussion."

"Mandy, it's all connected. If you are not in love with me, there's no need to discuss a wedding date. We have been engaged since Thanksgiving of 2009 and it's now Thanksgiving 2012. That's three years and you won't even talk about setting a date. It doesn't sound like someone who's anxious to get married. At least not to me," he stressed. "Not to mention I saw all the signs but I was in denial and didn't want to face the facts. It was clear to me then and it's clear to me now, that you jumped into this relationship with me because you were trying to run away from my brother," he stated firmly. "But my egotistical, conceited, overconfident pride wouldn't allow me to face the facts in the beginning. I know I'm a great catch if I do say so myself, and figured how could you or any woman not want to be with a great catch like me," he said arrogantly. "But all the pride in the world wakes up at some point!"

I kept staring across the table at him but couldn't speak as if my voice had abandoned me.

"Mandy, just admit it and be on the level with me. I'm not holding it against you because as I just said, I didn't jump into this relationship with my eyes closed. I had my suspicions about your feelings for Brad but my pride wouldn't let me face them. I convinced myself that I could make you love me or you would grow to love me. But my eyes are now wide open to that myth," he stressed strongly. "I see very clearly that love doesn't work that way."

"But Todd," I stared at him and paused. "I do love you," I mumbled sadly.

"I'm sure you do. I don't doubt that you love me. But I know you are not in love with me and you never were."

I stared silently across the table at him as tears rolled down my face. I couldn't dispute what he had just said.

"Mandy, I'm sorry, but I don't see any other way but to break off our sham of an engagement." He shook his head.

"Wow, you think of our engagement as a sham?"

"Frankly, that's what my father calls it. He said any engagement that last longer than two years is a sham against one of the parties involved."

"And I guess you believe your father that the sham is on you?"

"Mandy, can I see it any other way? It is what it is and it's not working." He rubbed both hands down his hair and stared at the ceiling for a second, and then looked at me. "You need to move on with your life and try to find some happiness and I need to move on with mine and find some happiness. I want to be with a woman who can give me all of her heart. I'm not pleased to be in a relationship with you giving me just a corner of your heart while the rest of it is consumed with the longing of my brother," he sadly explained. "And the fact that you have put off setting a wedding date for the past three years has spelled it all out where your heart is."

I nodded. "Todd, I admit you are right about one thing."

"Just one thing," he snapped arrogantly.

"Just one thing," I snapped back at him.

"Okay, Mandy, what's the one thing that I'm right about?"

"I agree that it shouldn't take as long as it has to decide on a wedding date."

"Thank you for admitting that much," he said. "But if you can admit that can you now tell me why it has taken you all this time?"

"Todd, my best answer to you, something is holding me back but I'm not sure what that something is." I held out both arms. "I know you think it's because of Brad. But I cannot sit here and say it's because of Brad, because I don't know that for sure."

"Well what do you know for sure?" he asked firmly. "Are you over my brother or not?"

I gave him a long stare with sad eyes before I mumbled sadly, "Okay, I admit I don't think I'm over Brad. But I know I do love you."

"Okay, where does that get us? You love me but you're not over my brother doesn't sound like a good recipe for a marriage."

"I know you're right. It's not a good recipe for a marriage, since I know I do still have feelings for Brad. But I'm not sure how deep or what my feelings are for Brad; and I cannot sit here and say I don't want to marry you. I'm confused about my feelings for you and your brother. Everything inside of me tells me that I want to marry you and have a life with you, but then something is holding me back. I'm not sure if that something is Brad."

"You may not be sure if that something is Brad, but I'm sure he's at the core of it; and you need to make up your mind Mandy about what it is that you really want. You need to do what you need to do to help put your feelings in perspective," he urged. "If you think there's still a chance for us, I'll hang in there and wont' throw in the towel. But how are you going to clear your head of your confusion? We have been in a holding pattern for three years now, and I can't deal with this rut we're in," he stated seriously. "And Mandy, what makes it worse, all the comments from my family and friends on why you are dragging your feet," he said sadly and held up one finger. "But I do have an idea."

"What's your idea?"

"I'm thinking, maybe you need to take a trip to clear your thoughts."

"You mean take a trip somewhere?"

"Yes, take a trip somewhere. Go on a retreat or whatever it takes to clear your head and mind of who and what you really want," he suggested.

"I would have to take a leave of absence from my job, but I don't see any problem with that. Because actually, I think a trip is a great idea," I agreed.

He nodded. "I'm glad you think so because at least it's a start of something instead of sitting still and doing nothing to remain in this holding pattern."

"Yes, I agree. I think getting away to clear my head sounds like the best medicine to get me on the right track to help clear my thoughts; and I think the sooner I leave town to clear my head, the better for our relationship. I'll go on a retreat somewhere or maybe I'll visit some of my relatives?"

"Which relatives?" he asked.

"I'm not sure, yet. Maybe my Aunt Bonne kids: my chatty first cousin, Emma, or my very quiet first cousin, Melissa. They are around my age. I think they are a couple years older than me."

"Where are they?" he asked.

"Melissa and Emma both live out in Oregon, but my Aunt Bonne lives here."

"What part of Oregon, Portland?"

"Yes, Portland, but I'm not sure if I'll head to Oregon or drive down state to visit my grandmother for a few weeks."

"Drive down state for a few weeks?" he asked. "This trip is starting to sound involved. A few weeks sound like a long visit?" He lifted an eyebrow. "You need that much time to clear your head?"

"Yes, Todd, I think I do need that much time. Besides, it was your suggestion that I take the trip; and it was a very good suggestion because I think it will do the trick," I said encouraged with more perkiness to my voice. "I promise you when I return, my head will be clear and I will be ready to set a date for our wedding. Just give me this time without any calls, emails or text messages."

He held up both hands. "Okay, you got it. I won't bother you. I'll give you this time if it's going to help you clear your head and make up your mind about whether we have a future together. I'll be here waiting when you return."

Chapter Twenty-Four

It was straight up noon, on that peaceful Saturday in mid-January 2013. I was smiling with liberation since I had just arrived at Grandma Hanna's estate in the heart of Springfield, Illinois. Sitting in her driveway looking out at the familiar surroundings, I felt a million miles from home. I was so close to home, but yet I felt so far, in thought and in mind. I killed the engine and just sat there looking out at the old homestead. And after a few minutes of taking in the calm scenery of my Grandma Hanna's front yard, I stepped out of my blue Lexus and leaned up against it with my arms stretched over my head, taking in the cold morning air. It was great to have finally reached my destination. It had been a long, restless drive and it seemed as if I had been on the highway longer than four hours. Somehow my mind already felt clearer. The realization that I was so many miles from home; and my reasons for traveling so far comforted me. I had to get far away from Barrington to focus on putting my life in perspective to figure out where Brad fitted into my heart; and if he still lived in my heart, to figure out away to cut him out so Todd and I could set our wedding date and get on with our lives.

It was time to be crystal clear about my feelings. It was just as Kathy had told me a month ago. Taking a trip and getting away from home would be like a retreat to reboot my brain and clear up the cob webs in my mind. It would be a time to look ahead to the future and let go of the many painful memories that clouded my thoughts, especially the hurtful memories of my parent's failed marriage; and how my father broke up our happy home by leaving my mother to marry another woman. It was time to stop racking my brain with disappointments about how I couldn't make Brad love me, and try to accept my future with the knowledge that Todd did love me.

It was pass my lunchtime and I was starving, but as I stood against my car staring at the huge homestead where my father was born, I noticed that Grandma Hanna's white Lexus wasn't parked in the driveway. No doubt, she was probably at a church service. She was a devoted Catholic and never missed her church services.

I had always loved my grandparents' estate, and how the warm scent of dried roses always filled each room. All fourteen rooms were always filled with the scent of soft delicate roses. And ever since Grandpa Daniel's death, Grandma Hanna had remained in the big white house alone with the company of three live-in staff members: Florence and Harold Stanley and Lara Nole. The large rooms were bright and sunny with long cedar green sheer curtains sweeping to the floor from every single window.

Driving down to visit every summer was always one of my most treasured events. Being at my grandparents' house always seemed to bring me comfort and clear thinking; and just two weeks after my move to Springfield, it was very clear in my mind to stick to my promise of focusing on my relationship with Todd so I could go back to Barrington with a clear mind about moving forward with my future with him. However, by thinking felt unclear again when I saw Brad at the bank in town. I walked into the bank with Grandma Hanna. He didn't see me but I spotted him dressed in an elegant gray suit talking to another customer. He was seated behind a big fine desk explaining something to an elderly gentleman. Then on the drive back to Grandma Hanna's house I mentioned his name to her. I wanted to mention him to find out how much she knew about his move to Springfield. But she kept going on and on about a $4100 deposit that kept showing up in her account month after month.

I interrupted her continued talk about the incident when I said. "Grandma, I noticed that Brad is working at that bank. Do you know how long he has worked there? I had no idea he was living and working here in Springfield."

Grandma Hanna heard me, but didn't answer as she kept complaining about how the bank hadn't figured where the $4100 was coming from to end up in her account. However, when she pulled into the driveway and killed the motor she placed both arms on the steering wheel and looked at me and smiled.

"Your young man moved to Springfield awhile ago to manage that branch. But he isn't just head of that branch, he also my neighbor who lives nearby." She smiled.

"He lives nearby," I repeated as my heart skipped a beat. "How near by?" I asked.

"Oh, just across the street," she replied quickly. "That's the first Chase Court, you know. It's as old as this place. Brad's father, Ron Chase, decided to re-open the old Chase estate after he remarried and moved back here. The old house is named Chase Court just as all the other properties they own. I know there's a Chase Court in Barrington, but this Springfield property remained empty for years after the premature death of Brad's grandparents. It had been maintained by a monthly in-keeper. But now I'm pleased to say the property is being lived in again by the Chases. Brad lives there with his father, his stepmother, Paula and their staff."

After Grandma Hanna's announcement had a moment to sink in, I grabbed my face with both hands. "Brad Chase lives across the street?" I pointed across the street. "Brad lives in that huge palace?"

Grandma Hanna nodded. "That's correct. You are visiting me to get a perspective about setting a date to marry one Chase, and now you realize you have moved across the street from the other one."

I grabbed my face in shock. "Grandma Hanna, this is a big shock. How long has Brad lived across the street with his father?"

"Let's see, it's been about eight months. He drove down here last summer at the request of his father. Ron had mentioned that he needed one of his boys to manage that branch and then the next thing I noticed, Brad was down here handling it for him. He has always been and still is a polite young man just as he was when he and his brother were small and used to come down with Ron and Connie to visit Ron's parents' every summer before Ron lost his parents to that freak accident. Ron's parents were good friends with me and your Grandpa," Grandma Hanna explained and paused. "Yes, my dear, I'm glad you are here, but I hope having Brad so nearby doesn't interfere with you doing what you came here to accomplish."

I shook my head. "Out of all the places I could have visited, I picked the one place where Brad is now living."

"I'm surprise Todd didn't mention it to you."

"He didn't mention it because when we talked about my trip, I wasn't sure if I would visit you or one of my cousins. I mentioned Emma and Melissa, who lives in Oregon, but I never mentioned you. This is crazy." I grabbed both cheeks and shook my head. "I had absolutely no idea Brad was living across the street from you."

"I'm sure you didn't, but this is a small world we live in, my dear Mandy." Grandma Hanna slightly laughed.

"Grandma Hanna, why are you laughing?"

She gave me a firm stare and nodded. "News gets around and I am aware that when you were both much younger, you had a big crush on Mr. Brad Chase and not his brother, Todd." Grandma Hanna nodded.

"How did you figure that out? I don't think Mom ever figured that one out."

"I have my ways," Grandma Hanna smiled. "Long story short, I was surprised when you announced your engagement to Todd Chase." She smiled. "But that's all I know sweetheart. Do you care to fill me in?"

"There's nothing to fill in." I turned my back to Grandma Hanna so she wouldn't see my face. "I did have a crush on Brad years ago, but that was then and this is now, and now I'm engaged to his brother and I'm not interested in getting myself wrapped up with another Chase."

"Okay, Mandy, dear, but who are you trying to convince me or yourself?" She opened the car door and stepped out of the car. I followed her inside and into the kitchen where I stood with my back against the kitchen counter.

Grandma Hanna stepped over to the coffee pot, poured herself a cup of coffee and took a seat at the kitchen table. But I didn't join her, I kept standing.

As Grandma Hanna set there and enjoyed her cup of coffee, I had a taste for hot chocolate and prepared a pot of hot chocolate, placed it on a serving tray with two cups and headed outside.

"Grandma Hanna, it's really mild outside this afternoon. Do you care to join me for hot chocolate out on the porch?" I said heading out of the kitchen.

"Not right now, sweetheart. You go right ahead and enjoy your hot chocolate. I'm having coffee."

Sitting at the little white table that seated two on the front porch, I watched Brad closely that unusually warm February afternoon. With a cup of hot chocolate in my hand, I kept looking across the road watching him as he stood there on the front porch looking toward me. I wasn't sure if he had actually recognized me or if he was just looking my way. Then he waved at me and rushed off the porch and headed down the long walkway. At the end of the grounds when he headed across the road toward me, he was smiling with that sexy smile and those sensuous eyes that had always mesmerized me whenever I was in his company. It was obvious that he had recognized me and was coming over to say hi. He walked quickly up the walkway and stood at the edge of the porch smiling.

"Mandy, Mandy, Miss Mandy Clark," he said, smiling. "What a real surprise to see you down here so far from home. At first when I spotted you, I thought my eyes were playing tricks on me. But it's really you. You are here," he excitedly, smiling. "Mandy it's great to see you, but it really is a surprise to see you down here."

"It's great to see you too; and believe me that when I headed this way for my visit I had no idea you had moved here. What are you doing here in Springfield?" I asked with a permanent smile on my face.

"I could ask you the same question," he teased.

"I'm just here to visit with my Grandmother for awhile," I explained. "But, Brad, tell me, when did you move down here?"

He paused in my eyes for a second. "I lost track but I have been here awhile. I needed a change of scenery and here suits me just fine." He held out both arms. "Plus, a few things back home got under my skin and I needed to get away."

"I don't follow," I said, waiting for more of an explanation.

He smiled. "I'm sorry I said that out loud because it has nothing to do with anything that you need to concern yourself with. So, please, pretend as if you didn't even hear me say that."

"Okay, but I would like to know what got under your skin and made you feel you needed to get away," I mumbled.

"No, it's okay." He held out both arms. "It's been too long to re-hatch old memories." He stared into space for a moment. "But it's darn good to see you again, Mandy. You still look just as beautiful as the last time I saw you."

"Thank you." I smiled. "You look just as handsome as ever yourself. It's good to see you too, Brad." I paused with humble eyes as I looked at him. "I'm sorry to pry and start with the questions before we even get reacquainted. It's just that I had no idea you had moved here."

"Otherwise, you would have picked another destination," he teased.

"No, it's really great to see you."

He nodded with a serious look in his eyes. "It's really great to see you too. Yes, this is where I am for now. I'm not sure for how long. I'm just getting one of the branches in order before I head back." He smiled. "But let's not talk about me. How are you, Mandy?" He glanced at my hand. "I know about your engagement to Todd and thought the two of you would have made it official by now," he said seriously. "So what brings you down this way? Are you two...?"

I hopped out of the chair and stepped to the edge of the porch where he stood. "Yes, we are still engaged," I mumbled, looking in his eyes.

"So when is the big day?" he asked, sort of looking into space for a second.

"That's why I'm here," I said and paused.

"Are you getting married here?" he asked, looking me straight in the eyes.

"No, we are not getting married here. I'm just down here to clear my head."

"His eyes seemed to light up with surprise. "Clear your head from what?"

"As you know, Todd and I have been engaged for awhile now."

He nodded. "I would agree that over three years is a while."

"That's because I can't seem to make up my mind about setting a date."

"And you needed a vacation to clear that up for you?" he smiled with a confused look in his eyes.

"What is that supposed to mean, Brad?"

"It doesn't suppose to mean anything," he said, smiling. "I'm just asking."

"Well, yes, I felt I needed to get away to put my thoughts in perspective." I stepped over and nervously poured a cup of hot chocolate and passed it to him. Then I stood smiling with both hands in the pockets of my short mauve jacket and watched as he turned the cup up to his mouth and took a long sip before lowering the cup.

He looked at me for a few seconds and smiled, holding the cup up to me. "This is what I needed," he said, taking a seat on the front steps with his cup in his hand.

I walked down the steps past him, feeling his eyes on me as I stepped out into the yard. I felt somewhat anxious and noticed how handsome he still was, wondering what he thought of me, and how he really felt about my engagement to his brother. I knew right then and there that I still felt something for him but I wasn't sure what that something was; and I had to be sure before I accepted Todd's hand in marriage.

I looked around at him as he was still sitting there on the front steps, smiling and drinking the hot chocolate. He soon stood up, handed me the empty cup and then walked back across the road to Chase Court.

He looked around and hollered as he made it halfway across the road, "Thanks again for the hot chocolate."

"Sure, you are welcomed," I said, smiling.

After he left, I walked back to my seat, and I continued to sit there concentrating in great wonder of my overwhelming admiration for him. I still felt something special for him and I didn't even know why. A lot of time had gone by but something in the back of my mind kept telling me that the special way I felt for him stemmed from old feelings from years ago that had never died. Feelings I needed to put in perspective before I could marry his brother.

Chapter Twenty-Five

On a few occasions, during my visit to Springfield, I found myself staring out of the living room window at Brad when he would leave Chase Court or stand outside on the porch or on the grounds. I found myself fascinated by his comings and goings and would sometime peek through the curtains and watch him get into his black Mercedes and drive off the estate. I would also find myself glued to the living room window to make sure I didn't miss him pull back into the driveway. His car was the most beautiful car and it shined like crystal as the sunlight beamed down on it. It amazed me how seeing his car made my heart race. Todd had a red Mercedes that was almost identical to the one Brad owned, but only Brad's car appealed to me in that extraordinary way.

It had been years, since my high school days that I had felt true love for someone, deep within my soul lighting up my heart. And I had only felt that special way for the sophisticated, gorgeous, Brad Chase, who had touched my heart in a most wonderful way. Now he had touched my heart again, but the overwhelming fear of rejection was still there. He was a fairy-tale Prince, who was the rich Chase brother to my fiancé, but the two of them, was as different as day and night. He had stolen my heart all those years ago and when we were all grown up and I had my chance to be with him, I chose his brother instead. I wasn't courageous enough to stand up and rebuff the pain of having my heart broken by Brad, therefore I chose his brother. And although they were brothers, Brad and Todd had unique differences. They were both handsome but with distinctively different appeal. Neither Brad nor Todd was a real Prince, but yet, I felt like a fairy-tale princess in their presence.

My visit to Springfield had allowed me to get to know Brad better, and accepting and acknowledging the love that I had once felt for him had bonded all the broken pieces of my heart. I was whole again. Admitting in my heart that my love for him was now in the past, I could see clearly and my insides felt untangled and free of knots. And in just a matter of a few weeks of moving to Springfield, it was as if Brad and I had never been apart. It was as if we had stayed friends and had known each other forever. We shared many evenings together around Grandma Hanna's kitchen table talking and having tea or sitting on Grandma Hanna's front porch visiting with each other talking about different things. I shared with him my deep hurt and disappointment over my parent's divorce and how in my heart of hearts I still wanted my folks to find their way back to each other.

We were finally best friends and felt comfortable talking to each other about any subject. I could put our past relationship in perspective and accept my engagement to his brother. When I headed to Springfield in search of clarity at Grandma Hanna's house, I had no way of knowing that Brad was going to be the one to clear the cobwebs in my brain allowing me to walk straight toward Todd. But being with Brad and spending time with him had somehow melted all my misery of the past. It was like I got out of bed one morning and felt as light as a cloud, as if I could float in the air. All the hurt and pain from our high school days had been lifted off of my shoulders. It had all vanished and disappeared from the depth of my heart. The only thing left inside of me was an undeniable special friendship for Brad. Everything felt right and I could go back to Barrington and plan my wedding with Todd!

Chapter Twenty-Six

It was a clear, cool, Wednesday afternoon in March; Grandma Hanna and I had just finished lunch when Florence Stanley, the cook, served us egg salad sandwiches and pea soup. Now Grandma Hanna was busy in the kitchen. For as long as I could remember, she always had someone else to do her cooking. Plus, she confessed that she had never actually made a meal for herself since she reached adulthood, not even a simple sandwich. She was born into a household with servants and as an adult; she always had her own servants. And although my livelihood was similar with servants in our home since I was a toddler, I had achieved an accomplishment that my grandmother had not. I had made a meal for myself and felt I was a fairly decent cook. Yet, Grandma Hanna had never learned to cook without a recipe. However, for her elderly disposition she was quite active and in the best of health. She never even complained of a headache. And although she was quite elderly at 81, she seemed to be in better health than many younger women. For instance, my mother, who was much younger than her, from time to time complained about some kind of ache or pain. But Grandma Hanna never complained about any aches or pains. She prided herself in keeping active by working in her flower gardens in the summer and spending time in the kitchen when she wasn't working outside. She often said how spending time in the kitchen trying her hand at different recipes was her all time favorite hobby.

On this particular afternoon, Grandma Hanna was assisting Florence. They were making homemade pies and cookies. She and Florence had baked an assortment of cookies and pies for the Church Craft Day coming up the next day. She and Florence were up late busy baking most of the night and all morning. They had baked two apple pies, two peach pies and two cherry pies. Florence and Grandma Hanna had also finished a dozen of oat meal cookies and a dozen of sugar cookies. They were now busy baking a sheet of chocolate chip cookies.

The wonderful scents from the kitchen filled the cool fresh air. I had just received a letter that morning from Kathy, but had held on to it until I could sit and give it my undivided attention. Now relaxing in a chair at the little white table that seated two on the front porch, I was excited and smiling as I began to read Kathy's letter. I kept asking for a real letter instead all the emails and text messages and finally it arrived:

Friday, March 1, 2013

Mandy Clark
C/o Mrs. Hanna Clark
3311 Maplewood St.
Springfield, Illinois 60442

Dear Mandy:

I hope this letter finds you and your grandmother in the best of health and spirits. And as you can see, I stuck to my word and mailed you a real letter as you asked. You didn't want another text or email; you wanted me to put some work into my efforts of communicating with you. Well, I'll tell you it was real work. First of all, I had to go out and buy some writing paper and envelopes and make a special trip to the post office. Smile!

A lot has happened in my life since your long visit to Springfield. I hardly know where to start. And will start by saying, I miss you like crazy. It's not the same around here without you. I hope you make your way back home soon. I have been crazy busy, working the night shift, but did I tell you I left Barrington Medical Clinic last week and got hired at Barrington hospital three days later. So when you make your way back to work you won't see me there. I chose the hospital because they are offering better benefits to their nurses than the clinic. I would have written sooner, but there has been so much commotion with this new job and things going on in my life, which I'll mention a bit later in the letter. And by-the-way, I received your letter. You know what; you didn't say anything about when you are coming back home. Like I said, you are deeply missed; and Barrington isn't the same without you. Your parents miss you too. I saw your father the other day at a supermarket in the area. I was surprised to see him there since I know he and your mother divorced several years ago and he remarried and has lived in the Chicago area ever since he was elected Mayor. And although, I know you never wanted to talk about it back then and didn't think much of him serving in pubic office, but the four years he served from 2005-2008, I read he did a good job. Anyways, he is still considered somewhat of a celebrity to the community. A couple people in the store were asking for his autograph. I did get the opportunity to speak to him and he said hello. He looked the picture of health. Does he still have those back problems? Just wondering since he gets around so well. But I guess he should since he is still quite young.

Mandy, where does all the time go? It just seems to fly. Here I am only one week away from my 28th birthday and it seems as if my life just slipped through my fingers. I often think about all the fun you and I had in high school. Yeah, those were fun days for us. Remember that New Year Eve's Party at Brad's house when you got a chance to spend some time alone with him? That's when you thought he was the only fellow for you. Those were perfect years for us, but now we are all grown up and it makes it all seem like a hundred years ago.

Mandy, time has even turned our community into a rather quiet place. Remember when we were in high school how it was so lively and full of noisy teenagers from all around. You and I and the Chase girls and boys, especially Molly and Lynn and how they sort of controlled the temper of other kids at school. And in case you haven't heard, Molly and Justin are engaged and planning a Christmas wedding. And Lynn and Kent are engaged and planning an autumn wedding. Rachel, Cody and Wesley are all still at home with my folks. Wesley finally finished his two year internship residency at the hospital. He's now a full-fledge brain surgeon. My folks are glad to have him around to take care of their aches and pains but they realize his time at home is limited now that he's a practicing doctor. Cody is still single, dating but no one special. Rachel said she would never fall in love again after her two year marriage to Jeffrey Horton ended so badly. But she's in love again. She hasn't mentioned his name and being very tightlipped but said she doesn't want to mention his name just in case it doesn't work out. But from the very content look in her eyes this mystery guy could be her next husband.

I'm about to give you a bit of very exciting news. Ricky and I finally found each other again. He asked me to dinner and I accepted, and it all started from there. And all during dinner and all during the movie, I had this incredible urge for Ricky to kiss me. The chemistry between us was overwhelming. And the look in his eyes and his manner told me that he felt the same as me. We kissed at my door, and knew after that one kiss that we were meant to be together. Guess what, we are engaged and plan to be married on June 18. We felt it was only fitting to marry on the day that we broke up on ten years ago. Everyday since he proposed to me, I have to pinch myself to make sure I'm not dreaming. And I know this

*is all incredible to you, because you figured with my stubbornness
that I would never talk to him again after you confessed that he
behaved like a drunken fool after that New Year's party. But we
were all kids then and yes, he made a stupid mistake, but he is so
sorry about that. And I regret that it took me so long to be a bigger
person and forgive him for the mistake sooner. We have lost so
much time together, but now we have found each other again and
I'll never let him go. I'm so excited about our upcoming wedding
and I know you are too. So hurry home because I don't want my
maid of honor to be absence from the ceremony.*

*Mandy, I just want you to know that Ricky and I are so happy.
We were just talking about you the other day when I told him that
I hope you will soon make a clear decision about who you really
love, Todd or Brad. My advice to you is to just let go of the past
and start looking toward the future.*

*Mandy, I almost forgot to tell you, Ricky finally landed a vice
president position at one of his family banks. Isn't that wonderful?
And just yesterday he went out and purchased a brand new
silver 2013 Mercedes-Benz. Now every Chase guy I know owns a
Mercedes-Benz.*

Friends Always, Kathy

It was splendid to hear from Kathy and read the wonderful
news that she and Ricky had found their way back to each
other. But at the same time, her letter brought sadness to my
heart. Hearing about the happiness of other couples and her
happiness and newfound love made me focus on the fact that
my happiness was still yet to be. It made me reflect on my life
and how I had put things on hold to travel to Springfield to sort
out my feelings. Now they were sorted out and in perspective.
Brad was someone I had loved in the past that I had found a

solid friendship with and Todd was someone I loved now and had a future with.

I sat at the little table on the porch for ten minutes more, but after no sign of Brad's car pulling into the estate, I glanced at my watch and noticed it was two-thirty. Brad always arrived home from the bank around that time, but since he hadn't arrived, I decided to take a walk out back near the clear-water creek. After watching an assortment of ducks splash about in cold blue water, I walked over and took a seat on the nearby bench that was surrounded by evergreen bushes. The old wooden bench had been painted white many times over the course of years; and the newer coat of paint had started to peel and it seemed to catch my attention and held it as I thought about my life and how nothing stayed the same. How time had a way of peeling away everything in our lives that felt familiar. It had somehow painted over the dreams that were once in the depth of me for Brad to replace them with new dreams for Todd.

Seated there in thought with the clear sky and bright sun above me, I was alertly aware of what a cool, quiet, peaceful afternoon it was, but inside of me there was a storm blowing at high speed. I couldn't seem to shake myself of the thoughts of the past and what Brad had once meant to me. I was seated there daydreaming about Brad, when I glanced up and noticed him walking toward me. He had both hands in his jacket pockets as he headed toward me smiling. He was looking at me with those sparkling eyes. My face flushed and my heart raced, pounding in my chest from his sudden presence.

"Hi, Mandy, I thought I would find you out here," he said, smiling. "You look radiant like something from heaven sitting there on that bench in the sun. I have never seen you look more lovely than you do right now with those exceedingly beautiful eyes of yours sparkling from the sunlight." He complimented.

I stared up at him slightly frowning from the sun in my eyes. "Brad thanks for such a lovely compliment. What did I do to deserve a compliment of exceedingly beautiful eyes?" I laughed.

"Just being yourself. That's how I see you, Mandy. Your eyes are indescribable!"

"Thanks again, but what are you doing out here? Not that I'm complaining about the compliments you are giving out," I uttered in a low voice that wasn't quite my regular perky tone.

He examined my face closer and his smile vanished to concern. He looked handsome wearing black slacks, a blue shirt and a stylish black suit jacket.

"You've been crying. What's the matter?" he asked, placed his hand on the arm of the bench and took a seat beside me.

"I guess I thought things would have turned out differently for us," I uttered.

"That's life. I thought it would have as well, but you chose my brother and I have to live with that. It's him you are in love with and not me," he said with a regrettable tone to his voice.

I nodded. "I know, but I'm so glad we are finally the best of friends."

"I'm glad we are too and believe me if I hadn't been so clueless back in high school and realized what a treasure you were things may have worked out differently for us. But that's water under the bridge. You made the visit here to clear your thoughts and that you have done, is that correct?" he asked.

I nodded. "Yes, my thoughts are clear."

"Meaning, now you are sure about your engagement to Todd?"

"Yes, I'm clear about my engagement," I mumbled.

"Okay, I can only wish the two of you well," he said and patted my shoulder. "Thanks Brad."

"I'm not sure what you are thanking me for."

"Thanks for being here and being my friend through all of this. You are a very remarkable man. Do you know that?"

"I'm not sure I know that or why you are saying it, but thanks anyway."

"I'm saying it because you could easily resent me for being with your brother. Even though things didn't work out for us, you could have easily resented me."

"That was never going to happen. Why should I resent you for my own shortcomings?" he said seriously.

"What do you mean your own shortcomings?"

"I'm referring back to high school. If I had opened my eyes at that time and noticed you for the angel you are. Then maybe?"

"Then maybe what, what were you going to say?" I anxiously inquired.

He shook his head and looked at me. "Mandy, nevermind what I was about to say. It won't change anything. Besides, our time has missed us," he said and stared out toward the creek.

Sitting that close to Brad the delicate scent of his sweet cologne overwhelmed me. The past flashed in my head during our high school days when he was all I wanted. And years later I purposely started dating Todd in an effort to get over him. Now I was deeply sadden that what I had set out to do really caused me to let Brad go. But in the past I couldn't confess my feelings to him because he hadn't given me the slightest reason to believe he wanted me in his life. If only he would have confessed his love in the past we might have gotten our happy ending. Now I was about to marry his brother and our time had missed us.

"By the way, when are you heading back home to plan your wedding?" he asked after a short period of silence between us.

I heard him but didn't answer as I was engrossed in memories of the past.

He touched my shoulder. "Hey, where did you go?"

"I'm just thinking, what did you ask me?"

"I just wanted to know when you are heading back home."

I didn't answer again. I just stared out toward the creek.

"Mandy, are you sure you're okay? You seem sort of sad. What has gotten you so down in the dumps like this? Tell me, won't you? Maybe I can help in some way," he whispered, took both hands and turned my face toward his.

"You have tears in your eyes," he whispered. "What's the matter? I don't think I have ever seen you look this sad. Are you still sad about things that happened in the past with your parents; their divorce and all of that?" He released my face and I placed my focus back toward the creek.

I nodded and dried my tears with my fingers. I knew my parents weren't the reason for my tears. I was crying for what could have been, but missed us.

He gently held my shoulders and looked me in the eyes.

"Mandy, seeing you cry breaks my heart." I could hear the frustration in his voice as he shook his head and spoke in a whisper. "Please don't shed another tear." He paused and during the silence I could hear my heart pounding. "You have to stop dwelling on the past and concentrate on your future and being happy."

"Brad, you are right. I know I need to snap out of my funk. I really have a lot to be excited about," I said with more perk to my voice.

"Yes, you do, like going back home and planning your wedding," he said, smiling, looking me in the eyes as we sat there on the bench facing each other.

"Thanks for making me smile."

"Anytime, I'll be your smile dial up guy," he laughed.

"That's funny, but I might just hold you to it," I laughed.

"Okay, are you ready to take off? I'll walk you back to the house. And I won't pretend to know how you are feeling, but I have an idea," he said seriously and continued. "Mandy, I'm sure you are probably anxious and nervous about planning your wedding and also about the marriage," he said and paused. "I'm sure you are happy about it but you are probably plenty nervous as well."

"You are right, I am anxious and nervous," I agreed. "But I'm looking forward to getting home and jumping right into it."

"So, tell me, when you are heading home?" he asked.

"I'm heading back on Sunday," I mumbled.

"What a coincident," he grinned. "I'm heading back on Sunday as well. I have wrapped up all my business at the branch and will head out of here first thing Sunday morning."

Something inside of me was glad to hear that he was heading back to Barrington as well. "That's great," I mumbled in a low voice.

"Yes, it is great. I can't tell you how glad I am to be finished down here."

"So you never had intentions of making roots here?" I asked.

He shook his head. "No, I never had those intentions. It was always just about getting a job done. Not to say I wasn't glad to spend some time here with Dad and my new stepmother, but it was never about staying any longer than I had to," he assured me. "It's time to get back home."

"I'm more than ready to leave to," I said. "I needed a break from Todd to figure things out, but if you hadn't been here when I arrived, I doubt I would have stayed this long," I admitted. "It's been two months already."

He stared in my eyes for a moment as if he wanted to say something, but he said something else instead. "Your presence here also helped me. It was good to be able to see you and talk to you, Mandy." He nodded. "Your pleasant visit here made the rest of my stay go quicker, but I can't believe I have been here for nearly a year now."

"Time goes quicker when you're having fun." I hit his arm in a playful way.

"That's true, but I wouldn't say my bank project was fun. But spending time with you certainly qualifies as fun." He stared at me for a moment and then looked away. "Of course, Dad isn't ready for me to head back home, but he'll cope. He knew I was taking off once I took care of that business at the branch," Brad said and stared into space for a moment. "Time can be a pro and it can also be a con. It has away of just flying by," he stated seriously. "We both ended up staying here longer than we had hoped. I'm sure my arrogant brother will have something to say about your lengthy stay here," he said, smiling.

"I'm sure he isn't pleased with my two-month schedule away from Barrington, although he has given me this time I needed."

Brad grinned. "Yeah, I know. That was considerate of him. He can be a good guy every blue moon," he teased. "I'm sure he'll be ecstatic when you arrive back in town."

Chapter Twenty-Seven

Thursday morning sunlight was slowly creeping across the big Illinois sky, highlighting the manicure grounds and the well designed evergreens that lined the outskirts of Grandma Hanna's property. I was fully awake lying in bed in the spacious yellow guestroom, holding the satiny white bedspread up to my chin, looking through the crack in the long yellow curtains. It was plain to see that it was a clear day on the horizon. It was soothing to see the new dawn slowly moving out as the ray of light rolled in. Scattered in a far distant were clouds that stretched across the blue sky like thin layers of cotton candy, thinning out, and making way for what promised to be another bright day. It seemed that from the guestroom window, the Illinois sunrise was always enchanting. But this particular morning the lovely sunrise seemed to warm me even more, knowing my step-brother, Dale Smith, was asleep under the same roof, right down the hall in the huge lime green guestroom from me. Grandma Hanna and I were both very happy about his visit. His visit was a complete surprise. He didn't call ahead of time to say he was driving down; but we were both happy for the opportunity to spend time with him and get to know him better as an adult.

Dale Smith was my stepmother, Doris's, only child and Dale and I were close in age and the two of us had met when I was eleven and he was eight. We became good friends and played games together many times when Doris would bring him to Mandy Manor when she first started working for my father and babysitting me occasionally. Now Dale's mother was married to my father and now I had a brother and now he had a sister.

I had awaken much too early. Now, I lay waiting for the clock to strike seven so I could get up and about and help Florence, if she would let me, make breakfast for Grandma Hanna and Dale. When the clock struck seven o'clock, I jumped out of bed, showered, dressed and rushed downstairs to the kitchen. Florence greeted me with a smile and graciously allowed me to help with breakfast; and by eight o'clock Florence and I had breakfast on the table: Pancakes, maple syrup, scrambled eggs, bacon, mixed fruit, coffee and orange juice. Grandma Hanna, Dale and I lingered at the breakfast table talking and sipping on coffee and orange juice until late in the morning, and then shortly after one that afternoon, Dale and I were both all set to play tennis on the tennis court on Grandma Hanna's property, but we just ended up sitting out on the porch talking.

We had our tennis racks in hand as we both were seated on the edge of the porch, swinging our racks about. Then after conversing for awhile, we headed back inside and grabbed a few of Grandma Hanna's photo albums. Tennis would wait since we had decided to look through some of the albums before heading to the court. And while sitting on the front steps talking, laughing and having fun discussing the pictures in her old photo albums, we looked up and Brad was headed up the walkway. I smiled at him as he stood near the end of the yard. He was wearing a pair of well-pressed expensive looking jeans and a pullover dark blue sweater beneath his expensive looking black leather jacket.

"Mandy. Hello there." He waved at us. "Is Mrs. Clark home? I brought her wine opener back," he said with an apologetic expression on his face as if he was interrupting us from something.

"Hi, Brad. Sure. Grandma Hanna is here. Come on up." I beckoned to him.

Still seated on the front steps beside my step-brother, I pointed to him. "Brad, I would like for you to meet my little brother, Dale, who drove in from Chicago last night," I said, smiling.

Dale slightly elbowed me, "I wish you would stop that little brother stuff," he said, smiling. "It was fine when I was eight and you were eleven. But now, Mandy, look around, I'm a big boy. I'm almost as old as you are," he teased.

"Don't be silly, Dale. When you were eight and I was eleven, you were not my brother then and I was not your sister," I said jokingly.

We all laughed and Brad extended his hand, "How are you, Dale? I'm Brad Chase, your sister's annoying neighbor who borrows wine openers." He smiled.

"Don't listen to him, Dale. Brad is a complete gentleman."

"Wow, thanks for that compliment. I don't think I have ever been called a complete gentleman," he said, smiling.

"I don't know why not, because that's what you are," I assured him.

"This must be my lucky day. I walk over here to return a wine opener and receive the nicest compliment ever," he nodded and winked at me.

"You are most welcomed, of course," I said, smiling.

Brad passed me the wine opener. "Don't ask why I borrowed it, because I was just informed by my father's bold housekeeper, Miss Sonya Lee, that we have seven wine openers in that house somewhere," he said, pointing across the road to the big house.

"Wow, seven and you couldn't locate any of them," I teased.

He grinned. "That would be correct. But I made the mistake of saying to Miss Lee that seven couldn't help me if I couldn't locate them," he said, laughing. "I think she chewed me out in her foreign language."

"Did she really chew you out?" I asked.

"That's fine, that's just her way. She chewed me out for being annoying to Mrs. Clark, imposing upon her for a wine opener when we have seven, Miss Lee said."

"That's no biggie," I quickly said. "Grandma Hanna didn't mind. Besides, Miss Lee shouldn't expect you to find anything in that big house. It's not like you actually live there."

Brad smiled. "I agree with you but try explaining that to Miss Lee. She runs that house and does a darn good job and lets everyone of us know it," he laughed. "She's quite entertaining in her way."

"Maybe she is, but you're not annoying," I said.

"I'm not; okay, great." Brad winked at me and pointed across the road. "Now go and tell that to Miss Lee," he teased.

"Maybe I will." I smiled and felt a rush of blush to my face since it felt like Brad and I was somewhat flirting with each other.

Dale and Brad shook hands and Dale glanced across the road. "So, Brad, that's your house across the road there?" Dale asked.

Brad nodded. "Yes Sir, that's one of them. That's the old homestead. Apparently, it's where my father was born too many years ago," he laughed. "Now it's the gift that keeps on giving. My grand folks gave the place to my father as a gift when they packed up and moved to California before the family was devastated by their accidental death."

"Grandma Hanna mentioned something about your grandparents dying in some kind of accident. What really happened to them?" I anxiously asked. "My grandparents on my mother's side also died accidentally. It happened during the hot summer of 1985, two years after they had just given Mom and Dad the wedding of a lifetime. I was just a seven-month old infant at the time, but my parents told me their cruise ship was destroyed by a hurricane that came out of nowhere."

"That's too weird," Brad said with words filled with sympathy. "My grand folk's accident happened on the water as well. It happened while they were out canoeing on a fishing trip. I don't know all the details but apparently they lost control of the canoe and the lifeguards didn't reach them in time. I was a little boy at the time, but it was a devastating, shocking accident that really crushed my family for awhile," Brad explained with deep sorrow in his voice. "And although I was just a young kid when they died in that boating accident, having this opportunity to live at the old homestead with my father and my new stepmother has given me a chance to get to know my grand parents through their surroundings. The house is still decorated with all their original furniture, paintings and books. It's truly the gift that keeps on giving."

"Some gift that spread is," Dale said seriously. "I'll take a gift like that any day. I tell you, that's what you call a palace! Isn't it Mandy?" Dale exchanged looks with me and nodded.

"That's Chase Court," I nodded. "I agree it looks like a palace, but no more than the other palace they own in Barrington. It's also called Chase Court."

Dale paused at me for a moment. "I can't recall seeing that one, but if it's anything like this one, it's priceless that's for sure," Dale said, smiling.

"It sure is, and I have told Brad so many times," I said, smiling, looking at Brad.

Brad glanced over at our tennis racks and smiled. "This is a perfect day for a game of tennis. Are you two getting ready to head to the court now?" He exchanged looks with me and Dale.

"Yeah, this will be my first time trying to beat her in tennis since forever," Dale chuckled.

While they were talking and hitting it off really well, suddenly my mind went back to December of 2002, the night Brad and I had spent together in his room. It was the only time in the past that he and I were truly alone. Looking at his handsome face now and knowing I was engaged to his brother somehow seemed unreal. That time with him so many years ago felt like we were in a world of our own. He had told me that he wasn't in love with me and he had said I wasn't in love with him. He had explained that we hadn't known each other long enough. But now so many years in the future, if we were throw in that room together again, the argument couldn't be made that we hadn't known each other long enough to be in love. But the present can not be placed in the past. Brad and I took different paths toward the future that led us away from each other, but we managed to stay in each other's circle of life. When we were teenagers, he was adamant that we were not in love with each other. Now many years later, we are still not in love with each other. However, back in 2002, he meant the world to me and that time we spent alone with each other was the closest thing to paradise I had ever felt before and since.

Watching him converse with Dale, I wondered how much of that night stayed with him. Did he remember and was it still in his memory as a special time. It was a night of many first times for us: our first kiss, our first drink together and our first time alone. It was also our first and only time of ever admitting that there was something between us. We never figured out what that something was, but we admitted on that night that there was something between us.

Brad and Dale laughed out and interrupted my thoughts of yesterday. I hopped up off the steps and took the wine opener from Brad.

"I'll take this inside to Grandma Hanna. She's probably inside helping Florence in the kitchen. They were up until the bewitching hour last night baking."

"They are probably still at it," Dale remarked.

I glanced over my shoulder and smiled toward Dale. "I'm sure they are. I'll be right back."

When I stepped back outside a few minutes later, Dale excused himself and stepped inside. Brad and I took a seat on the front steps and he looked at me and smiled. "Now that we are both about to head back home, I was just wondering about something," he said.

"Okay, what's that?" I asked.

"I guess I'm more curious than anything." He touched my knee. "You know back in high school you liked me a lot and I liked you too. But I probably didn't do a good job of showing it. I guess what I'm trying to say is how did we end up like this?"

"What do you mean?" I asked.

"Our lives ending up this way with you being engaged to my brother; it's funny don't you think? Well, not funny, but something," he said. "Yesterday when you were sad and crying over your parent's divorce, you mentioned how you thought things would have turned out differently for us," he said curiously and paused in my eyes. "When you said that, were you referring back to high school or when we reconnected in 2005? Because back in high school I didn't realize what a treasure you were and when we met again in 2005, I realized what a treasure you were but I never got a chance to tell you since Todd beat me to the punch and won your heart. So, I'm curious to know if you were referring to back in high school or 2005."

"Maybe I was referring to fate in general. Life happened and took us in different directions," I mumbled.

"I guess life did happen, or maybe I was kidding myself a few years ago when we ran into each other in 2005 for the first time after high school," he said.

"Kidding yourself, how?" I asked, sort of nervously.

"Well, at the time, I was under the impression that there was still something between us. But I guess I was wrong because you chose Todd."

"Brad, this conversation is kind of awkward."

"I'm sure it is a bit awkward but we should be able to discuss this now. You are engaged to my brother and about to become apart of my family but I'm still trying to figure out where the two of us went wrong back then. Yesterday when we were talking I got the sense that you regretted things didn't work out for us in high school; and if I had known then what I know now, I would have held on to someone as special as you. I'm sure I would not have allowed someone like you to get away from me. I guess what I'm getting at, is that I'm aware of how we were crushing on each other in high school but I want to be clear about 2005. I just want to know was it all in my mind or did you have feelings for me back then as well?" he asked.

"Brad, why is that important now? Would it have mattered?"

"Can you just humor me? I'm just curious to find out if I was totally off the mark about what I thought you felt for me back then."

After a brief silence and him looking me right in the eyes, I answered him. "You were not off the mark." I looked away from him. "I did have a crush on you back in high school."

"I wasn't referring to high school. I was referring to 2005, but your non answer is my answer. You most likely had washed me out of your system when we meet again in the summer of 2005 since you chose to go out with my brother and not me," he said and nodded. Then he looked at me and smiled and to make light of it he continued. "I admit to having a bruised ego that summer after you chose Todd over me, especially since I'm the better looking brother," he said teasingly and looked at me and paused. "But it's all good now. Your happiness is what counts and if my arrogant brother makes you happy then we're all happy, right? Besides, that's water under the bridge and really doesn't matter whether you had a crush on me back in high school or not. I guess we were just kids then."

As he paused looking out into space, I wanted to ask him how did he feel about me back then but I couldn't find the courage to ask since I wasn't sure if I was ready for his answer. Then he looked at me and continued.

"Yes, Mandy, we were just kids back in high school. You grew up and fell in love with my brother, but at least we are still good friends," he said, stood to his feet and headed across the road to Chase Court.

After dinner, Dale packed up and headed back to Chicago taking a letter from me to give to my mother.

Thursday, March 7, 2013

Francis Redford-Clark
650 E. Hillside Avenue
Barrington, Illinois 60010

Dear Mom:

I know you don't like emails and text messages so I'm writing you a real letter as you requested. And I hope this letter finds you doing great. I miss you a lot and I also miss Dad. But I must say I have really enjoyed my visit here in Springfield with Grandma Hanna. I feel driving down here was the best medicine for me. I needed to clear my thoughts to make sure my marriage to Todd was the right choice and I feel now that it is. Traveling many miles from home seemed to have solved that problem. But Mom, you'll never guess what. I moved here to put distance between myself and Todd so I could clear my head, but during my entire visit I have lived right across the street from Brad.

I had no idea that huge brick palace across the street from Grandma Hanna belonged to the Chase family. When I was small and you and Dad would drive down here to visit Grandma Hanna and Grandpa Daniel I always wondered who lived in that big house. But at that time I don't think anyone lived there. Grandma Hanna said the estate was closed up for many years until Mr. Ron Chase reopened it when he remarried and decided to move back to Springfield. And as I mentioned before, Brad has lived across the street in the Chase mansion with his father and stepmother. I haven't met his stepmother but her name is Paula and apparently she is much older than his father, which is unlike Doris being ten years younger than Dad.

Dale was here for a short visit and it was great to spend some time with him. And as you see, he was nice enough to drop this letter off to you. He looks well and I'm glad the two of us have built a relationship. We had a long talk and he told me about Dad and Doris union. He mentioned that they seemed happy for a few years, but now they are having some serious problems in their marriage. He said they can't seem to agree on much lately. When he told me that, it reminded me of how it was around the house with you and Dad before he moved out and you two divorced. Dale was living with them, but because of all the tension between them, he moved out a couple months ago and now lives in Barrington. But he still works downtown at Lakeland Investments where Dad works.

This might be wishful thinking on my part but I have always wanted the two of you to get back together and I'm sure just because Dad and Doris are having some problems doesn't mean they will divorce and if they do divorce it doesn't mean you and Dad will get back together. But as imperfect as your marriage was back then, I always wanted my mother and father to stay together; and now here I am a grown woman and I still want you together. I have come to the conclusion that I'll always feel this way. Therefore, I'm keeping my fingers crossed that the two of you will find your way back to each other.

I plan to head back home early Sunday morning. I'll see you sometime Sunday evening.

Love always, Mandy

Chapter Twenty-Eight

I surprisingly enjoyed my stay in Springfield with Grandma Hanna. Being away from my job, my family and friends, didn't weigh as heavy on me as I had thought, especially since the time at her house had been uplifting and a much needed trip to help me sort out my life and put things about my future with Todd in perspective. But it was wonderful being home at Mandy Manor, sleeping in my own bed and planning my long overdue wedding to Todd. However, I was swamped with all the things I still needed to do before the big day. And even though my plate overflowed with a to-do-list, walking down the isle with Todd wasn't the only thing occupying my thoughts. I was also preoccupied and mesmerized by the unforgettable estate called "Hillside Palace" on the corner of Hillside and Lansing Streets that stood marvelously on a hillside that covered a stretch of three acres that bordered the manicure grounds with a white picket fence. I couldn't stop thinking about and visualizing the fabulous domain as the residence that Todd and I would share as newly weds.

And with all the planning and not a minute for anything else, four months later, after coming home to Barrington, that very warm Monday afternoon on July 8, standing on the sidewalk waiting for Todd to find a parking spot. I asked Todd to park on the street instead of pulling into the long driveway. I wanted to slowly walk up the driveway to take in all the magnificent surroundings of the beautiful estate. At the entrance, I paused up at the beautiful house which set a block away on the beautiful green hillside. I admired it with a longing stare. Suddenly my admiration for the lovely estate was cemented in my brain. I couldn't shake the thought of making the place my home. It was such a stunning multi-color brick house, brilliantly designed with black shutters on all the many windows. The place was flawless with immaculate landscaping.

"Oh, my, this place is picture perfect," I thought to myself, "I hope Todd falls in love with this place the way I have. If only he and I could live in this beautiful house. If only Todd would like it well enough to give up the idea of living at Chase Court."

I opened the tall white gate and strolled quickly up the long brick walkway. In enthralled in the place, I found myself running toward the house; and when I reached the front door, I quickly turned the crystal doorknob and rushed inside not waiting for Todd. The real-estate agent had phoned to let us know that the front door would be unlocked for our visit. I walked inside in awe as if I was seeing the place for the first time. I lingered excitedly in the foyer, which was one big sun room as the sun poured through the three sky lights overhead. This was not the first time I had paid a visit to the elegant estate. I had visited the property several times since my return home from Springfield. It seemed as though I couldn't stay away from the place. Everybody knew I had fallen in love with Hillside Palace and finally I had persuaded Todd to allow me to give him a tour of the lovely domicile. Which he agreed to after I promised to stop talking his ear off about the property. Literally it stayed in my thoughts constantly. I kept thinking about the insides and remembering the huge living room with its soft pink walls and woodwork, its floor to ceiling windows, and its cozy fireplace that was positively guaranteed by the real-estate agent to be the best design ever with the frame built of solid white marble. I kept remembering, too, the exact appearance of the spacious library, the dinning room, and its glass wall to the south. As for the five bedrooms upstairs, the large one in front with one wall of windows and one brick wall that showcased an elegant fireplace and built-in brick shelves, and the three guest rooms decorated in shades of light green and pale yellow.

I went out to the huge kitchen area and lingered there in happy thoughts as I looked around and admired the sunny spacious room. Then I paused and stood there looking outside through the glass wall at the soothing outdoor scenery and the towering oak tree, until footsteps sounded in the living room. Then excitedly I hurried into the spacious room with a big smile on my face.

Todd wasn't smiling. But I assumed that since this was his first visit to see the magnificent piece of property, he needed to familiar himself with the place. I had asked him several times to view it with me, but each time he had declined. He had shown no interest in seeing or purchasing a home for the two of us to live in after our wedding. He was standing by the white fireplace mantel and turned facing me as I came toward him, and before he could say a word. I looked at him and smiled.

"This is going to be our home after we are married. How do you like it, sir? Isn't it fabulous," I said excitedly, with both arms stretched out. "Todd, there is something about this place that makes me feel good inside and happy about our future together." I held my chest with both hands. "It's like the kind of home that I have always dreamed about owning one day."

Todd glanced about the living room and nodded. "I'll admit. It's worth dreaming about, but what about the home you already own?"

I stared at him speechless, not sure what he was referring to.

"Mandy Manor will one day be yours," he reminded me.

"I know, but right now it's my mother's home and she is still very young and will be living there for many years to come!"

"I suppose you are right," he agreed, and then held out both arms. "So this is the wonderful house you have visited and talked about non-stop for days?"

"Yes," I looked at him anxiously. "Don't you think it's super wonderful and just perfect?"

"I wouldn't go as far as perfect," he quickly replied. "But I will agree that it's okay as far as houses go," he mumbled with no excitement.

"Just okay, you don't think it's superb?" I asked, searching his face for any sign of interest. "Just look at this priceless house," I said excitedly and stretched out both arms.

"No." Todd shook his head. "I wouldn't say it's superb. It's nice, big and roomy, but it's similar to the rest of the houses in this area," Todd said, looking me straight in the eyes. "Priceless, maybe, but show me a house around here that's not priceless. This is a deep pocket area, you know?" he said arrogantly.

All the excitement seemed to have been drained immediately from my face. I had an overwhelming desire to scream out in tears, but managed to keep my tears from falling. After all, Todd had not yet really seen the entire house. Surely, when he took the time to look around and inspect all of Hillside Palace, he would fall in love with it as much as I had. So I was eager to show him around to every room and every inch of the entire estate.

I grabbed him by the arm. "Look, Mr. Sour Puss," I teased. "By the time I'm done showing you around this place, you will love it as much as I do."

"Don't bet on it, Mandy," he said. "You know I'm not easily persuaded."

"Maybe not, but in this case it will be different. Because there's no way you won't fall in love with this house once you see the entire place."

"Sweetheart, I really hate for you to waste your time showing me around when I'm quite sure I won't change my mind."

"But you took the time to come here and you promised you would tour the place with an open mind," I reminded him.

"Yes, I did take the time to come and I did promise you that I would look at the place with an open mind; and I will, but it still doesn't mean I'm going to change my mind and want to buy the place," he said in a manner as if he felt the house was beneath him.

"Maybe not, but can you please do me a favor and reserve your pessimistic views for the end of the tour?"

"Okay, you have a deal."

"Okay, good, let's get started." I led him by the arm. "I want to show you the entire house, room by room."

Eagerly I led him throughout the house and felt no real-estate agent in the entire state of Illinois could have described the estate in a more desirable light than me, as all the excitement of hoping to one day own the place was bursting inside of me to come out. Therefore, with great excited effort, I dragged him to every room and explained every exquisite feature about the house, but it all seemed like a waste of time. Todd never showed an ounce of interest or excitement toward the place. No matter how greatly excited I was, none of it penetrated his thought. He failed completely to catch even a fragment of my interest.

"Mandy, I appreciate that you have taken the time to show me around the place. And honesty, I can see that this is a really nice house, but after touring the entire place, I have to ask, where is all your excitement coming from? There's no way this house can compare to Chase Court," he remarked arrogantly.

"Yes," I agreed completely. "Of course it doesn't compare to that museum you live in. I never said it compared to Chase Court."

"You didn't have to say it; it's how you carried on about this place. In away, touring the place was almost disappointing because I thought you were comparing it to Chase Court."

"Todd, that's just great. You cancel out the house because it doesn't compare to your family home," I snapped, shaking my head at his attitude.

"I'm sorry, Mandy, but you put this house up too high. You made me expect more than what it is. But if it will make you feel any better, it could have been a palace and I still wouldn't want to live here," he admitted. "I'm just being honest."

"Thanks for your honesty, not that it makes me feel any better. Frankly, because I just don't understand you." I threw up both hands.

"What's not to understand? I prefer my family home over this would be mansion." He held out both arms. "Why should I live here when I can live in style at Chase Court?"

"Well, you just said it could be a palace and you still wouldn't want to live here."

"That was just a figure of speech, since most likely no house around here is going to compare to Chase Court."

"You got that right, most houses don't compare to that fortress with twenty bathrooms and fourteen fireplaces," I said, smiling to make light of it. "Besides, we cannot compare an average house like this one to Chase Court or Mandy Manor for that matter." I held out both arms. "But, Todd, we are not trying to buy a house to compare to our family homes. We are just trying to buy an average house that we can call our home that will make us both happy," I stressed my point.

Todd shook his head. "This place is not Chase Court or Mandy Manor, but it's not an average house either. It's on a grand scale. But that's beside the point," he said firmly and stared at me for a moment. "Mandy, I'm sorry but we are not buying this house. It's not going to happen, not ever, okay. Now, can we please drop the subject of buying this place and get past this issue?" he said, giving me a serious stare as if I had asked him to move on Mars.

"Just like that you decide against it? Just think about it for awhile, please!"

"I don't need to think about it," he said firmly. "My decision is final. I'm not going to change my mind," he said seriously, looking me in the eyes without blinking. "But at the same time, I don't want you to get all upset about this decision I have made," Todd said firmly. "It's a family tradition for the Chase family to remain at Chase Court and raise their kids and those kids raise their kids and the list continues," he explained. "You'll love living at Chase Court."

"I'm sure you're right; but I want a home of my own," I stressed. "I want this house. We can start our own tradition for our kids. We can name the place Chase Court III or whatever you like. If it were too expensive for us or anything like that, I wouldn't insist. But it's on sale for a steal. And, after all, the odds are good that I'll probably spend much more time in the house than you will, so if I'm willing to take care of a big house why not?"

"Mandy, can we not have this conversation," he said arrogantly. "Because what you fail to realize is that I'm not willing to manage all the staff that is needed to take care of all the yard work and other odd jobs that fall to the hand of a man who lives in a big house like this," Todd said coldly. "If we couldn't live at Chase Court it would be different. I would buy this house because you want it, and I would make the best of it. But Chase Court is my home and my folks expect me to raise my family there. It's huge with plenty of empty rooms, an absolute modern convenient that will make everyday life a lot easier for both of us."

I blinked hard and forced my tears to stay inside. I dared to stand there and let him see me fall apart emotionally. Todd hated to see tears fall from a woman's eye more than anything. It annoyed him to the point of anger, ever since the time he watched his mother cry for days after his father left home. Seeing a woman cry brought that hardship back to his mind. I had promised to never let him see me cry. But it was so hard to stand there and not show emotions as though the very floor of the house was slipping away from beneath my feet. It was so hard to accept the fact that I would never make the lovely house my home as I longed to decorate and buy furniture for all the many spacious rooms.

I took a deep breath and swallowed hard. "Listen Todd, I could take care of the yard work," I said anxiously. "Besides, I love gardening and yard work. It wouldn't be like work to me."

Todd looked at me. He had an arrogant look in his eyes that I had learned to dread. "For goodness sake, Mandy, please let this idea go; and please do not cry over this," he said firmly. "Besides, you know very well that you couldn't take care of the yard work and I wouldn't permit you to if you could. Besides, how would it look, you my wife, working on the ground?"

"Who cares about how it looks?"

"I care, okay," he said. Besides, you may like yard work but you are not a landscaper, and I'm sure you don't know the first thing about taking care of grounds this size."

"I could try," I insisted.

"No you won't try because you don't know how to use the equipment or any of that stuff. I'm surprised you would even suggest such a thing. Taking care of a yard this size is a huge task even for those who do know what they are doing. That suggestion on your part was just a childish attempt to have your own way."

I considered what he had accused me of, while still trying to hold my tears in and keep my composure. Perhaps he was right and I was somewhat spoiled and wanted my way, but being spoiled had nothing to do with wanting my own dream house. I wanted the house because it was exactly what I had pictured my dream home would look like. But I swallowed hard and figured there was no use thinking any more about it. Todd had made up his mind not to buy the place and that was all there was to it. Besides, it wouldn't be too exciting living in a house that I loved and he hated. His resentment toward the place would make me feel guilty and responsible for his misery.

Todd walked with annoyance to the living window room and stood there looking out. Just then my cell phone rang, which was in my purse sitting on a counter at the rear end of the huge kitchen. I rushed toward my purse and pulled out my phone and answered it.

"Hi Kathy," I mumbled sadly, hanging my purse on my shoulder.

"So tell me, are you and Todd still looking at that gorgeous house?"

"Yes, we are still here," I mumbled with no excitement to my voice.

"Don't tell me he doesn't like the place."

"You guessed right. He doesn't like the place."

"Why not, it's perfect as far as houses go."

"It doesn't fit into his family tradition," I explained.

"What family tradition is that?" Kathy asked.

"I guess a Chase can only live at Chase Court," I explained.

"That's sounds ridiculous and a bill of goods from him I'm sure," Kathy shouted through the phone. "I hope you told him so," Kathy said with an upset tone.

"I agree, it does sound ridiculous," I mumbled.

"I'm glad you do agree because Todd Chase needs to get a clue. He is being too difficult. You are his new bride to be and if you like the house, he should buy it for you to make his new bride happy," she paused for a second, and then shouted in my ear. "If you ask me, I think you picked the wrong brother: the difficult one!"

"Maybe, but I have to believe that everything will work out for us. How could it not work out?"

"Mandy, only you can answer that."

"Kathy, I know things will work out since I know Todd is truly the man I want to marry. I must love him deeply to have given up Brad for him."

"If you say so, but it still doesn't erase the fact that Todd can be quite arrogant and quite difficult to reason with."

"Okay, I know how Todd can be difficult and not always that easy to reason with; and yes, he's being difficult now, but he's not always his way."

"But really, Mandy, why are you being so understanding and letting him off the hook so easily? I know how much you love that place. You haven't been able to stay away from that house since you got back from Springfield."

"Yes, I do love it, but what good would it be to have him buy the place and be resentful about it afterward? So, I'm just going to forget the place and live at Chase Court the way he wants us too."

"Okay, if that's what you want," Kathy said sadly.

"It's not what I want, but that's the way it has to be. I love the man and I'll be happy with him wherever we are."

"Well, you don't sound happy now," Kathy said.

"Of course, I don't sound happy. I'm so disappointed because Todd is so stubborn. He turned down the idea of buying the house flat. He refused to even consider it."

"If he's that stubborn and won't bend to make you happy, maybe you should rethink marrying the guy," Kathy teased.

"Stop kidding around. There's nothing to rethink. It's just a house, right. I'll be happy with Todd wherever we live, okay?"

"Who are you trying to convince?" Kathy asked.

"I beg you pardon."

"Mandy, that's the perfect answer, but do you really mean it," Kathy asked.

"Yes, I mean it, why wouldn't I?"

"I don't know, Mandy, but there's something in your voice. But nevermind me, I'm sure you and Todd will work it out and have a wonderful life together wherever you end up living."

"Thanks for wishing us well because I am happy with Todd After my soul searching in Springfield I realized its Todd I wanted to be with," I assured her.

"Not when he's in one of his arrogant moods. The man is drop dead gorgeous and no doubt every woman's dream, and no disrespect meant, but sometimes Todd thinks he owns the world. I know you don't like his stubborn, arrogant ways."

"Of course not, but nobody is perfect. Besides, I don't let his stubborn arrogant ways get under my skin. I can deal with that," I said firmly. "Besides, he isn't always stubborn. You know there are times when he's perfectly charming and adorable."

Kathy laughed. "And when is that?"

"Are you kidding me? You don't find my soon to be husband charming and adorable?" I asked teasingly.

"Well, the jury is still out on that one," she teased. "I'm just kidding of course. Todd can be very charming and according to Rachel he can do no wrong."

"I wouldn't go that for, but Rachel has always thought of him as the Prince Charming among the Chase men. She even told me that I needed my head examined for leaving town and putting my engagement to Todd on hold."

"Did she really say that to you?"

"She didn't say it in those words, but that was her point. She had to voice how wonderful she thought Todd was."

"That's my big sister, always looking on the bright side of Todd. Plus, we both know how she has always carried a torch for that one. Back in high school she had a huge crush on your husband to be back then," Kathy explained, laughing.

"I remember, but I don't think her crush was huge for Todd back then," I said.

"It was huge and more," Kathy laughed.

"Okay, if you say so, but she did end up marrying another Prince Charming," I reminded her.

"I guess so after Todd never even asked her out back then," Kathy laughed. "Believe me; Rachel only married Jeffrey Horton because Todd didn't ask her."

"This feels a little weird discussing how Rachel used to have a crush on Todd. That was then and this is now. And now Todd and I will be married soon. I don't feel too comfortable discussing Rachel's old crush on him. "

"Okay, sure, we can drop it. I didn't know it was getting to you," Kathy said.

"It's not really getting to me. I just need to stop complaining about his ways. I love him and regardless to my disappointment over losing the house, I have to keep in mind that I'll get over losing the house and Todd and I will be happy."

"Mandy, if you're happy, I'm happy for you."

"Yes, I am happy. But I have to hang up now. Todd is waiting and I'm sure he's anxious to leave," I said abruptly and ended the call.

I stuck my cell phone in my purse and slowly headed in the direction of the living room. When I stepped back into the living room, Todd was still standing with his back toward me, looking out of the huge north window that covered almost the whole section of that wall. Seeing him standing there, I felt suddenly displeased with myself. Maybe I was being too pushy and unreasonable insisting that we buy a house that he clearly had no interest in. And my discussion with Kathy wasn't fair toward Todd and somewhat disloyal to speculate about my possible unhappiness in the future with him if he did give in and buy the place.

Then with a sharp stab of dismay, I remembered that Brad had also returned home back in March when I returned; and now it was summer, the second week of July and I wondered how he felt about my upcoming wedding to his brother that was scheduled to take place on Saturday, July 20th. We had both stood up at his cousin, Ricky's, wedding to Kathy just a few weeks earlier. But during the reception we didn't get a chance to mingle or talk much. We had not had an opportunity to talk as openly and as freely as we had when we were both in Springfield together. At that time he had accepted my marriage to Todd. After all, Brad and I had never been in a real relationship; I had merely promised that we would stay friends and I would give Todd my answer when I returned home from Springfield.

Now the wedding was only two weeks away. I felt cautiously excited and a bit overwhelmed, as well as disturbed. For despite my very long engagement to Todd, deep down I felt like I still didn't know him as well as I should. I had known him long enough to have suffered quite a bit from his superior moods. And although, we had an in depth conversation and I had explained to him that I was sure about how I felt about him, I sensed that he was not completely convinced. His uncertainty about my commitment to him could have been the root of his resentment and egotistical moods. There were times when it seemed to me that Todd was completely at the mercy of jealousy that showed through his eyes and from the tone of his voice. On those few occasions he seemed distant toward me. Especially, since my return from Springfield he seemed even more distant than usual as if he was keeping something from me. I couldn't question him about my hunch since it could have stemmed from my own insecurities. But I couldn't allow his distant moods to come between us, since his distant moods were not that often. He was mostly attentive, charming to be around and well respected in his social circle and in the community.

"Todd is an absolute perfect vision of a man. He is so different from the other men we know," Rachel had pointed out during a conversation a couple days before I left for Springfield. She couldn't understand why I needed to get away to put things in perspective before marrying Todd. "Of course Brad is all right too," she said. "In fact, Brad is nearly perfect, but you carried a torch for him most of your life. I guess that's why he couldn't give you that secure feeling that you probably get from Todd. I'm just telling you that if I was engaged to a man like Todd, I would marry him before he had a chance to change his mind. Who cares about his stubborn streak and arrogant moods? That's just because he is so charming and different. No one person can be flawless or have everything even if they are insanely good looking and happen to be a Chase man."

I remembered that conversation as I headed across the room toward Todd, I felt confident that Rachel was right about the things she had said about Todd. He was a charming and delightful person. His stubbornness and arrogance was the product of his uniqueness. No person could have everything and I had no right to expect perfection from Todd that we would always see eye to eye on everything.

"Todd, I'm ready if you are," I muttered softly, "I won't say any more about this house ever again. I get it. You just don't like the place."

"That's not true, Mandy," Todd snapped. "I neither like nor dislike this house." Todd stared at me as if I knew I had not spoken the truth. "As I have told you an astonishing number of times, I think we should just live at Chase Court."

"All right, I get it," I said. "We'll live at Chase Court."

He nodded. "I'm glad you do get it. It's about time; now are you ready to take off?" he asked with his eyes smiling with relief that I had dropped the subject of buying the big house on the corner that he didn't want.

Todd pulled me in his arms and gave me a tender kiss on the lips. Then he held me tight for a moment and then looked at me and nodded. It was his way of showing me his gratitude for my cooperation. He was smiling and seemed in a better mood now, but there was something different about him. He seemed distracted lately as if something else was heavy on his mind. And it was obviously from the irritated look in his eyes that he had not yet recovered from his resentment of being forced to tour a house that he wasn't interested in viewing. I looked at him and forced a smile. Deep down I had accepted the decision for the two of us to live at Chase Court, but I was also deeply hurt that he had closed the door on the purchase of the house of my dreams.

He grabbed my hand and squeezed it and gave me a serious stare. "So, are you okay with washing your hands of this house and moving into Chase Court?"

"Yes, I'm okay," I assured him.

I didn't want him to know how disappointed I was, after all he could be nice when he wanted to be and of course I did love him. I content with him I told myself determinedly. But it was clear to me that Todd had somewhat changed since my visit to Springfield. He didn't seem as interested or excited about our upcoming marriage as he had seemed before I left town.

Nevertheless when we stepped outside of the house I tried not to think negative thoughts. I wanted to keep the tears that wanted to fall inside of me from Todd's sight. And I tried to push from my mind the thought that this was my final goodbye to my dream home.

Chapter Twenty-Nine

As Todd and I strolled leisurely down the long walkway, I glanced about at the well-manicure grounds, bushes and trees that surrounded the property. When we made it to the end of the walkway and stepped through the tall white gates of the elegant estate, Todd and I noticed Brad standing on the corner. We were both surprised to see him standing there engaged in taking pictures of the place. Then he looked toward us as he heard the clicking sound of the gate that closed behind us.

"Hey, you two," Brad said, smiling and stepped over near us.

"Hi, Brad." I smiled. "You are a few blocks from home aren't you?" I glanced toward the street corner where Todd had parked his car. "I don't see your car. Did you walk all the way over here just to take pictures of this house?"

He shook his head. "Not really, this is my exercise routine."

"It's your exercise routine to take pictures of strange houses?" I teased.

Brad laughed and shook his head. "Of course not and you know. But as I said it's my routine to try and walk at least six blocks a day."

"Really, you are doing better than I am," Todd grinned.

"Why you say that? You can get off your butt and walk just the same brother," Brad grinned. "But back to the point, I admit I conscientiously decided to walk this way to see what all the fuss is about. And I can see why you two are into this spread; It's a sight to be seen; and I figured I would snap a few pictures, since it might end up being apart of our family history."

"Did you say family history?" Todd drew an attitude.

"Why yes, Mom said you two were seriously considering buying this place. Is that not true?" Brad smiled with a confused look on his handsome face.

"It's not true," Todd said firmly. "You wasted your time taking those pictures. Mandy and I have just decided that we are not buying it. Chase Court will be our home," Todd snapped and headed toward his car in a rush.

Todd glanced over his shoulder as Brad and I followed behind him. "Do you plan to walk six blocks back? If not, hop in and we'll give you a lift."

Todd drove past Chase Court and drove the three of us down the street to Mandy Manor. Todd and Brad didn't really exchange more than four words between each other before Todd pulled into my driveway. And when Todd pulled into the driveway he left the motor running as he quickly stepped out of the car, walked me to the door, and then showed me inside with a quick kiss on the side of the face. He had a business appointment to attend and said he would be back later for dinner. Brad followed me inside.

In the living room we found Rachel, sitting on the sofa with a glass of red wine in her hand. She immediately hopped off the sofa and smiled with pleasant surprise in her eyes to see Brad. She was spending a lot of time at Mandy Manor lately helping us with my wedding plans. After all the time that had gone by since high school she was still a very attractive slender woman with long black naturally curly hair and dark brown eyes. Her hair was super long, reaching down to her waist and she had never allowed it to be cut. She was one year older than Kathy and moved back home with her parents after her two year marriage to Jeffrey Horton ended in divorce last year.

I was so pleased she was lending her services and filling in for Kathy, since Kathy was still on leave from work enjoying her honeymoon.

"Brad Chase!" She said excitedly. "How absolutely splendid it is to see you again! Did you have an incredible wonderful time in Springfield? It's great to have you back in town." She turned the crystal glass to her mouth and took a sip of wine. "I still can not get over how much you and Todd look alike."

"What look is that?" Brad smiled.

"That drop dead gorgeous look, if I do say so myself," Rachel said from her relaxed feeling of a glass of wine.

"Do tell, who's gorgeous and who should drop dead?" Brad teased.

"Seriously, Brad, you both are too cute and you know it," Rachel said and took another sip of wine. "Todd is engaged to Miss Mandy here." She pointed toward me. "You are one lucky girl, Mandy. And then there's you, Brad."

"What about me?" Brad asked.

"Well, you're not engaged, but you might as well be, since you're otherwise engaged." She narrowed her eyes at Brad.

Brad lifted an eyebrow. "What do you mean by that, Rachel? I don't think I follow," he said, smiling.

"I mean for as long as I have known you, you have only had eyes for one woman." She took another sip of wine.

"And who might that be?" he asked.

"I'm not calling any names, but it's shameful it's not me," she laughed in a low soft voice. "I can't get over how you and Todd look just as fine as you did back in high school," she said, smiling and looked toward me. "I know you agree with that, Mandy."

I nodded. "Yes, I do, one hundred percent."

"See Brad, I guess we are teaming up on you because Mandy also agrees that you and Todd look just as fine as you did in high school," she said excitedly and paused. "But after some thought, I would like to rephrase that. Because time has served you both well, and I didn't think it was possible, but the two of you look even finer than you did back in high school."

Brad smiled. "Wow, Rachel, you know how to boost a man's ego. I don't think I have ever known you to be quite so complimentary. Maybe I should have a glass of the fine wine you're drinking," Brad said jokingly.

"I'm just calling it the way I see it. When you got it, you got. Some of us have it and some of us do not," she said arrogantly.

"That's true and present company definitely has it," Brad stretched both arms in either direction of me and Rachel.

"Thank you, I accept that compliment," Rachel continued all smiles.

"Rachel, you are welcomed and flattery is great, but with all the boys trying for your attention back in high school I doubt you even gave Todd and me a second look."

"Believe me, I did notice but your brother didn't."

"That's funny," Brad laughed. "I remember him thinking the same about you. He had a crush on you back then but thought you weren't into him."

Rachel smiled. "You are kidding, of course. I didn't get that memo. Besides, it's water under the bridge. He's about to be a married man." Rachel held her wine glass with both hands and took a sip. "Anyway, enough talk about high school. I know you have been back for a few months now, but I hope you enjoyed your time away."

"Pretty good," Brad said. "But it's great to be home. Like the saying goes, there's no place like home."

"Especially when home is Chase Court," Rachel smiled.

"So tell me, Rachel, what's been happening with you since I saw you last?" Brad asked. "I heard about your divorce. I'm sorry."

Rachel didn't comment as he continued. "I see you left the branch and now at the other one working for and with my arrogant brother," Brad teased. "Come to think of it, Rachel, you were a really good worker. Now that I'm back managing the branch will you consider returning?"

"I have a news flash for you. Working for your arrogant brother is not that bad," she said teasingly. "However, I will seriously think about that," Rachel said, "With you back it's a great possibility I could reclaim my old office at the branch where you manage. But you should know that the most exciting happening around here is Mandy's upcoming wedding to Todd in two weeks, but of course you know that."

There was a moment of complete silence and then Brad spoke. He was standing, before Rachel with a surprise look on his face.

"In two weeks, really," Brad commented and looked toward me. "I knew about the wedding, of course, but not the exact date. I hadn't heard it was taking place in two weeks," he said quietly.

"I haven't had time to tell you," I quickly said, running fingers over my hair in a vague attempt to hide my anxious nerves.

"Rachel," Mom called from the dinning room, "Your cell phone is ringing here in the kitchen."

"All right, I'll be right there, Mrs. Clark," Rachel responded, heading toward the kitchen, then glanced over her shoulder and said, "I'll see you later, Mandy. I'm staying for dinner."

Then Brad and I were left alone. I spoke first, still anxious. "I would have called or texted you about the wedding date, Brad. But I sort of figured you knew. I thought maybe Todd or your Mom had mentioned it to you."

"My mother, Todd or nobody on the staff mentioned it. They probably thought I knew since copies of your invitation were all over the house. I saw one of the invitations on the kitchen counter the other day. But dared to pick it up and read it."

"Why didn't you?" I asked, but he didn't comment as I continued explaining myself. "But as I was saying, since we have been back I have been so busy with getting my job back at the clinic and with all the wedding stuff. Plus you have been so crazy busy getting settled back into your downtown office. I didn't want to bother you."

"That's all right, Mandy," he smiled. "I understand that we have both been busy. I'm just happy for you and Todd if he makes you happy."

"If he makes me happy," I repeated nervously. "Of course he does make me happy and that's why I'm marrying the man."

"Yes, you are marrying the man. Please, excuse my manners. I didn't mean it to come out that way. But just standing here looking at you like this and knowing you are about to walk down the isle with my brother, something just hit me."

"What do you mean something just hit you?" I asked.

"I'm not sure how you're going to take hearing what I have to say. Because until this moment I didn't know I was going to say it."

"Okay, I'm waiting to hear what it is."

He stood there speechless and stared at me for about ten seconds as if the words that were on the tip of his tongue wouldn't come out.

"What is it, Brad?" I asked, looking curiously in his eyes.

Then he blurted it out quickly. "I don't want you to marry my brother. Now there, I said it."

I grabbed my face with both hands, stunned and speechless for a moment before I collected myself. "You don't want me to marry, Todd?" I asked with my heart in my throat, waiting for him to say he was just joking or something of that sort. But from his manner and the look in his eyes I could see he was serious.

Lost for words I just stared at him and after a long moment said, "Did you mean what you just said? Are you being serious right now?" I asked, still stunned at his confession.

He nodded with love pouring from his eyes. "Yes, Mandy, I mean every word I just said. Of course, I'm being serious. I have never been more serious in my life. Ever since the first day I laid eyes on you, you have been the one precious thing on my mind when I open my eyes to a new day; and the last beautiful thing in my head when I close my eyes at night. You are my optimism and my motivation; and I can't imagine a life without you. But more importantly than all of that, you are the love of my life."

"But Brad, you never said anything to me like this before."

"But I should have. I have deep feelings for you, Mandy. If the truth be told. I never wanted you with my brother. I wanted you for myself, but I never took a stand to convince you of that. But I'm wearing my heart on my sleeve and the truth is finally out. I'm simply flown away by your radiant beauty. How you overwhelm and baffle me all at the same time. How you amaze me sweetly beyond my dreams. And now, out of the blue when I least expected it, you own my heart; and I can't keep this love inside of me anymore."

I stood there shaking my head with both hands still holding my face. I was really confused now. After all I had cleared my head and knew I wanted to marry Todd and not Brad. Now my thoughts were cloudy again. But they were only cloudy for a short moment before I collected myself and took a deep breath.

"Stop it, Brad. Just don't."

"Don't what, Mandy?"

"Don't look like that. I can't bear it. It isn't my fault that I have fallen in love with Todd. When I wanted to be with you, you never said anything like this to me. I would have never gotten together with Todd if you had loved me back then, but you didn't love me back then and now I love Todd and we are about to be married in two weeks. Plus, even when I visited my grandmother and explained to you that I was there to clear my head to decide if I really wanted my marriage to your brother, you said nothing about having any feelings for me then. Knowing you cared could have helped in my decision making at that time. I wasn't sure I loved Todd enough to marry him. Plus, at the time he felt something was missing and that's why he convinced me to take the trip to figure things out. I practically grew up loving you and wanting to be with you and that's why it was so hard to be sure if I really loved you or your brother. But I made a decision in Springfield and that decision was that I did love Todd enough to marry him. And isn't it a good thing I did make sure? It would have been terrible if I had decided to be with you and then figured out that I loved Todd?"

"Yes, that would have been awfully tragic but obviously this is just as painful, too. You see, Miss Mandy Clark, I realize I love you more than anything I could have ever imagined," he said with deep conviction in his voice. "And don't ask me why I never told you so." He held up both arms. "I'm just figuring it out and putting it together for myself. All I know is right now this minute I just can't imagine life without you being apart of it."

"Brad, please don't tell me these things now," I stressed, holding out both hands. "It's too late. Our time has missed us and this kind of talk will only make me cry," I said, looking him straight in the eyes. "So, please stop saying all those wonderful things that I always wanted to hear from you before I start crying."

"Mandy, I'll stop. I don't want to make you cry," Brad said. "I just couldn't keep my feelings inside any longer. Yet, they come too late for any good. But you must never shed a tear for me or any other guy for that matter. I don't think there's a man alive worth crying for, Mandy. If I thought that I had ever caused you to cry it would bother me a lot. My mother cried enough tears over my father to last a lifetime," he said seriously. "So we'll have no tears, okay?"

I nodded, looking in his eyes. "Okay, no tears from this girl," I said lighthearted, still shaken by his confessed. And just then, the doorbell rang and after a few seconds it rang again. No one answered the door, so I excused myself and rushed across the room toward the foyer to answer the door.

"I'll see who it is," I said. "Wait here for me, Brad. I'll be right back."

When I opened the front door a few minutes later, I greeted two anxious teenagers selling Girl Scout cookies. Luckily I had money in my dress pocket, I purchased four boxes and they were on their way. Afterward I rushed upstairs to my room and stood looking in my dresser mirror brushing my hair. Suddenly I felt like I was in a daze. Brad had just confessed his love to me but I wasn't available to love him back because I now loved his brother. Instead of things become clearer they seemed to be more confusing. In the course of the day, I had experienced an assortment of emotions: Todd had broken my heart and pulled the plug on all chances of me living in my dream house, which was a huge letdown. And then, out of the blue, Brad confesses his love, something I have always wanted to hear him say. But he says it when my heart belongs to someone else.

I stood there in the mirror for a moment longer and took a deep breath. Now collected, I headed out of my room and leisurely walked down the hallway and the staircase with my thoughts more at ease. Then as I reached middle ways the staircase it dawned on me that I had rushed to answer the door, leaving Brad alone waiting in the living room.

"Brad is waiting for me," I thought to myself, as I hurried down the rest of the staircase and rushed toward the living room. "I should not have kept him waiting so long. It slipped my mind that he was waiting for me." I thought to myself.

But when I stepped into the living room, I stopped as rapidly in my tracks as if I had walked blindly into a brick wall, and stared in blank astonishment at Brad and Rachel standing in the middle of the living room floor, wrapped in each other's arms kissing passionately.

I stood there motionless staring at them as they seemed to be lost in each other's arms. I was stunned since only a few minutes before, he had confessed how deeply he loved me and couldn't imagine his life without me being apart of it. Then suddenly, a wild, unreasoning anger erupted inside of me. I wanted to scream and throw something across the room to get their attention so he could take his arms from around her and she could take her arms from around him. But as I stood there boiling with anger, listening to the sound of my own heartbreak, Rachel glanced around and saw me. When she spotted me, she jumped away from him as if he was fire. Her reactions caused him to look in my direction.

My mouth fell open as I grabbed my face with both hands. Liberation such as I had never known in my life completely saturated me when I realized that the man who had just kissed Rachel was not Brad. It was the man I was engaged to, Todd. I grabbed my mouth with both hands. For a moment I was speechless just staring at him. Todd looked confused and thrown off balance as he rushed across the room to my side and attempted to explain himself.

"It's not what it looks like, Mandy," he suggested. "But why are you looking so peculiar and laughing? I don't find anything the least bit funny? Besides, we were just kidding around anyway," Todd tried to explain. "You know Rachel and I work together now, and we became quite close while you were in Springfield."

"I can see that," I said firmly.

"Don't take that the wrong way. I'm just saying, she was giving me a kiss for the wedding," he awkwardly explained.

"She decided to kiss you two weeks ahead of time instead of at the ceremony." I waved my hand. "Now that is funny," I laughed. "Wouldn't it be funny to you if the situation was reverse and it was me explaining why I had just kissed another man?" I paused in his eyes. "As a matter of fact, you probably wouldn't find it funny at all, just like I don't really find it funny, but it's so outrageous that you would kiss her in the living room of my own home, until it is funny." I shook my head. "A kiss for the wedding, a passionate kiss at that; and I'm supposed to buy that? You couldn't think of a better lie than that, Todd Chase?"

"Mandy, don't take what just happened between me and Rachel serious. You know you're the only woman I love."

"But I'm just not the only woman you'll pull in your arms and kiss; and just two weeks before the wedding at that! The nerve of you, Todd Chase; risking it, knowing I was in the house!" I fussed. "You are smarter than that, so maybe the joke is on me and you wanted me to catch you to give you an out."

"Mandy, just calm down and don't make something out of nothing," he stressed.

"Oh, don't worry. I am calm, Todd," I collected myself. "I'm not the least bit upset with you, so don't worry about me making a fuss about that kiss."

"If you are not the least bit upset about it, then maybe I should be worried," he said anxiously and lifted one eyebrow.

"You're right, Todd. I shouldn't have said I'm not upset, because I am upset. But what I'm trying to say is that I'm not upset about what you think I'm upset about."

"You are not making any sense because I think you're mad about the kiss you just walked in on," Todd said.

"Yes, I'm upset that you showed me so little respect to have the nerve to kiss Rachel in my home, but I'm not upset that it was you kissing her; because, if you're kissing Rachel, she's probably who you want to be with. Maybe you two are madly in love and don't even know it," I snapped.

"Mandy, you are not making any sense," Todd stressed.

"I think I'm making a lot of sense. I paid close attention earlier when Brad spilled to Rachel that you had a huge crush on her back in high school, and everyone at school knew that she had a crush on you back then. But apparently for two smart people, neither of you knew about the other's crush. So now, I guess you have finally found each other again. I wished you had filled me in since I thought we were getting married," I argued strongly.

"Calm down Mandy. It was just a misunderstanding that you walked in on. I know it looks bad but she really was giving me a kiss for the wedding. Besides, Rachel had a little too much to drink."

"Okay, she had too much too drink. But what's your excuse? I'm sure you don't have one except it was what you wanted. That's why you have been so miserable with me since I returned home. I couldn't put my finger on it, but you haven't been quite yourself since I returned. Among other things, you haven't shown as much interest in the wedding."

"Mandy, you are not making any sense. Of course, I'm interested in my own wedding."

"It really doesn't matter now, but I'm sure I'm right about it all."

"Mandy, what are you trying to say? I have explained to you how that kiss was not what you think," Todd tried to convince me.

"I just said I don't care about that Todd. You see, I thought you were Brad. That's what made me so upset and hurt me to the depth of my heart. I was so relieved when I saw who you were, that's why I was so stunned. The fact that I was relieved that it was you and not Brad, when you are my fiance, seemed bizarre and weird that I wouldn't be offended and upset to see you kissing another woman. Either way I was stunned but I wasn't hurt when I realized it was you."

"You thought I was Brad?" Todd repeated, clearly confused.

"Yes, I did, and I know it sounds odd but I was upset when I thought you were Brad kissing Rachel," I explained. "You and Brad are about the same height and size and you're both wearing white shirts this evening. Anyway, I thought you were Brad and it made me feel furious and deeply hurt inside. So you can see for yourself that I can't go through with this marriage. If I feel that way about Brad, it all boils down to the fact that I'm in love with him and not you."

Todd grabbed his head with both hands and stared up at the ceiling for a moment. He collected himself and looked at me shaking his head. "I hope you know what you're saying is ridiculous," he said firmly. "Granted to walk in on me kissing Rachel was shocking since it looked worse than it really was? But based on one simple kiss, you are suddenly out of love with me!"

"It wasn't one simple kiss. It was the kiss of love," I explained. "That's what it was. It was the kiss of love."

"Just listen to me a minute, Mandy," Todd firmly suggested. "What do you mean; it was the kiss of love? I don't follow you."

"I know you don't follow me, but I know what it means. That kiss made it clear in my head who I really love!" I stressed to him.

"Mandy, I think you need some time to think this through. You're not thinking clearly right now," he stressed.

"Todd, no, you are wrong. I'm thinking clearer right now than I have since we started dating," I assured him.

"Well, I happen to disagree. You are clearly upset with me about that kiss, but we have been together and engaged for too long for you to let this one incident tear us apart. I hope you will not allow this incident to come between us. You witnessed a harmless kiss between friends, but now it's over?" he pleaded, clearly caught off guard that I had blurted out I loved Brad and not him.

Todd ripped off his neck tie and walked closer with shock in his eyes. "I tell you, Mandy; you don't know what you are saying. Don't let your jealousy rob you of your good sense and make us both miserable in the process. You may think I should not have kissed Rachel, and you're right, I know I shouldn't have kissed her. And I won't blame it on the wine or being caught up in the wedding bliss. But at any rate, it was a harmless kiss and it didn't mean anything," he explained. "It didn't mean anything to me and I'm sure it didn't mean anything to Rachel."

"Well, I think it did mean something to the both of you. Because I know it meant something to me!" I snapped.

I caught him off guard with my remark. "What?"

"Not what! Why? I can tell you why that simple kiss meant something to me?" I stated firmly.

"Mandy, can we please let this go and get on with our lives?" Todd pleaded.

"No way, Mr. Chase; that simple kiss may not have meant anything to you, so you say! But it meant a lot to me, especially, if the man I'm engaged to think it's okay to kiss other women," I stressed strongly. "And if you are not clear on where I stand, let there be no misunderstanding. I would never marry a man who thinks its okay to go around kissing other women in my face or behind my back."

He shook his head. "You won't listen right now and I can't make you understand."

"That's right, but in this case, I'm not refusing to marry you for that reason." I held out both arms. "I'm not jealous and I'm not hurt. I don't' care how many times you kiss Rachel Gross or any other woman because I just don't love you," I said heartfelt and grabbed my cheeks with both hands and looked at him in silence for a moment. "Even though I caught you in the arms of another woman, I'm still deeply sorry to say this to you. Because I sincerely thought I loved you, but I realize now that I don't. It was that kiss that opened my eyes. It took me back to the conversation we had last Thanksgiving. You looked at me and told me I was still in love with Brad and that I needed to clear my head about whether I wanted to be with Brad or you."

"Okay, we had that conversation last year, but you left town and decided it was me?" Todd held out both arms. "That's why we are about to be married in two weeks."

I looked up at the ceiling for a moment and then stared down at the carpet for a second. Then I looked at him and sadly said.

"You are right. I did decide it was you. But I was lying to myself and just couldn't see or didn't want to see the truth. But it's been Brad all along in my heart!" I stressed in a heartfelt manner. "I'm sure you are hurt and confused right now about my complete change of heart, but if you'll think for a moment you'll realize that my feelings for Brad has nothing to do with your indiscretion with Rachel, but all to do with the fact that I never stop loving him."

"Mandy, these things you are saying may be true, but why here and like this? Were you looking for an excuse to get out of marrying me? Why tell me like this, two weeks before the wedding, after all the preparations and time and effort that went into putting it together."

I grabbed my face and held it as I stared in his confused eyes. Then I glanced around the room and noticed that Rachel had taken a seat on the sofa, pretending to look through a magazine but she could hear every word we were saying. But suddenly my heart went out to her because she was probably living the same lie I had lived, denying my feelings for Brad for all those years. She had apparently loved Todd all her life. As that probability dawned on me, my thoughts were interrupted when Todd asked me again.

"Are you going to tell me why here and like this?"

I looked at him and nodded with compassionate eyes. "It's not because of the kiss, but it's because of the affect of seeing you and Rachel kiss." I glanced at Rachel but she kept her head in the magazine. "As I mentioned, I thought you were Brad kissing another woman. It woke up my brain and made me open my eyes to my love for Brad."

The point that I loved Brad had finally sunk in. Todd's face was overtaken with shock and confusion as he stood there in silence; suddenly he was at a loss for words. And just then, from the dining room, came the sound of Brad's voice coming from the kitchen area.

"I hear his voice now," I said, excitedly, looking toward the glass French doors that connected the dinning area. "I thought he had left, but I'm so glad he's still here." Then I turned back to Todd and slowly pulled my engagement ring off my finger.

"Todd, please take your ring. I'm sorry about this lousy timing and all I put you through with my indecisiveness for all these years. But I'm sure you realize that we can not go through with this wedding." I glanced toward Rachel who was now standing near the fireplace looking our way with shock on her face.

He didn't reach for the ring. "Mandy, don't do this. We can still work things out," Todd said. "Think of all the planning and preparations that went into this."

I shook my head. "No, we can't work things out. Not after what I have just told you," I stressed seriously. "I just told you that I'm in love with Brad and not you. Therefore, no, I can't marry you, Todd. You were right last Thanksgiving when you said I had never loved you because I really loved Brad. I think you have known all along, but it has taken me this long and an incident like what happened with you and Rachel to show me that truth. So go on and take your ring, please!"

He reached out his hand, took the ring and stared down at it for a moment before dropping it into his shirt pocket. He glanced over his shoulder at Rachel and then back at me and shook his head. The room was quiet enough to hear a pin down as he suddenly, turned on his shoe heels and headed across the room toward the front door. Rachel and I stared at each other for a moment before she turned her back to me and quickly headed across the room toward the front door as well. My heart skipped a beat and I grabbed my chest with both hands when I heard the front door open and close. Todd had left in disappointed shock and Rachel had left to probably comfort him. I was left to deal with the realization of what I had done and how it would affect my future. I suddenly felt so filled with life and excitement and needed to find Brad to let him know what I had come to realize.

I hurried across the room and burst into the dinning room with tears in my eyes that hadn't rolled down my face. I wanted to stay collected until after I had located and spoken to Brad. Mom and the entire staff would soon know that my wedding to Todd was off, but I wanted to talk to Brad first. Mom and Mrs. Lawson glanced at me and smiled as they were busy getting the table ready for dinner that would be served in an hour. What they didn't know was our dinner guest list had shrunk since Todd and Rachel had left the house. Mom and Mrs. Lawson glanced at me as they both had a pie in their hands that they were just placing on the serving table. And according to the menu it was one apple and one blueberry pie. After they placed the pies on the serving table, Mrs. Lawson nodded toward me and then turned and headed back toward the kitchen area.

Mom wiped both hands on her long white apron and stared at me with concerned eyes. She could sense that something was the matter and she could no doubt see the water in my eyes.

"What has happened, Mandy?" she asked anxiously.

"It's nothing bad," I assured her, drying my eyes with my fingers. "It's actually something quite wonderful or it will be just as soon as I talk with Brad."

"Why do you need to talk to Brad?" she asked with a curious look on her face.

"Mom, it's nothing to be concerned about."

"But, Mandy, dear, why do I get the feeling that it is."

"Mom, really it's not. Everything will be fine once I talk to him. Is he still here? I just heard his voice coming from this area a few minutes ago."

Mom nodded standing there waiting for more of an explanation that I didn't give. "Sure, Sweetheart, Brad is still here. He's staying for dinner, you know. Last I saw him, he was sitting out on the back patio," Mom said quickly. She had always preferred Brad to Todd but looked greatly confused as she headed out of the dinning room toward the kitchen.

"Thanks, Mom," I said, rushing away from her toward the French doors that were already opened to the patio. I tore outside to find Brad standing there looking out at Mom's flower garden.

"Brad," I said excitedly as I hurried toward him where he stood at the edge of the patio. "My wedding to Todd is off."

"Did you just say your wedding is off?" He stood there motionless.

"Brad, you heard me correct. I just called off my wedding to Todd," I said breathless, wiping my falling tears with my fingers.

"Mandy, did something happen? Why are you crying?" He reached out and touched my shoulder.

"I'm crying because I'm over the moon filled with happiness."

"You just called off your wedding but you're happy?" He stared in my eyes. "I'm not sure I follow what's going on."

"Brad, remember when we were together in your room years ago at the end of 2002 when we were still teenagers?"

He nodded. "Yes, of course I remember, but why do you ask?"

"I was just wondering if you remember what you said to me about there being something between us."

"Mandy, I remember that, of course, but I guess we never figured out what that something was."

"But we did figure it out. You just told me this evening that you love me, but I wouldn't listen or accept your decoration of love because I was still confused and thought my heart belonged to Todd."

Brad swallowed hard. "What are you trying to say, Mandy."

"I just figured it out in my heart what that something is. Brad, I love you," I said, looking his straight in the eyes as I grabbed my cheeks with both hands. "I don't love Todd. I love only you!"

He stared at me as if he was frozen in his spot. I kept looking longingly in his eyes, smiling with the kind of joy unlike I had ever known. He looked down searchingly into my eyes. "Mandy, what did you just say?" he asked with confusion in his voice. "I don't trust my ears."

"So, let me repeat myself. I love you and not your brother."

"I thought that was what you said, but as much as I want to pull you in my arms and kiss you, I need to know what just happened here? Less than an hour ago, I told you how I felt and you said you wanted to be with Todd. Apparently something happened between that time and now. Do I dare ask what in fear that you could slip away from me again?"

"I will tell you everything and I will not slip away again," I said lovingly as we stood facing each other, holding hands.

"It's kind of strange the way it all happened. I walked into the living room and caught Todd and Rachel kissing."

"You what," Brad said with shock. "You walked in on Todd kissing Rachel in a compromising position?"

"Yes, believe me, it wasn't just a friendly kiss. Although, Todd tried to explain that it was just a friendly kiss."

"I'm ecstatic that you have called off your wedding and want to be with me instead of my brother, but did you break off with Todd because you caught him kissing Rachel? And are you sure it wasn't just a friendly kiss? I want to be with you but not because of a misunderstanding," Brad explained.

"You are so honorable. That's the difference between you and Todd. You are the man I respect because you have so much respect for others. I'm standing here telling you I love you, but you want to make sure Todd isn't getting a raw deal. But I'm positive about the kiss between him and Rachel. It wasn't just a friendly kiss, and whether it was or not is not important."

"So, I guess that's not the reason you broke off the wedding?"

"No, Brad, it's not. I broke off the wedding because I realized I love you."

"And Mandy, I realized that I love you, but when I shared this with you an hour ago, you gave me no indication that you shared my feelings. You were still determined to go ahead with your marriage to Todd."

"I know I gave you no indication that I shared your feelings because an hour ago I didn't know what I know now. Once I explain what happened and how I came to my realization it will all make sense to you. I promise."

"Okay, let me just ask you one question before you start with your explanation. Is Todd aware that you have called off your wedding to him?" Brad glanced about the Patio. "Is he still here?"

"Yes, he's aware that the wedding is off and he left the house awhile ago and so did Rachel."

Brad smiled. "Okay, good." He held out both arms. "Now, please proceed," he said excitedly. "I'm on top of the world, but I need to know how I got here. I need to know how you went from being in love and two weeks away from a marriage with my brother to calling off the whole thing. Especially, when an hour ago you thought you still wanted to marry Todd. When I shared my decoration of love it didn't seem to move you."

"It moved me, but I just didn't know it moved me," I assured him. "I love you."

"Okay, Mandy, tell me what happened to make you realize all this?"

"The key here and what's important is that I thought he was you kissing Rachel."

"You thought Todd was me kissing Rachel?" he asked.

"Yes, Brad, I thought it was you kissing her."

"What gave you that idea?" he asked.

"I'm not sure. You two are around the same height and size; and I think you're wearing the same color shirt. I just know his back was to me and I thought it was you. And within those few seconds of thinking I was witnessing you kissing Rachel; it tore at my soul and hurt me more than anything I could have ever imagined. To stand and watch you kiss another woman hurt me to the depth of my soul."

"I'm sorry you had to go through that," he said.

"But Brad, I'm not sorry. I know it was the most agonizing pain I have ever experienced, but I'm glad I experience it since it opened my eyes. It made me realize that it was something that I couldn't live with. I would never be okay with you with another woman. I knew that right then and there."

"What about when you realized it wasn't me? I guess you chewed Todd out for his transgression and his indulgence in your living room with another woman." He shook his head. "I can't believe he was that bold to do something like that in your house knowing you could walk in on him. His arrogance has gotten worse instead of better," he pointed out. "So I guess the two of you had an argument, did you not?"

"Yes, we did, but it didn't get out of hand. Because frankly, I was too released that he wasn't you to be too upset. I was mostly disappointed that he had shown me such little respect to take a chance kissing Rachel in my living room."

"So, the bottomline here is that seeing him kiss Rachel didn't bother you as much as it bothered you when you thought it was me?"

"That's exactly correct. When I realized it was Todd kissing Rachel and not you; it didn't bother me in the same way. It made me see clearly who it was that I truly loved. Brad, that scene in the living room between Todd and Rachel was the kiss of love. It finally opened my eyes to the truth: an actuality that I had buried deep inside of me that only time could pull to the surface."

"Mandy, when I think of all the years we wasted because we couldn't see what was staring us in the face; it hurts the depth of me." He stretched out his arms and gathered me up in them. "We missed our time and a twist in fate brought us back to each other, because it was a one and a million chances that you would have walked in on Todd and Rachel kissing in your living room. I'm so thankful that we are finally together," he said with his voice filled with love as he brought his lips down on mine and swallowed me up in a demanding adoring kiss.

A flood of indescribable joy poured through me liked electric water. I knew without a shadow of a doubt that I was in the arms of the man I loved. And when his lips moved from my mouth to the side of my neck I thought I would lose my balance.

"Brad," I whispered softly against his face, "How could I have doubted my love for you for even a moment? I just couldn't see it because my heart was so afraid that you didn't love me back. I kept thinking about the time when you told me that you were not in love with me. I was too fearful to allow myself to love you because I was too afraid that you would never love me. But deep inside of me I have always loved you. I have never been content in my life without you. Even when I thought I was content with Todd I really wasn't. I know the difference and I haven't felt contentment until now. All those years without you, I was just going through the motion of living. I have never been really alive until this moment with you, right now."

Brad held me tightly in his arms and kissed me again and again. His demanding kisses found my neck and he whispered softly against my skin. "Mandy, deep inside of me, I think I have known that, just like I have silently always carried you in my heart. And my biggest regret is that I wasted so much time without you. When you first asked me all those years ago if I was in love with you, I thought it was sensible and politically correct to say no. Afterall, we didn't really know each other that well. But looking back at that time and comparing it to now. I loved you just as much then as I love you now," he admitted with his voice filled with love. "From the moment I first saw you, I always felt something for you." He kept holding me in his arms. "It was always there, that something between us."

"You are so right; there was something between us from the start. I remember how my eyes use to light up at school whenever I saw you. You were it for me even back then," I admitted with my heart overflowing with joy.

"You were it for me as well. But I allowed life to get in the way of finding my way to you sooner. For years, I tried to ignore that stirring, that flame that grew and grew," he whispered against my cheek. "But that flame overtook me and the closer it got to your wedding day with Todd, there was no more denial," he said softly against my face. "Is this really happening? I was dreading somehow getting through the next two weeks leading up to your wedding to Todd. Now just like a miracle from heaven, you tell me, you love me and not him!"

I nodded with a big smile. "That's true. I love you and not him."

"Mandy, hearing you say those words are indescribable beautiful." He placed his hands on both of my shoulders and looked me in the eyes. "I know you have one wedding to disassemble, but will you make me the happiness man in the world and say you'll be my wife. Will you marry me?" he whispered softly against my lips.

"Yes, I will marry you," I said breathless.

He grabbed me in his arms and brought his mouth down on mine and swallowed me up in a deep passionate kiss. When he pulled away from my lips, he led me by the hand to the patio table and we took a seat at the patio table.

"Wait here, I said and got up from the table. "I want to sneak inside and grab us a couple beverages. Is iced-tea okay?"

He nodded and smiled. "Iced-tea is fine, just hurry back. I miss you already."

I rushed toward the kitchen but looked over my shoulder and threw him a kiss. I was overflowing with happiness as I sneaked inside the kitchen, carefully not to make any noise. I lightly walked across the floor to the refrigerator and eased the door open. I grabbed two bottles of iced-tea from the side shelf and then eased the door shut. After which, I walked across the room and stood against the kitchen counter and twisted the top off of one bottle and took a swallow of iced-tea. After I lowered the bottle, I glanced about the kitchen very quietly trying to detect any movement near the kitchen. I didn't want to be spotted by Mom or anyone else, since I didn't want to answer any questions about why Todd and Rachel had left the house and wouldn't be joining us for dinner. Brad and I would share our great news during dinner, and we would also share the incident that took place with Todd and Rachel.

I rushed back outside to the patio to find Brad standing propped against the patio table with his arms folded. He was smiling at me.

"What took you so long? I thought I was going to have to come looking for you," he teased. "He glanced at his watch. "You were gone for five minutes but it felt like forever. Get over here."

"I feel the same way. I don't want to be away from you for a second," I said, smiling and handed him a bottle of iced-tea.

"Thank you." He took the bottle and pulled me in his arms and held me close, kissing my face and neck.

When he released me, he took a seat in a chair at the patio table and before I could be seated in the chair next to him, he grabbed my hand and sat me on his lap. "This is where I want you." He twisted the top off his drink and took a sip. "Mandy, sweetheart, now that you have agreed to be my wife, I was just wondering about something."

"What are you wondering about?"

"Something that's important to the both of us," he said.

"Okay, what is it?" I looked at him. "You're not worried about what Todd is going to say about our engagement are you?"

"Nope, it's not that, besides, after the dust settles, our getting together may not be as big of a shock to him as it is to us."

"You know, now that you mention that, before I took my trip to Springfield he told me that I was still in love with you."

"He actually said that to you, but still wanted to go through with your wedding plans?"

"Yes, because I was still in denial at that time and told him it wasn't so. But that's why he wanted me to take that trip so I could soul search and make sure I truly loved him and not you. I was so confused. I loved you, but I had convinced myself that I loved Todd. But he could sense that what I felt for him wasn't the real thing. He tried to get through to me and told me that I wasn't happy with him because I really wanted to be with you. So you're right. It's probably more of a shock to you and me than it was to him," I said and kissed the side of his face.

"That was the one time you should have listened to my brother," he smiled and playfully poked me in the side.

"You are absolutely right, but back to the thing that you are wondering about; you never did say what it is."

"I'm wondering about our home."

"What do you mean our home?" I asked.

"The place we will call home after we are husband and wife," he said. "Have you given any thought to where you would like to live once we're married?"

"Anywhere with you will be perfect." I took a sip from my iced-tea bottle.

"And anywhere with you would be perfect, but have you thought about it at all? I know you and Todd was considering buying a new home."

"We did consider it," I said.

"Thinking of a new house, I've been wondering," Brad said against my hair. "What do you think of that house off the corner of Hillside and Lansing?"

"You mean the Hillside Palace estate?" I asked casually.

"Yes, where I ran into you and Todd today?" He took another sip of iced-tea.

"I think it's a beautiful place, but Todd didn't think much of it."

"I actually stopped by there the other day and got an opportunity to tour the house." He nodded and kissed the side of my face. "I didn't mention it but today wasn't my first time paying a visit to the estate.

"Why were you touring the place?" I curiously asked. "Were you also in the market to buy?"

Brad shook his head. "No, I wasn't in the market at the time. I was just curious about the old estate after Mom mentioned it. She had told me that it was a possibility that you and Todd might buy the place," he explained.

I shifted curiously on his lap. "So, tell me. What did you think of the place after you toured the old house?" I asked excitedly.

"The question should be what I didn't like about it? And I can't think of a single thing that I didn't like about the house. I was actually blown away and quite impressed by the exterior and interior of the place," Brad said with conviction. "I'm not really into houses, because I figured if you have seen one big house you have seen them all, but it was something rather unique about the place that set well with me."

I placed my half empty bottle of iced-tea on the patio table and grabbed my face with both hands. I turned and smiled at him. "I can't believe you just said that. That's exactly how I feel about the old estate."

"Good minds think alike," he smiled and continued. "All I know is that I was drawn back to the house and found myself standing on the street corner looking up at the old estate with approving eyes, thinking it would be a great piece of property to own if you and Todd bought it. That's why I was standing there taking those pictures when you and Todd made your way back down that long walkway and met me on the street corner."

"Brad, this is incredible that we both like the old house."

"Yes, I do like it, but why is that incredible. What's not to like?"

"Nearly everything according to Todd, but you really like it?

He nodded. "Yes, I do, Hillside Palace is a gem to me," he said sincerely. "I was just impressed with the whole layout and that's what really inspired me to take those pictures." He placed his half empty bottle of iced-tea on the patio table. "Of course, my folks wouldn't consider it a Chase original because we didn't build it from the ground up, but that place is exactly the sketch I would have wanted for my home if it was built from scratch," he humbly explained. "With that being said, I know you and Todd decided against the purchase, what turned you off?"

"Correction, nothing turned me off." I held up both hands. "Todd decided against the purchase and I accepted his decision. I wanted to buy the house, but he found every excuse why we shouldn't buy it. He even made a speech about how we were expected to live at Chase Court."

Brad grinned. "He told you that? That's a bunch of garbage. We are not expected to live at Chase Court. We have a right and a privilege to live at Chase Court for as long as we see fit."

"Todd made it sound mandatory and expected; but you're saying it isn't?"

"That's exactly what I'm saying," Brad said seriously. "We are asked to live there, but by no means are we expected or have to live there if it's not what we want. What my brother failed to tell you is that he wants to remain at Chase Court so he doesn't have to lift a finger to fend for himself."

"I won't disagree with you. Todd was adamant about never leaving home."

"Now, that we have cleared that up, might you reconsider?" he asked.

"Reconsider," I repeated anxiously.

"Yes, would you reconsider buying the old estate?" he asked.

"Yes, I would reconsider, if you want to," I said with subdued excitement.

He nodded and smiled. "Yes, I want to buy it."

"Brad, it's exactly what I want," I screamed excitedly.

"It's exactly what you want?" he asked.

"Yes, Brad. It's exactly what I want! I can't wait to live in that dream house."

"So, you consider it a dream house?" Brad asked with surprised in his voice.

"Yes, Hillside Palace is my dream house. I just didn't want to let myself get to excited when you first mentioned it because I didn't want to get my hopes up to be let down again."

"Mandy, my bride to be, say no more," he said softly and kissed the side of my face. "You will have the house of your dreams because I'm going to buy it for you; and anything else that makes you happy." He playfully poked me in the side. "Afterall, what makes you happy makes me happy," he whispered against my hair.

"Brad, I love you to infinite. You make my life feel complete," I whispered breathless, wrapped my arms around his neck, and my lips touched against his. "I have loved you all my life."

"Mandy, I love you to eternality," Brad whispered against my lips. "I have loved you from day one, when our eyes connected in that high school cafeteria. From that day on, a stirring in me longed just for you. Now that we are together, my life is flooded with happiness," Brad whispered breathless as he pressed his mouth over mine and devoured me with a loving passionate kiss.

Would you like to see your manuscript become a book?

If you are interested in becoming a PublishAmerica author, please submit your manuscript for possible publication to us at:

mybook@publishamerica.com

You may also mail in your manuscript to:

**PublishAmerica
PO Box 151
Frederick, MD 21705**

www.publishamerica.com

Lightning Source UK Ltd.
Milton Keynes UK
UKOW05f1833020115

243864UK00001B/41/P